The Territories

Book five in the Sword Masters' Universe

Book one *Sword Masters*
Book two *Jabone's Sword*
Book three *The Burden of the Crown*
Book four *The Twins*
Book five: *The Territories*

Selina Rosen

Yard Dog Press

The Territories
Selina Rosen
First Edition Copyright © Selina Rosen, 2023

Published by Yard Dog Press at Kindle

Print Version ISBN 978-1-945941-34-4
The Territories
First Edition Copyright © Selina Rosen, 2023

Yard Dog Press
710 W. Redbud Lane
Alma, AR 72921-7247

http://www.yarddogpress.com

Edited by Lynn Rosen
Technical Editor Lynn Rosen
Cover art by John Kaufmann

First Print Edition January 1, 2023
Printed in the United States of America
0 9 8 7 6 5 4 3 2 1

Table of Contents

Chapter One

Rea had been seasick for the very first time in her life on her way from the Kartik to the Territories. She'd thrown up most of the three-day trip and it wasn't until her feet touched the ground of what would be their new home that she realized why. The last time she'd made a trip by ship this far was to fight the Amalites in the Hive. Her Fadra, Madra and brothers had been with her, and her Fadra had made sure she drank the seasickness potion all Kartik sailors drank before making a voyage.

She hadn't remembered for herself. That all by itself made her immediately feel like she was out of her depth and destined to fail in a huge and horrible way.

With an ache in her heart she realized she was alone now. Her family were all across the sea, and she was to head the Marching Night here which meant she was basically in charge of the whole shebang. It was overwhelming. The entire Katabull fleet—twenty ships strong—were here now, and before it was over they would return twice more. When it was done two-thousand Katabull and all the supplies necessary to start the colony would be here. All fifty of the Marching Night who were coming were with her now. The Great Leader was counting on her to make a new Katabull home here. It was an immense responsibility.

Meanwhile Rea had done nothing in her life to that point to earn the trust and respect of anyone. And what had both her Fadra, her Madra and the Great Leader told her more than once? That if you missed your mark with your arrow just once, you would have to hit a bull's eye ten times in a row before anyone would think you were a good archer. She had shot arrows everywhere and often struck people who were doing nothing but minding their own business.

No one thought she was a good match to be Captain of their pack in the Territories. The only reason they weren't all yelling it at the top of their lungs was that they trusted Tarius's judgement. Though being Katabull and followers of the Nameless God they didn't at all think Tarius was

1

infallible. So they were willing to give Rea a shot, but she couldn't afford to make any mistakes.

So what did she do? She forgot to do something as simple as drink the seasickness remedy and then did nothing but puke for three days.

She needed to trust herself, but she was supposed to oversee the building of a Katabull settlement in the Kartik-held Territories of what had once been the Amalite, and what did she know about doing that? Nothing. Tarius sent the Marching Night that were going in the first wave to help get things started with her in charge because she was the only member of the Marching Night going that was from Tarius's own household.

There was a lot riding on Rea and what was her first act upon stepping foot on their new homeland? To throw up on it. She had been too sick on the ship to do any sort of "leading," and even now she was too sick to really think clearly, but her pack and Tarius herself were counting on her so she needed to pull herself together.

She had disgraced her family enough over the last few years and this was her chance to show them that she was something other than an irresponsible dumbass incapable of staying sober long enough to get anything of real value done. What had she done so far? Prove to all that had come with her that she was an irresponsible dumbass incapable of getting anything of real value accomplished.

The truth was Rea wished she was just one of the settlers. She didn't want to be in charge. It hadn't been her intention to be the leader of anything and certainly nothing this important. But Tarius had insisted that she be Captain of the Marching Night in the Territories or not go at all. The latter wasn't a choice because no one at home could stand the sight of her, and the temptation of the bars in Montero called to her twenty times a day.

She had no desire to be Captain in the Territories or anywhere else, but of course for her people this fact did nothing but make her a prime candidate for leadership. Because of course who could be a better leader than the person who didn't want to do it at all? She was Katabull yet she still didn't fully understand what older Katabull seemed to fully comprehend when they spoke it.

Rea needed to change the course of her life, but she really felt moving to the Territories would have been enough. However there was no sense at all in arguing with the Great Leader once she had made up her mind. Explaining just how much she didn't want to be in charge, and that she couldn't possibly do a good job... well, being Katabull the more she didn't want to do it the more they would have been sure she was the perfect choice.

Rea didn't understand Tarius on most days. She knew her, respected and trusted her, but she just didn't understand her. That she had the infuriating quality of usually being right about everything only made Tarius that much more difficult to understand. What by the Nameless One did Tarius see in Rea that she couldn't see in herself?

Even for a Katabull the Great Leader said confusing things. But she'd say them, you'd be hell bent to know what the hell she meant, and then days, weeks or sometimes months later you'd pop yourself in the forehead because when you finally understood it... Well, she was just always right.

At that moment Rea just hoped Tarius was right about her.

They had landed in the Territories not long after sunrise, anchoring their ships just in front of what was left of the docks. The Kartik fleet had sacked this port during the Great War. Most of the village attached to the port had been burned. The troops that landed here would have been well on their way to the front before the order came down that they had decided to keep the ports whole. After all this was the farthest point from the border of the country. So the docks and most of the town were in ruins. They would have to move people and supplies from the ships to what was left of the docks in rowboats.

Even sick Rea took one look at the harbor and knew why Tarius had chosen it for the colony. It was a near-perfect horseshoe cove almost exactly the size and shape of the Katabull harbor in the Kartik. And here, as at the compound, the shape of the harbor would keep them safe from most storms. Also—even with the overgrowth of vegetation—she could clearly make out where a large river ran into the sea, so it had a source of fresh water.

Mostly the forest around them was beautiful and no doubt filled with game. In the distance she could make out a wooded mountain range. Still, as Rea stepped out of the rowboat, managed to walk five feet then puke, she looked up at what was left of the village that had been burnt and then allowed to grow up in brush for over twenty-five years and immediately felt like the task they had been handed was impossible.

It was a lot to take in all at once, and where did they start? She'd helped to build the Great Wall, but that wasn't a whole colony. Hell, she'd been mostly drunk for the last five years.

And why—besides the harbor—had Tarius picked this dead place for a Katabull Colony? Because it was far away from the Jethrik and its territories, and it was on the coast so far from the Barbarian nations that it would take a full month to reach them on horseback. The Katabull would be alone here; there were no humans of any kind closer than several days ride away—no close settlements of any kind. Of course this also meant there was nowhere to ride to for help or information concerning the area. Whatever they didn't bring with them or couldn't find here they just weren't going to have.

Of course she had overheard Jena saying that one of the main reasons Tarius choose it was that there were snakes in every other part of the Territories but none here. Rea had never seen a snake; the Kartik didn't have them. She hadn't even seen one when she had come to fight the Hive. But she had heard her Fadra, Madra, and the Great Leader tell stories about them, and she was glad they would not have to deal with the horrid things. They were like a lizard but with no legs, long and thin with fangs that they used to inject you with death. Some even had rattles on their tails so that they could taunt you before they killed you.

Rea looked it over—burned husks of buildings barely peeking through decades of growth—and in the moment, feeling like ass, could see none of the good. "No doubt no one moved to reclaim it, and even snakes won't live here because only a moron would want to live at the butt end of nowhere," Rea said, looking at it with a sigh.

"What's that, Captain?" Fleat said at her back, putting the lilt on the end of "Captain" the way he'd been doing ever since the Great Leader gave her the title. Fleat was the oldest living member of the Marching Night—nearly three hundred years old—and as far as she could see he had no intention of dying as long as he could get a rise out of her. So they were friends, sort of, at least he was as close to a friend as Rea had managed to make in the last few years.

She turned just enough to glare at him over her shoulder. "I said, you ancient, deaf pain-in-my-ass, there are no humans here because no one in their right mind would want to live here."

He patted her on the shoulder and laughed. "Ah girl where is your spirit of adventure?"

"Right there," she said, pointing at the puddle of puke she'd just made. "And in the ocean from here all the way back to the Kartik."

Fleat laughed loudly and smacked her on the shoulder so hard he damn near knocked her over. "So what is your first request?" Because of course they were all Katabull and the Katabull didn't take orders. "Captain, oh my Captain."

"To have you drowned at sea," she said but managed a smile. "Oh why for the sake of the Nameless One did Tarius put me of all people in charge?"

Fleat laughed. "We have all been very bad and must be punished?"

"Starting with you." He was right about one thing she needed to be lining them out, but she felt like crap. She suddenly remembered something she had nearly forgotten which didn't seem likely. She was the Katabull; she didn't have to walk around in this sick human body. She called on the night and in seconds felt great. She needed to calm down, *I am so worried I'm going to screw up that I am doing just that. I have to stop second guessing everything and just act. I grew up at the Great Leader's feet. My fadra was her runner, my madra her most trusted captain; they are all leaders. What do they all do? They don't try to do it all themselves; they pick the right person for the right job. They aren't afraid to ask the person who knows more than they do what they should do.*

5

Fleat smiled at her and said, "You look very like your madra in your human form, but like this...were you bigger I don't think I could tell you apart."

"No doubt because you are nearly blind." She smiled at him fondly. "So... I feel better but I still don't have any idea where we should start." She looked at him expectantly.

"So what? Will you listen to the old man and then pretend like it was all your idea?"

"I will listen to you, consider what you have said, make a better plan and tell them you helped me a little."

Fleat shook his head. "You have just as smart a tongue as your madra as well." He scratched his grey head and thought for a minute, then said, "We are supposed to send the ships back as quickly as possible. That means we need to make a shelter and off load all our supplies as soon as we can."

Rea nodded. "We should send scouts to see if any of the buildings are sound enough to be used. We have huge tents, but we would first have to clear areas to do that and looking at this mass of plants and thorn bushes I think that would take longer than the Great Leader wants the ships to be here."

"And this, dear Rea, is why the Katabull always choose the one who most doesn't want to lead. They don't want to lead because they alone fully understand all that must be done."

As understanding washed over her like a wave she realized she was already changing.

By the end of that first day their scouts had returned with the news that the center of the town had taken very little damage. It seemed that a street that ran in a circle around the very center of town had stopped the fire from burning most of what was there, and several buildings seemed to have weathered fairly well over the last twenty-five years.

They spent most of the second day clearing a trail to the buildings they had decided to use. There was a huge structure in the very center that had held up well. It was big enough to house all of them and store their supplies. It would be tight sleeping, but they could do it. Most of the surviving buildings were stone, but this one was massive with a tile roof—very like the houses in Montero. Because of this the interior had taken very little damage. If the roof had leaked at all they couldn't find where. It was well built and had obviously been constructed for defensive purposes.

The building was the tallest in town. Three stories with a walkway around the top that was in disrepair but could be easily fixed at some later time. Because of its size and strategic position, it would be the perfect place for The Marching Night to inhabit.

They found another building in good enough shape and moved their horses—they only had twenty-five—into the makeshift stable. Then they threw up a quick fence out of lumber they gleaned from the fallen structures.

The next day they draped a couple of the tents they had brought over the roof of the "stable," finished unloading the ships, and by nightfall they were ready to send the ships back to the Katabull Compound. The ships left with skeleton crews, the members of which would eventually wind up back at the compound when this was done.

As she watched them sail away Rea was filled with a moment of panic. Now they were stuck here. It was nearly dark when, as a group, they walked silently back to the huge fire they had built just outside the three-story structure they were all bunking in. There was a huge fireplace and hearth inside but though it wasn't as warm as it was at home it was far too warm for a fire inside. They were all exhausted, and Rea got the feeling she wasn't the only one that was wondering about their decision to move here.

This place was nothing like the island. That had been driven home today. While they were working to clear the "stable" a bear decided to walk up and attack them. Big mistake for the bear. They had all been in their Katabull forms most of the day because they could get a lot more done, so when the bear took a slap at Jagon, and he and two others had the bear down and dead in seconds.

The bear had been dressed out and cooking on sticks the rest of the day. As they had walked up to the fire after the long, hard day, they each grabbed a stick full of meat to eat and sat down anywhere they could find. They had hauled up sections of logs; they had even found some chairs and a table. The table had made the cook's life easier. Trin was the Marching Night's cook, but for now he was cooking for all of them, and he had been so happy about the table when they brought it to him to use that he had nearly cried.

Most of them had taken their human forms back by now, but a few hadn't. Turned out bear blood tasted funky to them. They had wondered about whether the meat would be any good, but as she heard the sounds all around her she wasn't afraid to taste it, and it was really good. She found a piece of log and sat down. She was exhausted, but she felt less overwhelmed. There was so much to be done but she remembered something the Great Leader always said that suddenly made perfect sense. "You can remove all the sand from the beach if you do it a cup at a time."

Out of the corner of her eye she saw something. She stood up and looked, and something moved. She walked towards it.

"Where you going?" Fleat asked at her shoulder.

"To take a leak if that's alright with you," she said,

"I suppose it is but leave more than you take."

She walked towards where she had seen the movement. She didn't want to tell him she saw something because then if he didn't, if none of them did, it would be yet another reason to doubt her. If she could kill something all by herself to eat that would go a whole long way towards gaining their trust and respect. They were doing what she asked them to do but not without arguing with her about everything. Frankly though they were getting a lot done they could get a lot more done if they would stop questioning everything she asked of them and of course it wasn't so much the old ones like Fleat—because after all they were the ones she was asking how to do things. It was the young ones who just had to know the why and how of things, that had reminded her over and over that she wasn't Tarius, and who slowed down progress.

Like most Katabull even in her human form she could move almost silently. She sniffed the air; she could smell something that wasn't them. She moved towards the smell and soon she saw something move again. Not watching where she was going, she got snagged on one of the thorn trees they had been avoiding for days. She tripped and one of the thorns went deep into the muscle of her arm. Rea pulled free of the thorn, but dropped her skewer of meat and cussed a blue streak. Rea saw a flash of white race away. She had managed to scare off whatever she'd been tracking.

"Gods and spiders." Blood was dripping down her arm. She turned and headed back for the fire. It was wood so if it wasn't treated quickly, she was going to get an infection maybe one bad enough to keep her from shifting.

Back in the light of the fire she called for their medic, "Garret!" He was young and energetic, trained by Yuri. He knew what he was doing but didn't have the experience Yuri or any of the other Marching Night medics had because he had yet to be on any battlefield as a medic. He ran over, poured way too much Montero Spring water onto the wound, rubbed enough ointment for six cuts onto it then used about a yard of gauze to wrap it. Rea looked at Katrina—whose arm was also bound in enough gauze that it looked like a cast. Katrina had run up on one of the thorn trees earlier that day when she was helping to kill the bear. They exchanged a grin and Rea shrugged.

"Thanks Garret," she said.

"You're welcome. Those things area dangerous; we need to get rid of them," Garrett said.

"I couldn't agree more." She looked around the fire and was surprised when all the idle chatter stopped and they all looked at her. They were waiting for her to make a decision about the hated thorn trees. "Tomorrow let's work first on getting the area around this structure, the stables, and the path to the docks free of these things. It's not that bad a cut but my arm is already throbbing as bad as it did when I took a sword blow in the Amalite Hive." She looked at Katrina for confirmation that she wasn't just being a whimp.

"Worse than any blow I have ever taken, and I am running a fever bad enough I doubt I could shift right now," Katrina said,

"That's what I was afraid of. Kadid told me we need to rebuild the docks so it will be easier for us to unload when the others get here." She looked at the old man and he nodded. He had been a sailor and a boatwright most of his life. He wasn't Marching Night and including him made the other packs see that she wasn't showing favoritism. "But we also need to get the paths cleared of these things. We will break into two teams tomorrow; one team will work on the docks, and the other will work to clear these hateful things away." Rea walked over and got a skewer of meat off the fire. "Worse than piercing my skin it made me drop my dinner."

They all laughed. It felt like acceptance which was a step closer to respect.

The next morning it was hard to say whether her arm was badly swollen or it was just Garret's dressing that made it look so. What she could attest to was that it was swollen, hot and painful. *Great we're here less than four days and have discovered a plant that is poisonous to us.* Still when she tried to shift, she was able to do so, and when she did the pain in her arm was all but gone. However, when she saw Katrina, she had still not shifted, and when Rea asked her about it she said she couldn't. When Rea put her hand on Katrina's head, she was running a fever.

"Go and lie down. Get some rest. I will send Garrett to take care of your wound," Rea said.

Katrina didn't argue about laying down, so she obviously felt as bad as she looked. She did roll her eyes and asked, "Do you have to call for Garret? I'm afraid this time he will wrap me from head to toe."

"Better safe than sorry." Rea laughed.

When she talked to them as a group after they had eaten a breakfast of more bear meat she told them about how she felt and that Katrina was even worse and doubled down on their need to cut down and burn up all the offending trees. She quickly broke them into two groups by saying, "Everyone on that side of the fire work on the docks. Kadid will tell you what needs to be done. Everyone on this side will work with me on getting rid of the thorn trees. Be very careful that you don't get cut by them. I feel like crap, but Katrina cannot even shift."

She started working in the direction of the tree that had gotten her because, revenge. The first thing she noticed as she was cutting away the briars to get to it was that she didn't see or smell the bear meat she had dropped the night before. She figured an animal, maybe even the one she had been tracking, had found it and eaten it. She took her axe and slung it into the tree she now considered to be her enemy. The trees were small and it came down in three chops. She moved to grab it so she could drag it to one of the many fires they had started to burn them up when she saw something in the dirt that made her drop her axe and move to get a better look.

Moving a piece of briar out of the way, she took in a deep breath and let it out. It was a human foot print—five toes no mistaking it with anything else. It wasn't one of them; she could smell it wasn't. Besides, with all these thorns everywhere and wood cuts poisoning a Katabull's system, they weren't very likely to be running around barefoot in the dark. She found two more.

There were no human settlements anywhere near here not for a three-days' ride away. It didn't make sense. She sniffed the air; the smell wasn't strong enough for the human to still be close. She wondered about telling the others but decided it wasn't really a problem. If they all thought Rea thought a bare-footed human was something worth worrying about well they might wonder more than they already did about Tarius's choice of her as leader. After all she was Marching Night. If there was a huge human contingency close by they all would have smelled it. Her pack, more so than any other Katabull, didn't worry about attack from humans. They were cautious, not afraid.

Now a splinter...that was a whole different matter. She grabbed the offensive tree and her axe and drug the tree over. She threw it in the fire where there was a huge blaze burning and felt vindicated. Apparently the damn things were filled with some sort of oil that made them highly flammable.

Just one more reason to rid the land of the hateful things, Rea thought.

By the end of the day they had cleared and burned trails all around the buildings they were using and another crew had cut and pulled in all the logs they would need to rebuild the docks. They had kept five fires besides their own burning brush and unusable building debris all day and now as the night closed in on them the fires shot light into the sky.

Anyone less that a day's ride away would be able to see the smoke and now the flames, Rea thought. They had killed yet another bear and were roasting it on the fire. *One thing is for sure Tarius wasn't wrong about the amount of game there is here. Between them they saw five deer, two elk, and some weird animal none of us has seen before even bigger than an elk. We are eating bear because we decided it was smarter to eat the things that want to eat us first than the things we want to eat. These animals—none of them—are afraid of us at all. If there were humans hunting here surely the animals would run when they see us and they don't. Yet I know what I saw was a human footprint. I know what I smelled was human.*

Katrina came to the fire and announced she felt fit again as she grabbed a skewer of meat off the fire.

"Did you try to shift?" Rea asked. "When I shifted this morning it stopped hurting, and when I shifted back to my human form this evening," she pointed to her arm where both bandage and wound were gone, "...it had healed."

"So not as bad as wood," Garrett said.

"Not for me," Rea said.

"I still can't shift," Katrina said.

Rea moved to put her hand on Katrina's head and announced, "She is still hot."

"Was she cut worse than Rea?" Fleat asked Garrett.

"No, Rea's cut was actually deeper and worse than Katrina's was."

"I noticed there were two kinds of trees," Roushe said. "Nearly the same but different."

"Great! So we are dealing with two plants—one bad and one worse—what a great place," Rea said, thinking out loud.

"But Captain, oh my Captain," Fleat said, "at least there is plenty of game."

There certainly was, the next day they wound up bagging a lion—which wasn't nearly as good as bear—but they weren't having to get into their food stores much at all. They were also finding plenty of edible plants, and there were probably a lot more they could eat but they didn't know the foreign plant life as well as they knew their own.

Katrina's condition got better and then worse for days until when the next ships landed with their personnel, horses and supplies, they offloaded them as quickly as they could. Then they put Katrina on the ships heading back to the compound so that she could be taken to the springs of Montero to heal.

This time as she watched them go Rea didn't feel panic or even an aching to go home. Something had shifted in the short time they'd been there. The Territories already felt like home to Rea, and she didn't think it was only her.

When she had brought Katrina to the ship she'd be going home on she was still saying she didn't need to or want to go.

"You have to, Katrina. I cannot let you continue to get sicker, and your wound is not healing," Rea told her.

"I will be back as soon as I can. I want to be here and will not let some thorn keep me away. I will not abandon you or my pack that is here." She caught Rea's hand and held it. "Rea, I hate to tell you, but when Tarius put you in charge...well I thought she had lost her mind. I thought you would not last a week. Then when you got sick on passage over I thought you would quit and plead to go home before you stepped off the ship. But you are not only doing a good job but an admirable one. I will come back and help you build this colony."

"Thank you, Katrina, that means more than you can know. May the Nameless One bring you back strong and healthy. I will miss you because," Rea grinned at her, "you know—too much quiet." Even sick Katrina talked more than any three people she knew.

Katrina's words had touched her more than she could say because it meant people were noticing that she had changed. Rea really just needed to be alone for a minute which seemed to be harder and harder to do these days. When Trin said he needed someone to haul off the bone carcass she immediately volunteered and waved away offers of help.

They had been carting the bone carcasses far into the woods because they didn't want to encourage the bears to come into their camp any more than they already did. When there were more of them and better cooking pots they would start boiling the bones down to get every bit of food out of them. For now they were just eating meat—great gulping amounts of it in a way they hadn't been able to indulge in years—which was good because they were all working their asses off from morning till night.

As she neared the boneyard she smelled something first and then saw movement. She stood stock still thinking this would be her chance to finally kill something and bring it to them to eat. So far, though they had killed something nearly every day, she had yet to be in on any of the kills. She put the bones down, drew her blade and started toward the figure. As she got closer and could both smell it and see it better she realized with a start what she was looking at. A human woman in tattered clothes was crouched down chewing on a bone. Which, well Katabull didn't leave a lot of meat on the bones. But with as many bones as they were making she would have been doing alright for herself.

There was something about the way she acted, looking around her, eyes darting here and there as she ate. *Like an animal.* Her blonde hair was ratted up, and it was impossible to guess at her age because she was covered in soot and grime. She was gaunt like she had been living on harsh rations, which explained why she was chewing on their bone pile. How long had she been here? Was she alone?

The woman intrigued her. What the hell was she doing there? She had to be an Amalite, but she couldn't have known anything about what that meant to the Katabull. Was she drawn here by their "human" occupation now, or had she always been here? Did she even know what a Katabull was? Either way, what did she think of seeing so many of them all at once?

Rea didn't know how long she stood there watching the woman but it was long enough that someone came looking for her. She heard a twig snap and turned to see Fleat coming up on her. The woman heard, too, and she was gone in a flash as if she had never been there.

"I think she is a feral human," Fleat said conversationally, as if it was something they ran across every day.

"I saw it the first time the second day we were here when I got stabbed by the thorn tree. In fact, she's the reason I got stabbed."

"And you didn't tell anyone because?"

"My guess would be my reason is the same as yours."

"It's only one human," he said, shrugging. "She is of the Everything and harmless if left alone. I saw her a few days ago down in the harbor going through the sand we had stirred up in constructing the docks. She was looking for clams."

"Should we tell the others?" Rea asked.

"Do you think she's a danger to us or them?"

Rea laughed. "One skinny human girl against hundreds of Katabull? No, I don't think so."

"I think she is a creature of the woods like the monkeys at home. We should not kill and eat it because it is too much like us. Like the monkeys she has a right to live unmolested by us," he said.

Then he got that look in his eyes—the one she had seen in her own parents' and in Tarius's that she had not understood till right then when she saw it reflected in Fleat's eyes. It was pain—not physical pain, but the deep, deep kind that never completely went away. She thought of her own mother and how her death still twisted her gut. But *they* had all lived through the Great War. They had all been, not splashed, but *covered* in blood—theirs their enemies', sometimes the blood of those they loved most. They carried that with them and the oddest thing could trigger it. Who knew why seeing and talking about this feral girl caused Fleat's grief to surface?

She let him soak in it for a minute while she went back, got the bones, took them to the boneyard and dumped them. Then she took the sack and walked back to where Fleat was still staring blindly into the woods. Who knew what he was seeing in that moment? Part of her wanted to ask, but the rest of her had no desire to know.

"Come on let's get back to camp." He nodded and fell in beside her. Why, why did she suddenly know something she had never known before?

Because until my mother died I had never lost anyone who wasn't ancient. I was born just before the Great War

15

started; I was too young to even realize my father had died. After my mother died I drank my feelings. I just acted on my base instinct and never let myself feel it. Then I was in the battle in the Hive and I killed many but they were such an abomination I didn't see them as human at all—the same with the keeps—and no one I cared about was even seriously hurt. They all lost people they cared about on a fairly regular basis and they killed all day for days. They blank out like that because there are times when it crawls out of the hole they put it in like my grief over my mother crawls out of its hole. But I have lost one person, and they have lost many.

"I am sorry, Fleat," she said,

"What for?" he asked, a chuckle in his voice.

"I am sorry that I never understood that other people have pain. That I did things that made their lives worse without ever considering what they—you—have been through, how much you have all been through."

"So you are apologizing to me because you can't apologize to your fadra and madra?"

"No, I'm apologizing to you for anyone who has ever treated you the way I treated my parents."

"When we are young we make many mistakes because we think we know things that we don't. You do not have to apologize for being young, just as I don't have to because we all do it." Then he grinned wildly and said, "You could apologize for just being an asshole in general."

Rea smiled back and said, "But I'm not sorry for that."

Katrina didn't get to come back right away, and they were actually on their own for months because of the volcano, earthquake and tidal wave that hit the Kartik. They only knew about it at all because of a note Jestia sent them on a bird. It was a good thing the land of the Territories was so rich because for most of the first three months they were there they were basically on their own. They only had the two ships that Tarius left them to fish with, and they just did without supplies they hadn't already brought with them or couldn't find there. They all assumed it was because the island was so busy rebuilding they couldn't spare any time or supplies.

Rea was proud of herself; she was doing a good job. She learned to delegate where she could and make hard decisions when she had to. Fleat was always there to aggravate and help her when she needed someone with more experience than she had to guide her.

They scavenged the remains of the town and timbered the woods to rebuild the buildings in the town center. They split logs and shingled rooves. As they finished repairing a dwelling, people moved out of tents into the new house. They had drawn lots, and as their names came up they got rooms in the central building. Soon no one was living in a tent. There wasn't much that two-thousand Katabull couldn't achieve.

They cleared pastures and fields. They plowed and put in crops. They hunted; they fished. They weren't there by any large stretch of the imagination, but Rea was sure they would be weathered in and have plenty of supplies laid back by the time the cold weather hit. It was starting to get cold at night already. None of them really knew what it was going to be like to have ice and snow. For one thing most of them had never even seen it. Everything they knew about the winters in the Territories they had learned from fishermen, Tarius, Dustan and other bards. The Great War had been waged during the summer, so not even those who fought in it had been in the Territories in winter. They knew they had to have lots of firewood and indoor fireplaces.

They all worked nearly all day everyday but took time to celebrate festivals and to mourn their dead. They had lost two people both were very old and as luck would have it they died in horrible hunting accidents. One was killed while trying to kill a bear with a hunting knife. The other was mauled by a lion after he speared him—not deeply enough—but refused to let go of the spear.

They celebrated mating exchanges, anniversaries of such, and birthdates. But mostly they worked.

Rea had a hobby of sorts; she was trying to tame the feral human. She would bring actual food at some distance away from the boneyard. It hadn't been safe at all for the human to go there as so did every bear in the forest. When all the settlers got there with more stock pots and workers, they started boiling the bone carcasses then burning and grinding the bones to use on crops, so there wasn't anything there anyway. So Rea had started bringing meat and sometimes a wheat cake or two. She would put it down on a stump or rock then move away from it. Rea was pretty good at sniffing the human out; she would wait. The human normally searched for food close to sundown when the moons weren't full, and shortly after when they were. Rea knew why; the human was avoiding them by coming when they were done for the day but not hunting in full dark because that would make her an easy target for the predators. If anyone besides Fleat had also seen her no one had said so, and Rea sort of treated her like a pet.

Slowly the human became used to her, so Rea kept getting closer till now the woman would look at her but continue to eat. Being able to get closer to her Rea realized two things: the woman was probably exactly the same age she was or close to it, and she looked less gaunt. She was starting to put on weight; regular meals of meat were making her healthier.

The oddest thing was whether Rea was in her human or Katabull form didn't seem to matter to the woman. One day their eyes locked, and Rea smiled at her. The woman attempted to smile back, but it was obviously so foreign to her that it looked odd. Still it showed in her eyes. Rea was sure the woman actually liked her, and she remembered what Fleat had said about the monkeys in the Kartik.

It was almost exactly the way the monkeys lived in the compound—not with them but around them. They had their nests in the jungle, but they came to the compound to eat what the Katabull threw away. Many of the Katabull had a monkey or two that they fed that wasn't tame but didn't act wild unless you tried to catch it. Rea was sure that was exactly where she was with the woman.

It was a pastime that gave her something to do besides worrying about everything. It served no purpose; it was just fun and different. She fantasized that someday she and the woman would sit and have a pot of tea and share a bone to chew on.

They were there nearly three months when her runner Arin came to tell her two ships were approaching. Both were

18

flying Katabull flags one also flew the Great Leader's flag. Rea ran to the docks as did most of the population to wait for them to arrive. All around her the Katabull were excited about the arrival of their leader.

"So how do you feel?" Fleat asked at her shoulder.

"I find I am filled with both excitement and dread. Excitement because I look forward to seeing them. Dread because I'm afraid Tarius will hate everything we have done."

"Have only excitement. You make your house proud, and she will have nothing but praise for the job you have done here."

Rea looked at him, a confused look on her face.

"What?" he asked with a grin.

"And?"

"And what?"

"Aren't you going to say something not helpful now?"

He grinned wildly and said, "Those things *are* helpful; they keep you humble. After all if your head got any bigger you'd need a porter just to carry it."

"That's better," Rea said with a smile.

Katrina was down the gangplank before the Great Leader was, and she hugged Rea as if they were not only friends from the same pack but blood relatives. As she patted the other woman on the back she tried to remember if she had ever slept with her. *Gods and spiders! I slept with so many people I just can't be sure but wait... Nope, she obviously likes me, and everyone I ever slept with can't stand me now.* Rea smiled. *Now I remember. I tried many times to sleep with her she always said no.*

Then Tarius was coming down the gangplank her baby on her hip and her two little boys hanging onto the edge of her shirt. Jena was right behind her, and then there was Rea's fadra and his husband and her brother Laz. Rea pushed the excited woman away from her and moved to wait at the end of the gangplank. She hugged the Great Leader but then nearly pushed her away, jumped around Jena, ran up the plank, grabbed her fadra and hugged him. She realized she was crying and tried to stop because she was the leader here, and she shouldn't show her belly to her people. Her fadra held her in a bear hug nearly too tight for her to breathe, and she found she couldn't stop crying. Why?

Tarius looked around at all those who had gathered making it near impossible for them to get off the dock. She saw all that they had built and said loudly enough that they could all hear, "You have all done better than I could have imagined." She then turned to Rea and whispered in her ear. "I knew, Rea, that you would make our family proud."

Her words did not help Rea stop crying as she moved to hug her brother.

Chapter Two

Tarius sat on her throne at the huge table they had made in the very center of the main hall of the building the Marching Night were using for their headquarters. Though not all of them lived there now most still did.

Tarius was filling them in on all that had happened on the island and, as always, she was weaving a brilliant tale. Of course Rea could only hear bits and pieces of it because Katrina was in her ear telling her version of events. She had reach Montero without incident and within a few days was feeling much better. In fact, she was ready to go back to the compound and catch the next ship to the Territories when the volcano erupted.

Rea was sure she had no idea why the girl was suddenly so attached to her. Maybe it was because they had both been victims of the poisonous thorns at the same time. Whatever the cause, Rea would have liked to talk to her fadra or to have listened to the Great Leader's tale, but she could do neither because Katrina would not shut up.

Her father whispered in her ear, "Your girlfriend reminds me of Jestia."

"She is not my girlfriend," Rea whispered back. "Hell of all the Marching Night I think I have spent the least time with her. She has always avoided me like the plague."

"Because she is a nice girl and you were always in full rut," Fleat said, not even bothering to turn away from the Great Leader's storytelling. When she looked at her fadra he was nodding in agreement.

Katrina was talking again, or closer to the truth, *still* talking. "...and it just kept spewing ash and lava. I was sure the whole town was going to be engulfed..."

Suddenly Rea couldn't hear her. All she could hear was Tarius as she said, "And then Arvon and Dustin were no more because the volcano had killed them."

Rea tried to process that and found she couldn't. "Oh, Fadra, I am so sorry!" When she saw the glint of tears in his eyes her own started to fall, and she hugged his neck. "I am so sorry for so many things. So sorry about our friends who have died and that you always seem to be losing someone you love."

She noticed Katrina had stopped talking. She decided to mark the day on the calendar.

Tarius, Jena, Harris and Elise, Laz, her fadra, and Hared followed she and Fleat around as they showed them what they had done and explained what they planned to do.

Tarius had Diana on one hip and Darian on the other as Pete walked along behind her hanging onto her shirt tail. Rea thought this was odd, but then Jena said, "Give me one of those babies, Tarius. Or better yet put Darian down and let him walk." Tarius handed the baby to Jena. Pete immediately moved to hold Tarius's hand, and when she tried to set Darian down he made it clear he wasn't having any of it. Jena turned to Rea, "They have been like this ever since the volcano. I blame Jestia."

Rea turned to look at her Fadra and he explained. "If your girlfriend had shut up you could have heard the whole story. Jestia took Tarius by spell. The boys saw her disappear, and everything was crazy until she came back, so ever since then the boys have living fits if they can't see her. Now that they are away from home it appears they must also be touching her." He sighed. "The baby she just holds all the time because she is a baby hog."

"Alright then." Rea led them a little further then stopped. "We left these two plants here so we would know what to look out for. This one is poisonous to us, but this one is worse."

Tarius smiled. "Yes your girlfriend told us all about it on the voyage here."

"Katrina isn't my girlfriend; I hardly even know her," Rea explained again. Then added in a mumble, "I never even slept with her."

"Well you were all she talked about all the way here," Jena said, rolling her eyes. "I've known her all her life and have never seen her so smitten with anyone."

"Rea this and Rea that," Tarius said, "till I was sure I'd get here and find that you now shit gold. Though I have to say you have done a fantastic job here, I don't notice you are leaving a trail of gold."

"Like a slug might," Harris said, and all of them laughed at her. A few months ago this would have sent her into a rage or to the nearest pub. Now she laughed with them because she knew it for what it was. She was part of their pack, and this was how they treated each other. For the longest time she hadn't felt like she was part of anything; now she felt like she was part of everything, and she enjoyed the back and forth.

"Well you know what I absolutely can't shit out? Holding court. So you're going to have to do that while you're here, Great Leader."

"Well now I'm not laughing," Tarius said. "Do they have a lot of complaints?"

"Not really, but the ones they have are very stupid."

Well the girl wasn't wrong, Tarius thought as she looked at the two men standing in front of her. "Say that again?" because of course she was hopeful it would sound less stupid when he said it again.

"I found a really pretty stick I showed it to him and he looked at it, said that's nice and threw it into the brush. I told him I meant to keep it and he wouldn't even help me look for it."

"But you found it."

"Yes, but he didn't help me look for it at all."

Youngsters. It was one of the reasons she had sent so many to the Territories; they were always getting their junk in a knot over some stupid shit. She had hoped that here where they would have more than enough to occupy their time they would have better things to do than fight over stupid shit, but here was the proof that some people would always willingly go out of their way to find something to bitch about. She shifted Darian, and when she did Pete momentarily lost his grip on her sleeve and was grabbing at her till he found something to hold onto. In a lot of ways Pete was worse than Darian these days. No doubt because he had lost his birth parents and was old enough to realize how close they had all come to dying. Jena must have known how angry she was getting because she felt Jena's hand on her leg. She looked over at her, and the look on Jena's face told Tarius that she knew how stupid this man's complaint was but she hoped Tarius wasn't going to rip the man's head off and shit in the hole in front of their little boys.

The baby was with Hared and Rimmy, who were visiting with Rea. Tarius admitted—at least to herself—that as big a pain in the ass as it could be to have the boys right on top of her all the time, she was really more comfortable when she could see all her little ones at once. She took a deep breath and let it out. She was glad this man was not part of her pack; it was embarrassing enough to have him be one of her people.

Finally she sighed then said, "Child, at home we were hit by an earthquake, a volcano and a tsunami as fast as I just said it. While you were here looking for your pretty stick, back in the Kartik thousands of people have done nothing but pick up the sticks that used to be their lives for months; whole villages have been wiped out. I very nearly died, my son's fathers were killed in a river of molten rock, and my young ones are still so traumatized that they won't let me take a dump without them."

She stood up with Darian and looked at the line of people awaiting her judgement; none of them were the old ones. Old people took care of their own problems; they didn't make mountains out of mole hills. "If none of you have any problems worse than this man's not-lost stick, please don't waste my time."

She looked down at the man in front of her then. "Why did you not just wrestle it out?"

"He would not wrestle over it. He said it was stupid," the young man said.

She sat down and looked at the other man in the dispute. "You are right and he is a moron. Now go." When she looked up she noticed she had half as many people as she had only a moment ago.

Jena chuckled and whispered in her ear, "You know how to clear a room, my love. I'm going to go get Diana, feed her, and put her down for a nap."

"Don't you boys want to go with Mama?" she asked them.

They both shook their heads. "No," Darian said.

Jena laughed and stood up. As she started out of the room Laz followed her.

"Aren't you boys bored?" Tarius asked them because she certainly was.

"Not leave you, Madra," Darian said, and Pete nodded.

"Who's next?" The rest of the cases weren't nearly as stupid, but they were all petty. They always had been; that was the good thing about Katabull. She had never liked this part of her job but these days she could see it as nothing but a waste of her time. Disputes they should have easily taken care of themselves. Something about being nearly dead in the nowhere, able to do nothing had left her with no stomach for other people's petty problems.

Jena walked out the front door and found Rimmy, Hared, and Rea sitting on chunks of logs around the fire in front of the huge building the Marching Night had refurbished for themselves to use as a dwelling and the town's center.

Rea was actually holding Diana who seemed perfectly happy to have her sister hold her. It wasn't really time to feed her, but Jena could just sit through so much court before she seriously wanted to stick her head in a rain barrel and leave it there.

Jena sat down on a chair next to Rimmy and Laz stood behind her. She sighed and said, "Sit down, Laz, we are safe here." Ever since she had been kidnapped Laz had stuck to her like glue on Tarius's orders whenever they left the compound and Tarius wasn't with her. "I see no difference between this place and the compound."

Laz took a seat next to Rea. The baby immediately looked at him and smiled. He made a goofy face that made her laugh. The baby obviously loved Laz.

Rimmy shook his head. "Seriously, the boys would rather sit through court than be separated from Tarius."

Jena sighed. "Apparently so."

"We have to put an end to this. It's ridiculous," Hared said.

"You think it's ridiculous! Last night we wound up with all three of them in bed with us," Jena said. "It was getting better at home, and they were alright on the ship. I don't understand why the minute we got here it started all over again."

Rimmy cut Hared a look, and Hared shrugged and looked at his feet.

"What, did you do?" Jena demanded.

"I might have told them about lions and bears," Hared said,

"Why would you do that?" Jena nearly shrieked. "You know what they have been like ever since the disaster."

"I was putting the boys down for the night. They knew we were coming, and Darian wanted to know if I had a story about the Territories, so I told him one Tarius used to tell me when I was a kid. It was my favorite story..."

Rimmy cut him off. "The one about how a bear and a lion were fighting in the road over a moose carcass and we came right up on them and they attacked us..."

Jena cut him off. "And Tarius shifted, jumped off her horse, and killed both of them while we were all trying to calm our horses down. So they aren't clinging to her because they are afraid she will disappear they are clinging to her because they think she is the only one of us who can save them from attacking lions and bears."

"And see," Rimmy said taking immediate offense. "Now I think it's ridiculous. I could kill a lion and a bear, too."

"Yes, Rimmy, that's the real problem—that the boys don't respect your ability to kill a lion and bear at the same time."

Rimmy reached over and took the baby from Rea. Rea didn't look too happy about it which sort of surprised Jena. Rea had never shown any interest in the baby till then. Rimmy held the baby up in front of him so that their faces were almost touching and said, "My sweet girl, you know your father could kill a lion and bear for you don't you, oh yes you do you do." Diana laughed and grabbed at his hair. He smartly moved his head so she couldn't get a handful.

Rea made a face, no doubt at how silly her fadra sounded talking baby gibberish.

Jena looked at the girl and sighed. "All day, every day, between he and Tarius and the only time I really get to hold her is when I'm feeding her."

Rea had seen her fadra act this way before, but she really thought it was because the baby was new. She had never really enjoyed little kids or babies, but as soon as Tarius stepped off the ship with her little ones Rea knew what it was that had been missing that she couldn't quite put her finger on. There were no children in the colony, none. Even though she had hardly paid any attention to them in the compound, she had missed hearing the sound of children playing.

The Great Leader hadn't sent couples with cubs for a reason. She wanted them focused on the work at hand. Cubs here in the last few months would have meant fewer people were doing the work or children weren't getting watched. Half-watched children and lions, bears, and wolves—because they had killed a couple of those now—were a recipe for disaster. They needed to tame the colony before it would be safe for cubs. Hell, they still had bears in town at least once a week. They were eating a lot of bear meat.

Being unaware of what they were talking about, Rea spoke her thoughts out loud. "The more bears we kill the more elk, deer and that weird animal—What did you say it was? A moose?—we see."

They all looked at her like she had a cat growing out of her ear.

"Give me that cub you get to hold her all the time." Rea reached over and plucked the cub out of her fadra's arms and the baby cracked up. She was a beautiful cub with her madra's fine features and blue, blue eyes. She had a head full of red curls and the Great Leader's smile.

"Hi Diana," Laz said, moving to put his face right in hers. She slapped at him and laughed. "She's not afraid of anyone or anything," Laz told Rea. "She even lets you hold her."

Rea knew why Laz said it. She had hardly paid any attention when Diana was born. Her father's husband was one of the birth parents—the baby had three due to one of Jestia's spells—so the baby wasn't really related to her, but then neither were Riglid or Laz. Jared had the same birth parents she did, but she was closer to Riglid and Laz than she was to Jared, especially to Laz.

She spoke to him in a whisper. The rest were busy having their own conversation about what to do about the cub's fear of lions and bears. "You know I have hardly noticed anything for five years because I was mostly drunk since mother died. I let my Katabull side run the show because I just couldn't handle my grief. My madra had a talk with me, and I stopped drinking. My grief enveloped me fully and it didn't kill me. I realized that being drunk all the time didn't make me feel better all it did was hold me in a state of dulled-down grief. It was only when I was able to own my grief that I was able to climb out of it."

"My madra's death hit us all hard in different ways. None of us were really there for you because we were too busy licking our own wounds," Laz said.

Hearing his voice the baby put out her arms and chuffed at him, and he took her from Rea.

"That cub loves you, Laz, and so do I. No one else's grief crowded everyone else's. Only mine did that because I choose to drink. I choose to screw everyone who didn't move fast enough. I choose to tear everything up. I am so sorry, Laz, for everything—for sucking the life out of our family, for all the times you had to come and get me in Montero, for the shame..."

"Stop right there. Rea, look what you have done. Look at who you are now. Don't you know why we were all so disgusted with you?"

"Because I was a drunken, irresponsible whore."

He laughed. "Well of course there was that." He got serious again. "No, Rea, we were so mad at you because we knew that wasn't who you are." He motioned around with his free arm and the baby mimicked him. "This...*this* is who you are. To know someone is capable of so much yet chooses to do nothing but tear holes in their own life and the lives of everyone who cares about them—that was what was completely unacceptable."

"I am still sorry for all I did that made things worse for you not better. She was your madra after all."

"That, as you know, doesn't matter. You're my sister; Diana is our sister; Riglid is our brother; it is all the same. Rea, you were always closer to Mother than the rest of us. You have to know that to her there was no difference between me and you."

She nodded. She did know that now. She hadn't before, but she did now. "Did you know this is the first time I have held Diana? Fadra and Hared adopted Pete, and I don't know him at all. I don't think I have ever even talked to him. Darian I have talked to just because he mostly demanded I do so. I was here for a month before I realized why I had pushed everyone away. I was afraid to care about anyone too much."

"I have done the same but different thing," Laz said. "The way Madra died—it took its toll on all of us—none worse than Mother, and I have to say—though if you ever tell her I said it I will call you a liar—I really see no difference between you drinking and causing trouble and her running around in battle trying to throw herself on someone's spear. Both are equally selfish; both would remove you from us when we most needed you. I look around me at this place; I look at you and I see that you have healed. I am trying, but I still haven't quite made it. I am afraid to get serious about anyone; I want to but the minute I start to have anything approaching real feelings for a woman I run away. So in this moment you are doing better than I am, and I will not judge you for your past if you will not judge me for what I am still doing."

"I would never judge you Laz," she hugged him.

Diana gave her the Great Leader's scowl. Rea laughed as she let go of her brother and said in the baby's face, "He was my brother first."

Jena stood up walked over and took Diana from Laz. "She's about to start crying because she's hungry." Laz started to get up and Jena patted him on the shoulder. "Stay right here and visit with your sister. I'm going right back to where Tarius is holding court. I'm going to flop my tit out and feed the baby and maybe then Tarius will realize this is the same as the compound... You know except for the lions and bears." She shot Hared a dirty look and walked towards the building.

Hared looked at them and said, "It was my favorite story when I was a kid."

It was one of Rea's, too. Tarius used to tell it to them and so had Dustan. Rea had to admit that she had always enjoyed Dustan's version better because he made Tarius much more amazing in it than Tarius did. She imagined Hared had done the same, so it was no wonder that in the Land of Lions and Bears the boys clung to Tarius.

Then she remembered Dustan was dead; Arvon was dead. She looked at Laz. "Just what the hell happened? I have only heard pieces because Katrina was in my ear and would not shut up."

"She's very pretty," Laz said with a grin.

"She isn't my girlfriend," Rea said. "Seriously, since we arrived I have not once thought about sex. I just don't have time. Now tell me all that happened."

Laz told her. It was a long story, and at some point her fadra and his mate had wondered off—no doubt they were in no hurry to hear it again having lived through it.

"What exactly happened to Tarius and Jestia?"

"I'm not sure even they know, but they both nearly died to dig a trench that stopped the lava from wiping out most of our side of the island. Tarius seems to be mostly the same, but Jestia... She is still physically weak, yet so powerful she nearly glows. She seems... I don't know... more removed from everyone, more connected to everything and less to anyone except the Great Leader. It's hard to explain really. Ufalla told me she feels like an extra wheel most days, like even she is somehow outside the space that Jestia now inhabits alone. But when she and Tarius are together you can see they live in the same space. I don't think Ufalla knows what to do about that at all. Where to put the fact that her wife is more tied to the Great Leader than she is to her. In fact, if I'm honest, I think Ufalla is worse off than Jestia right now. I mean Jestia isn't any crazier than she ever was though she certainly talks about things that are even harder to understand. But Ufalla doesn't know whether to shit or go blind most days."

"And I thought we were busy here." She heard cheering and knew what it meant she answered the curious look on her brother's face. "Someone has killed something which will be dinner tonight and breakfast in the morning." She sighed. "I have yet to kill even a rabbit."

"And yet they all still respect you," Laz said,

"Do they?" She didn't know that.

"Of course they do. Look at how they talk to you; how they do what you ask them to do."

She had noticed even the younger members of the colony spent less time arguing with her but hadn't really thought that was anything more than them accepting she wasn't going to back down if she felt she was right. "Let's go see what they got. I hope it's a bear and not a wolf or a lion, they are gamey as hell." Tarius came running out of the building Darian on her hip and Pete holding her hand.

"What have they killed?" Tarius asked excitedly.

"I don't know," Rea said. "How did you know they had killed anything?"

"I asked what the yelling was all about and they said it meant someone had killed something."

Tarius passed them even with both boys and Rea asked, "Riglid really could not keep up with her?" Of all the things Laz had told her this was the one she found most unbelievable. Because her fadra had been said to be the fastest Katabull on the Kartik, and Riglid had beat him in a foot race three years ago.

"It has something to do with the magic she has dragged with her from her past life. She says it is the reason that she is able to do all the things she really shouldn't be able to do but does." Laz added to the confused look on her face, "It doesn't really make sense to me, either."

"Why did Riglid not come?" It was a good question. After all he was the Great Leader's runner; he went everywhere she went. Rea could think of only one reason he wouldn't come and that was because he was still mad at her.

"Kaden broke his leg about a week before we left. Well actually crazy Kaseria broke his leg."

"I thought they were good friends."

"Oh they are best friends which is why when she told him to step into her cupped hands and she would lift him up so he could pick the mangos out of a tree he agreed. Long story short she still doesn't know her own strength in her Katabull form, and she wound up throwing him up into the tree instead of merely lifting him. Really it's his own fault; he knows she's crazy. Anyway Tarius said that father was coming and he could take his old job back for the trip and Riglid should stay home and take care of Kaden. I think she felt guilty because it was after all her daughter-in-law who crippled our brother's husband. Of course if he wasn't a scrawny human man..."

Rea nodded. She was just glad it wasn't that Riglid as still holding her a grudge. They came up on the kill site, and it was yet another huge bear. Her fadra was standing triumphantly over it, his sword bloody, and as Tarius came up with the boys he yelled triumphantly, "See boys I can kill a bear!"

"Gods and spiders," Rea cursed. "He hasn't even been here two days yet."

Finding she needed a moment by herself, Rea grabbed a big chunk of bear meat and headed for the woods. There was a big stump left from one of the trees they had used to make the timbers to build the docks, and Rea had started putting the food for the human on the stump. She stood away and chuffed a couple of times; it was how she had started calling the human to her.

In moments the human woman had come crawling out of the woods. She was always crouched as if ready to spring and run away at any moment, but she walked up and grabbed the piece of meat greedily. Rea smiled at her and she awkwardly tried to smile back.

What are you doing here? How long have you been here? What exactly is your story?

Not too surprisingly Rea did not hear her come up till she was whispering in her ear, "What are you doing?"

Rea jumped.

The human watched Tarius closely but didn't start and run away. She continued to eat. In fact, Rea was more startled by her sudden appearance than the human was.

"Fleat said he thinks she is a feral human," Rea whispered back.

"Oh at least that," Tarius said. In a low tone, but loud enough the human could hear, she muttered words Rea didn't recognize. The human looked right at Tarius and then she did something Rea had never seen or heard her do—she spoke.

"Erah," she said. She pointed to herself with the hand not filled with meat. "Erah."

"What did you say to her?" Rea asked in a whisper.

"Basically, 'Halt! Who goes there?' They are the only Amalite…" She spit out of habit, "…words I know. Did she just spit?"

"I think so," Rea said. "Maybe she is just copying you."

"Amalite," Tarius said. This time she didn't spit, but clearly the human did, and the look on her face said it all. "Now that is very curious. Where did she learn that? Her name is Erah." Tarius pointed at Rea and said, "Rea." The human looked at Rea, but she didn't try to say her name. Clinging to the meat she took off into the woods.

"Come," Tarius said.

Rea was afraid she was about to have her ass handed to her on a platter. She walked away from where she had been feeding the human.

"Am I in trouble?" Rea asked.

"For showing kindness to that poor girl? Not at all. But she has language."

"What does that mean?"

"Well clearly she is not Kartik. It means she would have been able to speak when the Kartik forces landed here, attacked her town, killed all her people who didn't flee never to return, and burned most of the place down. And we have no idea how old she was when that happened. She has some language, so she probably kept that going talking to animals, plants, inanimate objects. She would have had no chance of surviving as she obviously has unless she was at least three. But does she have a three-year-old's language skills or a six-year-old's?"

"What would be the difference?" Rea asked

"At three any horror would just be images she couldn't really tack onto anyone or anything. I was six when the Amalites…" She spit again, and so did Rea now. "…killed most of my pack, when they slit my throat." She pointed to the very visible scar across her neck as if Rea hadn't seen it nearly every day for most of her life. "I never forgot that moment. I can still clearly see images from that time. It drove me to be a killer of Amalites. It drove my whole life. If she was the same age I was—six or more—when our forces separated her from everything she knew... Well, humans, Katabull... we are built for relationships, and that poor creature has been alone for over twenty-five years. If she knows it's our fault..."

"So what should I do?"

"What you have been doing. But you should tell the others about her so that they don't accidently frighten or hurt her. So that she won't be able to sneak up on someone and maybe try to do them harm."

"Do you think she is dangerous?"

"All beings are dangerous, but I do not believe she has any malice in her. Only remember I was six when the event that turned me into the war lord of nations happened to me."

Chapter Three

It had been a year since the great mountain blew up and as far as Ufalla was concerned took her life with it. Jestia's power had consumed her and everyone around her. At least that was the way Ufalla saw it.

She loved Jestia and she knew Jestia loved her, but Jestia didn't *need* her. Ufalla worked at the Arvon and Dustan Swordwork Academy that Hestia had built in their memory. She trained young fighters, but for what? There was no battle. She made money doing it, but so what? Jestia as heir apparent had literally vaults full of gold. The money Ufalla made did little more than pay her own bar tab. Jestia didn't need her protection; Jestia was the great savior of the Kartik. What she and the Great Leader had done... Well that was all anyone had talked about for a year.

Possibly what grated most of all was that Jestia had done it with Tarius. More than feeling useless, more than feeling she could no longer really understand Jestia and that Jestia didn't need her, what bothered her the most at night when she couldn't sleep was that Tarius understood Jestia completely. That Jestia would talk to Jazel about things Ufalla would never understand she could handle; they were both witches. That Jestia would have longer and deeper conversations with the Great Leader galled Ufalla no end.

And that was what was happening right now. They had gone to the compound because Jestia just had to talk to Tarius. Of course she couldn't say about what, and instead of riding there which would have given them some time alone to just talk, there apparently wasn't time for that and so Jestia just popped them both to the compound. Ufalla supposed she was expected to be happy because at least Jestia didn't leave her at home this time. These days she would often come home from the sword academy to learn that Jestia had been and was already back from the compound.

But here she was sitting at her parent's table picking at her dinner while Jestia was off having yet another private conversation with Tarius. Almost more infuriating than all that was that it didn't bother Jena at all. Not at all, but then Jena knew she was the most important person in Tarius's life and Ufalla no longer knew that about Jestia.

"You've hardly touched your food," Elise said, worry in her voice.

"Can I have it?" her younger brother Tarence asked.

"Knock yourself out," she said, and pushed her plate over to her brother.

Her younger sister Hera called him a pig then tried to take some of the food for herself. That had them growling at each other which lead quickly to pushing and shoving. Elise reached across the table, palmed each of their heads and knocked them together.

"Ow mother!" they both said at the same time.

"Calm down," she ordered.

When Ufalla looked at her father he was grinning from ear to ear. He still thought the odd things her mother did and said were cute. She had wanted a relationship like theirs; instead she had whatever she had with Jestia.

"What's wrong?" her mother demanded of her. Her younger siblings were mumbling hateful things at each other Elise glared at them and they shut right up. "What's wrong?" Elise asked her again.

"What the hell am I? There is no war so everything I know is a waste..."

"I suppose we should start a war just so you can have something important to do," Harris said with a grin.

"I am no one; I am nothing."

"Because you did not dig a trench that saved part of the island." When her father said it he was no longer smiling, and he quit eating his dinner which was monumental. "This is not, has never been about you. But that's the problem, isn't it? What exactly is it that you want, Ufalla? You wanted nothing as badly as you wanted Jestia and you got her. Now you have her what? You can't stand that she is as amazing as you thought she was, or is it that her star shines so brightly you feel diminished by her light. Life isn't a contest."

Her older brother was an amazing bard and he told a brilliant story about their father. She found herself words from her brother's story against her father now. "That's easy for you to say. You never wanted more than to ride beside the Great Warlord and take up her slack. You never minded dwelling in her large shadow. Well I do mind, especially when my own wife prefers her company to mine."

She stood up and so did her mother. "Ufalla, calm down, sit down eat something."

"Yes that will fix everything!" Ufalla thundered.

Her father stood up then, caught her eyes and held them. "Do you know what your problem is? That you don't actually have a problem. There is nothing at all wrong with your life except you want to be the center of attention—not just to Jestia but to everyone. Tarius and Jestia went through something horrible that none of us can imagine, yet they are not the ones whining about their lot in life. It is you, only you. The rest of us also did nothing of real value that day, but we are just happy to be alive. We are happy that as bad as things were the worst didn't happen. There are still Kartiks living in the compound because they still have nowhere of their own to live, and what is your big problem? That your wife is talking to your godmother."

Her mother said nothing for a minute which meant she agreed with him. Which she proved when she finally said, "My darling girl. You have done nothing but complain for a year, yet as far as I know Jestia has not complained about you even once."

Ufalla nodded and sat down. She stewed in what they had both said for a minute then said, "You are both right." She took her empty plate away from her brother and put more food on it.

But knowing they were right didn't help her figure out what that made her.

Jestia sat on a bench by the lake looking up at Tarius who was standing in front of her. "The same dream has woken me up three nights now. Here's the thing—it isn't a bad dream, but it's making me nuts because I have no idea what it means."

"Can you tell it to me?" Tarius asked.

"If I didn't think so I would not have come here," Jestia said with a smile. "I am in my spring alone. It is night but both moons are full. The water starts to glow white and I can feel not just the silky warmth of it but suddenly the energy I feel is exactly like it was at the energy well behind Sedric's keep. When I wake from the dream it is always hours before sunrise and yet I feel completely rested as if I have been asleep all night. I get up, go to the apothecary and start working. I work all day and I am not tired at all. And as you know I was drained for weeks. Even when my magic power came back completely I was still physically weak for months more; I thought I might never feel my old self again. Then I started having these dreams, and when I wake from them I am as charged as I was when we stood in that place. It's as if I have gone to the energy well."

"I think you are, Jestia. Your magic has been growing stronger, and I think you have found a way to channel the energy of the well into you as you sleep. You are in your hot spring in the dream because I took you to Jazel's spring when you were drained and it saved you."

"Yes I think that's it. Jazel said it was just a dream."

"Just because it's only a dream doesn't mean it doesn't have power," Tarius said with a smile. They talked for another hour about everything from Tarius's kids to the new spell Jestia had been working on to try to detect Amalite missionaries.

"...the idea I'm working on would have them yelling every time they tried to preach so that they couldn't hide what they were doing. They have always infiltrated everywhere by sneaking around, whispering, gathering numbers in private. They can't do that if every time they try to talk to someone they start screaming at the top of their lungs now, can they? The tricky part of the spell is turning out to be trying to figure out how to cover the most area with it. Can I build it to cover the whole island? A whole country? I know I can cast it in an interior space, but I sort of feel like if it isn't big enough what's the point."

"Even a single dwelling spell like that might come in handy," Tarius said,

Jestia sighed. "I'd better go find Ufalla. I will be happy when she finally realizes that what happened didn't actually happen to her."

Tarius nodded. "You and I because of who we are understand things other people do not in a way they do not, and she is not you Jestia. She wants things you do not want and needs things you do not need. In a way she is doing to you what Jabone did to me; she is not who she wants to be, and she is blaming you."

Jestia shrugged. "She will get over it just like he did." She gave Tarius a quick hug and then she vanished. She popped up inside their hut. Ufalla was not back from her parents yet which was good. She loved Ufalla and she just wanted her to stop all her stupid selfish shit. Of course she couldn't say that. No she had to tell her how pretty and wonderful she was and hope that would be enough to make her stop whining about... well everything. To hear Ufalla talk everything was wrong and nothing was good and she needed Jestia to stop being connected to Tarius, stop being who she was, doing what she did, and what exactly? What exactly did she expect of Jestia? She was heir apparent. It wasn't what she wanted; it was her brother's fault for dying and her father's for accidentally killing him.

She was the most powerful witch in the Kartik, maybe the whole world. This also wasn't something she planned; it just happened. What Ufalla wanted from her she couldn't do. She couldn't be just some dumb girl who couldn't do anything better than Ufalla could.

She didn't expect Ufalla to change for her. She was alright with her doing whatever she wanted to do within reason. She better not cheat on her, and she wouldn't put up with her being drunk all the time. Both probably had more to do with her father who was both a whore monger and a drunk as well as an idiot, than any moral high ground.

She dreaded Ufalla coming home. When had she gone from being excited to see Ufalla to dreading her presence? *When the world came apart and she went from thinking the sun shone out of my arse to thinking everything I was and everything I did was wrong. I changed because I didn't have a choice, and she changed because she couldn't stand what*

39

I have become. Yet nothing that should be important to her about me has changed at all. I still love her, I am still devoted to her, I'm always here when she needs me. I can't help it that I now dwell in a place here but not here, or that I see things others can't see and know things I can never tell them.

Ufalla walked in the door, walked right over to her and hugged her. She hugged her back. "Has someone died again?" she asked carefully.

Ufalla laughed. "No, no one has died. I am sorry, Jestia, I have been acting an ass. I had a talk with my parents..."

"And they told you, you were being an ass?"

"In not so many words. Mostly they put things in perspective for me."

When they made love Ufalla felt like everything was going to be fine. It had felt like Jestia was fully there, not just physically but emotionally. She felt like she had finally come to terms with who she was and who Jestia was. They woke up the next morning and had breakfast just the two of them. They talked the way they used to about everything and nothing and then Jestia popped them home.

When they materialized in front of Jazel's, Ufalla immediately felt tricked. "I, I thought we were going home."

"I thought you have classes today?"

"I do but..."

"This is a closer walk than from our house and I am supposed to work with Jazel today, so..." She kissed Ufalla on the cheek and walked into Jazel's.

Ufalla stood there for a moment. Didn't she need to go home before she went to the academy? No she didn't. Her clothes were clean, and she had everything she needed at the academy. Still she stood there for a moment looking at the door Jestia had just closed. She had gone someplace she could follow but didn't belong. She took a deep breath let it out and started for the academy. How could she be so sure of something last night and even first thing this morning yet be so unsure of it now?

It's not about Jestia. I'm unhappy with me. I'm no one. What is my purpose, what is the reason for me?

Chapter Four

They had just made it through their first winter. At the start they had all been excited about the snow, having never seen it before. They had built their dwellings well enough and had put back plenty of food and firewood. They found they could hunt in the cold, but it had them wearing more clothes than they had ever worn in their lives. Fishing was right out. Most days they spent huddled around their fireplaces trying to stay warm, so by the time they had dealt with months of snow and cold, even resorting to chopping ice off the river to get water, they were ready for it to be over.

Then as the warmer weather started to melt the snow they had other fun problems. The river rose and overflowed its banks. One place was bad enough it looked like it might break threw and flood the colony, so they had quickly cut down trees and put up a temporary levy.

Then the ground had turned to absolute mush for a while. It rained nearly every day at home, so they thought they were used to walking in mud, but this stuff was sticky and deep. It had a high clay content, so if you walked in it for more than five minutes you spent ten getting the layers of muck off your boots.

And that was just the short list of the difficulties the Territories presented that the Kartik did not. It was an adventure. Yet didn't feel like it at all when all of them were sitting inside for most of four months with nothing to do but tan hides, feed the fires and cook meals.

Rea wondered how the human woman had made it all these years with the bitter cold winters. Along with food she had also brought the woman new clothes and some blankets and was not at all surprised when the next day when she went to feed her she was already wearing the clothes. Tarius had told her that the woman must be very intelligent or she would not have survived all these years. During the summer months the human had occasionally been clean so she knew to bathe. But during the winter she obviously did not bathe, and she smelled like smoke and was covered with soot which meant she kept a fire. Yet even from the catwalk no one had seen smoke besides their own, and Rea had looked.

The others all knew about the feral human now, but as Rea had asked them to they had left Erah alone. Rea would now bring the things to the stump, call her by name, and within minutes Erah would come running.

When Rea wasn't up to her ass in work she took care of the human and she hunted all over the surrounding woods. She had yet to even see an animal she could stalk for them to eat much less killed one. It seemed to her that every other Katabull in the settlement had brought down game but her. It wasn't true, but it sure felt that way.

They were still keeping a fire in the fireplace, as were most of the colonists, because it still got really cold at night, but they could now let it die down during the day.

Tarius had come twice—neither time in the snow, much less the heart of winter—brought them fresh fruit from the island—something they all missed—and other supplies they couldn't get or make themselves. It was always a thrill to get to visit with family and friends she no longer saw every day. Her brother Riglid came with his husband the last two times, and it was clear he held no ill feelings for her.

Tarius held court when she was there, and Rea wondered if Tarius was as short tempered with people in the compound as she was with the colonists. Tarius had no patience at all for any petty grievances they had and would tell them so.

The Great Leader would tell them what they were doing right and what they could do better. It turned out that Tarius's bigger plan was to have them break into three groups a day's ride away from each other, building two more compounds. Her reason was sound: by spreading them out the game would be able to replenish itself because they wouldn't be over-hunting the areas. There would be less fish inland, but by placing them close to rivers they would have both a source of fresh water and fish. There would also be less cold in winter and better growing conditions. Of course this meant a lot more work for everyone.

The fishing off the coast was amazing. They had put out a few lobster pots just to see what they would get and pulled up traps filled with the biggest lobsters they had ever seen. With only two ships they were able to bring in all the fish they could eat.

Their crops had done alright, not great, but alright. They would have to work the land for a couple of years and build it up to have better yields. At least that was what the old woman Rea had put in charge of gardening had told them. It turned out that most of the older members of their group had all fought in the Great War. They had been trained then about what was edible and what was not, and what they didn't know Jena and Tarius had taught them on their visits. Luckily the area was abundant in edible plant life. Though the winter had been long and cold, it hadn't been hungry.

They had rebuilt the catwalk around the top story of what they all now called Marching Night Keep, and they took shifts walking it. It had allowed them to spot bears and other dangerous animals before anyone could be surprised or attacked.

It wasn't hard to see why there were so many bears. Until the Katabull got there they were the top predator, and the rivers and sea were full of fish. But mostly the skeleton town left after the fire had made great dens. In fact one of their biggest challenges in rebuilding the structures had been getting rid of the bears that had lived in them first. They ate a lot of bear that first year.

The cleared fields the Amalites had farmed around the town had all grown in making them harder to clear than virgin forest would have been. The Amalites had planted berries, vineyards and fruit trees, all of which had grown in and taken over. They were careful not to destroy any of the fruiting plants and vines. It was different fruit than they were used to, but it was good, and they had eaten a lot of it.

So would have the bears.

It turned out that the thorn trees that made them so sick actually bore small limes filled with a multitude of seeds. It was no wonder there were so many of them. They were not in the woods and so they were something the Amalites had planted and that needed sun to propagate. Rea almost felt like it was the Amalites still trying to kill the

Katabull from the grave. The limes were incredibly sour but not bad in tea especially with enough honey, and honey was abundant here. They had several people who were good at robbing hives, though she wasn't one of them. In fact, she was just standing close when they were robbing one and she managed to get stung three times before she could get away.

It was very cold in the early morning, but it was supposed to be the best time to hunt, so that was what Rea was doing. She armed herself with a spear and headed out in her Katabull form. She went alone for a lot of reasons not the least of which was she wanted to kill something all by herself. She had always been a good hunter and this was ridiculous.

She wasn't far into the woods when she heard distressed screaming and knew instinctively it was the human woman. She ran towards the sound and saw that the human was being chased by a moose. It caught Erah on its antlers and threw her; she landed hard then jumped up and started running. Rea could see there was blood on Erah's cheek.

Rea ran after the rampaging beast, jumped up and drove her spear deep into the body of the moose aiming for its heart. She was sure she hit it, but it didn't stop so she jumped on it, bit the back of its neck, sunk her claws into its throat and hung on. It ran several more feet then dropped like a rock so that she had to let go and jump away quickly to stop the huge thing from falling on her.

But she didn't even get to do a victory dance over her kill because the human was obviously hurt. Rea sniffed the air then ran in the direction she knew the woman had gone. Rea didn't know how bad Erah was hurt. When the girl saw Rea coming she doubled her pace. She was fast, but she wasn't the Katabull. Rea easily caught her, but holding onto her was a different story.

"Erah, Erah calm down," she said. To her surprise the woman quit squirming.

Then Rea she realized something; Erah had screamed in the first place because she was in trouble and hoped she would come to help her.

"Let me see your wound." She knew the girl didn't really understand her, but she seemed to calm down even more.

The wound was bad and deep and had probably been caused by hitting a limb when she was thrown. The fact she was running as fast as she was meant she hadn't broken any bones. The wound needed to be treated because it went all the way through her cheek till, if she tried, Rea could see Erah's back teeth. But would she let Rea treat it?

Rea slowly released her hold on the woman. There was a moment when it was clear she wanted to run, but she didn't. Rea gave the wound a closer look; it needed a stitch or two for sure.

Slowly she reached into her pocket and pulled out her handkerchief. She caught the girl's eyes and held them then slowly raised the cloth and gently put it on the wound. The girl lifted her hand and held the cloth tightly to her own face, so she knew what to do about wounds. This close to her Rea could see why—the girl was covered in scars as if she were one of them, a sword fighter.

Garrett could stitch up her wound no problem, and he had powders that could knock her out so he could do it, but Rea was afraid bringing her into the colony was just going to freak Erah completely out. She had spent a long time gaining her trust and Rea didn't want to lose it now.

She looked around her. How far was she from the colony? She turned in the direction of the town and yelled out as loud as she could, "I have made a kill and I need a medic!"

The girl jumped and started to run off.

Rea grabbed her arm. "Shush," she told the woman, and she was still and quiet. Erah pushed the cloth harder against her cheek.

Rea listened and soon she heard Fleat yell out, "Yell again so we can find you!"

She did and in minutes Garrett was there. As she heard the triumphant calls of the Katabull who had reached her kill site she damned her luck that she wasn't right there to gloat.

"Come up slow," she told Garrett. "No sudden moves, and hand me the powder to knock her out." He did and she slowly reached in her pocket and pulled out the piece of bread she had wrapped in a cloth that she was going to eat if she got hungry while out hunting. She tore off a small piece then pressed the powders into it in her pocket and held it out to the girl.

"That isn't going to work," Garrett whispered in her ear. "How is she going to chew with a hole in her face?"

But of course he was wrong because he had never been hungry, and what had Fleat told her? "A man who has never been hungry will never know how a hungry man acts." Of course when he said it he was talking about people who couldn't feel other people's pain, but in this instance it worked as he had spoken it.

The human greedily grabbed the bread from her hand and stuffed it into her mouth. In seconds she was wobbling. She started to panic and tried to run off, but Rea grabbed her and held her till she was still. Then Rea laid her down on the ground and watched as Garrett poured way too much Montero spring water on it. It was a good thing Tarius brought it to them in barrels or he would use it all up in a week. He washed Erah's face then he looked at Rea and smiled.

"I had not seen her at all before. The others said they thought she might be pretty under the grim, but she is stunning." He threaded his needle and put in twice as many stitches as he needed. As she figured it, with the closeness with which he placed them it would take twenty or more, and Rea couldn't hold her tongue.

"Do not put in so many stitches, Garrett! Half that many will do."

"She is stunning, and smaller stitches will mean a cleaner scar," he said, not looking up from what he was doing.

"For the love of the Nameless One she is a feral human! I'm sure she doesn't care what she looks like. Those will have to come out in a few days, and I will have to catch and hold her or drug her again to do it."

"And pulling a few more will not matter," he said, and just continued. When he had finished he put too much ointment on it and wrapped her head in gauze until very little of her face could be seen. Rea said nothing but knew the creature wasn't very likely to leave any of that on after she woke up.

When he had finished Rea said, "Thank you, Garret, I know she is not one of us..."

"But she is Rea; all of us are part of the Everything. She thinks and feels just like we do, and frankly she was here first. We have come into her space." He packed his bag and stood up. "I saw your kill as I ran up here; it is by far the biggest animal anyone has killed yet."

"Thank you. Tell them I am sorry I can't help them butcher it out, but if they will leave the hide I will pick it up on my way home and take care of it myself. I need to stay with her until she wakes up at least."

"They will understand, but know we will start eating it before you get back."

Of course they would because it was something they hadn't eaten before. They had mostly been eating predators because they were trying to make the colony safe for children and livestock. All they had now were fifty horses, twenty-five of which belonged to the Marching Night because of course they were the ones who went out scouting and did patrols. But Tarius would bring goats and chickens when next they came, and they would have to have tight pens built for them and shut them up at night or they would get eaten in a week—and not by them.

"Tell them they can kill these things now. It turns out that this grass-eater will actually attack unprovoked. Since it is bigger than a horse it could probably kill us easier than a bear."

"That is good news... I hope it tastes like elk. I think we are all a little tired of eating bear." He left, and Rea wondered what she should do with the woman now. Lying on the ground she was bound to get too cold. She picked her up and stood there with her.

Well now what? She smells bad, but not like an Amalite. Of course that is because they throw shit in their streets, don't wipe their asses, and never really bathe. The smell of smoke is strong on her, so she has to have fire yet I have looked and looked and seen no smoke but ours. Maybe she is doing like the people in the Hive—building her fires at night and letting them go out during the day. But why would she do that? There have been no people here for twenty-five years, and animals... well they are afraid of fire.

Fire, that is the answer. I will find where she is living by sniffing out her fire. The wind is coming from the direction of the ocean; our smoke will be coming from there.

She turned, sniffed the air and soon she locked onto the smell of smoke coming from a different direction. She started towards it. Rea was surprised when she found a cave opening because it wasn't very far from the stump where she normally fed the woman.

As she walked in the smell of smoke told her she was in the right place, but even if it hadn't she would have known she had found the human's den and not a bear's. There was a wall some five foot in that had been built out of bricks. It went from the floor to ceiling and in the middle of it was a door with a window. Rea shifted her hold on Erah, opened the door and walked into a small, nearly-round room. The only light came from the smoldering fire and the window in the door. More than enough for her, but it would have been hard for a human to see. Then she noticed a candle sitting in a niche on the wall. It was warm inside and surprisingly clean. There were wooden boxes stacked three and four high around the room. From the look of the top box in every case they were filled with everything the human thought was useful that she would have scavenged from the village. She had a bed; she even had a chair and cooking pots.

Rea lay the woman down on her bed and added wood to her fire. When it started to smoke she knew why they hadn't seen any smoke from her fires. The back wall of the room was an obvious cave-in—a stack of crumbled rock—and the smoke drafted into it. Caves could go on for miles, they breathed. At least that's what someone had told her when they were about to fight in the Hive. The Nameless One alone knew where this smoke wound up, and of course a lot of it wound up in the room till the fire really took off. It probably drafted better with the door open but with bears, lions and wolves in the forest and the cold weather, Rea doubted the human left it open very much.

Rea wondered what would be best. Should she leave Erah to wake on her own wondering how she had gotten there? If Rea did was Erah going to right away rip off the awful dressing Garrett had put on her face and maybe the stitches, too? If Rea stayed would she be able to make her understand that she needed to leave her wound alone?

She had made her first kill in the Territories. It was huge, and she really wanted to be back there helping butcher it and maybe crowing a little bit. But she felt she should stay and wait for the woman to wake up and at least try to make her understand to leave the wound alone.

Rea was bored, so she wandered around looking at what the woman had gathered. There was cookware, jars, plates, cups. There was a stack of clothes and blankets all folded, but when she took a good look at them she realized they weren't much better than, if as good as, rags. Cloth didn't hold up well over as much time as had passed. These were the things she didn't wear anymore because they were threadbare and full of holes. She kept them anyway because until the Katabull had arrived, she had not seen another person in decades. She would have thought someday these might be the good things.

The human had a whole box of candles of different sizes and shapes and another filled with knives, hunting knives, skinning knives, eating knives. Yet Rea couldn't remember ever seeing the woman carrying a knife.

She walked over to the bed checked the girl over and found she had a knife tied on the inside of her pants. Why she wore it like that Rea could only guess. She covered the woman up. She was probably going to be shocky when she woke up and the warmer she was the better.

Rea's eye went to an odd shape against the far wall right across from the girl's bed it was covered with an old blanket. Rea walked over and pulled the blanket off. When she did she actually jumped. Under the blanket was a mummy. She moved closer to get a better look and realized what she was seeing. The mummy wore Kartik armor, and in what was left of her hand she held the handle of a Kartik broad sword. Rea covered the mummy back up, then turned to look at the woman.

Maybe that explained the spitting. Maybe this Kartik soldier was so badly wounded they thought she was dead but she wasn't. *They would have sacked this village and then rode out hard to get to their rendezvous point. This group would have had the longest distance to cover. They would have stripped the dead of their weapons... though she has her sword. But if she was badly wounded but still alive and unable to travel they might have left her, so they would have left her with her sword. She might have asked to be left behind. She might have gotten better. We don't kill noncombatants, so civilian inhabitants—that weren't their filthy priests—would have been allowed to flee from their burning village. In all the chaos, the girl could have been left behind especially if one or both of her parents were killed in the fighting. She might have hidden and been left for dead. These two would have been the only living people left. They would have depended on each other. But how long did the soldier live? Obviously not long enough to teach the girl our language but maybe long enough to help her build this, to get her up big enough to be able to fend for herself.*

The girl let out a groan and moved. Rea watched her wishing she could ask her all the many questions that raced through her mind. The clothes Rea had given her were way too big for her. Katabull were bigger than most humans even in their human form, and of course they wore their clothes big so they didn't rip when they shifted. Rea had never learned to make clothes or even take them in, but the woman had made do by tying up the legs of the pants and the sleeves of the shirt. She hadn't just cut them off, though she certainly could have.

Erah's eyes opened wide. She looked at Rea and rubbed at the gauze. "Rea," she said. Rea had been trying to get her to say her name for months.

"Yes." She pointed at herself, "Rea."

The woman poked at the dressing on the wound.

Rea moved slowly forward, gently took her hand and moved it away from the wound. "Leave it alone." She knew it was probably stupid to talk to the girl, but didn't know what else to do. Then she had a thought. She poked her own cheek made a face like it hurt then placed her hand over it as if to protect it. To her amazement the girl nodded her head; she understood her. "Garrett is not the best medic, but he'll learn... you know if he doesn't run us out of medical supplies first."

She pointed towards the door then to herself. She walked to the door and walked out then walked right back in. "I will be right back."

The woman nodded and Rea walked back out the door shut it and took off at a run towards the colony. On the way she passed six members of her pack who were still dressing out her kill. They cheered when they saw her.

"Will the human be alright?" Fleat asked.

"I think so. I am going to go get her some tea and honey; I don't think she will be able to really eat anything solid for a couple of days. Thank you all for dressing my kill. I am sorry I didn't help but..."

"You saved the human," Garrett said, "...and have brought in more meat than any of us have ever seen on one animal."

"That is the hide," Fleat said, pointing to a small mountain. He laughed at the look on her face. "Captain, oh my Captain, it took you forever to kill anything but when you finally did... Go take care of the girl, she is good luck for us and don't worry about carting your new tent." He gestured to the skin. "We will carry it back to camp for you."

"Thank you all again, especially you Garrett." She took off at a run.

When she got back to the woman's den she was still laying on her bed under the covers. Rea put on a pot of water, waited for it to boil, and then made a strong cup of tea with lots of honey in it. She put it aside to cool a little before she handed it to Erah. The woman sat up and wrapped the blanket she'd been under around her shoulders. She looked at Rea curiously. When the tea was cool enough Rea handed it to Erah who took it and started drinking it greedily, letting Rea know she was right not to hand it to her when it was hot. Erah made a face when the warm liquid touched the cut in her mouth, but it didn't seem to put her off drinking it. When she had finished it she handed the empty cup back to Rea and looked at her expectantly, so Rea made her another cup of tea which Erah also promptly drank.

Rea took the woman's axe went outside cut up some firewood and brought it all in. She put more wood in the fire. There was smoke in the room again, and she had an idea. She walked to the back of the cave and shifted one of the smaller rocks towards the top and rolled it out making a slightly bigger opening. When she did the smoke seemed to crowd the new hole, and soon the room had cleared of smoke. Rea liked to jump out of her skin when she heard loud clapping and turned to see Erah applauding her.

What do you know and what do you not know? No human could have moved even that rock, but it's easy for the Katabull. Hell, I could move every rock in this cave in in a few hours. It would be a stupid thing to do, but I could do it. You have been watching what we can do for months. I moved that rock and you seemed excited about it but not surprised. You are always cautious around me, but you are no more afraid of me like this than you are when I am in my human form.

And she seems to know we are the same person. Did the Kartik soldier tell her about our kind? Did she come close to us in the first place because she knew we wouldn't hurt her?

Rea set her up with wood for the night and made her one more cup of tea then ran back to her kill site. As promised, they had started a fire and had already eaten some of the meat, which was obvious when as she got there one of them shouted, "It is the best meat ever!" When one of them gave her a bite she had to agree.

She was there just in time to help them cart the meat and hide back to camp for which they seemed glad.

It was enough meat for the whole colony for a week which was saying a lot because there were a lot of them there.

The aroma of the cooking meat filled the whole camp. Because of course it was cooking everywhere. The Marching Night gathered around their fire pit out front of their keep, mouths watering as they waited for it to get just the right amount of done.

When it was they each grabbed a stick and started to eat the meat off it. It was by far the best meat they had eaten since they'd been there.

"It is better than elk!" one of them exclaimed.

They were praising her and thanking her, and as many of them were doing so because she had saved the human woman as because she had brought down so much good meat. She felt good and she wanted to just revel in it, but part of her was still worried about Erah.

Many of them had moved inside to sit around the great table and eat. Katrina sat beside her, and she had to work at not groaning. Katrina spoke to her every day. If Rea would have let her she would have talked to her all day every day.

"So you were quite the hero today. Of course to me you are a hero every day," Katrina said.

"Thanks," Rea said, chewing on a chunk of meat. She had taken her human form back when they brought the last of the moose back to the colony. It had been a long day and she was tired. She half thought she should go stay in the cave with the human tonight but then remembered what the Great Leader had told her about not dropping her guard. It would be really stupid for her to go there to take care of Erah only to fall asleep and have the woman kill her with one of the many knives in her box of knives. How did Rea know Erah hadn't killed the Kartik soldier? It was really unlikely, but she didn't know and how creepy was it that she lived with a dead body? But if you thought there were only two people in the whole world and the other one died you might keep them around just not to be alone. She didn't think she would, but you never knew. She remembered again what Fleat had said about a man who had never been hungry had no idea what a hungry man might do. Who knew what Erah was really capable of?

Katrina had kept talking but she hadn't heard her. In fact, she wasn't really listening to anything till she heard them calling her name over and over.

She looked at Fleat who sat across from her. "They want you to tell them the story about how you killed the moose and saved the girl."

"But... I have never told a story," Rea said truthfully.

"But you have seen hundreds of people do it. You grew up at the feet of the Great Leader, Dustin and Radkin; there are no better bards. No one else can tell the story only you and the human saw it, and she will neither come into the colony nor can she speak any words we might understand."

Then his tone changed. "You know unless you are too afraid to stand in front of us all and tell us what happened."

Katrina reached across the table and took her hand. "Tell the story; you will be amazing."

"Listen to your girlfriend, Captain, oh my Captain," Fleat teased her.

She cut him a dirty look, took a deep breath, finished the meat on her stick and stood up. She walked to the front of the room to stand in front of the roaring fire in the fireplace. She had been cold most of the day, and the warmth felt good.

She was not a bard and they could not expect her to tell as good a story as a bard could, but looking at them she knew all they really wanted was to know what had happened. Fleat was right; she had watched and listened to bards tell stories her whole life. She paced back and forth in front of the fireplace for a few seconds then stopped where she had started and launched into her tale.

"I went out hunting because—as you all know—I had neither killed nor even seen anything to kill since we have been here..." She told them the whole story right up to when she came back to the kill site and helped carry the meat back. She ended with, "...I will hang that hide to dry out and scrape it tomorrow. When it is tanned out.... Well, it should make a tent big enough to house us all."

They all cheered. She grabbed another skewer of meat out of the fireplace and went back and sat down where she had been.

"Not bad," Fleat said with a grin.

"Not bad!" Katrina exclaimed. "She is as good as the Great Leader herself."

When she looked at Katrina she realized the girl was more smitten than ever. She turned and glared at Fleat who was grinning from ear to ear. He thought the girl's crush was hysterical, and he did everything in his power to help Katrina pursue her. Everything from telling her just where Rea was all the time to getting up from sitting beside Rea when Katrina walked up and indicating she should take his seat. And why did he think it was so funny, because he knew that she had done nothing but whore around and drink for years. Rea had slept with anyone who showed her the least bit of interest and chased as Katrina was chasing her those who were not interested in her at all until they bedded her just to be rid of her.

"And now I am done in I am going to get washed up and go to bed." She handed her meat to Fleat because she hadn't really been hungry when she had taken it. She imagined now when she thought of it she took the meat to end her story which meant she really had learned more by watching bards then she would have thought. She stood up and started for her room. It was on the third floor because she liked to be able to get up first thing in the morning and walk around the catwalk checking out the colony. But tonight she seriously wished she were on the ground floor because she was tired and the stairs seemed a bit much. She got to her room stripped and poured water into the bowl and washed up. She went to her bed and crawled in.

She and Fleat both had rooms to themselves, on the top floor. She had one because she was the captain, and he had one because he was, after all, older than the Nameless One. The rest of the Marching Night slept in bunks three and four to a room. There had been enough room for all fifty of them in the building; the ones who had moved into separate dwellings had done so because they had chosen mates and wished for privacy.

Her room wasn't big, but it was private. There were only curtains for doors because doors would have kept heat from entering the rooms. As it was if she didn't have plenty of covers she would have been way too cold on the top floor. The fireplace downstairs was the only heat and the heat got upstairs through the stairwell. When in deep winter it had been its coldest she had also put a bear skin on top of her covers. It wasn't warm yet, but it was way too warm for the bear skin. And where did she get the bear skin? It was from her father's kill because until today she had killed nothing.

They hadn't actually known why all the bears had disappeared when cold weather hit; they thought maybe they had already hunted their numbers way down. But the last time the Great Leader and her family had been there Jena had explained that bears hibernated through the winter, and then she had to explain what that meant.

Rea was almost asleep when she felt someone crawl into bed with her. She sighed and sleep in her voice said, "Katrina, what do you think you are doing?"

"You killed something today and I know how randy we get after a kill, I thought..."

"Katrina..." She turned to face her. The girl was right. After a kill a Katabull always wanted to mate, yet she had absolutely no desire to do so. "I like you, I do, and I would never want to do something to hurt you." She could tell the woman was as naked as she was; Rea still felt no desire, none at all. It wasn't that Katrina wasn't a looker because she was gorgeous. "You know—because everyone does—that for years I bedded everyone, usually when I was too drunk to know what I had done with who."

"But I wasn't attracted to you then," Katrina said sadly.

"No doubt because you have a brain. I was good for no one and nothing. My madra told me that I didn't know whether I liked men or women, both or neither, and she was right. In this moment I can't tell you what I want except nothing right now. I think part of me is afraid that if I have sex with anyone I will go right back to what I was—as if I am as afraid of it starting me down the wrong path as I am that taking a drink might."

"Oh," Katrina said. "So, it's not me it's you?"

"That is not it at all, Katrina. I don't want anyone, not right now, not in that way."

"If you decide you do..."

"You will be the first to know."

"It's cold. Can I sleep here?" Katrina asked.

Rea knew what she was doing; she thought if she was laying with her naked it would break down Rea's walls. She wanted to tell her to go away that she just wanted to sleep, but, *How many hearts did I break? How many people did I hurt because they cared about me and I didn't care about them I just used them?*

"Alright, Katrina, but nothing is going to happen except I am going to sleep."

"I understand."

Rea turned over with her back to Katrina and immediately Katrina spooned her. It didn't feel bad. It was nice and warm, but she still didn't want to have sex—not with Katrina not, with anyone. She wasn't even worried about it, didn't miss it.

Katrina sighed contently. "This is enough for me right now," she whispered.

Rea felt bad because the girl loved her, she wanted her. Rea was sound asleep in minutes. When she woke up in the morning Katrina was still holding her and still sound asleep. Rea got up and looked down at her.

I am so sorry. I didn't mean for this to happen. I did nothing to make this happen. She got dressed and decided to let Katrina sleep.

As was her habit she walked to the door that led to the catwalk opened it walked through and quickly closed it behind her. They had learned the hard way that if the door was open any length of time it would suck all the heat out of the building. She started walking around and wished she had put her cloak on. Realizing how cold it was she remembered she needed to go check on Erah.

Erah was still asleep when Rea walked in. The fire had gone cold so she stirred it up and got it going. The cook had a pot of bone broth boiling on the fireplace, and Rea had grabbed a canteen of it and brought it with her. It was cold now so she dumped it into a pot and started to heat it on the fire. As it started to warm the aroma of it filled the air and she could hear the human sniffing. When she turned around Erah's eyes shot open. When she first saw Rea there was a moment of panic on her face, but she almost immediately calmed down. She sat up and pulled the covers around her. She pointed at the pot of broth on the fire then made like she was holding a cup drinking. Rea nodded poured her a cup and handed it to her.

Erah put her finger in it then shook it and said a word Rea didn't know but knew it meant hot. The woman than sipped the broth carefully. She made an attempt at smiling at Rea, and Rea realized, *She learned to smile but she hasn't done it in so long she is having to relearn how.*

Rea smiled back. "It is good, and it's the moose that tried to kill you so you are getting your revenge by eating him." She knew Erah couldn't understand, but she was never going to learn to speak their language if she didn't start talking to her.

She noticed the girl had made more tea by herself and thought, *she learns quickly, so maybe she can learn to talk to us faster than I think.* She pointed at herself. "Rea."

"Rea," she copied.

Rea nodded. She pointed at Erah, "Erah."

"Erah," she said pointing at herself.

"Pot," Rea said, pointing at the one now sitting by the edge of the fire. Erah looked confused. "Pot." Rea tried again, pointing.

"Pot," Erah said.

Then Rea pointed at the contents of the pot and said, "Broth."

Erah tried to say it, but every time she did it was garbled. Still, she was trying. Rea had no idea how long it took to learn a different language because she had certainly never done it, but she understood right away that the shorter the word was the easier it was for Erah to say it.

Erah sucked down cups of broth as Rea tried to teach her half a dozen simple words by pointing at things and saying what they were. Then Erah pointed at the dressing on her own head.

Rea nodded her understanding. "Yes, it is a ridiculous amount of gauze, but I need you to let me get it off, check your wound, medicate and dress it. I don't know if you will let me do it or bite the living shit out of me."

She walked forward slowly, knelt in front of the girl, and moved her hands slowly towards her face. Erah nodded. She didn't act like she was going to bite, so Rea started to remove the bandage. The gauze was soaked with blood and ooze, but when she finally got to the wound it seemed to be healing well for a fresh wound. Erah sat bone still as Rea cleaned and redressed the wound. When she finished Erah reached up, touched the bandage and smiled.

"Yes, I do wrap a wound better than Garrett does, but he means well."

She threw the dirty bandages into the fire then stood up. "I know you have no idea what I'm saying, but stay in today. The bears are starting to wake up again and Jena says they will be hungry and mean. But you know all that, don't you?"

Erah gave her a confused look.

"I have a million things I want to ask you that you can't answer." She looked over at the blanket she knew covered a mummy.

Rea got back to the keep in time for breakfast. She sat down with her plate and was glad that when she looked around Katrina was nowhere in sight. Fleat grabbed a plate and came to sit beside her. She could almost guess at what he was going to say from the grin on his face.

"So, I hear that on the top floor everyone saw your girlfriend walking out of your bedroom this morning."

Of course he had heard because the Katabull were the worst gossips on the planet.

"She is not my girlfriend, and she slept with me but I did not have sex with her." Then she thundered loud enough everyone in the room could hear, "If I had sex with her every person in the colony would have heard us—all of them—and some of you know that from experience." Because of course she had banged so many people that there were at least fifty people in town she had slept with including six members of the Marching Night that were there. She lowered her voice and glared at Fleat. "Stop encouraging that girl; she is going to get hurt."

"Oh, Captain, young people really don't understand anything. That girl is already deeply in love with you. She will either get hurt or break you completely down and have her way with you. What are you so afraid of?"

"I don't even know what if anything I want sexually. I don't love her, and I have used enough people."

He laughed. "I think it's obvious that she wants to use you."

Katrina walked in then and Fleat stood up pointing her towards where he had been sitting.

"Old man," Rea hissed in a whisper, "I will strangle you in your sleep."

He laughed and moved to sit across from her no doubt so he could have a front row seat.

Katrina got herself a plate of food and walked over to sit beside Rea.

"I'm afraid I overslept," Katrina said, then she leaned over and kissed Rea on the cheek as if it was something that happened all the time. Rea just stared at her like she had a cat crawling out of her ear, and across from her Fleat chuckled. Rea glared at him she half expected he had put the girl up to chasing her just for his enjoyment. Then as she heard the muttering all around her she knew the real reason the girl had done it. *By the gods she might as well be pissing on my leg. She is marking her territory.* Rea turned to glare at the room as a whole and the mumbling stopped.

Katrina said, "I have not slept that well since we have been here. How did you sleep?"

"Alright I guess." The mumbling started over again and again Rea glared at them and they were silent.

"How was the human?" Katrina asked.

"Better. I brought her broth. I told her it was like she was getting her revenge on the moose. Of course she can't understand a word I say, but I am trying to teach her some words." Rea stopped. *Oh my gods why am I talking to her? If I am nice to her and don't ignore her she is never going to leave me alone.*

As if to prove her right Katrina then started talking to her with more enthusiasm than she ever had before.

Rea ate as quick as she could then stood up. "I must go. We have a colony meeting today; I must prepare." She left the building and went to stand at the fire outside. She didn't need to prepare; she already knew what she was going to say. They had already scouted the territory and found two suitable areas to build other towns. They would build the one in the west this year and the one in the east next year. She hadn't been standing there for ten minutes pretending to think, when Katrina came running out.

"You forgot your cloak." She brought it over to her.

Rea tried to take it from Katrina's hand, but no, Katrina had to drape it over her shoulders then walk around in front of her and fasten the clasp. "We can't afford for you to get sick." She kissed her on the cheek again.

"Katrina, I don't think you understand..."

"I do, Rea, but if you really aren't interested in anyone at all, then if others think you are attached to me then they

60

won't come after you. I will always be attached to you. I would rather not have all of you than have none of you."

Rea sighed and nodded. Katrina kissed her on the cheek again and then went back in the building. When Fleat walked out of the keep a few seconds later he took one look at her pointed and started laughing. He walked to stand beside her and held his hands out over the fire to warm them still laughing.

"Old man, if I find you have put her up to all this…"

"I could not have made her do this if I had tried. You should know this better than any. Women have a way of getting what they want."

Chapter Five

Ufalla looked at the woman she was training; she was very pretty. Nothing like Jestia's beauty, but she was pretty enough. She was several years younger than Ufalla but an adult in every sense of the word. She had dark brown eyes and black hair that hung nearly to her waist, which wasn't practical and told you most of what you needed to know about Iris's personality. She was a nice girl but vain and vapid.

Her rich parents sent Iris to the academy before she was to do her stint in the military. It was easy to see why; her skill with a sword when she arrived at the academy was laughable. If you went into military service with poor weapon's skills you normally wound up with the job of cooking or cleaning the latrines—if you were lucky. If you weren't lucky and there was a time of war you'd likely as not be placed in the front to be mowed down to save better fighters.

As part of the pack of the Marching Night within the Katabull Nation, Ufalla had never done a term in service under the command of a Kartik general, but she had always been part of the Kartik military. When she fought in the Jethrik Territories she had first been under Kasiria's command and then Tarius's. When she fought here in the Kartik it had once again been under Tarius's command.

It was funny when she thought about it. Queen Hestia was her mother-in-law yet she had never been under Kartik command.

There was a battle inside Ufalla's head that was being waged without any commander. Even she didn't feel like she was in control of herself any more.

What did she really want? It used to be enough for her just to be with Jestia. Being with Jestia had been all she really cared about until it wasn't. Until Jestia became something she could never be, and she became nothing in comparison.

She needed something. Something that was hers that had nothing to do with Jestia. She needed to do something that was out of Jestia's control.

The first time she had banged Iris on the mats in the arena after everyone else had gone for the day, it had been completely impulsive. She'd had a moment of guilt and then terror. If Jestia found out she would likely kill them both. But Jestia had been busy in her alchemy when Ufalla got home. Ufalla bathed well and when Jestia finally came out of the alchemy she was way too worried about whatever she was working on to even notice that Ufalla was acting off. She had made love with Jestia later that night and Jestia still didn't have a clue. It gave Ufalla a rush she hadn't felt in a long time. Suddenly she felt alive again. It was dangerous, it could cost her everything she really cared about, it was something Jestia didn't know that she did. It was out of Jestia's control.

After that every time she did it and got away with it. She felt like she had just won a battle. In her mind she thought, *How smart and all-knowing is Jestia really if I can carry on right under her nose.*

After Ufalla finished Iris's final lesson they went to the supply closet and had a tryst. As Ufalla was pulling on her clothes Iris said, "I'm going to miss you."

"And I will miss this," Ufalla said, looking up and smiling at her. Iris was finished at the academy; she would be going back to her parent's home and then into military service in a few weeks.

"Is there really no way..."

"I told you Iris I love my wife. You are a nice girl, I like you this has been fun, but I love her and there is the whole she would kill us both in a horrible way if she found out." Which though Iris would never admit it had been as much of a thrill for her as it had been for Ufalla.

It wasn't until Iris had been gone for several weeks that Ufalla started to feel guilt for cheating on Jestia. But she also started to feel empty again.

Jestia noticed it before she did. They were standing in the hot spring. Jestia had worked her way over to Ufalla and was running her hands all over Ufalla. She had been so much in her own head she hadn't even noticed till Jestia stopped doing it and demanded, "What's wrong?"

"You spend more time at the complex most days than you spend here."

"I was only there three times, and every time I was home before you were."

She didn't understand, and she was never going to because she was the great and powerful Jestia. The Savior of the Island. The Heir Apparent. Ufalla was nothing, and worse than that now she was a liar and a cheat. She hadn't liked herself before, but now she hated herself, which only made her resent Jestia that much more.

It was the beginning of spring when someone yelled from the catwalk, "The Great Leader's ship approaches and there is a second ship with her that is flying the queen's flag!"

Rea looked up from the cement she had been mixing. They were working on putting a permanent levy where they had earlier built the temporary one. She looked up at Katrina who was working hauling the mud she was mixing over to the people laying the rock. "My madra is coming. Someone take over for me so that I can wash up." Someone quickly took her place and she ran in the direction of the keep, grabbed clean clothes, then ran to the river to bathe. In seconds someone splashed in beside her. "Katrina, what the hell?"

"Fleat told me I should wash up, too, to meet your madra."

"Katrina, you have known my madra all your life." Rea crawled out of the water and started drying herself.

"But not since I have been your girlfriend."

"Katrina, you are not my girlfriend."

"If you say so, my love."

Rea took in a deep breath and let it out then she got dressed and started stomping towards the docks. "Stupid girl," she mumbled. Katrina now slept in her bed most nights holding her though Rea still hadn't had sex with her and still had no desire to. It didn't seem to put Katrina off at all. She made sure everyone in the colony knew they were a couple even though they weren't. She would grab her hand and hold it, kiss her cheek when she found her or left her. The only time she actually left her alone was when Rea went to take care of and work with Erah.

In fact, maybe the best thing about Katrina was that she was smart and seemed to know just how far she could push things and what was a step too far. Katrina slept with her, she held her, but didn't try to do anything else. She kissed her on the cheek but never on the mouth. When Rea needed to be alone she didn't even have to say so, Katrina just slept in her own bunk. And she never even asked to go with her when she went to take care of Erah.

Erah had learned quite a few words though Rea was starting to be sorry she had taught her "no" and "mine." Erah's wound had healed quickly, and she had let Rea take the stitches out without so much as moving. Rea had to give credit where credit was due; Garrett had stitched her so well you could hardly see the scar. If she was dirty you couldn't see it at all. And Erah was dirty a lot—not because she didn't bathe; turned out she swam in the river so much that there was now hardly anyone in the colony who hadn't seen her. No, she was dirty all the time because she as a slob.

She was less afraid of all of them but still never came into the colony unless it was dark. They knew she came in because they often found her tracks in the dirt. Rea fed her so there was no need for her to come into the town. Rea guessed she did it because she was curious.

The oddest thing Erah had done yet concerned Garrett. He had been out hunting alone when Erah had walked right up to him and given him a very pretty orange stone about the size of a human fist. She had smiled at him, touched the side of his face where she had been injured, and then run off disappearing into the brush. Rea guessed she was thanking him for helping her. Garrett kept the stone on a table by his bunk; it was now his most prized possession.

The stone was very pretty, and they had all been looking for more of them ever since on the beach, in the woods, down by the river. They hadn't found another one like it yet.

Rea had lived her fantasy of drinking tea with the human. Turned out Erah loved tea with honey. When Rea would go to the cave to bring Erah food, Erah would make them tea, and then Rea would try to teach her some words.

Rea learned more about what plants were edible than any of the old Katabull knew by watching what Erah would bring in to eat. Erah would occasionally even have a fish or a rabbit on the fire which she would insist Rea eat. By "insist" Rea meant if Erah pointed at the meat and Rea didn't immediately grab a piece and start chewing on it, Erah would grab a piece and try to shove it in Rea's mouth. She had seen the girl catch a fish in the river. Erah would jump in with a sharp stick and spear it. If she didn't get one right away she quit. As for the occasional rabbit, Rea had found her snares, which were made from braided grass.

Rea knew someone had to teach her to do that. She was bright, but Rea doubted she could have figured it out on her own. Rea thought about the body in the girl's cave a lot. Once she had moved close to it to uncover it, and Erah had lost her mind, screaming things Rea didn't understand and showing threatening posture for the first and only time since Rea had found her. Rea walked away, and Erah calmed down but started to cry and buried her face in her hands muttering words Rea could not understand littered with the word no, no, no that Rea had taught her.

Rea knew why the girl said "no" over and over again. It was deep grief—the disbelief that the Everything would allow something so awful to happen to you as to sever a connection you still needed so badly.

"I know just how you feel," Rea had whispered.

Fleat had joined Rea on the dock shortly after she got there. "How oh how did you Captain oh my Captain garner a meeting with the Queen of the Kartik herself?"

"Ha, ha, Fleat, do not even pretend that you don't know my madra is banging the queen."

"Even I know that," Katrina said, joining her having dried and dressed so quickly she was still mostly wet. Everyone in the colony that wasn't working on something they couldn't leave was slowly making their way to the docks.

Rea looked from Fleat to Katrina. "Do not embarrass me in front of my madra. Embarrassing me in front of the Great Leader is bad enough, but do not, I beg of you, do it in front of my madra."

"I would never do anything to embarrass you my heart," Katrina said.

Rea looked at Fleat. "Nor would I, Captain oh my Captain."

Rea sighed. She knew they were both going to embarrass her, but only one of them would be working at it.

As their ship came into dock Radkin was as proud of Rea as she had ever been of any of her children and pleasantly surprised. Tarius had told her how good she was doing, but the size and scope of what the colonists had done under Rea's leadership spoke more than words ever could. Radkin didn't wait for the gangplank to be lowered. She took her Katabull form and jumped off the ship onto the dock.

"Could you not wait just a few minutes longer!" Hestia screamed after her.

For answer Radkin turned her head looked up and shrugged. Then she ran down the dock, grabbed Rea in a bear hug, lifted her off the ground and just squeezed.

"Madra, you are crushing me," Rea said as she hugged Radkin back.

Fleat looked at Radkin. "And she was afraid we would embarrass her in front of you," he said.

"A Madra's love can never embarrass a cub," Radkin said, and finally let Rea go. Then she turned and hugged Fleat. "Have you not died yet, you old fart?"

"I keep trying but alas, no," Fleat said. Then he added, "So have you met Rea's girlfriend?" He pointed at Katrina and Radkin let him go, grabbed Katrina, and hugged her.

"Of course I have met her. Her parents' huts are next to ours." She hugged the girl just as tight as she had done her daughter, which she knew was uncomfortably tight yet the girl did not say a word about it which meant Katrina was completely smitten with Rea. However when she looked at Rea it was obvious she didn't feel the same way. Radkin let the girl go and Katrina took a deep breath but still said nothing.

"She is not my girlfriend," Rea told Radkin. "I haven't even slept with her."

Fleat cleared his throat loudly and Rea shot him a dirty look before saying, "Alright I sleep with her, but I have never had sex with her."

"Which makes her extra special because I'm sure she is the only one in the whole colony you have not banged," Radkin said with a laugh.

"There are only about fifty I have, and…I have banged no one since I have been here. How was your voyage?"

Radkin laughed loudly at her daughter's attempt to change the conversation. "Uneventful, which you know to me means boring."

After they had all disembarked and she had taken them on a tour of the colony, showing them all they had done, Rea led them to the hall at the keep. Trin, their cook, was already preparing a special meal he had started the minute the ships had been spotted.

Her father and Hared had not come this time, but Riglid and Kaden were there as was Laz. Tarius and Jena had brought Darian, Pete and Diana what surprised her was that they also had Jabone's cub Arvon with them, but neither Jabone or Kaseria had come.

The colonists nearly lost their minds when they saw Arvon. There was a tremendous not very Katabull-like "Ahh!" that came from all of them as a group when they saw him. All the Katabull loved that baby because he was both Katabull prime and the Great Leader's grandson, but on top of that he was as blond as his mother which made him different from every other Katabull in the world. Because of this they counted him a good omen.

When she asked Jena why they had Arvon but his parents had not come Jena explained, "He is with us most of the time these days because if they are awake he and Diana want to be together. When we were leaving Jabone and Kaseria brought Arvon to see us off, but when Arvon realized we were all going and he wasn't he started throwing himself a wall-eyed fit. Since he is Katabull prime, well he is hard for them to control when he's mad. Kaseria took him, handed him right to Tarius and said, "Here take him with you." As a mother, Kaseria is a fine swordswoman. Anyway, Jabone started to protest but when he tried to take him back from Tarius Arvon bit him, and so... Arvon came with us. I don't mind watching him. Most days he is better for us than he is for his parents, and the cubs entertain each other so I can actually get more things done. But lately..."

"They have taken to climbing trees," Tarius interrupted, temporarily leaving the conversation she'd been having with Fleat about the levy they were building and why.

Rea didn't see what the problem with that was. They were both two, and that's what cubs did at two—they started trying to climb trees. Till then they climbed their mothers.

Jena shook her head. "I can see by the look on your face that you don't understand the problem. They don't *try* to climb trees; they *do* climb trees. Arvon can just climb them all the way to the top by himself. Because Diana can't climb them as well, he helps her. So twice now we have turned our backs for only a minute and Tarius has had to climb up a tree to the very top to get them both down. Hared nearly lost his mind the first time they did it. He just ran around the bottom of the tree the whole time Tarius was climbing it trying to be ready to catch them if they fell."

"We normally catch them before they get too high in the tree," Tarius said,

"By *we* she means Darian. He seems to know when they are up to no good before they do. He will come and get us yelling, 'Babies up a tree!' "

"My little monkey climbs good," Darian told her, "but sister will not bounce like he does if they fall."

"I guess not," Rea said.

"But she is one of Tarius's cubs, so any day now Tarius will teach Diana to shift," her madra said, "and problem averted."

"If she does that to this cub she will have a whole other problem." Jena swore. Rea remembered that Jabone, who was younger than she and her brothers, was taught to shift before any of them were. Pete, too, was shifting at six years old.

They all sat around the great table in the main hall of the keep. Rea noticed Tarius had Diana on one knee and Arvon on the other. Jena sat to her right and Darian sat to the right of her. Pete sat on Tarius's left. Rea wondered how the Great Leader could focus on anything when she always seemed to have arms and laps full of cubs. They were supposed to go to the new town in the morning to see the progress and were they taking all those kids. The trail went right through the middle of bear country taking horses loaded with cubs didn't seem like a good idea to her.

As always Tarius's ship had brought them fresh fruits, cheese, and butter—things they craved but couldn't grow there or make themselves. This time she also brought them fifty chickens and ten goats. They had just finished the pens for them and they had removed them from the boat and put them right into their new homes. Rea had already assigned the duty of shutting them up at night and watching them during the day to the Katabulls who lived closest to the pens. Soon they would have their own eggs, milk, cheese and butter.

The big predators weren't all they had to worry about with their chickens; there were the racoons and fox to deal with, too. Racoon were at least good to eat, but fox they ate only because they refused to kill something and not eat it. They hadn't even known they would be a problem till Jena had told them the last time they had come. The goat pen just had to keep out the big predators, but the chicken pens had to be made to keep out the small predators as well.

Tarius's ship had also been loaded with grain and seed, but the kingdom ship was loaded with cloth, barrels of nails, all the tools necessary for them to set up their own forge and black smith shop to make their own weapons and nails. But possibly the thing that was going to be the biggest boon to their colony was that they had brought all the parts to erect a saw mill that ran on a water wheel. The ability to cut their own lumber was going to make everything they built from there on that much easier. Rea thanked Hestia at length.

There was such a wealth of goods on both ships that the ships were still being unloaded as they sat down in the main hall to eat.

Rea sat next to Darian, Katrina and Laz started to sit in the chair next to her at the same time.

"Sorry," Laz said.

"No, no you sit," Katrina said, and moved quickly to sit next to Riglid across the table.

Arvon started to climb onto the table and Tarius said a sharp "no". He sat back in her lap looking as if it was all he had intended to do. Tarius gave him a piece of meat which he greedily started to chew on, taking out great huge chunks and growling. Rea grinned; he was really cute. Then Tarius handed Diana a chunk of meat and she did the same thing Arvon was doing except she wasn't snapping off huge chunks of meat.

"I could do without that," Jena said, pointing at the babies.

"They are just enjoying their food, Mama," Tarius said. "So Rea, tell us how the new colony is going."

"It goes well..." Then as they ate she told them what they had done, where they were on their projects, and what they had planned. They had started work on the west site first because there were more trees and wildlife there. The Marching Night had gone there first, clearing a trail to the town site, making a sizable clearing, and erecting tents on the site. Then they had sent the people who would actually live there to do the rest of the work. They had made the decision on who would move there by asking who wanted to go, and then she and Fleat had chosen them by the diversity of their knowledge and skills. The chosen residents of the new town had moved into the tents there and immediately started work on building permanent dwellings and planting crops.

When they had first arrived in the Territories, they noticed that some of the homes that were in disrepair and partially burned were made of logs that had been notched and stacked to make walls. The rooves had been covered in spilt-wood shingles. This is how they were constructing the buildings of what they now called West Town.

"Eventually there will be a stone building two stories tall—very like this dwelling just one story shorter—in the center of town. It will be a defensive post, a meeting place, and a safe place to go in case of storms or fire."

"I look forward to seeing it," Tarius said.

"Tarius I'm telling you again," Jena said, getting the Great Leader's attention which was never hard for her to do. "I do not want to ride across a forest full of bears with these four cubs without their fathers to help."

"Why did my father and Hared not come?" Rea asked curiously.

Laz laughed as if it was the funniest thing ever.

"It isn't funny, Laz," Riglid said. But then he would say that because he was always so serious and rarely thought really funny things were. Beside Riglid, Kaden was grinning, so apparently he thought it was funny, too.

"Are they alright?" Rea asked.

"Yes and no," Tarius said. "They got food poisoning eating meat off a street vender's cart in Montero. They were moving at both ends for three days so they didn't feel like making a trip on a ship. In fact just talking about the idea of the ship rocking made Rimmy puke."

"They did send their love," Laz said,

"Can you handle all four of them alone?" Tarius asked. "It is a half day's ride away. We will leave early and come back late."

"I can help her with them, Great Leader," Katrina offered.

"You poor, sweet child, do you know what you are getting yourself into?" Tarius asked.

"I can help as well," Kaden offered. No doubt he was afraid to go into wild country being only a weak human man.

"There are many here that would gladly help you with the cubs, Jena," Rea said. "This place has no children so they are always a sight for sore eyes for all of us."

"I noticed that is about to change," Tarius said,

"Aye. There are two couples expecting cubs in the next few months," Rea said.

"You know how straight people are. They do not make real plans regarding when they have cubs. They just go at it, forget birth control, and have babies," Fleat said.

He was right. Cross-paired couples planned their families with great care. When they would have them; who would carry them. As far as Rea was concerned it was still too soon to be bringing babies into the colony because it was still too wild and they had too much work yet to do. But the cubs would be their parent's problem, and since it was their decision to use no precautions they could deal with the repercussions. The rest of them would just enjoy having cubs around without having to be responsible for them.

They all started talking amongst themselves and Rea turned to Laz. "How have you been?"

"I'm good, you know, aside from being an irresponsible straight person." He grinned then shrugged. "I'm tired of being alone but still don't seem to be able to commit to any relationship, so just like you and your not-girlfriend."

"Not just like me. She loves me, and I didn't do anything to make her do it. In fact, just the opposite is true. I don't love her and I never pretended to. In truth I don't know that I am capable of loving anyone that way." She added in a whisper so low he was the only one who could hear it. "Plus I don't have a giant crush on Jena."

Laz whispered back if anything even lower. "I do not have a crush on Jena."

"Do and always have," Rea whispered back. "Why do you think Tarius choose you to be Jena's personal guard? She knows you'd die for her. You would never act on it, and I know it is more wanting someone just like her than it is wanting her. But Jena's stunning and pretty amazing. That mold has been broken and that is never going to happen."

"I will settle for what I can get when you do," he said with a smile, looking with meaning at Katrina.

Darian reached over pushed her plate out of the way and was soon sitting on the table in front of her looking at her expectantly.

"What?" she asked him.

"Tell me about the girl in the woods," he said. "Madra says there is an animal girl that lives in the forest. That she talks to you."

"She doesn't really talk," Rea said. "I have taught her to say a few words."

"Why is she there? How did she get there?"

"I don't know," Rea said.

"How long has she been there?"

"We think since the Great War."

"Where does she live?"

"In a cave with a brick wall in the front with a door." Rea turned to look at Laz.

"He is completely enthralled by the idea of her. He did nothing but ask us a bunch of questions we don't know the answers to all the way here till I think we all wanted to thump Tarius for telling him about her at all. Pete is nearly as bad. You know what the problem is—has always been with all of our parents and their friends—their generation tell such good stories it makes kids want to do everything they have done."

Rea nodded and whispered, "At least they are no longer so afraid of bears and lions they have to always be with Tarius. I have to tell you I was not looking forward to carting four kids with us across the Territories tomorrow."

"We are not afraid of them because Father killed one. He said it was easy," Darian said.

Rea looked at Laz in shock.

"That sort of proves what I just said," Laz said. "Hared tells them one story they are scared shitless. Father tells them another and they aren't afraid at all. It might be nice if there was a happy spot in the middle."

"It wasn't that. He heard me and I was Katabull whispering." Which meant she was whispering only for Laz's ears so low no human could have heard and only a close Katabull could have.

"Oh, the wizard's hearing is better than any Katabull's." Laz went a little white then when he remembered what they had been whispering about before. He looked at Darian.

Darian reached over and patted him on the head. "It's alright, Laz. Everyone loves Mama. Not as loudly as Madra does, but we all do."

Jena waved and watched as Tarius rode away with Riglid, Rea, Radkin and Fleat. Two other Katabull were driving a wagon loaded with some of the supplies from both ships. *That wagon is where I would have been stuck with the babies if we had gone, no thank you.* Arvon was hanging on one leg and Diana was on the other. This was perhaps the only time she wished she didn't have so many babies. When Tarius had to do something and she couldn't go with her because... well Tarius would have taken them all with her but it would have been a nightmare and it wasn't really safe.

She didn't really get to think about how unhappy she was to be left behind as they were leaving because Darian had thrown himself a nifty little fit when he realized his Madra wasn't taking him and Pete with her. Because of course Pete and Darian were worse about being separated than the babies were. Darian had given it up when Tarius scowled at him. Then in that dramatic way only Darian had he asked Laz to pick him up so he could see his Madra as long as he could. Now she was out of sight he looked at Laz.

"Please put me down." Laz set him down and Darian looked at Pete and said, "Come on Pete." He started walking away and Pete followed.

"Where do you to think you're going?" Jena asked. Darian shrugged. "I know that look, mister, you are up to no good. You stay right here around the fire where we can see you."

"We just wanted to go see the horses, isn't that right Pete?" Darian said.

Pete nodded.

Jena gave Darian a look that would peal paint. "Did you talk about that before or after you raised hell to go with your madra?" Darian was only five but filled with magic and more precocious than any five-year-old she had ever known except for Jestia. She knew better than to treat him like any other five-year-old. He was clever and almost too quick witted. Right in this minute he realized he had messed up and was trying to figure out how to tell a better story.

"We talk about it before, then I forgot because I wanted to go with Madra and..."

"You are full of crap," Jena said. Behind her Hestia laughed. "Well he is." She focused her attention back on Darian. There was no sense at all in blaming Pete or expecting Pete to act like the older brother. He was eight but he never ran the show it was always Darian who instigated things. Pete would watch out for him and protect him, but he would also go along with his plans no matter how hair brained they were. "You just stay right here and behave yourself."

Jena walked, dragging the cubs that were hanging on her legs with her. They both started laughing; it was their favorite game. Tarius, Jabone, Kaseria, Rimmy and Hared all let them do it so she did, too. They were all Katabull, though, and what was easy for them was hard for Jena.

"I swear I must have the strongest legs of any human," Jena said as she sat down on a log close to the fire.

The cubs gave her a look that said they thought her a traitor but then let her go and started playing in the dirt. They would be covered in filth in seconds but she'd dump them in the river later swirl them around and call them clean. Out of the corner of her eye she could see Darian whispering in Pete's ear and Pete nodding. "Ah hah! No you stop right now."

"We weren't doing anything." Darian shrugged. His mannerisms and facial expressions were so much like Tarius's it was scary when you knew he was actually blood related to none of them.

"I could take them on a walk around the colony, or down to the beach," Laz said. There wasn't a lot for cubs to do there because of course there were no kids in the colony.

Jena looked at Darian. "Would you like to do that?" He nodded. "What about you, Pete?" Pete nodded. "And will you behave?" They both nodded. She wasn't buying it; they had something up their sleeve. "I don't know."

"I could help him watch them," Katrina said.

"Alright, but you boys don't give your brother or your sister's girlfriend any trouble or you will be in it deep."

"In what deep?" Darian asked.

"You know what," she said.

Laz took Darian in one hand and Pete in the other and started walking. Katrina fell into step behind them.

"So where do you want to go?" Laz asked.

"The stables," Darian said.

Hestia moved to sit on a log across the fire from Jena. She looked at the babies playing at Jena's feet. "So you have your hands full."

"Yes, and I love it till Tarius is going someplace she has to go that I would like to and I can't because…three cubs of my own and then…" She pointed at Arvon. "…that little thug. I was actually surprised that you didn't go with them."

Hestia shrugged. "Radkin needs to spend some time with Rea, and Rea… Well I don't think she has ever approved of me as a replacement for her mother in Radkin's life. She thanked me profusely for the items I brought but... I do not wish to push things with her."

"Each child comes with their own problems and gifts. Of course the cub that gives us the most trouble is Darian. I don't have to tell you what trouble a magic child is," Jena said.

"No, but Jestia didn't really come to her magic till she was in her teens. We knew she had an ability but I don't think any of us knew how strong it was going to be. Your little one started out doing things normal humans can't do as a toddler."

"He has the most gigantic heart; no one loves as completely as Darian does, but—the poor baby—his head is always going and he is made for mischief. No!" She reached out and grabbed Arvon's hand as he started to put a handful of dirt in his mouth. And of course she had no sooner shook the dirt from his hand then Diana picked up a handful and started to stick it in her mouth. Jena grabbed her hand and repeated the process then sighed. "For one thing Darian was the one that taught them to eat dirt."

Hestia laughed then stopped took in a deep breath and let it out. "Jestia has changed since the disaster. She is both more present and more distant. What of Tarius?'"

"She has changed. In some ways she seems calmer, but at the same time she has absolutely no patience at all for unnecessary drama. Her holding court now is mostly just her dismissing most of their problems as petty and telling them not to waste her time. But she seems to accept things in a way she never has before."

"What do you mean?"

"Well now that I know so much more about Katabull anatomy and how toxic wood is to them, I realize that not only was it a wonder that Tarius saved Arvon's leg but it was a wonder he lived at all. I will not go into the gory details, but his leg was rotting, which meant the toxin would have flowed all through his body. When he started to age faster than other Katabull, we thought it was because he was half human, but Tarius always knew it was because of his injury. She even told me once that no half Katabull she'd ever known had aged like a human did. He should have died of that injury; the only reason he didn't was that

Tarius loved him so much she cared for him day and night and willed him to live. Yet when he was killed on the mountain she hardly reacted at all. I have to admit it took me awhile for my grief over their deaths to really hit me because I very nearly lost Tarius and she wasn't really well for a very long time. Besides, the world as we knew it had come apart. When Arvon and Dustan's deaths did hit me I cried for a week, and I still tear up as I am even now doing when I think about them.

"But I don't think Tarius ever has grieved the loss like that, and I know she doesn't still mourn either Arvon or Dustan. When I asked her about it she said that if she had lost him at the time he was injured, when she most needed him, it would have put a huge hole in the Everything, in her life and in all of ours, but when he died he had already done everything he was supposed to do and so it was alright that he died."

Hestia nodded. "As the Katabull say, it was his day to die. They don't just say those things; they mean them."

The boys were walking down the middle of the stables talking to the horses.

"I can't imagine why they wanted to come to the stables. We have many more horses at home. They don't seem to care about them one way or the other," Laz said to Katrina.

"I had wondered that myself. Maybe it's because of the building."

The stable was pretty impressive. It was long with walls that closed on the sides and only a few openings for the horses to go in and out to the pasture. The middle section of the building had fences down both sides, twenty feet apart. They had stored the winter hay here and could feed the horses without having to open gates.

"After all horse sheds back home are four poles with a roof." Katrina shrugged. "We have to have something more substantial here because of the winters."

"So... what made you fall in love with my stupid sister of all people? I thought you were smarter than that."

"So did I," Katrina said with a grin. "I don't know." She sighed. "As soon as we stepped on the ship to come here she was just a different person. She forgot to take the seasickness tonic and was super sick all the way here. Yet one day I saw her standing at the bow of the ship just looking at the water. She is beautiful of course, but in that moment there was such a look of sadness on her face that I just wanted to hold her and make her every pain go away. Then of course she retched over the side of the boat and the moment was gone.

"When we both got hurt, but I was hurt worse than she was, she sort of took care of me. She was so sweet to me. When I had to go back because I wasn't getting any better, there was no part of me that wanted to go and leave her here. When in Montero I got a front row seat to the disaster, none of it seemed real. All I thought about, all I wanted, was to be back here with Rea, even if she didn't want me.

"I tried to play it cool, I really did, but I just couldn't. The more I try not to talk to her the more I do. I tried to full-on seduce her and she wasn't having any part of me, but she lets me sleep with her and... Well I more enjoy just sleeping with her than I have enjoyed full-blown passionate sex with any other woman, so..." She shrugged. "Do you have any ideas?"

"Don't give up on her, Katrina. I know her and I know you; I think you are a good match. No one took my Madra's death harder than my sister, not even my mother, and Rea's stupid-ass choices just made her pain last much longer. She is just now feeling more like herself—just now figuring out who she is. Truth is she had so much sex with so many different people I just think it's the last thing on her mind right now."

"She as much as told me exactly that." Katrina sighed again. "It's still the best relationship I've ever had. Mine have always been one sided. At least your sister isn't pretending at feelings she doesn't really have."

Because of course Katrina had gone through a period where she had a thing for human women. It had taken Katrina awhile to realize that they just wanted to have the experience of sleeping with a Katabull; they didn't want to have a relationship with one. They would lead her on for a while because the sex was good then cut her loose the minute she got serious—which happened fairly quick.

"But enough about me. How have you been?" she asked.

"Alright. Doing the same but very different thing that Rea is, but I think my grief is starting to dull, too."

"They are busy talking. Let's go," Darian said to Pete.

Pete shook his head.

"Come on, Pete."

"Mama will be so mad. Madra will beat us. Laz might get in trouble."

"Mama will get over being mad, Pete. Madra has yet to beat us, and we have done worse things. It isn't Laz's fault that we don't mind, it's Madra's because she doesn't really beat us and Mama's because she doesn't stay mad at us."

Pete nodded and followed Darian down the middle of the stable out into the pasture and then over the fence where they ran into the forest.

"Gods and spiders those little turds!" Laz exclaimed as he ran into the stable.

"Crap," Katrina followed him.

"They wanted to come to the stables because the pasture is next to the forest and they could sneak out. Jena is going to kill me." He called on the night and Katrina quickly did the same. Laz knew what they were up; to they wanted to find the feral human.

They ran into the forest and Laz sniffed the air. "This way." They started running towards the scent.

Pete knew he shouldn't always go along with Darian, but Darian always had better ideas than he did.

"Rea said she lives in a cave, but it has a door," Darian said.

"Let's go back before we get eaten by a bear," Pete said. Their parents would be so mad if they got eaten by a bear.

"Don't be afraid, Pete. You are the Katabull. Father killed a bear; he said it was easy."

Pete nodded and continued to follow his brother. After all Pete was the Katabull.

"I have to find her," Darian said. "The Everything wants me to find her; it called me in my dream."

Pete nodded again as if that made sense. Though he rarely understood things that Darian was sure of, he also knew his brother's magic was strong because when he was in his Katabull form he could feel it. He continued to let Darian lead the way. Pete somehow knew this was always the way it would be—him following Darian.

Darian stopped, turned to look at Pete and said, "Shush! She is following us."

Out of the woods ran a bear, and Pete immediately was sure Darian had been wrong about a couple of things. Pete shifted and pushed Darian behind him. He roared at the bear, and the bear stopped charging but didn't run away. Pete roared at the bear again, and this time Darian joined him. Darian could sound like a Katabull anytime he wanted to. The bear just stood there looking at then as if sizing them up.

Then there was a flash of color and a blond human ran between Pete and the bear. She had a wooden spear in her hand, and she threw out her arms and yelled at the bear. The bear—feeling outnumbered—turned and ran away.

The creature turned to them and grunted then motioned for them to follow her.

Darian didn't even pause; he just started following her, so Pete followed Darian.

"Darian, we should go back to the compound right now," Pete said.

"We can't, Pete. We are supposed to go with her. Look!"

He pointed ahead of them and Pete saw a cave with a wall with a door. He had half thought it was all just a story. The human opened the door grunted at them and pointed for them to go in. Darian went in so Pete did, too.

Pete watched the human then. She was pacing back and forth looking like she didn't know what to do with them. Pete hoped she didn't decide eating them was a good idea.

"This is the nicest house ever," Darian said to her.

She stopped pacing and smiled at him. When she did she wasn't nearly as scary.

"Our sister is Rea."

"Rea," she said, and seemed to be completely calm now.

Pete relaxed a little.

The human put her spear down and pointed at a pot beside the fire. "Pot?"

"Yes, we'd love some tea," Darian said.

"Darian, we should go," Pete said.

"We can't go now; they have to find us. She is making tea, and it would be rude."

The woman put the pot on the fire then turned and pointed at Darian's head and then touched her hair.

"Yes, we both have the same color hair. Mine is cleaner. My mama has white hair, too. But we are all still Kartik because that's who found us."

They lost the boys' scent for a moment when another, stronger scent crossed their path.

"That is bear. Maybe I should go back to the colony and sound the alarm," Katrina said.

"Wait! I have found them again, but what... What is that other scent?" Laz asked.

"I'm not sure, but it might be your sister's pet human," Katrina said. "Should I go back?" she asked again. Meanwhile they kept running in the direction of the smell of the boys.

"Yes you'd better," Laz said.

"No wait, look!" Katrina pointed, and he saw the cave with the brick wall and the door just as his sister had described it.

He started running double time.

"Wait, Laz. Slow down. I will wait here. She is very flighty. I have never even seen her, but they all say she spooks easily. If you need my help—I doubt you will—but if you do you can call for me. I will be right here."

Laz nodded and slowed down till he was just walking as he reached the door. He wondered what he should do. In his mind he heard the words of the Great Leader, "Always follow your belly." His belly told him to knock on the door, so that was what he did.

When the knock came on the door Pete and the human both jumped, and she almost spilled the cup of tea she was handing Darian.

Darian took the cup. "You better pour another cup of tea," Darian said. "That is my brother."

"We are in so much trouble," Pete whispered to Darian

She started pouring another cup of tea. Could she actually understand Darian?

"Come in, Laz!" Darian yelled.

Slowly the door opened and even more slowly Laz walked in.

"That is Laz," Darian said pointing. "Laz, this is Erah."

Laz didn't know what he expected when he opened that door, but it wasn't this. The boys with sitting with cups of tea being served by a feral human. The woman gave a cup of tea to Pete and then pointed towards Laz and Pete handed him the cup. Laz lifted it to his lips and took a sip just to be polite. Then he smiled because it was obvious his sister had taught her to make tea; it was way too sweet.

He looked at her and smiled, and she smiled back. When she did it made his heart feel light in a way it hadn't in years. There was something captivating in her eyes, so much pain but so much light.

He didn't know what to do except stand there and sip the tea and look into her deep blue eyes.

"Laz," she said, pointing at him.

He nodded.

"Her name is Erah," Darian told him again.

"Erah," Laz said.

She smiled, nodded then said, "Yes."

"He is Rea's brother, too," Darian said.

"Rea?"

"She went with my madra; she will be home tonight," Darian said.

The creature nodded at the boy.

"Darian, does she understand you?" Laz asked.

"Yes, I think so. She has been sad a long time, but she is happy now."

"We have to get you both back before they send out a search party," he said in a whisper. He set the empty cup down on a box, then said to Erah, "Thank you. I hope to see you again soon. Come on, boys; let's go."

"We have to go, Erah." Darian quickly drank down his tea as did Pete. Darian looked at the woman and said, "Laz says thank you for saving us, and that we will come back to visit."

84

As soon as they were all outside and the door closed behind them Laz started laying into them. "I didn't say we were doing anything. You are in so much trouble you little hooligans. I'm going to be in so much trouble because you did this."

As they reached Katrina where she waited for him Darian looked up at him and said, "I won't tell if you won't tell."

"What! You are rotten to your very core. You will be in more trouble than I will be. Your mother told you not to give us any trouble." He turned to Katrina. "We were running all over the place looking for them, worried they'd been eaten by a bear or a lion or some damned thing, and they were hanging out with the feral human in a cave having a tea party."

"Rea taught her to make tea," Katrina said with a grin.

"I could tell because it was more honey than tea," Laz said.

"That's the way I like it," Darian said, but Pete made a face that said he preferred his tea to be tea.

"Why are you the Katabull, Pete?" Pete was quiet. "Why?"

"A bear tried to eat us," Pete mumbled.

"But it's alright because Pete and Erah saved us, and if we don't tell anyone what happened they won't know and none of us will be in trouble."

Katrina laughed and Laz cut her a look. "It is not funny."

"He is almost too cleaver," Katrina said.

"No *almost* about it," Laz said. He wished he could have told himself that he didn't think for even a minute about taking Darian up on his I-won't-tell-if-you-won't-tell deal.

As they rode along the trail to the colony, Rea rode between her mother and her brother Riglid.

"We work on it every time we travel on it, but as you can see it wants to turn to muck every time it rains and keeping the kids from riding on it when it is like that... Frankly they screw everything up," Fleat was telling Tarius from where he rode beside her.

Fleat thought every problem they had with the colony was because young Katabull were stupid and rash. In fact, daily she heard at least one argument between the young members of the colony and the old ones. According to the young the old were too cautious, too slow, and insisted on doing things their way or not at all, and the old accused the young of being careless, rash, and rushing things that needed to be done right instead of half-assed. But most days they worked well together in spite of all their bitching. Tarius had been right to send the young and the old together. The old had the skills and the patience; the young had the drive and the strength.

"This is beautiful country," Radkin said.

It was, hilly but not so much that there wasn't workable land, and it hadn't been hard to find a level enough area to snake in a road.

"You should see it with the snow on it," Rea said. "It's breath taking. But it is so cold here, and not just when it snows but for months before and after it. In winter we would get used to it and then it would be even colder. It was so cold at one point most of us were sleeping in our Katabull form just to stay warm."

"And you even had a nice girl to keep you warm," her Madra teased.

"She is not my girlfriend."

"I'd like to know why not," her madra asked.

Riglid spurred his horse and moved up quickly to ride with Tarius and Fleat.

Radkin looked at Rea and smiled. "Your brother does not like even the hint of conflict. Never has. Yet as Tarius's runner you know he is soaking in it most days, all day."

"Other people's problems and gripes are different from our own," Rea said.

"I see you have been learning from Fleat."

"I hope I will not become as antagonistic as he is," Rea said with a smile.

"Changing the subject is no better than moving your horse. Both are ways of avoiding a conversation. Why are you not all up in that girl?"

"Madra, I..." She didn't have a really good answer that she thought her Madra would understand.

"Did you wear it out?" Radkin asked with a wild smile.

"Maybe," Rea shrugged. "I have zero desire for sex, and that's as good a reason as any. She has feelings for me that I don't return. I care about her and wouldn't hurt her for the world. Now can we please talk about something else, anything else?"

"Are you ever going to embrace Hestia as my mate?"

Really! Anything but that, Rea thought. She took a deep breath, let it out and said, "I thanked her for all she brought to us; I am very grateful."

"That isn't what I asked you, daughter."

"I have and do accept her as your mate, but seeing you with her... It makes me remember Mother is dead. I don't have a problem with Hestia, and I don't begrudge your happiness. I admit I did but I don't anymore. Since I stopped drinking and whoring around I have worked to come to terms with a lot of things. I have been able to accept that mother is dead and that life goes on for the rest of us. I am not quite there yet, but I know I will get to a place where I can see the two of you together and not have it put a cut in my heart."

Her madra smiled, nodded and said, "I can't judge you for that. For years Hestia told me—sometimes many times a day—how much she loved me, and I never once said it back because to do so would have made me feel like I was cheating..."

Rea smiled broadly and said, "Yet shagging Hestia three or four times a day didn't?"

Radkin laughed. "That is exactly what Jestia told me. Anyway what I am saying is that I get it. But don't be afraid of love Rea, and if you get the chance to feel it then say it."

When they arrived at West Town Rea was happy to see how much progress the colonists had made. The inhabitants were all excited to see the Great Leader and her madra.

The amount of progress they had achieved told her they were working well together. There was nothing Katabull couldn't build when they cooperated with each other, and they would get nothing at all done if they were arguing all the time.

"I made Terak and Larad co-mayors of West Town," Rea told Tarius. Rea looked around to make sure Fleat was nowhere close enough to hear her. "Never tell him I told you so, but I would be lost without Fleat, and I thought if I put one young person and one old in charge that would better serve everyone who lives here as it does us. They seem to be doing a good job of following the plans and running the town."

One of the town's residents had just killed a bear, so that was what they had for lunch.

Sitting on log benches around the central fire pit eating, Tarius said to Terak and Larad, "Clear a good space the height of a tree if it fell between your furthest buildings and the tree line. Make the cleared space your pasture land; plant crops on it." She added, "If there is a forest fire that will save your town, and if a building in town should start on fire that should keep it from jumping into the woods. You have already built them far enough from each other to keep fire from jumping from one house to another."

Larad, the older of the two mayors gave Terak an "I told you so" look which meant he had already suggested this and Terak had said it was unnecessary.

Rea had not done that. She was, and always had been, happy to listen to what Fleat and the other elders had to say. She was being neither reckless or careless in her decisions yet she was a good ten years younger than Terak. Why? *Because no one was more reckless and careless than I was. Hell, I know all about house fires because I burnt at least one house to the ground, not sure if the second one was actually my fault because I was too drunk to remember. And all my elders—all of them—kept telling me that I was screwing up and just how I was doing it. I didn't listen, not because I didn't know they were right, but because I didn't want them to be. I want to do things the right way, the safe way, the considerate way because I have lived through the fall out of what happens when I don't.*

As they were riding back home two things were running through her head. First that it felt much better to have her elders tell her they were proud of her than to have them telling her to get her head out of her ass and turn her life around. Second was that her libido would probably come back only when she was sure she wanted to have sex for any reason besides pissing other people off.

Laz found Jena, Hestia and Kaden sitting around the great table in the main hall. Arvon and Diana were sleeping on a pallet they had made on the floor for them. The way the cook and his crew were tiptoeing around, it was for sure they didn't know these babies. They could sleep through a hurricane which he knew was about to hit when he told Jena that he had lost track of the boys and what they had done.

He once again found himself wondering about taking Darian up on his I-won't-tell-if-you-won't offer, but when he saw Katrina take up a guard position at the door just to make sure the boys couldn't sneak out the front door he knew he had to tell Jena.

"Did you have a good time?" she asked the boys.

"Yes, a very good time," Darian said. He could have gotten away with it for sure if Laz didn't tell on him, but Pete looked as guilty as if he had drowned a nest full of baby birds.

Jena looked from Pete to Laz. "So, what did they do?"

When Laz finished telling her she looked right at Darian and said, "What is wrong with you, child? You nearly got you and your brother killed. And Pete, when are you going to learn not to go along with the stupid-assed things your little brother wants to do?"

Pete looked at his feet and shrugged. Not a big talker, Pete.

"Laz and Katrina were nice enough to offer to take you someplace. They took you right to where you said you wanted to go and then how do you repay their kindness? You wait till they aren't looking right at you for a second and you take off and run them all through the forest."

Laz guessed he wasn't quite as mature as he would like to think he was because he really wanted to yell right in Darian's face, "Ha, ha I told you so! I told you you'd be in more trouble than I was."

Instead he said, "I shouldn't have taken my eyes off of them. I know how they are."

"They are old enough they should not have to be watched like babies," she told Laz. Then looking at the boys said, "When your madra gets back you will both have to tell her what you have done."

From the look on the little wizard's face he didn't like that idea at all, and he proved it when he said, "No, you tell Madra. We've been bad. We shouldn't get to talk to her. We will go right to bed without any supper."

Pete just nodded his head in agreement.

Hestia giggled and Jena said, "He has always done this—offer to be punished so he can do what he wants to do. No, mister, you will both sit here at the table doing nothing till your madra gets back, and then you will tell her what you have done."

"But she will be mad at me." Darian started to cry.

"Knock that off and sit your butts down," Jena said.

Darian stopped crying and sat down, and Pete sat down, too.

"What if we have to pee?" Darian asked.

"Then Kaden or Laz will take you to the latrine or the nearest tree."

"I have to go," Darian said.

"Me, too," Pete echoed.

Kaden stood up from where he had been sitting and walked over to Laz. "I'll take Pete," he said quickly.

Laz glared down at Darian. "Alright. Let's go. You pee. You shake it off, and then it's right back to the chair with you."

It was nearly dark when they got back home. They stabled the horses and then went to the keep. The Marching Night were filing in getting plates and then walking out the door to eat around the fire pit, leaving the hall mostly empty to accommodate their guests. They stepped aside to let them in.

When they got inside Tarius immediately thundered. "What did you do!"

Rea looked around—as she was sure nearly everyone did—hoping they hadn't done anything to incur the wrath of the Great Leader. Then she realized Tarius was looking at the two small boys sitting very still at the table without any plates of food.

"Tell her what you did, Darian," Jena ordered.

"It is not that bad, Madra," Darian said. He looked as contrite as Rea had ever seen him look.

"Then you won't mind telling me." Tarius walked over close to the two boys and towered over them, her fists on her hips.

Rea had always thought there was no one more frightening than her Madra, but she had been wrong.

When Darian was done telling his story Tarius thundered, "You might have both been killed!"

"The Everything told me…"

Tarius cut Darian off. "If you had told me and I thought you weren't lying I would have taken you myself."

"We will go to bed without dinner," Darian offered.

"Child, you slay me," Tarius said. "How will you waking me up in the middle of the night to tell me you are hungry punish you? You will eat your dinner and then continue to sit there till we go to the ship to sleep. If anyone sees you so much as raise your butt from that chair they will pick you up and stuff you right back into it. And you will apologize this minute to your brother and Katrina."

"I'm sorry Laz, sorry Katrina," Darian said.

"Sorry," Pete said.

Beside her Laz nodded but then leaned in to Rea and whispered, his lips nearly touching her ear, "They are such little turds but now they look so sad I feel sorry for them."

Rea nodded.

Katrina walked over to her and kissed her on the cheek. "Did you have a good day? I missed you. What did you do?"

"My day was alright. We went to West Town. That is all," Rea said, then turning to her brother said, "I have to bring food to Erah and check on her."

"Can I go with you?" Laz asked.

Rea thought about it for a minute, but apparently he had already been in Erah's cave and she hadn't freaked completely out so, "Yeah sure." She went to get a bowl of food to take to the human.

As she walked through the dark with her brother part of her felt like the specialness of her bond with the human was broken now that others had spoken to and shared tea with her. She said as much to Laz. "I know it's silly, but..."

"I'm sorry. Do you want me to go back to the colony, or wait for you outside?"

"No, Laz, it's good for her to start to get to know other people. It's a good start to her having a better life. She has been alone for a long time. Just so you know, though, there is a dead body... Well a mummy really... in the cave. It's under a blanket. Do not touch it; she loses her whole mind..."

"A dead body, what the hell?

"It is in Kartik armor. It is holding a Kartik sword. I thought at first it was a woman, that it was woman's armor, but I have only seen it once and I'm no longer sure it was a woman. Now I look at the size of the lump under the blanket I just don't know. I think Erah was very young when our forces hit the town. I think the soldier was probably badly wounded and got left behind. I think when the town was burned, the townspeople fled, and our forces left, that they were the only ones here. She has been here alone ever since the soldier died. It was long enough ago that there is nothing left of the soldier but skin stretched over bone."

"Why did she keep him in the cave with her? How did she do that? He would have stank to high heavens."

"I think, well I don't think she could bear to be all alone. If he died in the winter she would have been running a fire all the time, and till I fixed it a lot of the smoke from the fire stayed in the cave. It might have dried the body out." She shrugged. "It might have stank and she just didn't care as long as she wasn't alone."

Laz nodded as if that made sense, but it really probably didn't. "I don't know it's not like I can just sit and talk to her. I keep thinking if I can teach her to talk she'll be able to answer all my questions."

They reached the cave and Rea could see light through the small window in the door. Before she got to the door it opened and a hand motioned her in. "She just started doing that," Rea said.

Rea walked in first and Laz followed her.

"Rea, Laz," Erah said.

"That's right." Rea was some shocked. She had expected Erah to be at least wary of Laz, but she was smiling all the way to her eyes.

Erah had two candles burning for light; she had let the fire all but go out. She walked over stirred the coals and put on a pot of water. Then she held her hands out greedily for the bowl Rea was carrying and Rea handed it to her. She sat down on her chair and motioned for them to sit on her bed. They did so and she immediately started stuffing the food in her mouth any way it would go in.

Laz smiled. "She eats like a Katabull," he said.

"I am not that messy but you are," Rea said.

She finished the bowl of food in a few minutes and then she was looking at them. She was obviously trying to think of a way to say something. Finally she held her hand up and held it at one height then held it at another. Rea was lost as to what she wanted to know. Erah seemed frustrated but did it again and Laz looked at Rea and smiled.

"She is asking about Darian and Pete." He looked at Erah and made the same signs she had then pointed towards the colony. "You know what's odd; Darian taught her my name but not his."

"Oh she couldn't have learned his name quickly. It would have taken her days. Short words she picks up pretty quick, but... well she still can't say broth."

"Brot," Erah said.

"See what I mean?" Rea said. "And it was one of the first words I tried to teach her."

"She's listening to us," Laz said.

"I think she wants to learn to talk to us almost as much as I want her to be able to talk."

"You know, Rea, I don't think Darian could understand her, but when he talked to her she seemed to understand him."

"That's too bad," Rea said.

"Why?"

"Because Tarius is never going to let him come back to the cave after what he did."

Laz nodded. "You are probably right."

"Laz," Erah said, and handed him a cup of tea.

"You know Erah you have only just met Laz. Maybe you shouldn't be so forward."

Chapter Six

It was the third night in less than a week that Ufalla had come home stinking drunk after Jestia had given up on her and gone to bed. When Ufalla got into bed she was all over Jestia, and Jestia shoved her roughly away and got out of bed.

"What's wrong with you!" Ufalla yelled at her.

"What's wrong with me? What by all the gods is wrong with you? You are drunk as a rutting goat again. You come home hours after I have given up on you and gone to sleep then climb all over me as if I am some common whore. You are always crying 'Oh woe is me! I am no one; I am nothing,' and going out of your way to prove it."

"You have changed, Jestia. You don't see it but you have, and what am I to you what am I to anyone? You are better at everything than I am. Hell I'm a trained sword woman, trained by the greatest fighters in the Marching Night and I can't even win a sword fight with you because you cast a spell you don't even know you have cast and then... well not even Tarius the Black could touch you... Oh but wait she probably could because as far as you're concerned the sun shines out of her ass and what am I?"

"A spitting, hateful drunk just like my damn father, that's what you are." Then Jestia popped off to Jazel's.

Jazel felt her arrive in her alchemy and walked in closing her robe just a few second later. Jestia was crying uncontrollably. Jazel didn't say anything about how late it was or being woken up, she just walked over and hugged Jestia patting her back and let her have a good cry.

A teapot and cups popped into the air beside Jestia and drying her eyes she had both cups poured. She sniffed then took a cup and took a drink. Jazel took the other cup and together they went and sat at the small table in the room. "Eerin must have heard us fighting and made me a pot of tea. Oh Jazel what am I going to do about Ufalla? She is completely out of control! We fight all the time now."

"There is nothing you can do about what is wrong with her, Jestia, because it is not your fault. It would indeed be great magic if we could wave our hand and heal what is broken in another person. Her pride is the only thing that is wounded in her. She is blaming you for the way she feels, which is perhaps the one thing you cannot control. You want to have the same kind of relationship as you see the people around you having but you are amazing, not normal."

"Each witch is completely individual. There has never been a witch like you Jestia, and when you are gone there will never be another like you again. That—and only that— is what is wrong with Ufalla."

"For a witch to stay in a relationship with a normal human she has to be willing to make compromises she might not want to make. Only you can decide if you care enough about her to make them. If she is worth this amount of heartache. You may have to let her go, Jestia."

"I don't know if I can," Jestia said. "No one ever really loved me until she did. And I love her, at least I love who she used to be. I need her to be who she used to be."

"But Jestia, she might not be able to be that person again as long as she is with you."

"I spent most of my life alone. I don't want to be alone again."

"We would never let that happen, Jestia."

"I wish there was some spell I could do, to turn back time..."

"And do what, Jestia? All of this started after the volcano erupted. What would you go back and do? Let this entire town full of people and most of this side of the island perish so that Ufalla wouldn't have her feelings hurt? You did and have done nothing wrong. Jestia, I—Jazel—can't suffer the luxury of not trusting myself. You for *sure* can't. You are too powerful to let something like Ufalla's need to be better than you drive your thinking. We walk a tightrope as witches. If we let someone pull us into making even one bad choice everything starts to fall like leaves in a gale."

Jestia knew that was true, but she still didn't know what to do about Ufalla. She could be perfectly happy; she had been, but now Ufalla was making Jestia miserable.

Ufalla stumbled out of the house, and Eerin ran to catch up to her. "Ufalla you have got to stop all of this. The drinking is bad enough, but I know about the women. If I know it is only a miracle that Jestia hasn't figured it out yet."

Ufalla reached out and shoved him so hard he fell down. She started walking back down the street. Behind her Eerin got to his feet and ran to catch up with her again. "She will kill you, Ufalla, she will kill you."

"I don't care," Ufalla growled, and then she turned around and hit him in the mouth. This time he didn't fall; he caught her eyes and held them.

"Well I do. I do care. You keep screaming at her that she has changed, but she hasn't changed in any way that hurts you. You're the one who has changed. We are friends, you hit me because I say things you don't want to hear. Where is my friend? You don't care if you die that is fine, it is your life. But if you still care about Jestia at all... If she kills you it will turn her into something she doesn't deserve to be."

Ufalla's answer was to punch at him again. This time he easily blocked her punch. It was something she had taught him to do. She started walking again, and this time he didn't follow her.

He knows because he cares where I go and what I do, Ufalla thought. *Jestia doesn't know because she no longer cares where I go and what I do as long as it doesn't interrupt what she wants to do.*

The longer she went without Jestia catching her the more careless she became with who she slept with and where. It became a game; one that she was good at.

She had picked the girl up in a bar, a stranger, someone she had never seen before and probably wouldn't again which made her perfect. She was pretty with long legs and bright red lips. Ufalla was still mostly sober when the girl talked her into her room in the inn. Ufalla had her shirt off before the door was all the way closed.

"Aren't you married to the witch Jestia?"

"I am but I won't tell if you don't tell," Ufalla said,

"Do you not love your wife? Does she treat you badly?"

"I love my wife, but it is just difficult." She had taken her pants off.

"Do you do this a lot pick up strange women for sex?"

"Two or three times a week." She walked over and kissed the woman who did not kiss her back, and Ufalla was starting to lose interest.

Then a force hit her in the chest and shoved her against the wall hard and held her there. She watched in mounting terror as the woman before her shifted until she was looking at Jestia.

Jestia was near glowing with the force of her rage. "It is difficult! I gave you half my life you worthless, drunken whore! You love me but it is difficult! I'm difficult! While what, you are so easy to love as you whine all day everyday about everything that isn't my fault and that I can't change? You are easy to love as you come home drunk after bedding some whore and use your words to hurt me because... I'm difficult!"

Ufalla had been wrong. It wasn't rage that consumed Jestia; her heart was broken. "Jestia, I am so sorry."

"Really?" Jestia's tears started to fall, running down her face and off her chin. "You are sorry! For what? For treating me like shit for going on years as you try to figure out who you are? Or for letting my needs go barely tended while you lie with every whore in Montero! For coming home drunk and being belligerent." She shook her head and now the rage Ufalla had only thought she saw earlier was there.

"I love you, Jestia."

"No, you really don't." Jestia raised her hand and a ball of light started to form. Ufalla had seen her cast this spell before it was a ball lightning spell—well at least she would die quickly.

And then the witch Jazel was between her and Jestia, her back to Ufalla. "Jestia you must stop. You know what it will do to you. Just go, go now!"

The ball of light in Jestia's hand vanished. She started crying again, and Ufalla felt herself released. Ufalla started to move to hold Jestia, but Jazel put out an arm and stopped her. "You have done enough harm."

Jazel looked at Jestia again. "You know what you have to do, Jestia. You must go now, right now."

Jestia glared at Ufalla with black hatred. Ufalla was sure Jestia was going to finish her off, but then she was gone. Ufalla knew where Jestia was going. Ufalla would get a horse and ride to the compound and talk to her wife. But when she tried to move, she found herself slammed into the wall again and then she couldn't move at all.

"No!" Jazel swore, then she turned and looked into Ufalla's eyes. "Were it not for Eerin you would be dead, girl. Ever since I figured out what you were doing I had him following you, casting spells to hide it from Jestia. Right now I seriously do not give a damn what happens to you, but if Jestia kills you it will not just destroy her—do you understand that?"

"Let me go!" Ufalla fought against the invisible bonds that held her. "I need to fix this."

"I wonder if you know Jestia at all," Jazel said with disgust. "You will not be able to fix this unless you are actually sorry about what you have done instead of just sorry you got caught."

Jazel left her there, near naked, hanging on the wall.

Tarius was asleep when Darian woke her shaking her arm. "Madra, Jestia is hurt, she is coming."

She didn't have time to process what he had told her before Jestia appeared between she and her wife.

"Jestia for all the gods..." Jena stopped when she realized the girl was crying huge, wracking sobs.

Tarius held Jestia and patted her back. She didn't say a word till Jestia started to calm down a bit. "What happened?"

"I almost killed Ufalla." She started crying harder again. She sucked in air then said, "She cheats on me. Ufalla cheats on me with any whore that will have her. She has been doing it for months maybe years and I had no idea till a day ago when she came home late and drunk again. When she undressed... I could see nail marks on her back that I did not put there. I feel so very stupid. She doesn't love me anymore and I don't know anything right now except how much I want her dead. How much I just want to kill her."

Tarius nodded her understanding.

"Jena, get up and pack. We must all leave for the Territories as soon as possible."

Tarius got up and brought Jestia with her, still holding her. As much to keep her from going back to Montero and finishing what she started as to comfort her. As long as Tarius had a hold of her she couldn't go anywhere without taking Tarius with her.

"Rimmy!!"

In seconds he was in the room with them. "Rimmy, tell Hared to pack for the Territories. Then go and get Jabone, Kaseria and Harris."

Jabone and Kaseria were the closest to their huts so they were the first ones there. Jabone was holding Arvon who was still asleep. Jena was already running around packing. Diana was still in her cradle; she had slept through the whole thing.

"What on earth has happened?" Jabone asked looking at where his Madra held a sobbing Jestia. "Has Ufalla died?"

"If it were only that we would not have to leave in the middle of the night," Tarius said. She sat Jestia on the side of their bed then held out her arms to Jabone. "Give me that cub."

Jabone handed him over and she immediately put the baby in Jestia's arms. Jestia loved Arvon better than anyone but Ufalla who she now wanted to kill. Tarius hoped that holding him would calm her down. She knew Jestia would not pop out and take Arvon with her.

Harris came limping in as fast as he could move. "What is going on?" he saw Jestia and the state she was in. "Has something happened to Ufalla?"

"No, but it will if we don't get Jestia off the island," Tarius said.

"She cheated on me; she's been cheating on me. She's been mean and drunk and then I realized why. She was cheating on me the whole time," Jestia started rocking the baby. "I almost killed her, only Jazel stopped me."

"Jazel... good that gives us a little more time. Jazel will not let Ufalla follow Jestia right away. Harris, when the spell Jazel has cast on Ufalla has worn off she will ride here as fast as she can." She looked at Jena and then her grown son. "We cannot be here when she gets here." Both Jabone and Jena nodded their understanding. She looked back at Harris. "You must not let Ufalla leave the compound by horse or by ship. If she follows us to the Territories I don't know what will happen, but it won't be good."

"I am so sorry, Jestia," Harris said. He moved to put a hand on Jestia's shoulder. He looked at Tarius. "We will keep her here no matter what it takes."

"Thank you, my dear friend," Tarius said. She wanted to make sure he knew any anger she had for his daughter did not apply to him. "We will take Arvon with us..."

"But Madra, how long will you be gone?" Jabone said, looking at his son in Jestia's arms.

"No idea," Tarius said. As she saw the look on Jabone's face she grabbed his arm and pulled him down the hall into the main room. "I am sorry, Jabone. I know he is your cub. But Jestia loves him and he will be able to help sooth her even if I can't. And you know he will raise living hell when he realizes Diana has gone without him anyway. I would say come and go with us, but Ufalla is your best friend. You may be able to talk sense into her better than her father or mother can. If Ufalla follows us to the Territories... Son," she lowered her voice still further, "Jestia is crushed and her instinct is to kill Ufalla and have it over with. If she casts a spell to kill Ufalla what she will become will be more dangerous than anything you can imagine. Her logical mind knows that, but the part of her that loved Ufalla that thought Ufalla loved her..."

"But she does love her, Madra."

"Does she? You don't do that..." She pointed back to the room where Jestia was. "...to someone you truly love. If Ufalla still loves her she will not come here to find her or try to go to the Territories, and I would bet the Great Wall that she will do both. If she still even cares for Jestia she will give her time to calm down, time to heal. She will take time to figure out why she has done the things she has done. You must make her understand that.

"Dammit I knew the way she was acting was all wrong, but I didn't think Ufalla would take things this far. I thought she'd play at the edge of the cliff but not jump off of it. There is something seriously wrong with her. Maybe you can help her figure out why she would do something both so hateful and so incredibly stupid."

Jabone nodded. "I will try Madra." He smiled then and shook his head. "But I don't know that anyone can fix that level of stupid. We will not let her leave here, *that* I can promise you."

"Thank you, and I will bring your son back to you as soon as I can."

Tarius went back to her room to start packing her own bag and Jabone followed. "Jabone, please help your mother pack for the cubs. You know that she thinks I do it wrong." Jabone nodded and started helping Jena.

"Kaseria, you will be leader while we are away," Tarius said.

There was a huge communal gasp in the room, but Kaseria was the one who said what the others were only thinking.

"But... I'm crazy Kaseria."

"You will be fine. You know everything that I do, and what you don't know Riglid does. You understand what it means to lead and you don't want to do it so you will do fine for now. Jabone wants to do it so he is not suitable and we do not have time for me to round up anyone else. It will be enough to round up a crew, decide who will be going with us and load supplies."

Tarius put together a quick crew, and in less than an hour they were on the ship heading out of the harbor. Neither Arvon nor Diana had even woken up. Arvon was sleeping on a bunk with Jestia, though Tarius doubted that Jestia was sleeping. Tarius stood on the bow looking out at the ocean, both moons were full and the night was bright as day. The sea was still and tranquil. She felt Jena's hand as it closed on her shoulder.

"Why don't you come with me to our cabin and try to get some sleep?"

"I will. Jena, look how still and peaceful the night is. And we are not fighting a war, there is no earthquake or volcano. Everything in our lives is good. We are not fighting; our cubs are all well and happy. But we must jump from our beds and take off into the night because our goddaughter is a moron."

"You really think Jestia would kill her?"

"I think she already would have if Jazel didn't stop her. I don't think she would want to, but Ufalla would not have to do or say much to make her killing mad again. Jestia is hurt, but she is Jestia. She has a vast knowledge of things not even Jazel or I understand, yet... Ufalla was cheating on her right under her nose. Her heart is broken, but that is not where the rage comes from. Jestia feels stupid; that is where the anger comes from. It is growing in the place where Jestia thinks she should have known and didn't. It will take her time to realize that she didn't know because Ufalla was being such an ass. Part of Jestia was ignoring Ufalla's coming and going because she didn't want to deal with Ufalla's hateful attitude."

"They were so in love. I wonder what happened," Jena said. She took Tarius's hand and started pulling her towards the cabin.

"They grew apart, Jena. They didn't grow together; they grew apart."

Jestia looked at Arvon lying beside her. He was smiling even in his sleep. He didn't know the world was a rotten, stinking place full of liars and cheats.

She wanted to tell Tarius all this get to the Territories thing was nonsense. That she could stay in the compound and control herself if Ufalla came there. But... *I very nearly killed her, and I still want her dead. I once risked my own life to jump in front of an axe meant for her with nothing but a spell I had never made work before to save her. I gave her half my years, but I could have killed her easier than I did either of those things even though I know... I know what the price would have been to me if Jazel hadn't stopped me. I don't know if—even knowing all that I know could happen to me—I could stop myself from killing her if I saw her right now.*

It was better to put an ocean between them. No chance of her doing anything they would all regret later. Tarius was right to give her Arvon to remind her that there was still pure love in the world. Arvon loved her as she loved him.

She felt a small hand on her back, turned and saw Darian standing there. "Shouldn't you be in your bunk?" she asked him.

"I have to tell you something." Without being asked he crawled into bed with her. "There is a wild girl who lives in a cave..." Darian started, and before he had finished his story Jestia had fallen fast asleep.

Chapter Seven

Jazel left the girl to hang on the wall till it was nearly midday. "I hope she has pissed all over herself and is starving," Jazel mumbled as she walked towards the inn.

When she walked in she could hear Ufalla screaming from the second story. "Go get the witch Jazel! Go get her and tell her to let me go!" She had probably been doing so for hours if not all night, yet no one in the bar or who were trying to sleep in the inn had come to get Jazel. They knew her, they trusted her, and knew she must have a damn good reason for locking the screaming girl there.

"I'm sorry. If I had realized she would scream all night I would have put a silence spell on her as well. Thank you for your patience," Jazel said to the three people in the bar. "I will get rid of her for you in just a moment and pay you for the inconvenience."

Jazel went up the stairs at a brisk pace, opened the door and said, "Shut up right now you willful, selfish brat."

Ufalla shut up. It wasn't a spell of course, but after all the girl was screaming for them to get Jazel, and there she was.

"Did you cry like a baby all night? How stupid are you? These people would never come for me. They know you have been whoring around. They knew it was only a matter of time till Jestia found you out, and they want no part of her or my anger."

Ufalla had pissed herself, so Jazel muttered a spell to clean up the piss on the floor but left Ufalla in soaked underwear.

"Let me go at once, old woman!"

"If this is how you talk to your wife it is no wonder she wanted to kill you. I want to kill you, and I'm not stuck with you."

"Let me go!" Ufalla jerked against the spell that locked her to the wall.

"Shut up and listen to me." This time it *was* a spell because she didn't wish to be interrupted. "When I realized

105

what you were doing I didn't tell Jestia because the outcome would have been the same. When I realized you were not stopping but becoming more reckless I had Eerin follow you and throw spells to cover up what you were doing because again if Jestia found out the outcome would be the same. When Eerin told me last night that Jestia knew what you were doing and was even at that moment entrapping you, I got here as soon as I could—not to save *you*, but to save Jestia. You have no idea what forces you play with. It is as hard for her to understand why you do the things you do as it is for you to even try to wrap your tiny, insignificant human brain around what she is.

"But I'm an old witch and I know why humans do the things they do and it isn't pretty. Everything you do, you do because you think the whole Everything revolves around you and what you want. At the end of the day you are—all of you—selfish creatures often bent on nothing as hard and as fast as your own destruction. It takes next to nothing to break you. And what exactly broke you, Ufalla? The earth shook, the top came off the great mountain, molten rock rained and poured from it. Jestia called Tarius to her and together they kept the worst from happening. Then when Jestia was all but dead it wasn't you but Tarius that saved her. You realized how small and insignificant you are and will always be in comparison to those two and how unimportant your bond is when compared to Jestia's with Tarius. You used to be a strong woman, a good-hearted woman, but this horror that you have become...it was always in you just waiting for the moment you cared more about what you wanted than what she needed. Jestia didn't do this to you, you did it to yourself when you made the choice to serve your ego.

"You had an amazing woman who loved you, and you destroyed that for what? To drink yourself sick and get your fingers and your tongue wet? You have become the nothing you only thought you were before.

"You think Jestia has unlimited choices, but that is as far as it can be from the truth. Witches don't have real choices. If we do the wrong thing there is always a price that must be paid, sometimes by others, often by us, but we don't really have choices. You have lots of choices, and what have you chosen?"

Then she raised her right hand into the air, her fingers spread and muttered an incantation. "Let her speak, let her go where she goes I will not know what she speaks where she goes I cannot say." She stood there only a second longer and then she vanished.

So she had walked there only to take her own sweet time and popped away so that she didn't have to listen to Ufalla curse her. Ufalla was soaked. She left her wet drawers there, dressed, and stomped out of the bar and all the way to their spa. She took off her clothes, relieved herself, then got in the spring, jumped out and started to dress. When she had finished Eerin appeared as if out of thin air, but she knew he didn't have that spell.

"Do not I beg of you go to the compound," Eerin said. "Leave her alone; let her cool."

"I can fix this; I must fix this."

"Do you just want her to kill you? You thought you were so smart, didn't you? That Jestia had no idea what you were up to, but the only reason she didn't figure you out long ago was that Jazel and I were covering for you."

Ufalla took a deep breath and let it out, just now realizing that was what Jazel had said without saying it.

"Eerin, I love Jestia."

"If that were true you would not go to the compound, and I can see from the look on your face that you will beat me if I try to stop you. But you could only beat me if I let you. Unlike you I will walk away from a fight that will change nothing." There was a sad look in his eyes as he turned his back on her and walked away without another word.

In the seconds it took for her incantation to release Ufalla, Jazel muttered a third, silent spell, and really relaxed for the first time in months. She knew Jestia was on her way to the Territories because Jestia had mind spoken to her before the ship left the harbor, and now she knew there was no way Ufalla could follow her.

Jestia woke to the feeling of Tarius's hand on her shoulder. She knew it was Tarius because when they touched the magic connection they shared always made her skin tingle.

"Come Jestia," she said. "There is a pod of orcas following the ship."

When Jestia nodded and sat up she was surprised to see that she was alone.

To the look on her face Tarius said, "They woke early. I have already had to pull Arvon down from the main mast."

Jestia got out of bed and by magic changed the witch's robe she had been wearing into pants and a shirt, and then barefooted followed Tarius to the deck of the ship. She took a deep breath of the cool sea air and it brought up a strong memory of all the months she and Ufalla had spent on a Marching Night fishing vessel when she had been running from her mother and her duty as heir apparent to the Kartik throne. *And why was I running? To be with Ufalla, to be with her on our terms and not the kingdom's We were so in love. It was real; I know it was. It seems like so long ago now, but the memories are still strong. The touch, the feel, the smell of her, it was everything. Now there is darkness in my heart where she was.*

Her mind was about to go in a bad direction when she saw the whales. There were three of them, a pair and their calf, playing in the wake of the ship. Their energy coursed through her. So alive, so brilliant, so beautiful. She took in a deep breath of the smell of them and let it out.

Tarius said in a voice just above a whisper, "The sun always rises, my amazing sister. When I saw them I knew the Everything had sent them for you."

Jestia dried a tear from her eye and turned to look up at Tarius. "Thank you." She turned back to watch the whales. "I will heal, Tarius, this morning, just now, I know it."

"I never had a doubt, but it will take time and many things like this to dull your pain. I cannot, nor will I lose you again Jestia, I couldn't bear it."

"I will not leave you." She took Tarius's hand and held it. "I will fill the emptiness inside of me with moments like this." She motioned towards the pod of whales. "I will heal myself. It will be my greatest spell yet."

"Babies up a tree!" Darian yelled.

Tarius looked up and then took off running. When Jestia turned not only Arvon but Diana was half way up the mast. Jestia cast a spell and the startled toddlers found themselves sitting at the base of the mast. They looked at each other, laughed, and then started to go right back up the mast but Tarius grabbed Arvon as Hared grabbed Diana. Jena came running out of the cabin and grabbed Diana out of Hared's arms. From the look on her face as she said something to him Jestia couldn't hear, it was obvious Hared was supposed to have been watching them. Jestia walked up to them and found that the smile on her face was real.

The Everything is always looking for balance. It took a long time for Ufalla to break me; it will not take me as long to mend.

She took Arvon from Tarius and started walking with him back to the stern. When he saw the whales he clapped.

She didn't realize that the older boys were even there till Darian spoke.

"Look, Pete," he said, as if his brother couldn't see the huge animals swimming in and through their wake. "Orca. They bring good luck."

Pete nodded.

Darian looked at Arvon and shook his finger in his face. "You are a bad little monkey."

Arvon just laughed.

"I am surprised they could climb at all with these on." Jestia pointed to the life jackets all of the children were wearing.

"Oh nothing can stop Arvon climbing," Jena said as she walked up to join them in watching the whales.

Diana reached over and petted Arvon and then pointed at the whales. He just nodded.

"Unfortunately, Diana has to do whatever he does."

"He helps her," Darian said, turning to look at her. He looked at Arvon and smiled which didn't match what he said next. "You're a bad little monkey. Madra should beat you."

Jestia actually found herself laughing. To her surprise because she hardly ever heard him even speak, Pete started to sing a song about a whale. He had a decent voice. It was a song she knew, so she started to sing along with him.

Rea had just come back from taking food to Erah. Since the Great Leader's last visit a few weeks ago and Erah's meeting with Laz and the two boys, Erah seemed much more eager to learn new words. She would point at things and grunt wanting to know what they were called. Rea had even taken Erah hunting with her once, though she had yet to kill another stinking thing since the moose. So it was more like a nice hike wishing for something to kill. Erah was good company. For one thing, she didn't talk too much.

Rea wished there was a witch handy who had a spell to make Katrina talk less and Erah talk more. *Maybe something that takes words from Katrina and gives them to Erah.* She smiled as she filled her bowl and moved to the great table to sit and eat her dinner.

Katrina walked in, filled her bowl quickly, and all but ran over to sit beside her as if someone might sit in the seat next to Rea. Which no one ever did, not anymore, because Katrina had successfully marked her territory. As she sat down she kissed Rea on the cheek. Half the time Rea didn't even notice anymore. Katrina rarely slept in her own bunk; she was just always there and so was her constant talking.

"The levy is finished," she said as if Rea didn't know it. After all, she had been working right beside her all day listening to her talking and... well how did she always find something to talk about, and when did she breathe?

"What is the next big project?" Because of course they always had dozens of small projects going on.

"Erecting the saw mill," Fleat said, saving Rea the trouble.

"That's exciting making our own lumber."

"Why are we doing the saw mill before the black smith shop, Captain oh my Captain?" Fleat said. Rea could smack him. He knew why, hell it was his idea. He did this only to draw her into a conversation with Katrina which of course only made the girl talk more.

"It might be nice to have lumber to build the black smith shop with."

And then of course Katrina was off about how clever Rea was and what they could build and how. And who was clever was Katrina because it wasn't that she didn't have good ideas because she did. Mostly she was clever because she just kept asking questions so that Rea had to either talk to her or ignore her. Rea had learned the hard way that ignoring Katrina only got her asked the same question half a dozen times.

"Everyone is talking about wanting to build a pub, but I think after the important things are built we should put in a library. What do you think?"

"Well, I don't want a pub for sure," Rea said,

"No doubt because she lived in them for years," Fleat teased her.

"That, and I don't want to have to walk there every time I need you," Rea said.

He laughed as he got up took his bowl and went to wash it. He was limping; she didn't like it. Fleat swore he hadn't injured himself that it was just old age, but it seemed to her the limp was getting worse not better. She had seen Garrett give him powders more than once—her guess was for pain.

"What's wrong?" Katrina asked.

"I'm worried about Fleat's leg. Remind me to talk to Garrett tomorrow about what it is he is giving him and why."

"You are such a good Captain. I will remind you at breakfast tomorrow."

And that was possibly the only thing good about Katrina being always in her face and talking all the time. Katrina would tell her at breakfast. She wouldn't tell her when Rea first got up and was still groggy even if she had slept in her bed that night. No she would wait till breakfast. She never forgot anything, not ever, no doubt because it gave her yet another thing to talk about.

Rea finished her dinner. When she got up and started to grab her bowl Katrina took it from her. "I'll wash it for you."

Rea sighed. "Katrina you do not have to wait on me."

"But I want to."

Suddenly Rea got her sense of humor back. She leaned over and whispered in Katrina's ear, "Why don't you just piss on my leg and have it done with?"

Katrina smiled broadly at her and said, "I would if I thought it would work."

Rea laughed and walked outside to stand by the fire. It was already starting to get cold and it wouldn't be long till they would be forced inside which made all of them want to be outside as much as possible.

From the catwalk the guard on duty yelled, "There is a ship!"

That was crazy. Both of theirs had come in at dusk, it was already dark, and the Great Leader had just been there. Rea wondered if maybe they were about to be raided by pirates and almost laughed. Pirates would be unpleasantly surprised if they tried to raid a fully-armed Katabull town that included fifty members of the Marching Night. They didn't need to prepare, but still she was about to have the alarms raised when the sentry yelled down.

"It is the Great Leader's ship!"

Katrina was already at her elbow. Rea turned to her and said, "But they were just here with my Madra and the queen how many weeks ago?"

"Not even three," Katrina answered.

Rea nodded and started walking down to the docks to meet the ship. "Something must be wrong or she wouldn't come back this soon."

"Aye," Katrina agreed.

Rea realized the gravity of the situation when that was all Katrina said till on the docks Rea asked her, "What do you think it could be?"

"Maybe another disaster," Katrina said.

"It is dark night; the moons aren't even up yet." They had a Katabull crew, but it was a big ship. Their docks really could only take four ships, and theirs were at the dock which meant it was a tight fit. "Someone get torches and..." Suddenly there was a bright light emanating from the bow of the ship which lit up the opening into the harbor. "Oh crap. Jestia is with them."

"So?" Katrina said,

"So she is very powerful and she hates my guts. Tell the Great Leader I am ill. I'm going to go hide in my room."

Katrina watched as the gangplank was lowered and the Great Leader holding her daughter came down the gangplank followed by her wife and her two youngest sons and their fathers. Behind them came the princess Jestia who was holding the hand of Jabone's son, Arvon. Laz was bringing up the rear. The rest of the crew were behind him.

Tarius walked right up to Katrina and she felt honored. "So have we gotten here in time for dinner?"

"Just," Katrina said.

"And where is Rea?" There was an edge of worry to her voice.

Katrina started to tell her the lie Rea told her to tell but found she couldn't bring herself to lie to the Great Leader. She leaned in and whispered in Tarius's ear, "When the light shown from your ship and she realized Jestia was on board she told me to tell you she was sick and then she ran to hide in her room. She said Jestia hates her."

Tarius nodded then leaned in and whispered in her ear, "That was very wise. Jestia is in a mood; let us leave it at that for now."

Rea impatiently paced back and forth in her room wondering what horrible thing could have happened that Tarius was coming in after dark, right after having been here. With Jestia in tow, of all people. She was relieved when the curtain was drawn back and her brother Laz entered.

"What the hell is going on?" Rea asked as she walked over to hug him.

He hugged her back and said, "All hell has broken loose…" As they moved to sit on her bed he told her, "You were right to hide. She has never liked you, and she is devastated, murderous, and even madder than normal. She will be doing fine and then the craziest stuff will just come out of her lips."

"Hasn't it always?" Rea asked with a grin. "None of that explains why you are all here now."

"Apparently Jestia can't kill Ufalla from here."

"But she could kill me," Rea said.

"But she wouldn't because that would do the same thing to her that it would do if she killed Ufalla. Besides, she just dislikes you; you didn't cheat on her."

"Hello she 'dislikes me' because I slept with Ufalla," Rea said.

"But not while she was with Jestia."

"No, but that wasn't because I didn't try."

"She won't kill you."

"That doesn't mean she won't do something gods awful horrible to me."

"No, it does not."

Chapter Eight

Ufalla reached the compound in less time than it had ever taken her. When she had ridden through the gates both her father and Jabone were waiting for her. She'd jumped off her horse and held its reins.

"Where is Jestia?"

"Not even hi," her father said. It was clear he was furious with her.

"She is not here. Madra had to take her across the ocean to keep her from killing you. Madra said if you really loved Jestia you would not come here. I am sad to see that you have done just that," Jabone said.

Ufalla looked from her father to Jabone. "You just don't understand. I can explain…"

"Did you do it or not?" her father demanded.

"It isn't such a big deal. I do love Jestia, I just…"

"You don't love her," her father said. "You disgraced our family when you whored yourself out for your own pleasure. When, knowing what she is and what she can do, you brought her wrath down on your head. When you treated her so foully Tarius had to take her away."

"Tarius, Tarius, Tarius! I am so sick of everything revolving around Tarius!"

"How dare you put her name into your foul mouth. I would be nothing, nothing without her. I would still be pouring out the slop buckets and cleaning the latrines of rich morons who called themselves swords masters. Without her you would not exist to slur her name. I owe her everything, and so you owe her everything."

"I am sorry, Father. So sorry. I just… I need to fix things."

"You have broken your mug in too many shards to fix it," Jabone said.

"I will go to the Territories and get my wife."

"She is not your property, and no one in the compound will let you leave here by horse or by ship because my madra is the leader here not you!" Jabone stomped off.

She looked at her father. "Will you not even hear my side of it?"

"I already have, Ufalla. Your side is just that—yours. It isn't the truth, only the excuses you made to do the selfish things you have done. You have brought shame on me and on our house. You have treated your wife shabbily." Then he turned and walked away.

Ufalla had jumped back on her horse and tried to ride out the way she had come, but four Katabull stood in her way.

The biggest of them bellowed up at her, "Put your horse away! You will not be leaving the compound until the Great Leader tells us you can."

That was four days ago, and all her attempts to either get on a ship or leave by land had failed. She was sleeping in she and Jestia's huts, but none of the Katabull would even talk to her. They were all shunning her as were her own parents. She had thought that at least her mother would talk to her, but she had forgotten just how unforgiving her mother could be. When she had tried to talk to her brother he had told her flat out to go to hell.

She was pretty sure she was already there. None of them even wanted to try to understand; none of them were on her side.

She sat behind the crates out of sight; it was starting to get dark. There was a ship leaving for the Territories to fish first thing in the morning. The port they would be using was one she knew well. It was nowhere near the Katabull colony, but then nothing really was. Once there she would have to get a horse and ride up the coast.

If she could even get on the ship, if she could hide long enough for them to set sail, if she could stay hidden and get off the boat without being seen or smelled... just a lot of ifs. It wasn't a great plan, but it was the only one she had.

In the dark she was able to get on the ship undetected, but her feet no sooner hit the deck than she was thrown off it into the bay. By the time she swam to the shore and got out the Katabull were still laughing.

Feeling soggy and completely defeated she walked up the beach to sit on a rock. A few seconds later Jabone said from behind her, "So are you ready to stop trying to do what you know you shouldn't do?"

"Why are you all working so hard to keep me here when you know the witch Jazel has put a spell on me that keeps me from boarding a ship."

"We didn't know that till we saw you cast into the bay." There was a hint of laughter to his voice that she didn't appreciate.

"So can I leave now?"

"And go where, back to Montero to your drink and your whores? You know Madra told us to keep you here. You know that means there is no one here that will let you leave until Madra has told them to."

"Because she is the all-powerful Great Leader," Ufalla grated out.

"That is right!" Jabone thundered. "And do you know how she got that way? By earning their respect one deed at a time and by owning her mistakes. As long as you are playing the victim nothing will change for you and no one—let alone Jestia—will ever forgive you."

She didn't have to turn to know he had gone. She could hear him stomping away.

Rea woke to the now-familiar feel of Katrina's arms around her and the aroma of fresh fruit from the Kartik hanging in the air. After hearing how quickly they had left she wondered how they found the time to load fruit at all, and her guess was there wouldn't be much of it.

After talking to Katrina when she had first lay down last night, she realized there was no way of knowing how long the witch would be there. She couldn't very well run the colony from the safety of her room for weeks. Besides, who would feed Erah? Though she admitted Erah had taken care of herself for decades the girl now looked healthy instead of gaunt.

Speaking her thoughts aloud Rea said, "I suppose one day we should send Erah to live with her own kind."

Katrina moved and stretched a bit then went right back to holding her. "You can never do that."

"Why not, if she can learn to talk..."

"She will still be so different." Katrina moved her arm took her finger and moved Rea's hair out of her face pushing it behind her ear. "Humans... they always fear things that are different. In the Kartik we are revered, but in the rest of the world the humans tolerate or hate us they don't want to live with us. But even the Kartik don't really see us as equals. 'Better than' is almost as bad as 'not as good as.' You don't realize this because for the part of your life that you weren't drunk you have only ever known humans who do see us as the same as them, people like Jena, Harris and Hestia."

"But Erah is just like them; she is a human."

"She's a human, but she is not just like them. She is a creature of the forest, and she will never think, move or act like them. What Ufalla has done to Jestia, that is what humans do to those who are different."

"What do you mean?"

"Most humans want to control everything, and when they find something they can't control they punish it. Yet they never seem to be able to control the only thing that anyone can ever really control which is themselves. If Ufalla wanted to have other women she should have talked about it with her wife Jestia would have said yes or no. She took away Jestia's choice and made it all her own."

Rea nodded. "You really are very wise, Katrina."

"And I am fantastic in bed."

"Like a Katabull with a bone. Come on, let's go get some of that fruit before the pigs that live all around us eat it all."

Rea and Katrina filled their bowls with more fruit than meat, but she noticed as she looked around the table that those who had come from the Kartik had done just the opposite. It made a certain amount of sense. There wasn't enough game on their part of the island to let them eat big slabs of meat. Here it was the fruit that was a treat.

So far it was only the crew of the ship that had made it to the hall. Rea supposed they were the first ones up, and if nothing else the others had cubs to corral.

As if thinking about them had summand them, she could hear Tarius talking to someone outside by the fire.

Fleat who was sitting across from them heard her too and looked at Rea and smiled. "Don't worry, Captain oh my Captain. I will throw myself in front of you should the witch decide to fry you."

Katrina leaned over to her and whispered, "Remember that you wanted to ask Garrett about Fleat's leg." Her timing could have been better because right that moment Rea could care less if the bastard's leg fell completely off.

Tarius walked in with Diana on one hip and Arvon on the other. Rea wondered if she had realized that the cubs could walk now. Jena was just behind her with Pete and Darian. When Darian saw her he turned to run right over and climbed into the empty chair on her right. Standing in the chair he reached over and gave her a huge hug. She didn't know what had happened to make him decide he liked her so much, but when she saw Jestia enter the main hall she was glad he was there. Surely Jestia wouldn't fry her at the risk of hitting one of Tarius's cubs.

Jena got a bowl of food for Darian and set it in front of his chair. He let go of Rea and sat down.

Her fadra and his husband and her brother Laz came in next. Her fadra ran over hugged her and whispered in her ear, "I would ask where you were last night, but right now we would all like to hide from Jestia, and she likes us."

"Is she going to turn me into a rock?"

"Probably not because a rock can't feel pain," he said, and released her to go get his food.

"Jestia," Darian called.

She turned to face him from where she had been getting a bowl of food. "What, baby?"

"Don't turn my sister into a rock," he said while still stuffing his mouth with food.

"Your sister..." And then she saw Rea.

Rea wanted to crawl under the table as the witch's green eyes bored into her. "Rea," she hissed. "I didn't recognize you without your eyes bloodshot, puke in your hair and someone's undergarments around your neck."

Katrina started to protest, but Rea quickly whispered in her ear, "Do not incur the witch's ire on my behalf. What she has said is not untrue."

119

She cleared her throat looked at Jestia and said as calmly as she could muster, "Please forgive me."

"Jestia," Tarius said calmly, "Rea has changed, just like you have."

Jestia nodded and finished filling her bowl. Jena was sitting on Tarius's right. Jestia sat on her left, plucked Arvon off the Great Leader's lap, sat him in hers and offered him the bowl of food Rea had presumed she had gotten for herself. More than seeming just alright with Arvon splashing meat and fruit juice everywhere and all over her, Jestia was grinning at him as if he was doing something really smart.

Rea realized what Tarius had said was correct. Jestia had changed in the same way she had. They had both been wild; they weren't anymore. Suddenly she really heard what Katrina had said that morning. *Ufalla couldn't control anything else about Jestia, so she decided to make her miserable. I think that is the most hateful thing you could do to anyone.* Katrina was even smarter than Rea thought she was.

Having finished his breakfast Darian turned to Rea. "Could you take me and Pete to see Erah? Madra said it is alright if we ask and go with you because after all Erah is your special project."

Rea supposed that was exactly what Erah was.

"Please take them. Take them now," her Fadra pleaded as he leaned around the little Wizard to look at her. "He is driving us all crazy. It is all he has talked about ever since we last set sail from here."

"It is my best adventure Father," he said.

"It was very nearly your last adventure," her fadra told the boy.

"Can you please take us, Rea? We will be good," Darian said.

"They will probably not be good and don't try to watch them on your own."

He looked with meaning at Katrina, but then Laz said from across the table, "I will go with you."

Darian looked at Rea appealingly, and she nodded. "I will. She has actually asked about you and Pete more than a few times."

She had told them she would take them as soon as she had shown Tarius around the colony, but Tarius had said, "We were just here and can show ourselves around. Please take them. Take them right now," she said with a laugh.

Now Rea was walking through the woods with Laz and the boys. They hadn't gone far when Rea started to call Erah by name.

"She comes when you call her now?" Laz asked.

"Most of the time," Rea said. "Erah!"

They only walked a little further when Erah came running out of the trees to stop abruptly in front of them. She seemed super excited and held her hand at the height she usually did when she wanted to know about the boys.

"Yes, Erah." She pointed to the boys in turn. "Pete, Darian."

"Pete," she said. Her attempt to say Darian's name sounded like, "Daran."

"Close enough," Darian said excitedly.

"Laz," Erah said. Then she turned to him and to the surprise of them all, Erah actually grabbed Laz and hugged him tight to her.

"She likes you," Darian said.

"She is very strong," Laz said with a smile.

Erah did not let him go just kept hugging him, and Rea looked at her brother and grinned. "I knew when you were all she talked about she had a little crush on you."

When Erah finally released him she waved her hands around then started walking towards her cave. They followed. She kept turning around looking at them to make sure they were following. She never did that with Rea.

To Rea's dismay when they got to the cave Erah had a roasted rabbit on the fire.

"When she hands you a piece of rabbit eat it at once or she will shove it in your mouth; it is most unpleasant."

Erah handed them each a piece of meat, and they all put it right in their mouths.

Rea reached in her pocket and pulled out the orange she had brought her. She started pealing it and Erah watched her. She had never seen the fruit, and Rea wondered if she would eat it. Rea threw the peelings into the fire. The aroma of the orange was making her mouth water. She broke a slice out and ate it then handed the rest to Erah.

Erah took it and went and sat in her chair. She slowly tore all the slices apart and laid them out on her lap. She kept looking up at them and smiling. Then she took a slice and put it in her mouth. The look that came over her face was almost orgasmic. But she greedily ate half of it then looked up at them and held a slice in each hand out to them. They all shook their heads no except Darian who took a slice.

"Darian, I brought that for her you just ate a whole bowl of them."

"I really like oranges, isn't that right Pete?" Pete just nodded. He wasn't much more vocal than Erah. "Pete's cousin Jestia is here. She could make you talk; would you like that?"

Erah nodded.

"Do you understand him?" Rea asked. Erah just looked at her.

"Darian ask her if she understands you," Laz said.

"You understand me, don't you?"

Erah nodded excitedly, then said, "yes."

"That's why she kept asking about him. She can understand him."

"He talks to monkeys and whales, too," Pete said. "He can make them do things."

"And look he made Pete talk," Laz said.

Pete grinned and slugged Laz in the shoulder. Laz laughed and the next thing he knew Erah had punched him in the shoulder as well. He looked shocked for a minute then laughed even more.

"She really is strong." Erah started to hit him again, and he held up his hand and waved it "Once was enough."

"I can't *make* them do things," Darian said, shaking his head. "I *ask* them, and if they want to they do it."

"Ask her how long she has been alone," Rea asked.

"She will only be able answer easy things. She can understand me, but I can't understand her. You should ask Jestia to make her talk," Darian said.

"I think I had better make sure Jestia isn't going to kill me before I ask her for favors. Can you tell her that I like her; that we are friends?"

Of course it was Darian so he put his own spin on it. "We like you; you are our friend."

Erah nodded and tapped her chest with her fist then walked over and hugged Laz again.

"Seriously? I have fed you every day for years," Rea said.

"My sister wants a hug, too," Darian said, and Erah released Laz and moved to hug Rea. Rea hugged her back. "Now hug me." She hugged Darian then quickly stepped back and looked at him." She looked at Rea and started making a humming noise.

Laz and Rea looked at each other in shock. Humans could not hear a wizard or witch hum. Katabull hummed, too, though not as loud. She hadn't heard their hum, but she could hear Darian's.

Laz and Rea looked at each other and said, "She hums." They hadn't really noticed it when she hugged them because they were used to hugging Katabull—who hummed. But normal humans did not hum loud enough to be heard or felt.

"I'm filled with magic," Darian explained.

Erah looked confused then she started trying to form a word. When she finally said it, no one expected her to say what she said.

"Jazel."

"What the hell!" Rea said.

"You didn't teach her that?" Laz asked.

"No I didn't teach her that," Rea said. "Why would I?"

"Yes, just like Jazel. It's why I hum. I don't know why you hum, though." He pointed at Laz, Rea and Pete and said, "They hum, too, though not as loudly."

Erah bared her teeth, made herself as big as she could, and held her hands out like claws.

Pete giggled and Darian said, "Yes because they are the Katabull."

She stopped making the face and claws and nodded.

"She must have learned Jazel's name from..." Rea motioned with her head towards the lump under the blanket.

"Did you learn about Jazel from the dead guy?" Darian asked.

"Gods and spiders, Darian," Rea hissed.

Darian just shrugged.

Erah looked sad but nodded her head.

Darian reached out and patted her hand. "Jestia is like Jazel. She can help you talk, but only after she stops being so mad at Rea."

That night when Tarius and the rest of them were ready to leave the hall and go back to the ship Tarius took Rea aside. "Jestia wants to stay on land. Can you put her up here?" Jestia was a member of the Marching Night; it made sense for her to stay there, but she was also the heir apparent, so she couldn't be expected to share a room with others.

"I could give her my room. I could bunk with Fleat." Then remembering what she had learned about Fleat earlier that day she said, "No, I can share Katrina's bunk. I'll just go clean my room."

Katrina went with her to help. "It will be tight. The bunk is not as big as your bed."

"It will be fine."

"What did Garrett tell you is wrong with Fleat's leg?" she asked quietly, guessing that Rea's mood had more to do with that than it did giving up her room.

"There is nothing wrong with his leg," Rea said sadly. "Something happened in his brain. I did not notice but apparently that whole side of his body does not want to work. He might get better, but he might not, and apparently he could die at any moment."

"I am so sorry, Rea."

"Right now I am just going to believe he is going to get better instead of worse, but what he needs is good food and good rest. I doubt he would get that if I bunked with him, and since I mostly bunk with you anyway..."

"Though not on such a small bed or with three other people two of which snore." Katrina said.

"Aha! So now we learn the real reason you are always sleeping with me."

At the door Jestia cleared her throat and they turned to look at her. "This will do nicely thank you." Right then she didn't seem so dangerous she just seemed broken.

"I hope you sleep well, Jestia." Rea grabbed the dirty bedding and followed Katrina out of the room. The curtain had just closed behind them when a light came on in the room. Katabull could see in the dark. They had a few candles they used when it was really dark inside, but for the most part they didn't even use those. Jestia had cast the light.

As Rea climbed into the small bed with her, Katrina whispered, "I wonder why she wanted to stay here instead of on the ship."

In an odd turn of events she found herself spooning Katrina because there was no way for the two of them to sleep in the bed otherwise. "No doubt she did it just to make sure I would get no sleep at all though I guess that is better than being turned into a rock."

Katrina chuckled. "I think I read somewhere that it is easier for witches to center on land."

"Laz did say something about they brought her here because Jestia couldn't kill Ufalla from across the ocean. Maybe you are right; maybe we do need a library."

"This feels good," Katrina said in a whisper so low she could hardly hear her.

It didn't feel bad. Rea was surprised when she actually went right to sleep.

Feeling like she might be able to sleep Jestia doused the witch light and pulled the covers up to her neck. It was cold here and the bed was cold. It would warm up in a minute, but that didn't change the fact that it was cold right now. She closed her eyes and remembered her first trip to the Territories; it had been cold then, too. She had begged Ufalla to come get in bed with her to keep her warm, and she had. Both of them so young snuggled together on that tiny cot. Ufalla's love so wonderful so pure so unwavering. She never would have thought it would end, that it could end.

The bed was empty and cold. They had changed the sheets, but the covers still smelled like Rea and her woman. They shared warmth, and she was alone. There was another time she had felt like this, when Ufalla had been so mad at her she was sure she didn't love her anymore and that had been the plan. But she hadn't fallen out of love with her at all—not then.

But she had now, and now Jestia was alone in a bed and cold. She had seen a cover folded and laying on a chest in the room. She had it come to her and cover her up. In a few minutes she was plenty warm, but she was still alone.

Fleat had followed her down to the build site for the water wheel. They would have to take the wheel out of the water at the first sign the river would freeze, but it didn't freeze over till the very middle of winter. If they got busy they could have this up and running and have cut a lot of lumber before that happened.

She slowed down so that he could keep up with her. Now she knew what to look for she could see that even his face had fallen some. It broke her heart, so she didn't look.

At the build site they had cleared the trees away and had already laid the foundation timbers. The timbers had to be huge, but they had been easy for the Katabull to get and set. In their Katabull form they were ten times as strong as a human. When you had literally hundreds of Katabull there really wasn't much they couldn't accomplish.

Fleat stumbled, and she moved quickly and caught him short of falling.

"Dammit girl, I can…"

"Fall all the way down without help."

"You talked to Garrett, didn't you?"

"Yes."

"Then you know I could die at any minute."

"I always knew you could die at any minute. You are older than rocks and sky." Rea stopped walking and turned to face him. "But I still need you, Fleat, and I will be mighty pissed if you die and leave me to run the whole place alone. So when you start to fall I will catch you, and if you need help walking I will help you walk, and if all you can do is sit and tell me what to do I will listen."

He nodded. "And I will allow you to, Captain oh my Captain."

Jestia held Arvon's hand and walked with him down the middle of the stables stopping to talk to a horse or two. He had woken from his nap early and Diana was still asleep, so Jena said he might go with her and she had taken him. He really did not like to be separated from his aunt. His aunt. It was kind of funny when she thought about it. Tarius and Jena's oldest son was her age, and their daughter was the exact same age to the day as their grandson, but then they were Katabull... Well Jena wasn't, but she might as well have been.

"Bite," Arvon said as he watched the horse chewing on hay.

He said a few words now, but Diana had started talking in small sentences. They said she went right from saying Mama, no, yes and bite—bite was a big one for Katabull cubs—to *I don't think so*, and *Give me that*, in like a week.

"Up," he said, so she picked him up. He hugged her neck and then he wanted to reach out and pet the horse. He was a handful, so when he just wanted her to carry him so much she had tried to put a half weight spell on him. But of course he was Katabull, so it hadn't worked. Instead now she put a strength spell on herself when she had to carry him for any length of time. She walked with him out of the stables and into the pasture. She liked horses so much she didn't even mind stepping in horse shit. Of course she could always do a spell so she didn't actually step in it.

What did Ufalla want her to do? Forget what she was and what she could do? Why would she pretend to be weak and frail unable of taking care of herself? No one could touch her. She had her friends and her family, and maybe Jazel was right. Maybe what she really needed to do was not kill Ufalla but just let her go. Arvon wanted down so she put him down. No horse would dare to step on her godson. Out of the corner of her eye she saw the girl standing just in the tree line. She knew at once she was the one from Darian's story, the one all the Katabull talked about because of course she was blonde.

The story intrigued her. She wondered why the creature was watching her but then realized she wasn't watching her. It was Arvon she was interested in. Jestia reached down and picked him up again so that the woman could see him better. The human stood there for several minutes just watching them and then she turned, startled, and ran into the woods.

That woman was alone for decades living on what she could forage from the woods, and she had survived. Jestia was not alone. All that had happened was that the woman she loved no longer loved her, and if she was honest Ufalla was no longer the woman she loved.

It's just like when she hit her head and didn't remember herself, she wasn't my Ufalla then and she isn't my Ufalla now. She is someone I don't know, and I have been alone ever since she changed towards me. My sorrow has been close to this for a long time, but it is not really the problem. The problem is my rage... and why am I really so mad?... because she made me look stupid. If that is the case, what is the difference between her cheating and lying and drinking because her ego is crushed and me wanting to kill her because mine is? Still, I do not feel like taking the high road right now. In fact, I am sick of doing the right thing for the right reasons when it cost me the thing I love most.

In her arms Arvon chuffed and she looked at him.

No, that is wrong. Doing the right thing for the right reasons has given me many people to love who love me.

"Down," Arvon said.

She set him down again, he took her hand, started pulling, and looked up at her expectantly.

"Bite," he said again.

She laughed at herself when she realized what he wanted. "You want to go get some food?"

He nodded his head wildly then said, "Yes."

She started walking with him back to the keep. She thought it was stupid they called it the keep; it really wasn't like a keep at all. But they were Marching Night—all fighty and stuff—and everything was a fort or a keep or a compound.

Rea's bed had been comfortable enough, and she had made it more comfortable with a spell. But she could add a room to the top floor by reconfiguring the space, give Rea her room back, and make herself something nicer.

It was only around noon, but Rea was already tired. She took her Katabull form to keep working. Katrina wasn't lying about the snoring bunk mates. That coupled with neither of them being able to move all night—well she didn't think Katrina got much more sleep than she did. She knew she was right when she turned and saw that Katrina had catted out, too. They looked at each other, smiled, and went back to what they were doing which was using axes to hue logs into square timbers.

"How ironic is it that we have to hand hue the timbers in order to build a saw mill," Katrina yelled at her.

Rea just nodded.

"Less talky more worky," Fleat said from where he sat in a chair supervising the job.

Out of the corner of her eye she saw Erah watching them. When she saw Rea see her she smiled and waved. Rea smiled and waved back.

Then she caught Katrina's eye and motioned for her to come to her which, no surprise, was not hard to get her to do. "No sudden moves, but look slowly up and to your right and you will see Erah." Because of course Katrina was one of the only people in the colony who still hadn't seen her.

Katrina looked than looked back at Rea and smiled. "She... seeing her makes me happy, thanks." She took her axe and went back to work.

Jestia had spent the better part of the day reconfiguring the rooms on the top story of the keep. As she was finishing up she realized something. She wouldn't have done it unless she was planning to stay a long time, but why did she feel like it was going to take her that long to get her head straight?

A witch could twist raw materials into almost anything she wanted to make, so while the room wasn't big she made it beautiful and comfortable.

Tarius suddenly walked into the new room. She laughed when she saw the delicate nature of it, no doubt because it was in the Marching Nights keep.

"Jestia, your magic was making me tingle from way down by where they are building the mill. What on earth are you doing to Rea's room?"

"Oh this isn't Rea's room; her room is over there now," she pointed. "I added another room by taking a little out of all the existing rooms and the hallway and then reconfiguring them."

"Why?" Tarius asked.

Jestia looked at Tarius as if she were the one going mad and said, "Because I can."

Tarius told Rea she could have her room back, which made her really happy because she could use some sleep and she thought that meant Jestia was going back to stay on the ship. But no, when she got to her room it wasn't where she had left it. It was the same room, just in a different spot and the mattress was softer. It turned out Jestia had built her own room on the top floor and what exactly did that mean? How long did she intend to stay?

"I don't know, but I think the room is smaller," Katrina said.

Rea grunted. If it was she hadn't noticed. "It was sort of a waste of the witch's time to make another room."

"Yep." Rea agreed because of course that afternoon when they came home from working all day with little sleep she saw Fleat struggling to get up the stairs. He probably had been all along. Rea felt horrible that she hadn't noticed it before.

She'd had him sit down and called a bunch of them to help her move all of the things out of a room they had been using for storage on the bottom floor into an outbuilding they already used for storage, and then they had moved Fleat's things into that room. Now there was an extra room upstairs and an empty one.

"He didn't seem sad about moving," Katrina said.

Rea was tired and she just wanted to go to sleep, but Katrina was drawing her into a conversation. Still when she thought about it later she realized she had really needed to tell someone how she felt about it.

"He is very proud. He will not ask for help or to be treated differently at all. Yet if the decision is mine he seems more than alright with it. I imagine it was a relief for him not to have to walk up those stairs even one more time. But moving him... I know I am about to lose him, Katrina, and I still need him. I needed my mother when she died, and it made me a wreck. What if when he dies I become a wreck again?"

Katrina rubbed her shoulder. "I would never let that happen, Rea. Just know that I would never let you hurt yourself again."

Rea reached up took her hand and held it. "Thank you, Katrina. Now... shut up and go to sleep."

Katrina laughed then fell silent. In seconds they were both asleep.

As they sat down for breakfast in the great hall, Tarius noticed immediately that Jestia's mood was dark. Tarius filled her bowl and then moved to sit beside the witch. Jestia had a mug of tea in front of her but no food. "Have you eaten already?"

"No."

"Did you sleep at all?"

"A little... No, not at all," Jestia said.

"Here." She slid her bowl toward Jestia. "Make it whatever you want, but eat." She started to get up to get herself another bowl of food, but Jena handed her Diana.

"I'll get you a plate," Jena offered.

"Thank you," Tarius said, smiling up at Jena and then at their baby girl.

"Want down," she said. Tarius gave her a incredulous look and then looked around for her grandson. He was standing at the bottom of the stairs looking around ready to go up them.

"No, I know why you want down. So no," Tarius said.

Arvon started up the stairs, moving quickly.

"Jestia, snag him."

Arvon came flying through the air to land on Jestia's lap. Both of the babies cracked up laughing.

"Me, too," Diana said.

As if answering the question everyone wanted to ask, Jestia said, "The spell is not on him; it's on the air around him."

All around her Tarius saw all her people nodding. Magic could be used for and against the Katabull, but only in their human form. Arvon would not have a human form until they taught him to shift.

"Me, too," Diana said to Jestia again.

"Toss her up," Jestia said. Tarius did and Jestia caught her with the spell, flew her around for a minute, and then set her back in Tarius's lap.

Arvon chuffed.

"He wants to do it again," Diana said.

Tarius hoped she wasn't going to have to deal with Diana talking for Arvon the way Darian talked for Pete.

Jena set a bowl of food in front of Tarius and took Diana from her. To Jestia she said, "Do not do everything they want. They will expect us to repeat it, and we can't."

Jena set Diana in one chair and took Arvon and set him in the chair next to her. "Now sit still and I will bring you breakfast." Arvon started to climb out of the chair. Uh-uh, mister. You sit right there. Tarius, do not let those babies get up and run around like savages."

"I won't." Tarius glared at them both as if daring them to move, but not without a twinkle in her eyes.

Jestia laughed. "If it wasn't for Jena your cubs would be the biggest brats in the entire Kartik."

"Says the biggest brat I ever knew." Tarius started eating and when she did Jestia started to pick at her food which was a start. Then Rea and Katrina walked out of the stairwell, and Jestia smiled.

"Was I a bigger brat than Rea?" she asked.

"Nay, no one was as big a brat as Rea was," Tarius said, looking at Rea and smiling. "But you ran a close second."

Rea mumbled something under her breath even Tarius couldn't hear.

Darian and Pete were sitting across from her with Laz, Rimmy and Hared. They had been engrossed in nothing but their food, but the minute he saw Rea Darian jumped in his chair and started jumping up and down. "Rea! Jestia didn't kill you! Ask her to make Erah talk."

Tarius seriously wanted to sew her son's mouth shut in that moment. Rea looked like she was seconds from choking, but the look on Jestia's face was a mixture of despair and shame.

"I'm sorry baby," she told Darian. "That girl is so pure, so filled with the Everything... My energy... it is splintered. Do you understand what I mean?"

He nodded, and she continued. "I would not even go close to her right now, but later when I am better I will try."

Darian looked like he was going to say something else, but Tarius shot him a look and Darian didn't open his mouth.

To Tarius's surprise Jestia turned to Rea and said, "When my mind is less cluttered."

Rea nodded. "Thank you, Jestia."

Tarius heard what Jestia wasn't saying. Tarius couldn't just stay here forever. For the sake of the Nameless One she had left Kaseria in charge of the compound, and she had her son's cub with her. As much as the cub loved all of them and Jestia, he was starting to miss his parents. *Jestia built her own room yesterday because she plans to stay when we go. Is that safe? Is it safe to leave Jestia in the state she is in without me in the Territories?*

Fleat had just seated himself at the table with his breakfast. He must have noticed the sudden quiet tension in the room because he turned to Rea as she and Katrina were sitting down and said, "Captain oh my Captain." Rea rolled her eyes and Tarius smiled. "I wonder if I might get a window put into my new storage closet... I mean room."

"We can knock out some rocks to let in some light," Rea said. Then she grinned wickedly at him. "If we make it big enough the bears can eat you. What a great story that will be."

"I can make a window," Jestia said eagerly. She looked at Fleat and stood up. "Do you want it with or without a curtain?"

"Can the curtain be blue?" Fleat asked.

"Of course. Where is your storage closet?" Jestia said.

Fleat pointed to a door just to the side of the foot of the stairs.

Jestia jumped up and nearly ran to go in the room and put in a window.

Tarius looked at Jestia's bowl; she hadn't eaten a thing. How could Tarius leave Jestia there? How long could Tarius realistically stay before she had to get Arvon home and get back to the business of taking care of her people?

Jestia was back in minutes. "Done," she said. Then she walked over, sat down and immediately started eating. As the Marching Night all crowded the small room to see the window, Tarius realized something.

She will be fine here, because here there is so much for her to do. So much that she could help them with. Having a witch here will help them to thrive and it will give her purpose again.

Chapter Nine

Ufalla had to hunt by herself, cook for herself, and bathe by herself. They were all still shunning her. In fact if anything it was worse now.

One day she had been walking through the compound when her brother Tarius and Jabone came walking towards her. They didn't even look at her and moved to walk around her. She'd had just about enough of it. She moved to jump in front of them, took up a wrestling stance and growled.

"What is this?" Tarius had thundered. "I have done nothing to you. Why would you challenge me?"

"You have both of you turned your backs on me, but I don't challenge you, brother; I challenge Jabone. He has judged me without hearing my side of the story."

"Madra told me I might be able to talk sense to you, but you wouldn't listen if I tried. You refuse to admit that you are wrong. There is no excuse much less a reason for you to do all that you have done to your wife, but you cursed my madra when all she did was save your life and Jestia's."

"Will you wrestle me or not?"

"Seriously Ufalla," Tarius said. "Me you might win against. I doubt it, but you might. But Jabone will trounce you."

"Even in his human form? Because it will not be fair if he is the Katabull."

A crowd had started to gather which was more or less normal for when two Katabull were getting ready to wrestle.

"You have completely lost your mind, Ufalla. Look at him and look at you."

"If I have to trounce you to fix your head then that is what I will do," Jabone said.

Ufalla had been sure her rage alone would help her win. As kids they had been pretty evenly matched. But Jabone was a full-grown Katabull male now, and not pulling back because she was a pretty girl. He had her down with her arm twisted behind her back and eating a mouthful of dirt in less than a second. Around her the Katabull clapped, roared and then walked away. To them it was over. Jabone got off her and moved to let her get up; it was clear he also thought it was over.

"Now will you admit you are wrong?" he asked.

For answer she ran at him, head down, meaning to hit him in the stomach. Jabone reached out with a speed she could not match on her best day, palmed her head and held her there as she flailed her fists, trying to hit him. He shoved her backwards, and she fell on her ass. Then it started to rain.

He looked down at her. "Are you finally sorry for all you have done, or are you only sorry you got caught?" It was the same thing Jazel had said to her, and she found she was every bit as mad as she had been when Jazel said it.

"Your madra took my wife across the ocean so that I have no chance of fixing things. You are all taking Jestia's side, but you don't know what it is like to be married to her."

"I don't," Jabone said. "But you knew exactly what she was like when she was all you ever wanted. Jestia has never hidden anything from you..."

"She hides everything from me, everything. She tells your madra everything."

"The things she and my madra talk about none of us would understand. My mother never worries about what they talk about. She knows if it is something she needs to know Madra will tell her. And Jestia never shuts up, so if there was something you needed to know she would tell you, too. She often says things none of us understand, so I do not believe you when you say she hides everything from you."

"She can do anything; she doesn't need me. I feel like I'm nothing."

"Did she tell you that you were nothing? Did she mistreat you?"

"No but..."

"Then it is all in your head, Ufalla. You challenged me; I won. Do you accept that you are wrong or not?"

Ufalla wiped the rain which was turning the dirt on her face into mud off with a finger and flipped the mud in his direction. "It isn't that simple, Jabone. There are two sides to every story; will no one even listen to mine?"

"Gods and spiders! We just did. And it is all you have whined about since the disaster!" Tarius yelled at her. "Is there more? Something we don't know about how she mistreated you? Or is it all the same crap, she is Jestia you are nothing, she makes you feel bad when she talks to Tarius. You have been drinking like a fish. You cheated on her for your own pleasure. Now you want everyone to believe that you have some righteous reason, but it's the same crap you have been saying and as excuses go it's pretty weak. Come on, Jabone, our dinner grows cold, we are getting wet and she has no honor."

Jabone nodded and followed him away. Jabone turned and looked over his shoulder at her, and the disappointment on his features was painful to see.

Since that day they not only all shunned her but they gave her dirty looks and pulled their children away from her as she walked by. She had broken a sacred code. They wrestled and things were supposed to be settled. If they couldn't be you went to the Great Leader, but they all knew what the Great Leader would say.

And it wasn't because she had whored around. Hell, a big part of the Katabull had open relationships or group marriages. It was because that wasn't the deal she and Jestia had made. For them the cheating wasn't the actual sex act, the cheating was breaking the agreement, it was the lie.

She couldn't leave the compound. She had tried. They kept her there yet would have nothing to do with her. Even her younger siblings walked the other way if she was walking towards them. When she had tried to talk to her mother Elise had acted like she didn't even see her and walked away quickly.

What had she done? How could she fix it if none of them would let her even try? They wanted something from her that she wasn't ready to do yet. They wanted her to be contrite, but how could she be when they kept making her feel like the injured party? When everyone had turned their backs on her.

Tarius had just suffered through court. A rider had been sent to West Town to tell them what day she would be holding court, and so she'd had to deal with all of them again. The things they asked her to pass judgement on weren't any more important than they had been the last few times she had done it. She found herself more than once calling someone an idiot and telling them not to bother her with their trivial crap.

She was walking down the road just to clear her head. Court lasted so long she had moved it outside so that Trin and his staff could start to make dinner. It was late afternoon and starting to get cold. It still wasn't too bad yet, but the cold weather would be there before they knew it.

Walking towards her was the boy she had seen the first time she had held court there, the one with the stick. He was looking at something he held in his hand, wasn't paying attention, and almost ran into her.

She jumped quickly out of his way.

"I'm sorry Great Leader," he said quickly.

She smiled at him just to let him know she wasn't about to chew his head off. "What have you got there?"

He seemed reluctant to tell her, but finally he said, "It is the stick I was talking about in court."

Tarius sighed then said, "Let me see this amazing stick."

He handed it to her and she was shocked. It was about six inches long, bright red and orange, and about as big around as an arrow shaft. "Son... this is not a stick. This is rock wood." She handed it back to him. "I have only seen one other piece before. It belonged to the wizard Hellibolt. He told me that when the conditions are just right wood gets buried and over time it turns to stone. That is extremely rare. You best put it somewhere safe so you don't lose it."

He smiled brightly. "I am about to give it to the man who holds my heart. If he gives me something as well it will be his and I will always have it."

"I hope the exchange goes well; you'd best get to it." He nodded and she started to just walk away but she turned and took hold of his shoulder so that he looked at her. "I am sorry I dismissed your case so harshly. You were right to get so upset with your friend. He should not have thrown

138

that away like that, and when he did and you were upset he absolutely should have helped you look for it."

"Thank you, Great Leader."

She let go of his shoulder and he walked away. She watched him for a minute before she started walking again.

The world fell apart, hundreds died, Jestia and I were nearly among the dead. We went to a place that was nowhere and we were nothing and lived for a moment in our old lives. Arvon and Dustan died and everything was torn up. I lost my ability to see other people's petty problems as anything but that. I forgot that everyone's problem seems big to them. I forgot that the truth is in the details. His complaint seemed so asinine to me but I only saw a small piece of the whole picture. When I know what he was actually talking about and how he is going to use it...well it makes perfect sense that he would be so angry about his friend's callous actions that he wanted me to tell him he had done wrong. And that is all most of them want. For me to tell the person who has hurt them that they were wrong to do so. I will go back to doing that.

When a knock on Ufalla's door woke her up in the morning she didn't know who she expected to see when she opened the door but it wasn't Jazel's woman, Helen. She didn't ask to come in nor did she wait for Ufalla to invite her in or even for Ufalla to open the door all the way.

As she pushed her way in and immediately moved to sit at Ufalla's table Ufalla said, "Do come in, Helen. Make yourself at home."

"This isn't a social call, dear. You're in trouble big trouble."

"You mean because Jestia wants to kill me?"

"That, too, but mostly you are completely out of control."

"Helen, I am being held here by the Katabull and Jazel has made it impossible for me to even step on a ship. How can I be out of control?"

"That, that right there, that's how you are out of control. You do terrible things, you are mean and hateful when you are drunk, and you get drunk to have an excuse to be mean and hateful and to do terrible things. You think you had a good reason for everything you have done, but you don't...not at all."

"I do, too."

"Really?" Helen looked at her. "So you came here to try to talk to Jestia to fix things. And you want to go to the Territories to see Jestia to fix things, knowing that Jazel has told you what will happen to Jestia will be far worse than what happens to you if she kills you. You are willing to risk all of that, and tell me, tell me right now what you would say to Jestia that could fix all the hurt. What would you tell her?"

"That I felt useless and worthless. She can do everything and she doesn't need my money because she has the coffers of the whole kingdom at her disposal. That she is always going to Tarius and I used to be the one she talked to and now it is always Tarius and..."

"How would that fix anything? That is the same self-indulgent crap you have been yelling at her when you come home in the middle of the night dead drunk having barley washed the whore you just banged off yourself," Helen said. "The only chance you will have to 'fix things' is if you start with 'I am sorry, I was wrong.' But first you have to know it's true. You have to actually be sorry—which you aren't. You aren't sorry for what you have done to her because you are way too busy feeling sorry for yourself. Why did you start to screw around behind her back?"

"You're one to talk, you often pick up women for sex."

"Ahh, but Jazel knows I do. So I'm going to ask you again. Why did you—not me but you—start sneaking around behind your wife's back with one trollop after another?"

Ufalla started to spit out another nasty retort but then took a deep breath, let it out, and sat down across the table from Helen. "Because when I flirted with a woman and could get her to have sex with me just for a minute I felt like I was really good at something. It was like hunting. It was like stalking my prey and then landing something. Jestia knows so much that I don't, that I never will, and it made me feel good to think I was pulling the wool over her eyes."

"Now, was that so hard? Does any of that sound like you are the hero of this story?" Helen asked.

"No, but that is the problem. I will never get a chance to be the hero of any story as long as I am with Jestia."

"Does that sound like the kind of thing a hero would worry about? Not just doing the good deed but getting credit for it? You have done many things that were admirable. So have I, though not as splashy. People notice; they do, but there will be no great ballads about us. I have always been alright with that because the life I have had because I am with Jazel has been amazing.

"But our life has not been without problems. I will tell you a story about me that few know. When I met her I had a son, Fredrik. He was the product of a rape at the hands of Amalite raiders." She spit, though it was a Kartik custom not a Jethrik one, and Helen like Jazel was a Jethrik by birth. "I hated what had happened to me, but I loved my son. He was three when I met Jazel, and I was immediately head-over-heels in love with her. We lived a happy life together for decades till I realized Fredrick was aging faster than I was. When I asked Jazel how that could be, she told me what she had done. She had done the same spell on me that Jestia has done on you; she split her years with me. And so my son at forty looked like he was my father. I knew I was going to outlive my son, and I was mad at Jazel all the time.

She kept telling me she was sorry. She kept explaining that she loved Fredric as if he were her own. That she had always known she was going to lose him but lose me first, and she couldn't stand to lose us both.

Well, my son—our son—didn't die of old age. He was born because of Amalite raiders, and he died because of them. Jazel and I were filled with nothing but dread and grief. Jazel was heartbroken, but I nearly went mad. Somehow in all of that we found our way back to each other. We went to the middle of the woods and built a life there separate from other people. In my grief I began to see what Jazel had done to me as a gift instead of a curse. Nothing could have saved our son from the Amalites. I was always cursed to outlive him and that being the case having years to spend with my love to have a chance to grow and change seemed like an amazing gift. We were happy; life was good again.

"Till the day Amalites darkened our door yet again. They were after the Jethrik army, and they cut across our land and found us. When they realized what Jazel was they took me hostage. They made Jazel throw a spell that allowed them to ambush Tarius the Black and the Jethrik army she led. You know the rest of that story because you have heard the Great Leader herself tell it. What you don't know was what Jazel went through as we were traveling to the Kartik and even for years after we got here.

"The agonizing guilt she felt because men had died because of her spell. Good men had died at the hand of the Amalites who had raped me and killed our son. I have no idea, so I know you don't, what it is like to wield such power, to hold other's lives so delicately in your hand. And Ufalla, Jazel told me that Jestia was more powerful than she would ever be years ago. Since then Jestia's power has only grown.

"When I realized I was going to see my son die of old age I was so mad at Jazel I nearly destroyed us. I didn't understand her. But when Fredric died it all became very clear. Jazel chose to live her life with me. Even though she often had to go places I couldn't go and do things I couldn't do she always came back to me. I was her constant, the thing she counted on. Her being able to do what she needed to do when she needed to do it was dependent on me being there to hold her when she had a bad day and love her no matter what.

"Anything you say to Jestia that doesn't start with a sincere apology, an admittance of guilt, and doesn't end with *I love you*, will not fix anything at all. If you really love her—and I believe you do even if no one else does, because I have been nearly where you are—then you have to let it be her decision whether she chooses to go on with you or not."

Ufalla nodded, took a deep breath and let it out slowly as she tried to put her new knowledge into words. "Jestia almost died to channel the lava around Montero. If she had, I would have had to live the Nameless One alone knows how many years without her, watching everyone I love grow old and die. I was so mad because I can't protect her—not from herself—and I have no control over her or what she will do when the Everything calls her. But everything you have said is true." Ufalla started to cry, got up, walked over and grabbed Helen, hugged her and buried her head on her shoulder. She finally understood what she had done and why, but knowing that didn't help her know how to get Jestia back.

They were just about ready to put the wheel into place. Rea checked the plans again. She had checked the plans about a hundred times that day, and she kept having Fleat look at them to see if he thought they were doing it right. It was a lot of moving parts and more complicated than anything any of them had ever put together before.

Laz had come to the site to help them work as he had been doing every day. And at the end of every work day Laz went with Rea—and usually both of Tarius and Jena's boys—when she went to feed Erah. Erah had been hanging around on the edges of the build site watching them; she was obviously interested in what they were doing.

Rea called a break before they tried to set the wheel. She and Laz were getting a drink when Erah jumped around till she had their attention. Rea started to go to her, but Erah shook her head and pointed at Laz. Rea shrugged walked over and got another drink as Laz trotted over to Erah. Rea watched them. Laz walked up to her; Erah hugged him then she held her hand out in front of her palm up. Laz shrugged so Erah grabbed his hand, picked it up put it palm up and then placed something in to it. She closed his fingers over it and put a finger on his chest. Then she turned and ran off.

Laz came back to the site and walked right up to Rea. "Look what Erah gave me."

It was one of the orange stones almost identical to the one she had given Garrett. "What the hell, Erah!" Rea screamed into the woods. "I save you from a rampaging moose and tend your wounds, but I don't get a pretty rock!"

"She did stick a frog in your mouth yesterday," Laz said with a laugh.

"Don't remind me."

They started back to work and set the wheel. They thought they had it right, but when they took off the brake the blade went flying into the wheel axle and broke it. The wheel fell into the river, and it took ten of them in full Katabull form to fish it out again.

Rea called a stop to the day. They had obviously done something wrong, and they were going to have to build a new axle, so they would have to hit it again in the morning.

Katrina hadn't gone to the build site that morning. She was on sentry duty and had been walking around the catwalk most of the day. It was boring, but she didn't dare drop her guard because the minute she did it was a sure bet a bear would sneak in and eat one of the Great Leader's cubs.

They had been there almost two weeks, and Katrina wondered when they were going home. She loved them and enjoyed their company, but the cubs were a handful—one more thing to worry about. Nothing was really anything like normal with them here.

Jagon came to relieve her and she nearly danced she was so glad to be off the catwalk...until she walked through the door and the witch Jestia was all over her. She was so shocked for a second she did nothing. Jestia had thrown her arms around Katrina's neck and was rubbing her body against her. Then there was the other thing: the incredibly beautiful and sensuous witch Jestia was rubbing her body all over her, and Katrina hadn't had sex since they left the Kartik. Katrina felt her own arms go around the woman, but then she quickly pulled her arms off her and held her hands above her head.

"Jestia, I ah. I am very flattered, but I love Rea. I'm with Rea."

Jestia stepped back and looked into her eyes. "You know that I can do things she never could."

"I'm sure that you could and it would be wonderful, but later I would feel like I had cheated. I am sorry, Jestia."

"I'm the one who is sorry. I wish that my wife had been as loyal to me as you are to Rea."

"Rea is all I want. I... I am supposed to go to the build site. Excuse me."

Katrina stepped around her, nearly ran to the stairs and raced down them. She didn't have to go to the build site, but she felt like her heart was going to bust out of her chest and her blood was boiling. She was all the way turned on, and she just needed to find a nice, private spot far away from the witch so that she could stick her hands down her pants and take care of her suddenly urgent problem.

It was late, but Rea couldn't sleep. She had the plans spread out in front of her, and sitting at the great table alone by the light of the fireplace she was trying to figure out how they had all gotten it so very wrong. It was a wonder that no one had been killed; they couldn't make the same mistake again.

It's that piece there; we had it in backwards… no it was right. Maybe we forgot that pin. We might have forgotten that pin. I should just go to bed I will have better luck figuring out what went wrong if I get some sleep.

The Great Leader planned to leave the next morning. She would miss them all, but she would be glad to get things back to normal. She folded the plans, stood up, stuck them in her pocket and started for the stairs. At the bottom of them Jestia met her wearing a short blue silk robe and nothing else.

"Why are you up so late?"

"Ah… I was working."

"Would you like a drink? I could get you one." Rea could suddenly smell the liquor on Jestia's breath. That couldn't be good. A witch and liquor—that didn't mix well, did it?

"I don't drink any more, Jestia." Rea started to get around her to go upstairs, but Jestia barred her way. She stepped backwards to the bottom step, wrapped her arms around Rea's neck, then promptly kissed her right on the mouth.

She moved back and in a voice that could give a hen wood said, "Take me to bed."

"Katrina is in my bed."

"Then take me to my bed or on the table," Jestia said.

Rea hadn't even thought about sex in years; she sure hadn't wanted it, but she did now.

"Jestia, I am with Katrina."

"I hear that you sleep with her but don't couple with her. So what's missing?"

"Na... nothing is missing. I told her if I ever wanted it I would have it with her."

Jestia went to kiss her again, but this time Rea moved quickly to put her hands in front of her face.

"No. I would not hurt her or break my promise to her, and I don't want to be a part of this."

"Part of what?" Jestia asked.

"Part of the problems between you and Ufalla. Part of you thinking that sleeping with Rea will in any way make things even," Tarius said from where she had just walked in the front door.

Jestia let Rea go, ran to Tarius threw her arms around her neck and started crying.

Rea bolted up the stairs as quick as she could and ran into her room; when she got there Katrina was not there.

"Katrina, come here at once!"

Katrina came running in looking disheveled and still mostly asleep.

"Why on the night that I want you to be here are you not here?" Rea demanded and quickly threw all her clothes off. "What are you waiting for? Get naked and get in bed. We're doing this thing. We're doing it right now!"

Tarius let Jestia cry for a minute then said, "You told me it was safe for me to leave and leave you here. Then you do this. Do a spell and unintoxicate yourself because I know that you can." Tarius felt the spell.

Now sober, Jestia released her and went to sit at the table. She looked up at her. "How did you know what I was doing?"

Tarius moved to sit at the table where she was close enough she wouldn't have to speak loudly but far enough away she could look Jestia in the eyes. "Today as I was walking around the town taking one last look before we leave in the morning, I saw Katrina in tears leaning against a building where she thought no one could see her but of course she was wrong. I went to her and asked what was wrong and she told me that you had thrown yourself at her. That she had been very aroused but stayed true to her heart but had tucked into a space between the building—which like I said was not as private as she thought—to take care

of herself. She felt guilty about being so aroused by you."
Tarius smiled at Jestia. "I told her she should give herself a
break because you are a very beautiful and arousing
woman to start with, but that being Katabull your magic
makes us tingle anyway and all that together would be hard
for anyone to resist."

Tarius took a breath and all mirth left her as she said,
"I said to myself of all the women here why would you go
after Katrina and I knew it was to punish Rea but why?"

"Rea slept with Ufalla," Jestia said, as if that made
perfect sense.

"But Jestia, that was at a time when you yourself were
feeling your oats, before you and Ufalla were ever together
and when Rea was so drunk she didn't know what she was
doing or who she was doing it to most of the time. The girl
spent years Katabull more than she was human and except
in battle always because she was drunk. I knew when you
failed to punish her through getting Katrina in your bed you
would go after Rea next, so I only pretended to go back to
the ship. I waited in hiding outside the keep hoping I was
wrong and that you would have given up on this plot. What
on earth good would it do you to break Rea, to put her back
on the road to destruction—and it would have. How would
coupling with Rea somehow even the score between you and
Ufalla?"

"I don't know. I don't know." Jestia sobbed. "I think I
just wanted to hurt someone and make them feel as bad as
I do. And Rea might have slept with her long before we were
together but she flirted with her long after that. I think I
turned her into the essence of all the whores Ufalla has
cheated on me with. It didn't make any sense then; it sure
doesn't now. Those whores didn't make any promises to me.
I went after Katrina first because I thought I would make
Rea know what it feels like, but when I was all over her I
knew what I had heard was true—they had never sealed the
deal."

"So you went after Rea to break her. Rea has worked
hard and turned herself around. She has not only done a
good job with the colony but an admirable one. You would
what, sleep with her to make Katrina hate her, to make her
what she was before—a drunken whore. What was the end

game, Jestia? I cannot go and leave you here if your biggest desire is to punish Rea for the things Ufalla alone has done to you. These people—this community—they depend on Rea's leadership. They *trust* her, and after all she had done it was not a trust she won easily. I will not allow you to undo her.

"This morning when we spoke about my leaving you seemed like you were doing better—like you would be good here. It had been a week since you have even given Rea a dirty look. What on earth happened that suddenly made you decide to do this?"

Jestia had to think about it; it didn't just pop into her head, so she knew just how messed up her head still was. "I was walking out of my room as they were walking out of theirs. When I saw the love in Katrina's eyes when she looked at Rea I just saw red. I used to have that, now I don't, and I thought *Rea doesn't deserve it.*"

"But she does deserve it. I'm not sure she wants it, but she does deserve it," Tarius said with a smile. "She is not your enemy, and I cannot, I *will* not leave you here, I won't be able to go, if you insist on treating her that way."

Jestia nodded. "I get it. What I tried to do was terrible and I realize that. But, Tarius, neither of them would have me, and I would not have even tried to use my magic to force them."

"Not even when you were drunk?"

"I wouldn't," Jestia swore. "Katrina never even had more than a moment when she even considered having sex with me because her heart belongs completely to Rea, and Rea… Well Rea is not even in love with the girl yet would not break her promise to her—and she was full on aroused." She started to cry again. "They have never been together and yet they have more loyalty to each other than Ufalla has to me. What can I ever say that would have them forgive me?"

From upstairs the night erupted in sounds of passionate love making.

Tarius looked at her and grinned. "My guess would be that Katrina will hold you no grudge."

"And see? Even that sound makes my heart break. I miss having someone to hold, to touch."

"Jestia, there are many women here who would gladly bed you that have no ties to anyone. If you feel you must even the score do it with one or all of them, but do not, I beg of you, in any way go after your sister."

"Our mothers sleep together. I swear the way you Katabull tie family together..."

"...is right and altogether just. Think of this, Jestia, if you broke Rea it would knock a hole in your mother's relationship with Radkin. We tie family together the way we do for a reason, little sister. Our relationships intertwine, so you cannot pull a string from one sleeve without it reaching the other cuff."

Jestia nodded. When Tarius said it that way it made perfect sense to her. She took a deep breath and let it out. "I can't go home, Tarius, because what I did tonight proves I can't really trust my judgement. That I am still too wounded to face Ufalla without wanting to do her damage. But you must go home. I promise you I will not do anything to hurt Rea again and hopefully she can forgive what I have done."

A vocal louder than the one before interrupted the night and Tarius smiled at her. "And now, I doubt Rea will hold you a grudge, either. I will leave in the morning and when I come back you will be better. When you are ready—and only when you are—I will bring you home."

"What happened?" Katrina asked.

Rea had her arms wrapped around Katrina with her head resting on her back. She was happily exhausted and just wanted to sleep.

"What do you mean?"

"What happened that you all of the sudden wanted this?"

"Are you complaining?" Rea asked with a chuckle.

"Not at all, you were everything I thought you would be and more. I would just like to know."

"Well, you aren't going to like it."

"Tell me anyway," Katrina said.

So Rea told her what Jestia had done. To her surprise Katina laughed and said, "She did the same thing to me till I had to run into an ally with my hand down my pants. I don't care how it happened; I am just glad it did. I love you so much, Rea. I have wanted you for so long and..."

"Katrina, for the love of the Nameless One, shut the hell up." She moved and shoved Katrina onto her back and kissed her on the mouth, happy that she had finally found a way to shut the girl up.

Chapter Ten

Early the next morning they watched the Great Leader and all the others board the ship for the journey home—all but Jestia that is. The fact that Jestia was staying worried Rea but didn't surprise her. Especially since just two days before Jestia had reconfigured the rooms upstairs again by doing away with Fleat's old room. Now Rea's room was back where it had been in the first place and back to the size it had been.

They were getting ready to pull the gangplank when Laz came bounding down it with his bag in hand.

"What are you doing?" Rea asked him with a smile.

He embraced her as the gangplank was being raised and said, "I am staying."

She couldn't say she wasn't ecstatic about it, but she was surprised that her brother would step away from his job watching Jena and her cubs.

"As we were boarding I told Tarius that I felt I was leaving home instead of going home. She told me I should stay; that she will find a replacement for me when they get home." He was so excited he was near glowing.

Behind her Jestia said, "And she told you to keep an eye on me."

Laz didn't answer which meant that was exactly what she had said.

"That's what I thought," Jestia said. "Well, come on Laz. I want to go back to the keep and finish my breakfast."

When he followed her away it only proved what she had said. Beside her Katrina squeezed her hand; Rea squeezed her hand back, looked at her and smiled. They watched till the ship left the dock then they went back to finish their breakfast. Tarius, along with her family and crew had come to the keep early and eaten before any of them were even awake.

Rea had woken her limbs entangled around Katrina's, and somewhere in her all the pain she had still been carrying over the loss of her mother was gone. She didn't know whether she was in love with Katrina yet or not, but she did love her. So as she woke Katrina by kissing her cheek she had not been afraid to say so. That was what her madra's story had taught her. At her words Katrina had been all over her, so they had been late getting to breakfast in the first place. Which meant that when they had to go down to say goodbye to her family on the dock they hadn't eaten at all. As they walked into the keep the room was mostly full with people eating their breakfast. When they saw the two of them enter, as a whole they stood up and started clapping. Rea figured the applause was for Laz who had walked in with Jestia just ahead of them, but no.

The clapping stopped, they all sat down, and Fleat boomed from his place at the great table, "Captain, oh my captain you did not lie! When you coupled the whole of the town could hear you."

Rea looked at Katrina, grinned a crooked grin and whispered, "And yet I will miss him when he is gone."

Jestia didn't know how to begin to apologize to Rea and Katrina, so she didn't even try. She noticed they took seats far away from her and neither of them would even look in her direction. She knew Laz had already eaten but he sat beside her with a mug of tea anyway which just further proved she had—not a body guard really—but maybe a chaperone.

"You might as well know now if you don't already, the gods know the Katabull are no good at keeping secrets. I tried to seduce both Katrina and your sister last night. I didn't have any luck."

"Katrina is so in love with Rea I don't think anyone else would do for her, and Rea... Well she had so much sex she was tired of it. My guess would be that you jump-started her libido." He grinned, so he wasn't mad at her.

"How long will she stay mad at me?" Jestia asked.

"They were pretty happy last night—several times from what people are saying. They are not mad at you; they are afraid. Mostly Rea is afraid you are going to turn her into a rock."

"And you are here to help make sure that I don't."

"I am here because I want to be here. It was the Great Leaders idea that I keep an eye on you just in case... you should try to turn my sister into a rock."

He pulled something out of his pocket, brought it up on the table, and started rolling it around. It took a second for Jestia to realize what he had which sort of proved what a mess she was. She easily used a spell to grab it out of his hand.

"Hey, that's mine!"

"Where did you get it?"

He tried to take it out of her hand, but she easily moved it away with a speed spell she cast without even trying.

"The human gave it to me as a gift," Laz said, and tried to take it again.

"Do you know what this is? This is a giant piece of cornelian. It is a very powerful stone. I have never seen a piece this large. I need it."

"It is mine, Jestia, give it back," Laz said, proving that his sister might be afraid of Jestia but he wasn't. "She gave Garrett one. Go get his." Laz was getting mad, as in he was going to shift, rip her arm off and take it back if he had to.

"Oh." Jestia handed it back to him.

"Oh, what?" Laz asked, clutching the stone in his huge fist.

"You like this human girl; that's why you stayed."

Laz glared at her. "Jestia why must you always be you?"

She laughed and playfully punched him in the shoulder. "Ask your girlfriend to get me one of those rocks."

At the build site they were carefully going over the plans again. "I swear I cannot figure out what we did wrong," Rea said in frustration.

"Nor can I, and I got a lot more sleep than you did last night," Fleat said with a wicked grin.

"It was time well spent," Katrina said, unashamed.

Rea looked up and saw her brother and Jestia walking towards them. "Here comes trouble."

"And your brother," Katrina said.

"She a royal pain in my ass," Rea said.

"I like my window," Fleat said.

"This is quite impressive whatever it is," Jestia said, looking around the structure they had built to house the mill.

"Did you figure out what we did wrong?" Laz asked.

"No. According to the plans we did everything right... I think the plans and instructions are confusing."

"What's it supposed to be?" Jestia asked, looking at the pieces and what they had built to set it up on.

"It's supposed to be a saw mill, but yesterday when we sat the wheel and kicked off the break the only thing it sawed was its own main axle when it slung the blade into it," Fleat said. "We have made a new axle and fixed the pieces that were broken, but..." He shrugged.

"Can I see the plans?" Jestia asked.

Fleat pushed the plans across the table towards her. Rea watched Jestia as she just stood looking at it. Then the witch held her hand over it and an image like a model fully assembled stood over the plans. Rea looked at it and immediately knew what they had done wrong.

"We didn't anchor the axle properly. This allowed it to shift and become unbalanced. Once that had happened, and with the full power of the river behind it..." Rea said. Then she added, "Thank you, Jestia."

"I'm sorry," Jestia said. They all gave her an odd look and she said, "About yesterday. I'm sorry."

"I'm not," Katrina said with a laugh.

"I can build this with a little Katabull help on the big pieces," Jestia said. They all watched as the smaller pieces started to assemble themselves.

From the corner of his eye Laz saw Erah standing at the tree line. Jestia was busy, and it didn't look like they were going to need his help, so he walked up to meet her. When he got to her she hugged him and he hugged her back. When they parted, he walked further into the woods and she followed. Jestia needed a stone, and he didn't know if she might come running up there to question Erah and scare her off because when Jestia wanted something there wasn't much that could stop her.

When he was sure they could no longer be seen he took the stone from his pocket. He pressed it to his heart hoping she would understand that meant he liked it.

She nodded.

"Erah, where did you get the stone?" He held it out to her, but she pushed his hand back towards him.

"Laz."

He understood she was telling him *no it's your rock.*

"Yes, well you should tell the princess that; she wants to take my rock. If she needs it I should give it to her because she is in a state, but you gave it to me and its mine." He didn't know how to make her understand what he wanted. He remembered Rea had taught her the word more. He held the rock up and said, "More?"

She nodded excitedly, and he knew she understood him.

"Erah and Laz, more," he said.

Erah nodded her head, took his hand and started running. Laz followed willingly but had to admit that in his human form he was having to work to keep up with her.

The trail she took through the woods didn't seem to have any rhyme or reason, and if he wasn't Katabull he would have been lost for sure. Finally she stopped where a tree had blown against a cliff face but was still alive. She let go of his hand and started to crawl through the branches. He followed her and found himself in the mouth of a cave. His first instinct was to look quickly around for any sign of a bear or lion but he neither saw nor smelled one. Which was odd. You would have thought it would be the perfect place for a den.

Erah looked around in the shadows at the cave mouth until she found a torch. She took her knife out of her pants—they still had no idea why she wore her knife on the inside of her pants—then she struck a rock with it that made sparks and lit the torch. Laz was surprised it had started with just a few sparks, but then he smelled burning pitch.

Laz smiled at the girl. She held the torch out for him to hold then took his hand and led him into the cave. At least he thought it was a cave, but when he looked around he realized it had been chiseled out. It wasn't a cave; it was a mine. They hadn't gotten far when Erah grunted and

155

pointed. He was looking at a massive wall of the rock, and at the base of the wall was a cascade of the orange stones. He dug around in the pile till he found one even bigger than the one he had. If his was a good stone for Jestia, bigger would be even better.

"Thank you, Erah. My friend will be very happy." Laz knew the girl couldn't really understand all his words, but knew she understood his tone.

Erah nodded then started dragging him back out of the cave. By the time they got back to the entrance the torch was almost out, and he realized that was why Era was all *get in there get it and go*. She didn't want to be stuck in the cave without light. When he realized how much trouble it was for her to get the rock for him it made it that much more special.

He helped her make another torch to leave there. She wouldn't leave until they did, and he wondered why. But he helped her and learned how she did it. There was a certain tree that ran sap and she made the torch by wrapping dried grass around it and then covering it with the pitch.

When they had finished she took his hand—hers all sticky with pitch—and led him back to the town the opposite way from, the way they had come. They wound up at a spot on the tree line that gave him a clear view of the keep. She had taken him home. It took a minute because the pitch had kind of glued their hands together, but she let go of his hand.

He worried about her in the woods alone with lions, wolves and bears; she was after all just a human. He wanted to walk her home not the other way around, but she had lived here alone for decades. She smiled at him one last time and then ran into the woods.

"Goodbye Erah, be careful, may the Nameless One watch over you."

He put his hand on the big stone he had just gotten for Jestia. Then he took out the rock Erah had given him and looked at it. He liked his rock better.

If the witch needs the rock to help her heal and she gets better then she will try to help Erah talk to us. So the sooner she gets it the better.

It was nearly dark when the Katabull left the mill site and headed back for their homes; the moons were already coming up. Jestia didn't have to look up; she knew they would both be full. Tonight one would eclipse the other, and just for a moment they would look like one moon. She had erected the mill with the Katabull's help with the heavy lifting easily, but it had taken time and energy. She would never tell them, but they had put several pieces in the wrong place.

Once they had it running they had sawed several logs into boards then all roared in triumph as if they had just won a battle. Jestia didn't have the heart to tell them that if they had just pointed to a tree she could have turned it into a stack of lumber.

She was tired. The amount of casting she had done wouldn't have taxed her strength if she wasn't all broken inside and had slept more than a hand full of hours in the last two weeks. Still, as physically exhausted as she was, the triumph the Katabull felt when the mill ran, and the admiration and appreciation they had both felt and expressed warmed her in a way that was helping to heal her spirit.

When they got back to the Keep—she still thought it was a stupid thing to call the building—their dinner was already done. She got a bowl and got in line, but she found herself propelled by them to the front of the chow line—which was slightly unsettling as they thought it was alright to just pick her up or push her till she was standing at the pot and the cook was ladling a rich meat and vegetable stew in her bowl. She might have protested if she didn't know that to the Katabull to be pushed to the front of the line, physically, was them showing her high honor.

"Thank you," she said to all of them. Then she took her bowl and sat down. She was actually hungry, so she dug her spoon in and took a big bite. It was really good which meant the meat was bear, elk, deer or moose and not a wolf or lion which... Well she hadn't felt like eating anyway so she didn't even bother to make it taste like something else. The stew was well-seasoned with enough peppers in it to make it hot but not too hot.

She was feeling pretty good and then she remembered when she had been in the Jethrik Territories and at the garrison. *Every day it was stew, and they never seasoned it so that it was like eating dried leaves that had been soaking in hot stump water. At that time I didn't yet have the knowledge or power to make it taste any better; we just all had to eat it that way. Ufalla has always loved to eat, and I think she more than the rest of us just could not stand to eat such tasteless swill.*

Ufalla...back then I was all she ever wanted. I never doubted for a minute she loved me; I knew that she did. It wasn't all a lie; it couldn't have been. I did something I should never have done; I gave her half my life because I just couldn't imagine that I could ever live without her. I didn't ask her if I could do it; I just did, and now what? She will live perhaps hundreds of years. Because a witch never had any idea how long her life span would be. Unless some catastrophe took life from them a witch tended to live as long as the Everything needed them to. *She will live way longer than any human should, and she has turned into someone I do not know and certainly don't like. Will she just continue to degrade into something even worse? Can I do anything to stop her from sliding down the slope of the cliff she willingly jumped off of? If I am no longer enough for her to be happy how can I hope to make her happy? Is it over, do I have to let her go? I don't want her the way she is now, and don't know that I could ever forgive her for breaking the trust between us. Do I let her go and never look back? Hell right now I cannot get through a bowl of stew without reliving the past. How long will it be before I can do anything that I don't think about her, and how everything I thought we had came completely undone?*

She looked at her dinner; she had stopped eating. She took a deep breath and made herself eat. She even made herself enjoy the taste and feel of it in her mouth as she ate it. In minutes her thoughts stopped rattling in her head and she remembered something.

All I have to do is keep going, cling to normal things, keep moving and the healing will happen—in time.

Laz had heard them come in but he had laid on his bunk—which had been Katrina's he didn't figure she'd ever use it again so it was his now—for a minute looking at the stone he had gotten for Jestia. It was beautiful; the orange color of it shot through with hues of red and yellow. He had no doubt it held powerful magic. He couldn't feel it in the stone, but when he had been in the cave he could hear the humming of the Everything stronger than he usually did.

He missed his monkey. When he had decided to stay he knew there was only one thing he could do about Pogo. He gave him to Darian. He doubted even he cared about that monkey as much as Darian did. He would get lots of attention and be well cared for. Pogo couldn't live here. He was used to living with Laz but running around the compound and in and out of the jungle. There were no predators except humans and Katabull on the island, and Kartiks didn't eat monkeys, so he was safe to come and go as he pleased. It was too cold for him here. Besides, there were too many things that would want to eat him, and he wouldn't have understood having to live always inside.

Laz hadn't lied; he felt like he was home here. He felt like his future was here. Still, he would have liked to say that Jestia was wrong, mostly because it would have been nice for Jestia to be wrong about something, but he couldn't deny that he had feelings for Erah. She stirred things in him. In his mind he kept cleaning her up and putting clean clothes that fit on her. When he did she was every bit as beautiful as Jena, but mostly she had the same energy as Jena did. Rea wasn't wrong, either, he had always crushed on Jena, but never wanted her. That would have been sick, like wanting to sleep with one of his mothers, but Rea was also right that he wanted a mate just like her.

He lay there till he was sure most of them would have gotten their food then he stood up and stuffed the big stone into his pocket. It was a good thing he sewed huge pockets in his pants or it wouldn't have fit. As it was with both stones in his pocket it looked like he'd had a horrible injury that had swollen his balls six sizes. He grinned at the thought and headed out of his room.

When he got to the hall he was able to just go up and get his food because there was no line. He sat down next to

Jestia. "I got you something." He tried to get it out of his pocket and wound up having to stand back up to do so. He plopped the huge stone on the table in front of Jestia.

Jestia immediately grabbed it and held it up. "Thank you, Laz! This is just what I needed, right when I need it." She kissed him on the cheek.

"Where the hell did you get that?" Rea thundered. Because of course they had all been looking for one ever since Erah had given Garrett his.

"Erah showed me where they are, and no I will not tell any of you where that is because they are hers," Laz said,

"Seriously!" Rea thundered. "I gave her blankets and clothes. I feed her all the time."

"Such ingratitude," Jestia said with a grin. "Oh, what is a mother to do?"

"She didn't give me a pretty rock," Rea mumbled. She turned to look at Katrina. "I was going to take her food in a minute. You want to go with me?"

Of course I do. In fact I think I sort of feel like you do about no rock. You take Laz with you all the time and you took Tarius's boys with you but you never took me."

Rea could tell she was only half kidding.

The evenings were getting colder which meant she could walk right to the cave and knock on the door because when it got colder Erah went in early.

Erah opened it and seemed to check Katrina over then smiled at her and waved them both in.

"Laz?"

"He's home." She pointed towards the town.

Erah looked unhappy but nodded that she understood.

Rea pointed at Katrina. "Katrina."

"Kat," Erah said, not even trying the long name.

She held out her hand expectantly, and Rea handed her the bowl of food.

"See what I mean? She always wants something from me and yet... where's my rock?" Rea moved to sit on Erah's bed and she took Katrina's hand and drug her after her.

Erah set the bowl down. She had already made tea, and she poured it and handed them each a cup.

Katrina took a sip and made a face.

"What?" Rea asked.

"It's way too sweet."

"I don't think so." Rea shrugged. "You better drink it or she will pour it into your mouth. Don't know why, but if she gives you something to eat or drink if you don't get right on it she will *make* you eat or drink it. Like if you don't you are going to starve and die. I really have no idea why she does it; I have no idea why she does a lot of things. She could understand Darian but he couldn't understand her, so I didn't learn much."

"She can understand him? Why?"

"I don't know...because he's magic I guess. Apparently he can talk to whales and monkeys, too."

"I miss monkeys," Katrina said thoughtfully.

Across from them having finished everything in the bowl already Erah grunted at them. Obviously she didn't like to be left out of the conversation.

"Well," Rea said to her, "maybe we would talk to you more if you could talk."

They talked—well mostly Katrina did—as they walked back to town. It was dark but both moons were full and they were Katabull so they could see in the dark even in the dense forest and in their human form. They weren't afraid of even the biggest predators there because...well, they were Katabull.

Rea had just explained about the body. "Ever since I found it I have wondered. Why did she leave him there?"

"Because he died when she was too small to move a body," Katrina said. It was such an obvious answer that Rea hit herself in her forehead with her palm.

"Of course! That makes perfect sense."

"Once he dried out the way he did I imagine she just couldn't make herself get rid of it."

"I can't see how she could have made it on her own if she was much younger than five or six. Yet if she was, and he was with her for years—even months—why does she not speak Kartik?"

"He might have been a translator," Katrina said.

"A what?"

"A translator. During the Great War some soldiers were taught to speak Amalite."

"Why?" Rea asked.

"If they captured an enemy soldier they could question him and find out the position of the enemies' troops or supply lines, how many there were, how well armed and prepared they were. They could spy on the enemy if needed."

"That makes sense. Did you read that in a book?"

"If I say yes can we have a library?"

"Well did you?"

"No, it was in a story Tarius told. But a library would still be a really good idea."

"Still if he was with her for years why wouldn't he have tried to teach her Kartik at some point?"

"Really? Because you have been working with her for years and have taught her a handful of words," Katrina said. "If he could speak her language what would have been the point of teaching her his? In fact, the longer they would have been here without other human contact the surer he would have been that they were never going to see anyone else, that he was never going home."

Rea nodded. Once again that made sense, and she found herself wondering what other revelations Katrina might have told her in all the time she never shut up and Rea was always tuning her out.

"Why do you like books so much?"

"I have always liked books, but I never really had time to read many. When I went home wounded because of that stupid lime tree I had lots of time, and of course Montero has a wonderful library. Then everything blew up and shook and I was stuck there even longer. I didn't feel like drinking or even going to the pubs to listen to bards. I couldn't just spend all day every day pinning away for you..."

"It was not as bad as all that I'm sure," Rea said with a laugh.

"Oh it was. Once I wanted you I was pretty much consumed with thoughts of you. Reading was the only thing that kept me from spending hours a day with my hand in my pants fantasizing about you. Once I got back to the compound it wasn't quite as bad because I could talk to your family about you."

"You make me feel guilty that I didn't bed you the moment you got back to the Territories."

"As you should. It wasn't like it is that hard for you to make me happy."

"And when we get back to the keep I will make you happy again."

"Let's run," Katrina said, and took off, making Rea have to work to keep up. But she did.

When Jestia walked out on the catwalk one of the Marching Night was on look out, as one of them always was.

He nodded at her. "Good evening, Jestia."

"Good evening, Roash."

"Where do you want to be?"

"On the west side facing the Twins."

He nodded and continued his circuit, careful not to cross her path.

The Katabull were magic beings, so unlike humans they knew to give a witch space in which to do her work. Roush also knew that any of them watching from the tower was really Tarius being over cautious. She told them someone should be on guard at all times, but here what were they looking out for? Bears, lions, wolves? As predators none of them could compete with the Katabull. It wouldn't be long till the native predators knew there was a new king of beasts in their forest, and they'd start to steer clear of the towns.

She made a pillow then sat on it resting her back on the building. Then she folded her legs under her, held the stone in her hand, closed her eyes and waited.

She could hear the stone humming; it vibrated in her hands, warming as she held it. She envisioned her energy mixing with the stone's, swirling together inside it.

Then she heard Rea and Katrina going at it, and it nearly pulled her out of the space she was building, but she cast a simple cone of silence spell and continued her casting.

She moved her energy through the stone faster and faster. Going into the stone from her right hand, her energy entered, was cleansed, and then it went back into her body through her left hand. She did it over and over till the dark energy in her body was at its normal level. Then she opened her eyes. Seeing that the twins had eclipsed themselves she raised the stone towards the single light and recharged it. She took a deep breath, and as the Twins started to separate again she lowered the stone. She took another deep breath, this time releasing it very slowly. Finally she smiled; she felt whole again. She got up and, still holding the stone in both hands, she got rid of the pillow and headed for the door. Roush met her as she was getting ready to open the door. His eyes got big, not out of fear but a sense of wonder. When Jestia looked down she wasn't surprised to see that her hands and the stone were glowing white.

"It went well then," Roash said.

"Very."

He opened the door for her even though he knew she didn't need hands to open a door.

She walked to her room and walked inside where she set the stone down in the middle of the dresser she had made for her room. As she did the stone and her hands stopped glowing, but the way she felt—clean and balanced—didn't change. She walked to her bed, crawled in, and went right to sleep.

When Ufalla was convinced that it was Jestia's fault that she had done what she did and acted the way she did. When she had been sure that everyone else just didn't understand and weren't trying, and that she didn't deserve their shit, she had no trouble eating, and none at all sleeping.

But now she knew that she alone was the villain in her story, that she had crushed Jestia, ruined what they had, and that there was probably no fixing it. Now she knew that it was her own fault that her family and all her friends were mad at her, and now she could barely eat because nothing had any taste, and she couldn't sleep at all. She spent all day, every day, walking around avoiding all the people who had been avoiding her, trying to figure out what if anything she wanted now, and if there was any way that Jestia could ever forgive her. If she could forgive her, would Jestia take her back? Was that even what Ufalla really wanted?

Because if it wasn't then she needed to let Jestia go and leave her alone.

She hadn't been a hundred percent sure that she even still loved Jestia till she heard whispering amongst the Katabull that the Great Leader's ship had been spotted. At the simple thought Jestia was coming home she was filled with sudden hope. The thought of just seeing Jestia again made her heart race.

She found herself running to the docks and then hiding behind some crates in amongst some trees away from the prying eyes of the others.

The boat docked and she wanted to run and wait for Jestia at the bottom of the gangplank, throw herself at her feet when she disembarked and plead for her forgiveness, ask her for another chance. But those were all things *she* wanted, and being only concerned with what *she* wanted is how she had gotten here in the first place. She stayed right where she was because she needed to give Jestia her space and time to decide what she wanted, and whether that included Ufalla or not.

But as she stood there peeking out watching, Tarius and Jena their cubs and their cub's fathers got off the ship, but not Jestia. Laz didn't get off, either, and she kept waiting thinking Jestia would disembark with Laz, but neither of them came off the ship. When the whole of the crew had all gone down the gangplank and there was still no sign of Jestia, her first thought was panic that something had happened to her.

But as the Great Leader walked past where she was hiding Tarius turned, looked right at Ufalla and said, "She did not come back; she stayed in the Territories."

Ufalla nodded and stood up from where she had been crouching. "I am sorry, Tarius, for everything."

Tarius smiled at her, the first Katabull to do so in weeks, and said, "That is a good start." Then she and her family just kept moving. Jena didn't even glance her way.

Ufalla took a deep breath and let it out in that moment being unable to decide whether she was sad or relieved that Jestia wasn't there, and realized that was her answer. She wasn't yet ready to face Jestia; she still had work to do. But at least now she knew what she wanted; she wanted her wife back.

When Laz decided to stay in the Territories Tarius couldn't even pretend to be surprised. It might have been nice if he had decided at a point before they had all boarded the ship so that they could have talked in private about the damn monkey. Tarius was alright with Darian having Pogo. In fact, she'd had her eye out for years trying to find him a monkey. But from the moment Laz had asked Darian if he would take Pogo for him, it was all they had heard all the way home. When were they going to get Pogo, could he stay in he and Pete's room? He reminded them that the monkey was his and not theirs. On and on and on, all things monkey. Tarius didn't mind him having the monkey at all, but Jena said all they needed was one more living thing in their house throwing food and tantrums.

"Can we go get Pogo right now, Madra can we?" Darian said.

"For the love of the Nameless One, run as fast as you can to your brother's house and get the damn monkey." The funniest thing about it was that Jena said it before Tarius could.

His brother and his wife had not been there to greet them, and since they had their cub Tarius had been some worried. But shortly after she had spoken briefly to Ufalla here came Kaseria and Jabone in their Katabull form running as fast as they could. Since they had their bows with them it wasn't hard to figure out what they'd been doing.

When Tarius saw them she set Arvon down pointed and he took off running to meet them. Jabone got to him first, scooped him up and hugged him. Happy to see him, Arvon immediately climbed onto Jabone's head. Kaseria caught up to them, reached up to pet him and then he immediately jumped onto her.

Jabone walked up and embraced first Jena and then Tarius. "I was getting worried."

"I'm sorry, son." She kissed his cheek then patted him on the shoulder. "We... I had to leave her there, and I couldn't leave her there till I knew she wasn't going to blow a hole in the whole colony. Arvon has been very good, but he has been missing you both. We will never take him without you again."

"Because your son takes all of us to watch just him," Rimmy said with a laugh. "He is up masts and up trees and dragging Diana with him."

"We will not let you take him again," Kaseria said. "Jabone whined the whole time."

But Tarius could see that she was just as glad to have her cub home.

"Let us go home. We are all exhausted; we can talk as we walk."

Which they did. Turned out Kaseria had done a fine job running things and nothing had burned or been destroyed in their absence. Nor had Kaseria started a war just to have things to kill which apparently more than one of the other pack leaders had said they were afraid would happen when they heard Tarius had left Kaseria in charge.

"When did Ufalla get here?" Tarius asked.

"Hours after Jazel released her from a spell."

Jabone told her all that had happened concerning Ufalla, and when he had finished Tarius said, "You all shunned her? That is the opposite of what I asked you to do."

"You did not hear her, madra, and I have not told you all that she said because it was very hard to hear. There is no talking to her."

Tarius nodded. "Then I was right to leave Jestia in the Territories."

Chapter Eleven

After having eaten a good meal, cleaning her energy, and getting a really good night's sleep, Jestia woke feeling like herself for the first time since...she didn't. She stretched and looked at the light coming in the window. She guessed it was near midday from the angle of it, and the shadows the light cast. She stretched again and contemplated getting up. It was cold, so she decided to get dressed before she got up. She thought she would go on a walk in the forest so she did a spell to be dressed in pants and a tunic Marching Night black with red cuffs—quite smart.

She got out of bed and had brown stirrup boots appear on her feet. She realized as she did this what it was she planned to do. She looked at the stone on her dresser. She needed to carry it, but it was way too big to stick in her pocket; it would look like she had some strange growth on her groin. She shrank it and called it into her pocket. She smiled; it was still warm. It should help her keep her energy balanced.

When she got to the great hall everyone but Trin and his crew were gone, and it was way past breakfast. Still they found her something to eat and set it in front of her, so apparently they were all still happy with her over the mill. She ate and then decided to hunt Rea up. She popped up right behind her, and feeling her magic Rea jumped and turned.

"Dammit, Jestia! You liked to made me jump out of my skin."

"Then we are even. You and your girlfriend almost messed up my spell with your rutting." She grinned.

Rea looked at where the blade was spinning, cutting boards. "You shouldn't be popping up around things like that." She pointed at it.

"I didn't know you cared. I know where I'm going before I get there." She looked around. "So where is Katrina? I thought you and she were more or less joined at the hip... Well, maybe not the hip... More your face, her..."

"Jestia, what is it that you want?" she asked, but not without a smile on her face, so Jestia thought she probably had forgiven her.

"I am as good as I am going to get right now, and I was thinking if you could take me to her I could try to help the human speak. Can you leave here?"

Rea looked around her. She had been helping to roll logs down to the log sled, but they didn't really need two of them to do it; it was just easier that way. She looked at the man she'd been working with. "Rory, can you do this? I have to go with Jestia."

"No problem," he said.

She turned to Jestia, nodded, and then started leading her into the forest.

"It's the first time I have walked into the forest here," Jestia said.

"Why?" Rea asked.

"Well first off I am not as comfortable in the woods as you Katabull. But mostly because I did not want to accidentally run into your little human friend and scare her so bad she may never have anything to do with another person in her entire life. My energy was all screwed up, and she is still mostly like a wild animal. Something so connected to the forest, like animals, can feel energy. You know that."

Rea nodded. She did know it because she was Katabull. Animals seemed to know instinctively when a Katabull was just walking and when it was hunting.

"My magic is strong, and just like Katabull feel my magic, so would the human. Mixing strong magic with dark energy... Well there is a reason you were afraid of me. You aren't now, are you?"

She wasn't. Rea couldn't really say why, so she assumed what the witch said was correct.

"Anyway, the forest here is very ethereal, alive and brilliant in a way I was not expecting it to be."

"Why not?"

"Well, because Amalites..." They both spit. "...lived here, and then there was a bloody battle here. Thousands would have died—some of ours mostly theirs. The rest would have fled even as our forces moved on. This is nowhere near the port where Tarius, your parents and mine landed when they came to fight the Great War. But as I felt the energy of the town when I first stepped off the dock I finally realized what they rode into. It would have been a nightmare."

"Worse than the Hive?" Rea asked. They had both fought that battle.

"Maybe not as frightening as fighting in caves filled with cannibals, but we knew what we were fighting there. We knew what an abomination those things were, and we saved the innocents before the battle started. They would have ridden into these towns and most of these people would have just been people. People who had a horrible belief, but most of them wouldn't have been horrible people, just stupid ones.

"Look what they built. They built a town, they had docks, they sailed and fished. They planted fields, vineyards and fruit trees, and raised children. Your human friend is the proof of the horror our parent's rode into off those ships. Towns full of people, children who didn't have a chance. They faced thousands of soldiers trying to kill them mixed in a civilian population just trying to get out of the way. We have never faced that, not in the Hive, not at Rorick's Keep, Finias's Palace, or Sedrick's Keep. In those places, all the evil done to the innocent was done by them. We have fought terrible battles; they scarred us enough. But our parents...they fought a war."

Rea saw worry on the witch's face and she didn't like it. "What are you saying, Jestia?"

Jestia laughed then. "Oh, Rea, I am a witch. You never ask a witch what she is saying; you just try to figure out what she is *not* saying. And I guess what I was getting at was that I expected the town to feel worse than it did, and I expected the forest to feel just as bad. The town is not that bad even for me, and the forest has no residual negative energy at all. The energy..." She took a deep breath. "Every step I take fills me completely up."

The change in Jestia was so complete that Rea knew it must have been a hell of a spell. "I could call her, or we could go to her cave."

"Oh, let's go to the cave," Jestia said. "Maybe we will find more stones."

Rea nodded and kept walking in the direction they'd been going.

"You never did tell me where Katrina is."

"She is looking for a place to build a library."

When they got to the cave Rea knocked on the door. No one answered, and Rea started to call, but Jestia put a quick finger in front of her lips.

"No, don't call her, let me check out her cave first."

"You... you won't take her rocks if you find them, will you?"

"Of course not."

Jestia opened the door and walked in. The energy was good, powerful, the humming of the Everything resonated from the walls. It had nothing to do with the human that lived there or her hoard. She walked right over to a covered lump.

"Now what have we got here?"

"It's a dead body," Rea said.

"I know that. Why is it here?"

"We think it is a Kartik solder who took care of her. That he died when she was too little to move the body and then... Well he just sort of became part of the furniture."

"It's a man then?"

"I'm not sure; it's all mummified. I only looked at it once, and I was sure it was a woman because the armor looked like female armor. But look at the size and... all dried out most human women are not that big. Can't you wake him up and make him tell us?"

"Wash your mouth out!" Jestia said in a hiss. "Necromancy...no." She used magic to uncover the body. "I can read his energy from the room because he lived here and his story still lives in the walls. It is definitely a man, but he is wearing female armor."

"Why?" Rea said making a face.

"Asks the girl who has never been in a dress. His body was male, but he was a woman. She got separated from the others, took a belly wound, fell and was trampled by her own horse—her leg was crushed. She passed out. When she

172

came to it was dark and our forces had already left. She was afraid to call out because the Amalites might find her. She lay there for a day but didn't hear or see anyone, so she took care of her belly wound as good as she could. Used strips of her tunic to tie sticks to her leg and mostly crawled down to the river to get a drink. That's where the girl found her. She was only about three, but because the soldier spoke Amalite she was able to tell the girl what they needed to build camp.

"They depended on each other. The soldier's leg didn't heal right; she walked with a cane and a bad limp." Jestia smiled. "The woman was a bard. She would sit in this cave and tell the girl stories, lots of stories, many about the Katabull..."

"Now it all makes sense." Rea seemed excited. "She has never seemed to notice any differences between me whether I am katted out or not."

"She knew what you were as soon as she saw you because the soldier told her all about you. Eventually the injuries took their toll, and the soldier died right there. She did not have her armor on when she died, so the girl must have done that. The girl would have been about seven, maybe eight, tops."

Jestia stepped away from the body and covered it back up.

"I can't imagine what it must have been like for her to lose everyone she knew and then loose the person that replaced them."

Jestia could more feel than hear the sadness and fear in Rea's voice.

"Katrina will not die and leave you, Rea. You may care for her as much as your heart will let you. That girl is determined to annoy the living hell out of you till you die just to get away from her."

Rea went outside and called for Erah as Jestia continued to go through Erah's belongings.

"Jestia, I don't think you should just rifle through her things like that," Rea said through the open door. She wondered where Erah was. This was her part of the forest; she was normally well within yelling distance of the cave.

"Erah!" she called again.

"If she could hear you she would be here by now," Jestia said.

Rea walked back into the cave. "I wonder where she is."

"Probably in town chasing after your brother."

"She does seem to really like him," Rea agreed.

"The feeling is mutual," Jestia said.

"What do you mean?"

"Come on, Rea, are you so busy with being Tiny Leader..."

"Tiny Leader! What are you going on about?" Rea said and smiled, shaking her head. Like all witches Jestia was crazy, but at least today she was normal crazy for Jestia.

"You're the Tiny Leader because you aren't the Great Leader." Jestia shrugged, going through yet another box. "Laz is falling in love with the human girl."

"What makes you think that?" Rea asked.

"I don't *think* things, Rea, I *know* them. We all know he has always wanted a girl just like Jena, and let's face it, the feral human is about as close as he's going to get. It's obvious the girl is sweet on him because she gave him not one, but *two*, stones. She even showed him where they come from."

"She gave one to Garrett, too," Rea said,

"After he helped her."

"Yes but I didn't get one and I help her all the time," Rea said.

"That really burns your ass, doesn't it?"

"Well it hurts my feelings for sure," Rea said.

"We always take for granted the person who most cares for us." Jestia looked up from the box she was going through. "Relax, your little friend loves you; she is just attracted to boys. That's her loss; you and I both know men have no idea what they're doing down there."

Rea nodded; she did know that. Her madra had said Rea didn't know what she wanted or if she wanted anything at all. But now that she had been sober for more than ten minutes she admitted that she didn't find men attractive at all and probably never had.

Jestia put one box aside and started to go through another one.

"Jestia, what on earth are you looking for?"

"I'll know if I find it," Jestia said.

"You don't even know what you're looking for?"

"There is something emitting a strong magic signature. I can't pinpoint it because the whole cave hums with the Everything." She moved yet another box and started going through another one.

"Jestia can you not just cast a spell to find it?"

"What would be the fun in that?" Jestia said, digging through the contents of the box. "Well, this is kind of sad."

Rea walked up behind Jestia and looked into the box. It was filled with kid's toys, packed and well preserved.

"You really shouldn't be going through her things like this. Could you not do a spell to find her so that you can make her talk?"

Jestia looked at her like she had lost her mind. "If I do that I can't go through all her things."

Rea sighed and said none of the things she was thinking about just how crazy Jestia was.

Jestia went through the toys, then moved that box and started digging in the one under that which seemed to be full of paper.

"You are making a wall-eyed mess," Rea scolded.

"Which I can fix in seconds with a spell. Don't get your panties in a bunch." Jestia suddenly started laughing. She reached down into the loose paper, grabbed a book she pulled it out. "There it is."

"A book. Great. You can give it to Katrina for her damn library," Rea said with a smile. "Now can you put all this back so we can go find the girl?"

Jestia didn't even flick her wrist. In fact, she just kept looking at the book as all around her everything went back to where it belonged. Jestia held the book up and turned it around so that Rea could see the title—which didn't matter because it was in a language Rea didn't understand. Jestia was obviously really excited and looking for some reaction from Rea, who just looked confused and shrugged.

"It's a book of spells written in *Triad*. The people who inhabited this land before the Amalites stole it from them. The Amalites abhor magic, and so the question becomes where did this come from and how did it get here?"

"And see if we find Erah and you make her talk we can ask her."

Jestia stuck the book in her pocket before she followed Rea outside. In her last life she and her twin had been half Triad and filled with magic. It could not be a coincidence that she was here now and found that book in the last place you would expect to find it. The Everything meant her to find it here. When she thought of why she was there in the first place she was reminded of the price of magic. She looked up and Rea was looking at her expectantly.

"What?"

"Make girl talk," Rea grunted, and Jestia laughed.

She found the girl easily and then transported she and Rea there.

As Rea appeared beside her she was yelling, "What the hell, Jestia!"

The human started to run, and Jestia threw a spell to stop and hold her there.

"Your yelling scared the girl."

"Really, Jestia?" Rea said, patting herself down and looking to see that all her pieces were there and where they should be. She looked relieved then said, "For the love of the Everything, Jestia. I am used to magic and I'm surprised my pants are still clean. Erah is *not* used to the things you take completely for granted that you do."

Jestia nodded; Rea was right. And where had she found the girl? Standing with Laz by where the pasture fence led into the forest. Laz glared at Jestia.

"Let her go at once," he ordered.

"If I do she is going to run off, then I will not be able to do my spell to make her talk or understand us. Take hold of her so that she will be still when I let her go."

"She might bite me," Laz said.

"Don't act as if you will not enjoy it, and just take hold of her."

Laz walked behind Erah and hugged her to him. When he had hold of her good and tight Jestia released the girl from the spell. She started kicking and jumping around, but when she saw it was Laz holding her she calmed right down. When she did she looked at Jestia and started to make a loud humming sound.

"Yes, she hums," Rea told the girl.

"She can hear us hum?" Jestia asked.

"Well not us, but she heard Darian hum, and now I'm guessing she hears you." Rea moved to stand in front of the girl where she could see her she pointed at Jestia. "Jazel," she said.

The girl nodded.

"Really, me Jazel? That's rich, she's older than rocks and not nearly as beautiful or powerful as I am," Jestia said.

"Could you maybe focus for a minute Jestia?" Laz said.

Jestia nodded and moved to push Rea gently away and look straight into the human's eyes. She didn't speak her spells; she wanted things to happen and they happened. Which, of course, was the reason she was here, because she had wanted to kill her wife.

"Jestia," Laz prompted again.

The first spell Jestia cast cleaned the human up and untangled her hair. The second should allow her to talk if the girl had enough language in the first place for the spell to attach to.

"Only you of all the witches in the world would worry about what she looks like first," Rea said. "Make her talk."

Erah started making noises that weren't any language Jestia knew, and she was sure her spell had failed. She would have to try something else. Then the woman looked at her and said two words, "Thank you."

Laz started jumping around still holding the poor woman who was being jerked around like a rag doll in the Katabull's arms.

"You can let her go now, Laz, and you should before you break her neck," Rea said, laughing. Rea was so happy it radiated from her touching the edge of Jestia's magic in a way that felt like love. "Thank you, Jestia! Thank you," Rea said.

Laz let Erah go and spun her around and hugged her; she hugged him back. When they parted she turned to Rea and said, "Thank you."

"Yeah, that's fine, but where's my rock?" Rea laughed.

"I can get you rock," Erah said. Both of the Katabull laughed in a way that was so infectious that Jestia found herself laughing, too.

"This is Jestia," Laz started, "Jestia is our..."

"Sister," Jestia told the girl. "I am their sister."

Rea looked at her, nodded and said, "Yes, Erah, she is our sister."

They had been home several days but Tarius had not seen Ufalla again even once. She thought about going to talk to her but if what her son and the others told her were true about what the girl was saying she didn't want to stir that pot because it wasn't done simmering. Yet the woman she had seen by the docks had seemed honestly contrite.

She woke from a dream, not even really a bad one and yet she couldn't go back to sleep. Tarius was used to seeing Jestia at least once—sometimes as many as three or four times—a week, and they mind spoke nearly every day. They could do none of that with Jestia across the ocean and her here. Tarius found that not knowing what was going on with Jestia, not being able to hear from her and know that she was alright, was very unsettling for her.

She sat up, and threw on a loincloth and a shirt, and started for the door.

"You alright?" Jena asked in a whisper.

"I'm fine my love; just can't sleep. I'm going to walk around for a minute and see if I can make myself tired."

"Be careful," she said, and Tarius smiled.

It seemed like a lifetime ago when Jena had thought Tarius was a human male, someone she had to always worry about. Yet Tarius rarely left her side that Jena didn't tell her to be careful. Of course Tarius supposed she had given Jena more to worry about more often since she knew all that Tarius was.

The years came and went and yet every day changed you. Every minute of everyday something could happen that changed the way you felt about everything.

She found herself walking down to the lake. The moons were waning but bright enough that even Jena could see, and Tarius found she wanted to go wake her wife up and make her walk with her just because it was so peaceful and beautiful. She knew Jena would get up if she wanted her to. She would even enjoy the walk but she wouldn't get back to sleep and would be tired the whole next day. Tarius decided to let Jena sleep.

The water of the lake gently slapped the shore; there was no wind tonight just quiet calm. The more she thought about the dream the more nonsensical it seemed, and she knew it meant nothing. It was just her mind racing to sort her thoughts. She needed to sleep; maybe she would be able to after she walked around the lake.

She felt the girl before she saw her. Ufalla was sitting on a big rock that sat right on the water's edge. Tarius easily walked up on the girl unseen and unheard, but as she started to speak the girl didn't start. She had grown up there in this place she had no fear.

"So, what are you thinking, little sister?"

"I was actually remembering what you have always said about if you shoot an arrow and miss the target completely you will have to hit the bullseye ten times before you will convince anyone you can hit it once."

"So... I am not your enemy today?"

"You were never my enemy, nor was my wife. I was my enemy, only me."

Ufalla started to cry. She drew her knees up and rested her head on them. Tarius sat down beside her and put her arm across her shoulders and gave them a squeeze.

"When we are young we are always our own worst enemies. We think we know everything and know nothing. You are not the only one to throw a rock up and have it land on your own head. When I was young I thought the only thing I wanted was to fight my father's enemies, avenge my parents' deaths, make the Amalites pay for the scars on my throat, my chin, and my heart. I thought killing all day everyday would make me whole. But then I fell in love with Jena. I killed men many times, day after day all day. Yet the only thing that ever filled the hole in my heart was Jena—and I nearly destroyed us. I nearly died, she wanted nothing to do with me, and so I did not care if I died."

"But... everything worked out. The Amalites were put down because of you. You and Jena—no one loves like you do. You have a wonderful life!"

"Exactly right."

"I don't understand," Ufalla said with a sniffle.

"I didn't die. I did everything wrong yet Jena forgave me. Everything worked out exactly as it should have in spite of my best efforts to destroy my life and knock holes in everyone else's." She took her arm from around Ufalla. "It's a beautiful night, little sister; enjoy it."

Tarius stood up and started walking home. Now she could sleep.

Ufalla watched Tarius walk away. She didn't feel as all alone as she had just a few minutes ago and not as hopeless. *Because in a lot of ways Tarius is as magic as Jestia is. She's right; the night is beautiful, and I hadn't even noticed. I keep trying to think of what I can do to fix things; it's all I think of.*

She took a deep breath and let it out. Then she lay down on the rock and stopped thinking about anything external, concentrating on her breathing. Gradually she allowed herself to feel the stone under her and to look at the moons above her. She imagined all despair and sadness in her soaked into the rock under her; she imagined the light of the moons filled her with love and hope. She didn't know how long she lay there just focusing on pushing the darkness out of her and replacing it with light, but by the time she sat back up she felt as if a weight had been lifted from her and she really heard what Tarius had said. Ufalla couldn't *make* anything happen. All she could do was make it as easy as she could for Jestia to forgive her. Then see what happened from there and live with it, knowing that whatever happened it wouldn't be the end of her.

They had gone back to Erah's cave at her insistence that they should celebrate with tea.

"We not make the house in the cave," Erah said, in answer to Jestia's question as she made the tea. "Pandy found it. She said it was better than living in village because bad men could come back."

She had been young enough when she started living with "Pandy" that she didn't remember that it was her people who had been attacked by their forces. No doubt she had told Erah what the Amalites were and all the evil things they believed. She had been old enough when Pandy died that she had a full bank of language skills. Rea's lessons had helped, but Erah was still having to stop and think before she spoke because she probably hadn't spoken much since Pandy's death.

"So the wall with the door was here?" Jestia asked.

"Yes, and the bed and the cook pots," Erah said.

Jestia pulled the book out of her pocket. "Where did you get this?"

Erah shook her head; she didn't understand the question.

Jestia thought a second and reworded her question. "Where did this book come from?"

"It was here," Erah said. She handed a cup of tea to Laz. "Laz."

He took the cup and smiled at her. "Your hair looks pretty that way."

"You mean clean," Jestia said. She rolled her eyes. "The book was here."

"Yes, and the papers. Pandy said to keep them; they were important."

"The papers..."

Jestia had the boxes unstack and had the box with the papers in them come to her. Erah was so excited she almost spilled tea all over Rea as she was handing it to her. But this time she wasn't scared at all.

Rea wiped her hand on her pants and looked at Jestia. "Could you not just go get the box?"

"That would require moving," Jestia said from where she sat on the only chair. She started looking at the papers. "It's a diary." She did a spell to have the pages stack and go into the right order which had Erah jumping up and down for joy.

"Erah," Rea said, getting the woman's attention. "Jestia studied magic with Jazel."

"Can I study magic?" Erah asked.

Jestia didn't say anything, but she soon realized the others were looking at her. "She hums, so she has a slight magic ability, but that could be from soaking in this cave for years. If she has any actual power it isn't much. Let's let her learn to talk better before we try to teach her any spells." She looked at the diary before her and cast a spell that allowed her to read any language.

"She was a Triad witch; she escaped the Amalites."

They all spit and to her amusement she noticed Erah did, too.

"She has done that before," Rea said.

"Obviously ole Pandy taught her that," Jestia said. "The witch built this dwelling. It was her lair. it was far away from any settlements until it wasn't, and then she put a spell on it to hide it from view."

"What happened to the spell?" Laz asked. "We are human now, and we can all see it."

"When a magic user dies any spell that needs maintenance dies with them." Jestia shrugged. She put the book and the papers back into her pocket and again the human started jumping around in glee. "She's certainly easily amused, so she is just the girl for you, Laz."

"Come on Jestia," Laz said, embarrassed.

"Rea, let's go back. At any moment Katrina will have a search party sent out for you."

Rea nodded and stood up knowing Jestia was right. As soon as they stepped outside the cave Jestia popped them back to her room in the keep.

"Dammit, Jestia!" She started checking herself again> "You might at least warn me before you do that."

"Takes too long." Jestia started pushing her out the door. "I have things to do. Now go find your girlfriend but keep it down; I want to read my new book."

"What is it with girls and books," Rea said as she walked away.

Chapter Twelve

Jestia lay down on her bed made herself a light and picked up the first page. The spell book she could look at later; if there was anything she didn't already have it could wait. For now she was much more intrigued by the diary of the witch. But as she started to read she realized it really wasn't a diary at all.

"I came here because the cave called to me. I, Kasandra, having lived here many decades, having seen the Amalites destroy all that I loved and cherished, write these words as I count the end of my days. My hope is that one day someone will read my words, understand how hateful is the Amalite religion, and use my words to fuel their desire to end the Amalite reign of terror forever.

"They came like bugs in the night crawling into and onto and across everything, at first unseen. When they were seen my people thought they are not a real problem; there weren't that many of them. By the time they realized what they were looking at there were so many of them there was no getting rid of them, just like bugs. They must be stepped on as soon as you see them or soon you will have a full infestation.

"They drove the Katabull from this land, they killed every queer, every artist, and now, now I am all that is left of my kind, and I will soon be no more. I hear them now scratching, picking on the walls; they grow close. They are taking the essence of this mountain, the heart of the cave and this land. For the priest's greed cannot be quenched, and the people follow them blindly afraid that if they don't the gods will attack them. The people are as bad as the priests because they did not fight back they joined and became part of the problem. They are worse because they knew better but wished to believe the lies they were told. They continue even now to believe their lies even when they can clearly see that no blessings have flowed to them at all. They stood and watched as the Amalites killed or drove out the Katabull, the queers, the witches and wizards, everyone who mixed a potion, who sang a song, told a story or painted a picture. All the best things about humanity they call an abomination. They got rid of the creatives because they couldn't control them. When they killed the bards there was no one left to tell the people the truth about the priests, so their lies were allowed to be the only thing the people heard. When they killed the singers and the musicians there was no one to lift the people's spirits to teach them right from wrong, and when they killed the painters and burned their work there was no visual record of the atrocities they had committed here. Nothing to warn other nations of the death they bring cloaked in their religion.

"And the common man did not stop them. No, they joined them willingly. They wait for the reward they will get when they die and in the meantime do nothing but evil and hate their own lives. There is no reward for them in death, for those who live evil lives will return into a life worse than the one they have left. So it is written; so mote it be.

"All the pain has been caused by the short-sightedness of my own people. They sold today for the promise of something worthwhile later.

"When it first started I told our leaders, and others of my kind told them, but they had grown fat on the backs of the people. They didn't see the threat at all. It was, after all, only a religion. When the Amalites started making hundreds of converts to their filthy beliefs our leaders still did not see the problem; the people were still working, taxes were still being collected.

"They came after my kind first. Even as they were finding us and killing us when they could, the kingdom did nothing, after all it wasn't them. When they went after the Katabull in swarms so large that even the Katabull couldn't fight them, when the Katabull started to leave the country at its borders and cross the ocean for the Kartik, our leaders did not care. They helped the wicked to spread evil lies about the Katabull. As we and the Katabull were killed, left, or went into hiding, the Amalites continued to take over converting more people to their religion every day till slowly the priests of the cult took over most positions of power. By the time the royal line were being drug from their homes—

from their infants to their old people—and killed as a sacrifice to the Amalite gods, it was way too late for them to rise against the enemy, and there was no one left who had their backs.

"I stayed here in the forest in my cave. Thinking, wondering what I could do to step on them like bugs and rid the world of them. I can do nothing. I am one and my power limited. I can do nothing that could wipe them out or stop them or even slow them down, but I have seen the ones who will. I saw in the future that one would rise. One of our bloodline and my cast will rise in the land of the Kartik. She will be joined by many who understood the darkness and will help her fight against it. But one would have started the work that she will finish; a Katabull with a wizard's heart.

"Together they and their followers will fight the darkness whenever it rises. For the Amalite scourge will never end till no one who prays to their gods is left alive. This I have seen, how they are knocked down only to rise again and again in one land after another. But... When the twins converge on the well of power and shine with the same light, and the one bathed twice in blood walks with his royal Katabull brother through the valley of the Katabull and the Great Wall rumbles, those who do not rise against the Amalite gods shall perish at the hands of the one the Great warlord calls the Sword of the Nameless One."

Jestia took in a deep, shuddering breath. It was very nearly the same prophesy that had brought Hellibolt and Persius to the Kartik. The one supposedly written by her grandfather. The only thing different was the last line which might as well have called she and Tarius by name.

All this time I thought the prophesy was only about timing and making Persius realize he must work to keep the Amalites out of his country. It is more than that. Darian and Pete are not mentioned just to mark the time they are key parts of this prophesy. It is not over, that was just the starting point the event that put it into play... it is still in play.

As Jestia read on it was mostly information on exactly how the Amalites had wormed their way into Triad. Details about which royals had helped them, who had taken bribes to look the other way, and how all of them had lived while the people died. How the priests had richly "blessed" them...until they had taken over the whole of the country. Then they, the royals, were slaves to the religion just like everyone else. They were stripped of their titles, their wealth, and their lands. It was nearly exactly the same as every story she'd ever heard, every book she had read about Amalite conquest. No real surprises.

She picked up the last page and started to read.

"The picks are close now. They must destroy everything that is beautiful, everything and everyone that is special they hunt out and kill. I will not let them find me, and I will take as many of them with me as I can. Before they can break through I will collapse the wall that separates us on them, and on me.

She made the cave in; she is under the cave in. She had to be talking about a mine, but what were they mining for?

She didn't get a chance to think about it because then the page still in her fingers started to burn. She let it go, and it floated in front of her as new words were written on it with the fire.

Jestia quickly read the words before the page could burn up.

The sword of the Nameless One must dig my body up and collect my amulet.

"Great." Jestia hissed as she watched the paper turn to ash. "Now I get to move tons of rock to find a dead body... It had better be a really nice necklace."

Rea was just finishing her dinner when Jestia walked down the stairs and into the room.

"Well?" Rea asked.

"Interesting reading," Jestia said. Then she went and got herself a bowl of food and sat down across from Rea and Katrina.

Laz still had not come back, and Rea envisioned he and Erah sitting just talking which made her feel left out. When she had said as much to Katrina, Katrina's apparent answer was to talk twice as much as usual to make up for them not talking to Rea. She was mostly talking about the library. Though it should have been clear that Rea was now talking to Jestia, Katrina apparently hadn't noticed.

"I can't have been the only person in this town bored stupid when it was so cold we couldn't be outside for more than a few minutes. A library will give us all something to do on cold winter days. Much better than a pub."

Fleat grunted. "You will never convince the youngsters of that." He looked at Rea, rolled his eyes and grinned. "Of course this year when the cold comes I'm sure you will find plenty to do, Katrina."

Katrina giggled. "No doubt about that." She nudged Rea in the ribs with her elbow. Rea shoved her and Katrina laughed.

"Do you think the human will come into town now?" Fleat asked.

"Doubtful, at least for now. She is just now being domesticated. Talking will speed the process, but she will still be overwhelmed for a while by how many of us there are," Jestia said, obviously with a mouth full of food.

Rea looked at her and Jestia was eating... Well, she was eating like a Katabull; like it was her first and last meal.

Jestia must have realized Rea was staring at her because she looked at her and said, "My good courtly manners are a waste here anyway, and I'm hungry."

"What did you learn from the book?" Rea asked.

"About books... Jestia, do you think your mother would get us some books?"

"She would, but you'll not get them before this winter. We left in such a hurry I didn't take any blue birds with me, so I can't get a message back to the Territories."

Katrina looked disappointed, but not so much that she was finished talking. Seeing her start again Rea took a finger and put it over Katrina's lips. "No, Katrina, no. I asked Jestia a question; please let her answer it."

Jestia looked at her, obviously trying to remember the question.

"What did you learn from the book?"

"Oh, I didn't crack the spell book yet. I read the diary. Well, it wasn't so much a diary as a last will and testament. It was mostly about the Amalites laying waste to the country of Triad. No real surprises there, they basically did what they always have done. So no real shocks except when there were huge ones. A prophesy about me and Tarius that we previously believed had been written by my grandfather but apparently was originally written by Triad witches. Then when I finished the last page it caught fire and wrote a message for me to dig up a body to retrieve a magic item I will apparently need because I am the Sword of the Nameless One." She sighed then looked at Rea. "So apparently I was supposed to come here and find it, but I would have rather I got curious about the Territories and came with Tarius just to visit then ran here because my wife is a drunken whore."

"My dear girl," Fleat said, "I have learned never to question the how of something and focus only on the why of it."

Rea looked at him, waiting to see if he would end with some smart-ass comment for Jestia like he always did for her.

He grinned. "Isn't that right, Captain oh my Captain? It doesn't matter how your woman talks, it's always just Why?! Why?!" So apparently he saved all his smart-assed crap for her. She was about to say as much when Jestia interrupted.

"The most discomforting thing about what I read was what wasn't there, and that I only realized as I was walking down the stairs." Of course, being Jestia, she just stopped right there and stared at things no one but she was seeing.

"What Jestia?" Rea asked.

"I should have thought of it before when I remembered who I was and how I came to be at that time." And again she just stopped talking.

"What, Jestia, what!" Rea demanded.

Jestia smiled. "I think I liked it better when you were afraid of me. This place we call the Territories—both those we own and those that the Jethrik claim—used to be the Amalite, but before that it was Triad."

"So?" Rea wasn't getting the significance of that at all.

"So... Where the hell did they come from in the first place?" Fleat said.

Jestia nodded. "Precisely. How many countries did they destroy before this one?"

Ufalla woke to the unfamiliar sound of knocking on her door. When she answered, it was Jabone with his cub.

"I am sorry, Jabone."

"That's what Madra said, so I thought we would come and cheer you up—or at least this one will." He handed Arvon to Ufalla. The cub hugged her neck, and she hugged him back. "Before he went this last time if we separated him from Diana he threw a living fit. Since he has been back he is less attached to her and more to us. Madra said she is glad because it is bad enough to have Pete and Darian joined at the hip. But Arvon still hardly talks; he just lets Diana talk for him. My sister will tell me what it is he wants. It is so bad that yesterday when he was cross and Kaseria could not figure out what he wanted, she marched him right over to my parent's house and told him to tell Diana what was wrong. Kaseria said he grunted a couple of times and Diana looks at her like she has a cat crawling out of her mouth and says, "His pants are too tight." Kaseria loosens the string on his loincloth, he makes this huge sigh, takes Kaseria by the hand and leads her back home again."

"I am sorry that you were separated from him for so long, sorry about the wrestling, and just sorry for everything I have done for over a year."

"Being sorry is only a start. You will have to stop doing the things you were doing."

"I have and I will."

"Can you?"

"I must, Jabone. I can't stand what I became. What I did to Jestia... how I almost wound up dead... almost ruined her. I was so afraid of not being enough that I became nothing."

Jabone smiled at her.

"What?"

"You sound like Madra."

Arvon started to play in her hair in a way that she knew would leave it a tangled mess she'd have to work to get out, but she happily let him do it. "I don't know about that, but I have remembered to listen to her again."

Laz and Erah had been talking, nothing earth shaking nothing important, just talking. She was as excited to be able to talk to them as they all were that she could.

Finally he said what was obvious to him. "We should really bury Pandy."

"Bury her?" Erah shook her head.

"That's what people do when people die; they bury them. We could mark the place we bury her," Laz said. He didn't want to tell her that it was creepy to keep the mummy in the same place she ate and slept. That was, after all, what he thought not what she did. "Look how much room you would have if the body wasn't there, and the dead don't care where they sleep."

"They don't care where they sleep?" She sounded confused.

"When someone dies there is nothing of them left behind. They don't care what happens to the body because they don't live there anymore," Laz said.

"The ground is cold," Erah said.

"Pandy can't feel, Erah."

She nodded. It was obvious, and part of her knew that was true.

"We don't have to bury her right now. But soon."

"If Pandy should be buried we should do it now. Later is the same as now."

So Laz took her shovel and dug a hole then he picked the mummy up. It was every bit as gross as he thought it would be, and the odor of it was oddly smoky-dusty-moldy. Tarius would have his hide, but he buried the sword with the soldier; she had died with it in her hand. If he tried to remove the sword the whole hand would most likely come off with it. That might upset Erah, and it wouldn't do him much good either. Afterwards he found a huge rock and placed it over the head of the body. When he looked at Erah she looked sad, and he thought maybe he had made a huge mistake.

"I could dig her back up," Laz offered.

Erah laughed at him then made a face and shook her head.

He looked up. "I guess I better get back; it will be dark soon.

"Katabull see in the dark," Erah said.

Laz nodded. "That's right."

"Strong like ten men," Erah said.

Laz smiled as he realized something. "Erah, was Pandy a bard?"

Erah nodded excitedly. Well, that explained why she knew all about Katabull and Jazel. Kartik bards loved stories about witches, wizards and Katabull.

"Are you a bard?" Erah asked.

"No, but my madra is, and lots of my friends and family are."

She took his hand and started yanking him back towards the cave.

"Erah, I really should get back."

"Tell me a story," she said, and drug him into the cave. She sat him on the bed and raced to sit in her chair.

"Alright, but I'm really not very good. What kind of story do you want?"

"Do you know Tarius the black meets Jazel?"

"Of course I do. You know about Tarius the Black?"

"She is the greatest fighter who ever lived," Erah said.

"She would tell you that was her father." Laz took a deep breath stood up paced back and forth and then launched into the story. When he had finished she clapped.

"Do you know Tarius the Black?" Erah asked.

"Yes, and Jazel." Laz smiled. "Erah, Tarius is still the Great Leader. She started this colony. She has been here several times."

Erah was very excited, "I saw her. She was with Rea. Her finger is in her sword."

"That's right." Laz nodded. "And now I need to go before Rea gets worried and comes looking for me. Because when she finds me and I'm not dead she'll scream at me that she's going to kill me."

"I don't understand," Erah said,

"That's alright; no one does."

Jestia put a spell on Erah so that Jestia could track the human's movements. Jestia was going to have to move all the boulders and debris at the cave in to find the body. She was pretty sure the human would flip completely out to have all her things moved out of the cave then to have boulders and debris moved through her cave to be stacked outside. Not to mention how she might react when Jestia found one or more mummies or skeletons.

For two days the girl stayed close to the cave. On the third day Erah went gone down to the mill to watch the Katabull saw logs into boards and no doubt to see Laz.

Jestia transported herself to the mill. Laz was catching boards and stacking them. Jestia walked up to him and silenced the noise of the mill, which made all the Katabull jump for a minute thinking the mill had broken until they saw her. Then they just kept working.

"What are you up to?" Laz asked with a smile, as he stacked the finished boards.

"Your girlfriend is here." She pointed to where she knew the girl was.

Laz looked up, smiled at the girl and waved. She waved back wildly.

"She's not my girlfriend," Laz said.

"Whatever. I need you to go get her and keep her busy away from her cave for the day."

"Jestia, I am supposed to work here all day and... What are you up to now?"

"I will do your work here, and you don't need to know what I'm up to. When I get done no one will know I was there. Except you know maybe I will make things better."

"Jestia, I don't think..."

"And you shouldn't. Don't act like you don't want to spend the day with her. Go hunting or fishing or something."

"You will not do anything that will upset her?"

"Well that isn't likely. I upset everyone eventually, but what I am doing today shouldn't upset her if she doesn't know I'm doing it."

"How will you do my work here and... whatever you are doing in her cave?"

Jestia did a spell and the next board he was to catch stacked itself.

He nodded. "Jestia, do not do anything you don't need to do in her home."

"You worry too much Laz. Now go," Jestia said.

192

Laz took off at a run. She removed the silence spell, left the spell to stack the boards off the mill and started to walk away.

Fleat looked back at the mill and thought with a grin, *The witch stacks lumber better than Laz does, and she isn't even here. I imagine she could turn the trees into boards if she willed it, but then we would not learn to use the mill. We are still having trouble figuring out how to use the brake to keep the blade at just the right speed, and Jestia cannot stay here forever. I wonder what she is up to now.*

Rea had just helped to roll a log onto the sled, but she left her post and walked up to him. "What is Jestia up to?" she asked, looking to where Laz was talking to Erah at the tree line.

He knew why she asked him; Fleat had been much closer to them than Rea was. "I was just wondering that myself. I could not hear them even though she silenced the mill. Your brother was more than happy to go, though, and it isn't because he hates work."

Rea nodded. She was obviously deep in thought. He could see the moment at which she figured it out and then she said, "I know what she's doing. Jestia has had my brother keep Erah busy so that she can go to her cave and dig through the rubble looking for the dead witch."

Fleat read the look on Rea's face. "And you would rather help her than roll logs?"

"You know if I go I will not have to help her, but I am very curious, and would like to be there to see what she discovers," Rea said. "But it would be the second time this week I walked away to leave my partner to do my job and theirs." She ran down to help them roll the next log onto the sled then ran back.

He could tell she was torn. "Go," Fleat said. "It is not every day someone digs up a long-dead witch to help them fulfill a prophesy. If you must justify it, we all know Jestia should not be trusted on her own."

Rea nodded and was off.

Fleat watched her go with a mixture of joy and sadness. Joy that Rea was doing something just because she wanted to. The girl worked all the time, and she needed to learn to balance work with play. Not everything had to have a reason. He was sad because he would have loved to go with her, but he could barely get to the mill site. And sitting on his chair and watch them mill, making suggestions if something went wrong, and telling them when to take breaks and when to go back to work was exhausting.

Fleat was glad he had come to the Territories. In a lot of ways it was the greatest adventure of his life. As a member of the Marching Night from its earliest days he had combed the beaches of the Kartik killing any Amalites they found there. They had gone to sea and captured Amalite ships and he had fought in the Great War, and the Hive. But battle, war—that wasn't really an adventure. When he was young he thought it would be, but after he had done it... Killing was not life affirming, and watching those you loved die sucked the light from your soul. After the Hive he knew he couldn't fight anymore. When Tarius called for the whole of the Marching Night to go to the capital he had gone with all the rest, but he had stayed at the palace to help protect the queen and Jena while the others had ridden out to do battle. Tarius had not needed him, and he wasn't fit to fight.

He had loved only once but long with a fire and passion. Heard had happily died fighting the Hive. Happily because he was even older than Fleat, and he had hoped to die in the battle. Their two children with their cross mates were now each over two-hundred years old, and he had four grandkids over a hundred.

None of them needed him, and he had been one of the first to be chosen to come here. *I came here ready to die; instead I have lived more in these last few years than any others in my life. Rea needed me, and I was an important part of helping this colony set roots. I saw it go from an idea in the Great Leader's and all of our heads to reality. A real new home land. Now my body is failing me, but I find I am no longer ready to die. I am enjoying my life even though I can't follow the young where they go anymore. I am still able to steer them in the right directions; they still seek my council. I have done more good here than I ever did when I was cutting people in half all day. But had we not done that we could not have done any of this. I have had a good life, and I am ready to die, but I no longer wish for it.*

He was not surprised when he saw a young woman come to take Rea's place. Rea hadn't wanted to leave them short-handed. She was a good leader, and he liked to think he had more than a little to do with that, too.

By the time Rea got to the cave, all of Era's things were sitting outside it, and small boulders were rolling out the door into a stack. When Rea jumped over one and went inside, she saw boulders that were too big to roll through the door had been stacked to the side. Jestia was standing inside the cave, her hands in the air apparently lifting the rocks out of the wall, setting them down, and then rolling them outside.

Jestia turned to her and yelled to be heard over the noise of rolling boulders. "I hope there is enough room in here to stack all the big ones or I will have to either shrink the boulders or make the door bigger, which seems like a waste of energy."

"Have you found anything yet?" Rea asked, also yelling.

"No. My guess would be that she will be on the very bottom of the pile and probably nearly to the back of the cave in. You know because... Life."

"Is there anything I can do?"

"You mean besides feed your own morbid curiosity?"

Rea nodded.

"You could use your Katabull eyes to watch for any sign of anything because I am working so fast I might miss something important."

Rea shifted to have the best eyes possible, and moved to stand beside Jestia to be the most out of the way. "Do you think you will have enough time before Erah comes back?"

"I'm sure our brother will keep her plenty busy. The problem is I have no idea how big this cave in is; could many be feet more, might be miles. I may have to give up here, put everything back, and try to find the opening to the mine go at it from that side."

"Mine?"

"Yes. In her notes the witch kept talking about the Amalites 'picking away at the heart' of the mountain. When they got too close she collapsed the roof of the cave onto herself and them."

"Do you know what they were mining for?"

"No idea. I'm almost as interested in finding that out as I am in finding out what the amulet does."

Laz had convinced Erah to go to the river to spear fish. She caught one; he didn't, and she right away wanted to take it back to her cave to cook it and eat it.

"No, no let's eat it right here. I'll make a fire." He pulled flint from his pocket and pulled out his knife. When he did, Erah jumped back. "Is something wrong?"

"Knives, swords, the glint off the metal." She shrugged. "I do not like it. When I see it, it makes my belly afraid."

"Is that why you wear your knife inside your pants?" Laz asked.

She nodded. "I know it is silly. We must use knives to live; swords are for fighting, Pandy told me that. Could you kill a bear with your sword?"

Laz nodded as he worked to get a spark and light the bundle of dry grass he had gathered. "A Katabull can. I don't think a human could." He got an ember, blew it into flame and started the bundle of sticks they had gathered.

He put his knife away so as not to cause her any more discomfort. She had been too young to remember the battle fought in the town, but it wasn't very hard for Laz to stick the pieces together. That battle would have been terrifying for a small child, but all she remembered was that the glint of sun on steal meant something bad. She reacted without knowing why.

Laz had been waiting with his madra and his siblings on the docks for his fathers and his mother to come home. But his fadra didn't come home; he had died. His father was no one he knew, and for the longest time his mother seemed to be only half there. It took them a long time to heal from what they had done and what they had seen. For the longest time Laz would not go to the docks; he would not watch the ships come in. He had never told anyone, but the most terrifying moment when they had gone to fight the Hive had been getting on the ship and watching his siblings, his madra and father get on the ship. He had just had the most horrible feeling of doom. But as soon as the ship left the dock he had been fine.

Erah had cleaned the fish down by the river and left the guts there. "I don't usually eat outside because food brings bears, but if one comes you will kill it. I had never eaten one of them till you got here, but Rea has brought me lots of bear meat, and... it is my favorite thing."

"Then I will kill a bear for you," Laz said with a grin.

Erah put the fish on a stick and held it over the fire. "After we eat we could go home and I could make tea."

"No," Laz said. too quickly. "We Katabull we like to be in the jungle... well forest here. I am too much in buildings and in town. Rea has told me that when winter comes there is not much to do but sit inside and try to stay warm."

"Rea is right," Erah said. Then she looked up. "I know just what we can do."

She had been standing there a couple of hours just watching when she finally saw something.

"Stop, stop, stop!" Rea shouted.

Jestia set the boulder she'd been moving down, and it rolled outside, but she didn't grab another one.

Rea ran over to where she had seen a hint of color, rolled a huge rock out of the way, picked up what she had seen and held it up.

Jestia smiled and nodded. "It was a cornelian mine. Dig around and see if there is anything else there."

Rea did and she found two more stones, both smaller than the one she had found before, which was much smaller than the ones Erah had given away. She moved some more rocks, found nothing else, and moved back to stand beside Jestia.

Jestia lifted yet another boulder, sighed, and shouted at Rea over the rumble it made as it rolled out the door. "I have already moved twenty feet of rock, and I am running out of room in the cave to stack the big ones. I may have to give up on getting to her this way, put everything back and look for the entrance to the mine. At least from that way I wouldn't have to worry about displacing Erah. Of course I'm not sure the witch didn't manage to collapse the entire shaft which means... Well, I could be at it for a while."

She looked like she was close to giving up and just putting back all she had already moved.

197

"Jestia, we just found the stones you think they were mining for. We may be close; just work on it a little longer."

Jestia nodded, moved a boulder towards the top and there was a loud rumbling as the whole wall came down. They had to jump out of the way to keep from being crushed. The air was full of dust, but of course Jestia didn't want there to be dust, so as quickly as it had filled the air it was gone. When she looked through the hole in the wall there stood Laz and Erah with shocked looks on their faces.

Laz was holding a torch in his hand, Erah had a big round piece of cornelian in hers.

"I only moved one rock," the startled human said.

Jestia looked from the girl and Laz to the pile of rubble she still needed to move. Because she still hadn't found the witch's body, and it had to be under the two foot of crap still on the floor.

"Fancy meeting you here," Jestia said.

"What have you done!" Laz said.

He started walking over the rubble, and Erah followed. She looked around the wreck Jestia had made of her home, walked over and handed the stone to Rea without a word.

"Erah, Jestia can put it back just the way it was," Rea told her.

"Except better," Jestia said. She looked at the girl and the clothes she was wearing, which had probably been Rea's, and were three times to big. She cast a spell to make them fit.

Erah looked at them then at Jestia.

"I will put it back just the way it was... except it will be clean, maybe bigger, and now you two need to get out of the way so I can finish what I started."

Laz put a hand on Erah's shoulder, but glared at Jestia as he said, "You had better put it back, Jestia. Come on, Erah, let's go."

Jestia watched as they walked out the front door then turned to Rea and said, "She finally brought you a damn rock, and you didn't even say thank you."

Rea ran out the front door to find Laz and Erah just standing there. Erah was just looking at the huge pile of stones. "Thank you, Erah," Rea said holding the rock up. She smartly jumped out of the way of a bolder Jestia sent rolling out the front door.

"This is nothing," Laz said, answering the awe on Erah's face. "Jestia once dug a giant trench to route a volcano away from a town."

"What is volcano?" Erah asked.

Laz took her hand and started walking away with her. "It is a mountain that spews molten rock so hot it burns everything it touches. The Great Wall rumbled, the earth shook, and the Great Leader stepped out of her house with her wife and kids took three steps and then vanished because Jestia needed her energy to cast the spell..."

Rea smiled, shook her head, and went back into the cave jumping over the boulders that were rolling out faster than they had before because Jestia was close to finding what she was looking for. If it was there at all. *Wouldn't that suck.* Rea thought. *To move the entire cave in just to find nothing. If the witch was killed in a cave in that killed others they might have dug them all out then left the rest of the boulders. I will not tell this witch that because she would be pissed off. If that's what has happened, let her find it out on her own.*

But that fear went away as they found a human mummy. Jestia tossed it aside like cord wood. "That is not her." They found three more that Jestia threw away because they weren't the right ones. Suddenly Jestia stopped moving rocks. "Rea, come over here and very carefully move those rocks there, please."

Rea did so, glad to have something to do even if she didn't fully understand why Jestia couldn't just move these stones, too, and half thought she was having her do it just so Rea wouldn't feel useless. As she moved the first one she could see the feet of a fourth mummy. Crushed by the weight of the stones that had fallen on all of them, they were sort of flat, and looked a lot like slices of jerky—thin, twisted and dried out. Rea imagined the smoke from the constant fire Erah had kept for decades had cured them. She had to move three more stones before the mummy was completely uncovered. It was wearing some kind of purple robe.

Jestia used magic to lift the mummy up, but she didn't toss this one aside. Under where what was left of her head had been was a brilliant red stone held in a gold clasp.

"Pick it up," Jestia said. When Rea did it she could feel the magic in it.

"Why did you not just pick it up?" Rea asked.

"Half way through the excavation I realized that if some witch wanted to keep the Sword of the Nameless One from stopping the Amalites this would be the perfect way to set a trap."

"So you had me pick it up?"

"Relax. You are in your Katabull form; magic can't hurt you."

Rea nodded. "Well, now what?"

"How does it feel?"

"I can feel the magic in it," Rea said.

"And is it good energy or bad energy?"

"How am I supposed to know that?"

"Because you are the Katabull," Jestia said, obviously disgusted with her. "Does the energy feel good to you or bad?"

"Good I guess; it makes me tingle."

"Like good sex?"

"Well yes," Rea said.

"Good," Jestia reached out and grabbed the amulet from Rea's hand. She looked at Rea and smiled.

"Well?" Rea demanded.

"When I wear this amulet an Amalite cannot hide from me, and no one who wishes to do me harm can hide their intentions. It is not only a good item for the Sword of the Nameless One to have, but it is very good for the heir apparent to have as well."

"Great, so you are even more powerful," Rea said, giving Jestia a crooked grin.

"Better than that I am more protected." She made a leather thong for it and slipped it around her neck.

"Now to clean up this mess," Jestia said.

"Will it take as long to put it back as it took to destroy it?"

"No because we do not need all that rock back in here. I have plans," Jestia said.

"Should I go and find Erah and bring her home?"

"Yes. By the time you get back I should be finished."

"Jestia, do not change it too much."

"Just go. Anything I do that she doesn't like I will put back to the grubby way she had it," Jestia said.

It was clear Rea was being dismissed, so she left.

When she found them she said to Erah, "You may go home now."

She looked at Laz and added, "She found what she was looking for, and surprise! Jestia is even more powerful than she was before."

Rea held up the stone, looked at Erah and said, "Thanks again."

They started to walk away and Rea yelled after them. "Do not be surprised if it is very different. Jestia said she had plans."

So as they walked through the forest towards the cave Laz tried to explain Jestia to Erah. "Jestia is very good and very powerful, but she is also crazy."

"What do you mean?"

"She..." He tried to remember how Tarius had explained it and then change it so a human might understand. "Witches and wizards know too much, and the knowledge makes them think in a way different than other people."

"She said I might have magic. Will it make me crazy?"

"She said you might have a little, so probably not enough to make you crazy. Jestia wasn't really crazy till she became so incredibly powerful. Anyway, she will build your house back the way she thinks it is better, but if you ask her—for the Nameless One's sake don't *tell* her to do anything—but if you *ask* her to put it back the way it was she will do it. Jestia always means well."

Erah nodded and said, "Different isn't bad. Pandy moved into the ground, and it made my house better."

As they neared the cave entrance Laz knew Jestia had made big plans. There was a stacked-rock fence so tight you couldn't get a knife blade between the stones all around the front of the cave to make a fenced yard, and there was a window in the front wall.

Far from looking agitated, Erah seemed really excited. Which was good because when they entered nothing was the same. Where the floor had been rough before it was now smooth. Jestia had built a wall in the back of the cave some ten foot further in than the cave in had been. There was a door in the left part of it and a huge fireplace with a hearth on the right side, the chimney of which went into the mine shaft. The fire was blazing, and there was no smoke inside. Erah's boxes were all stacked neatly against one wall and her bed was clean and neat.

"I didn't do anything with Pandy. I don't know where she got off to," Jestia said.

"We buried her," Laz said.

Jestia opened the back door with magic and said, "Out this door you have your cache of stones which you can now easily access." She closed it back. "If you don't know how to use a fireplace and hearth, I'm sure Laz or Rea will gladly show you."

Erah ran across the room and hugged Jestia.

Jestia looked at Laz, "She is really strong. And now I need to get something to eat and go straight to bed."

Jestia popped up in her room where she walked over and flopped on her bed. It had been a triumphant day; she should be on top of the world, so why did she suddenly feel gutted?

When Erah hugged me in that altogether too tight way... That is the way Ufalla used to hug me. When she did I always felt like nothing could ever hurt me. Who would have thought she would be the very thing that would hurt me worse than I have ever been hurt before? I will be doing better, feeling like I'm more myself, and then... the littlest things still have me doubting myself. That is a luxury I can't afford; I can't not trust myself. I knew her better than I have ever known anything till I didn't know her at all. How can I ever again trust what I know if I could be so wrong about something both so important and yet so simple?

Rea had still not taken her human form back. In fact, she was just about to suck down a vial of blood and shift back when she felt Jestia return to the keep. She sucked down the vial of blood, took back her human form, and was about to go downstairs when she got the feeling she needed to check on Jestia. She went to her door and knocked.

"Come in." Even the tone of her voice did not sound right.

Rea opened the door—the only one on the floor—and walked in.

"You alright, Jestia? Is there something wrong with the necklace?

"I am fine; just tired from all the casting." But she didn't look at Rea. "It was a victorious day."

"Then why do I hear tears in your voice?"

Jestia looked at her then, and the intensity of her sadness was such that Rea had to work to not look away. "I was happy, so happy, but... The slightest thing makes me remember why I am here, all that is wrong with my marriage. Then I doubt myself; I can't, but I do."

"We all doubt ourselves from time to time."

"But I can't, Rea. Don't you understand ?I can't. I *have* to trust myself. I *have* to because the power of the Everything flows through me. You cannot wield that kind of power and have doubt."

Rea walked over and sat on the bed beside her. She took Jestia's hand, squeezed it, then let it go saying nothing. Rea didn't know all the rules of being a witch, and she wasn't about to pretend to. But in the last few weeks she had gotten close to Jestia, to respect—not just her power but her person. "I trust you completely."

"Really? Because you thought I might turn you into a rock." Jestia laughed even as she cried.

"I didn't really know you then."

"And you do now?"

"I know your spirit."

"I tried to sleep with you and your girlfriend just for spite."

"She was not my girlfriend then, it didn't happen, and I'm sure if you had really been trying I would have had to shift to stop you," Rea said.

"I trusted Ufalla completely. I thought I knew everything about her and even when it became clear she had changed I just thought it was a temporary thing, that she was still who I thought she was. If I can't trust Ufalla, I can't trust me."

"You can and you should." Rea took a deep breath and let it out. "My mother was the whole world to me because my father died in the Great War. When Madra and Fadra came back without him... For a long time it was like they hadn't come home, either. I was the youngest of their cubs, and I didn't have all of them; I just had Mother for the first part of my life. My mother kept us all tied together; she took care of us all till my madra and fadra became themselves again. I was just a teenager when mother got a wasting sickness, and she started dying—not all at once but in stages. I couldn't deal with my grief over losing her in stages because she was still alive, and I had hope that a miracle would happen. But it didn't. She was in hideous pain, and then she went into a coma, and then she was dead.

"I hated everyone and everything. I blamed the Nameless One, my parents and my brothers—everyone—because they weren't my mother. None of them knew how to make me feel better, and they didn't have time for my grief because they were filled with their own. So, did I try to work out what I was feeling? Did I try to deal with it and find a way to move on? No. I drank, and being Katabull I didn't have to drink much till I was no longer responsible for what I did.

"I slept with everything that moved because it was also a way of not dealing with my real problems... of just not thinking. It was just like the drinking, just as intoxicating, and even more destructive to others.

"Ufalla is not the Katabull, but I have to believe being mostly-always drunk does the same thing to humans. It becomes the excuse to worry only about yourself, to wallow in your selfishness.

"I know why I became a drunken slut. I can't say why she started drinking and whoring around, but once she had started on that path, Ufalla wasn't at *all* the person you trusted because she wasn't herself. I know this because *I* wasn't *me*. I did all the things she has done. I wasn't married, but I don't think that matters when you are broken inside and decide that instead of dealing with your pain you will just cover it up with being an ass.

"You were right to trust her; you weren't wrong. What you have been dealing with—that isn't the woman you love—it is the thing her actions have made her.

"No one could stop me. Not my parents, not my brothers, not the friends I turned into enemies, not even the Great Leader. I had to *want* to do better. In order to reach that point I had to be so low that there was nowhere to go but up. She lost you, Jestia. You are here and she is there because you wanted to kill her. If that isn't her bottom, then she is more stupid than I think she is. Maybe now she will start to climb up."

Jestia turned to look at her. Rea could not read the look on her face, but hoped she wasn't about to be turned into a rock. Then Jestia hugged her neck with one arm, drug her head down and kissed her on the cheek. "You are very wise."

"I don't know about all that," Rea said in embarrassment.

"Don't worry; I will never tell anyone."

"Will you come down to dinner?" Rea asked.

"I will in a minute. Thank you."

Rea stood up and left the room. As she closed the door Katrina ,who was in the hall, was all over her. Rea pushed her away. "What the hell, Katrina?"

"I heard what you said to Jestia, and... You are the sweetest thing ever."

"Really, Katrina, you spy on me now?" She started for the stairs.

"Only when I realized you were in Jestia's room with the door closed. I was afraid you were coupling."

"And what would you have done if we had been coupling?" Rea asked, shaking her head as she started down the stairs.

"Been really, really upset," Katrina said. Because of course Katrina wasn't stupid and would not want to incur the witch's wrath.

"If I wanted to have sex with someone else I would tell you," Rea said. "But why would I want to when you give me more than I want?"

"What's that mean—more than you want?" Katrina asked as they hit the bottom floor and headed to take their place in the chow line.

"It means you want it even when I don't. That doesn't mean I don't enjoy it; just means I don't think about it all the time like you do."

"Oh," Katrina said.

"And see? I can tell by how quiet you are and the look on your face that you are thinking about it even now... Will you at least let us eat some dinner first?"

As they waited their turn in line Katrina started to fill her in on the progress with the library. "Having lumber and nails is huge. We are almost finished with the build on the shell. I've been asking around and lots of people have books they are willing to put in so that we can share them. That should give us something to read this winter until we can fill the shelves in the spring and..."

"The only thing you like better than sex is talking," Rea said.

Everyone in line laughed.

Katrina grinned. "That is not true; I like sex better than talking."

Fleat laughed louder. "If that is true, the Captain's fingers will be worn to nubs in a week and she won't be able to sit without pain."

Chapter Thirteen

Rea took twenty of the Marching Night and the witch to go with her to West Town to help them prepare for winter. She had planned to take them wagons filled with lumber, but as they were starting to take the wagons to the mill Jestia had cleared her throat and said, "That won't be necessary. I can turn trees into lumber and with less waste."

Fleat had laughed and said, "I thought as much."

They were all riding horses, except Fleat and Roash, who were on the wagon they had filled with pumpkins and apples. They couldn't grow apples in the Kartik; it was too warm. But they had always eaten them because they imported them from the Territories and before that they had received them in trade from the Jethrik. The town site had been filthy with apple trees, and since they had cleared away the brush and started to take care of them, they had more apples than they could eat. They stored well in cold rooms and would last most of the winter, and they would still have enough to send home with Tarius when she came.

Their pumpkin crop had been really impressive as well. As they were loading the pumpkins and apples into the wagon, Rea had turned to Jestia and said, "Should we even bother, or can you just make these, too?"

Jestia had shrugged and said nothing, which meant she probably could make them out of algae and tree bark. Having the witch there had certainly allowed them to get a lot of things done in a hurry.

Katrina rode beside her, and Jestia rode just behind them. The witch was singing, and Rea would have liked to listen, but... Katrina.

"We have only ridden about an hour yet look how different the trees are here. Not nearly as tall and thick as our trees."

Jestia stopped singing and said, "The dirt here is not as thick nor as rich." Then she started singing again.

"We should get our own house you know after we make the exchange," Katrina said.

"I have not said anything about making an exchange," Rea said.

"Which is why I am saying we should make an exchange and then get a house."

"Katrina, I have no desire to leave the keep. I am perfectly happy there, and as captain of this colony it's where I should be."

"But you would make an exchange."

Behind them Jestia started laughing loudly.

"Woman, that is not what I said at all!" Rea bellowed.

"It's what I heard," Katrina said with a grin. "So, when do you want to do it and do you want something private or to have guests while we do it?"

"I have not said yes, Katrina."

Suddenly Jestia was between them where there had not been room for a horse just moments before. She looked at Rea and grinned wildly. "You might as well say yes. You weren't going to have sex with her, and look how well that worked out."

Then as if Rea were not there at all, or had said yes, Jestia and Katrina started to plan a ceremony for their exchange.

She could hear Fleat laughing from the wagon right behind her, and when she turned Roash was grinning from ear to ear. She slowed her horse till she was riding behind Jestia and Katrina. She looked over her shoulder at the two men and said, "I did not say yes."

Fleat laughed all the louder, and Roash started laughing as well.

Rea sighed and moved to ride beside the wagon. "Well I didn't." Then loud enough that Jestia and Katrina could hear her yelled at the back of their heads. "I don't want to make an exchange with you, Katrina! I don't want to make an exchange with anyone!"

"But you will," Fleat said. "That girl has owned you ever since the first time you told her no and she didn't go away." Then he laughed still harder.

"You become more senile every day, old man," Rea hissed.

"But he's still right." Roash laughed.

"In the keep or in the forest?" Jestia yelled back at her.

"What?" Rea yelled back.

"The exchange ceremony—the forest or the keep?" Katrina yelled back.

"Oh for the love of the Nameless One," Rea mumbled.

"She says the forest will be fine!" Fleat yelled.

She turned to glare at him. "Old man, I will smother you in your sleep."

"As long as you tell everyone I died in a horrible hunting accident."

And why had she taken the old reprobate with her at all? Because his condition was not getting any better, and she didn't want him to die when she wasn't home. She didn't know why; she just didn't.

"You are a horrible turd," Rea told Fleat.

"Katrina, I did not tell you I would make an exchange!" Rea yelled up at her.

Katrina pretended not to hear her, so she rode her horse back up to ride on the other side of Katrina, turning her head to glare at Jestia across Katrina.

"Don't you think we should?" Katrina said.

"Why? Why would we do that? Things are fine the way they are now," Rea said.

"Come on, Rea," Jestia said. "You know you will bind yourself to her sooner or later because she isn't going to give up. And it would give Fleat both great pleasure and a since of relief for you to do it before he dies."

"Only because he loves nothing more than to see me squirm." But Rea looked back at him and for a moment could see the pain etched across his face. She looked back at Katrina. "Alright, we will make the exchange, but try not to make a huge, complicated mess out of it."

Rea turned to Fleat and yelled, "I said yes, you old fart! Are you happy now?"

"Ecstatic, Captain oh my Captain."

Rea brought Erah a bowl of food though she knew she would rather Laz brought it. She was glad Erah could talk and that she now combed her hair she had always cleaned her teeth. She still only half washed her hands. Rea was glad she had a better place to live, but she missed the time when she was the only one Erah talked to; when Era was still her project. As she walked in Erah put the kettle on for tea because of course Jestia had turned some old pot Erah had that had a hole in it into a beautiful tea kettle. Then she had taught her how to use it.

Rea handed her the bowl of food.

"Thank you." Erah said as she took it and went to sit in her chair.

Rea moved to sit down on the bed. "So, Katrina and I are going to make an exchange."

"What's that?"

"I will give her something I love; she will give me something she loves, and we will be bound to each other."

"What will you give her?"

"A necklace of rare stones my mother made for me." She took it from the top of her shirt where she wore it. "Truthfully, I have worn this since my mother died, and I think I will feel a little naked without it. But since I will always be with Katrina I will always have it, and you know very little sleep between the sex and the talking. The constant talking."

Erah nodded her head up and down excitedly, just understanding what Rea was talking about. "Bound... together."

"Yes. It wasn't really something I ever wanted, but she asked me and now that I know it is going to happen it seems like the most natural thing in the world. Now I just want it over with. We could have done it simple just the two of us, but no. She wants to have a ceremony with our friends and family watching, so would you like to come? It will be in the forest, and you would not have to get close to the crowd. It will be over quickly because it is already starting to get cold."

As Jestia had told them, the girl still didn't want to be around the town or a lot of them at once. She would hang at their fences and the tree line and watch them. She would wave at them, even yell "Hi!" at random Katabull, but she still had no desire to be part of their society, and Rea admitted she probably never would. She would most likely spend the rest of her life in this cave which since Jestia had fixed it up was nicer than anything Rea had ever lived in, so who could blame her.

Erah didn't answer her question about the ceremony. Instead she asked her own question. "How do... people bind?"

"I told you," Rea said, not understanding.

"No, *bind*." She slapped her hands together.

"Do you mean sex?"

"Yes." Erah nodded. "How do sex?"

"Me and Katrina?"

"No, man and woman." She slapped her hands together again. "Bind."

"Great, I get to be the one to tell you about sex. Well, at least it's a topic about which I know everything."

And so she had the sex talk with a woman damn near as old, if not as old, as she was who knew literally nothing about it. As Rea explained, Erah asked questions, and she ran the range of emotions from interested, to turned on, to disgusted—which meant Rea had done a thorough job.

As soon as word spread around the compound that Ufalla was sorry for what she had done, her family and all the Katabull stopped shunning her. She would have to prove herself to them, but for the moment she was part of them again which meant she was also expected to do her part.

She was working on one of the roads through the compound filling the holes with rocks and gravel. They all took turns doing it. It was Jabone and her brother Tarius's turn to do it, so they volunteered her to help. She didn't mind; in fact, it felt good to be doing something she used to do when she lived there. Good to work hard and not really think.

Something they had just said finally registered. "The colony has its own ships?"

"Yes, we gave them two," Jabone said.

"So Jestia could come home anytime she liked."

Both her brother and Jabone got very quiet in the way people did when they thought they might have said too much.

"She's not ready to come home yet," Ufalla said.

"And now you know how much she wants to kill you," her brother said with a laugh. Jabone cut him a look and he just shrugged. "Roughing it in the colony. Does that sound like Jestia at all?"

"He is right," Ufalla said. "Now I know." She kept scooping the gravel out of the wagon and throwing it on top of the rocks they had just put in the hole. "Of course what you are forgetting is that Jestia no longer has to rough it anywhere she goes. She can make whatever she wants from raw materials. She could live however she wanted to live there; she would never have to come home."

"It will be alright, Ufalla," Jabone said. "I think...I think she would not want to kill you so much unless she really loves you, so in time she will forgive you and not want to kill you anymore."

Ufalla laughed at what he had said. "Thanks, I feel better now."

"You know what I mean," Jabone said.

"It's the way you said it brother." Young Tarius laughed.

"What you said was worse," Jabone said.

"Yes, but I was trying to be an annoying turd," Tarius said.

"And you succeeded beyond your wildest dreams." Ufalla laughed.

"Well, not my wildest dreams. Those include half a dozen naked dancing girls and a bucket of blackberry jelly," young Tarius said.

They were working, cutting up and laughing. Normal felt good. It made Ufalla feel like she really would survive no matter what Jestia decided.

The ceremony was held on the edge of the forest, and most of the town was there.

Fleat sat in a chair in front of them and said, "Rea, daughter of Radkin and Rimmy, Tweed and Irvana, what do you bring to exchange with your love?"

It was cold, but Rea's face was sweating, and her hands were shaking. Why on earth was she so nervous? Fleat looked at her expectantly and smiled. She nodded that she understood she was supposed to do something now and then stumbled over the words she had practiced for a week and that weren't all that hard to say.

"This necklace, made by my mother's hand for me that I have worn every day since she died." She put it around Katrina's neck.

Katrina had tears in her eyes that she didn't shed, and when she smiled at Rea, Rea relaxed a little.

Fleat turned to Katrina. "Katrina, Daughter of Riley and Mazen, Len and Drazel, what do you bring to exchange with your love?"

"This stone plucked from the rivers of the Jethrik during the Great War by my Madra and given to me as a shifting gift that I have carried in my pocket ever since." She took the blue stone and stuck it in Rea's pocket.

"And now two are bound in love and friendship. May your lives be a journey you both want to take." Fleat, obviously choked up, lowered his voice just for them and said, "May you live and love as long and as hard as Heard and I did."

"Thank you Fleat," Rea said.

"Well maybe not as hard; I once put Heard through a wall."

Rea smiled, "Braggart."

Erah had come to the ceremony. She was standing well off in the forest just watching, and when Laz saw her he went to join her. He hadn't been sure she would come at all. She was worried that he was standing with her instead of closer, but he had assured her it was alright. But she wasn't really comfortable with it till at the start of the ceremony Rea had found them and looked right at them and smiled. As soon as the ceremony was over they all started back to town.

"Is it over?" Erah asked.

"The ceremony is, but they will go back to the keep now and there will be a huge feast with dancing and singing."

"It was very nice," Erah said.

"It was. It's only about the third exchange ceremony I have been to; most Katabull just do the exchange with their mate alone. This was the best one I have ever seen, but that might be because there was a time when I thought my sister would never be happy. That she would make all of us miserable for the rest of our lives."

"Rea?" Obviously Erah couldn't imagine that Rea could ever do anything wrong.

"Yep she used to be a wall-eyed mess. Trashing out her own life and everyone else's. I have to go to the party; I wish you would go," Laz said.

"I'm afraid."

"I understand. But there is really nothing to be afraid of, Erah. There will not be all the people that were here; it will just be the Marching Night. No one in the colony would hurt you, but certainly no one in the Marching Night would. They wouldn't want to, but even if they did, Rea is in charge and she would not allow it. Jestia will be there, and she would not allow it. *I* would not allow it. There will be so much food. Our cook Trin and his staff have been working for two days. There will be dancing and singing."

"I want to go Laz, but..."

"Then go with me. If you are afraid or even uncomfortable at all, you tell me and I will take you home."

"Well I'll be damned," Jestia said at her shoulder.

Rea turned to look where the witch was looking and said, "I will be damned as well."

Laz was walking into the keep hall with Erah on his arm. All fifty of the Marching Night that were in the Territories were in that room. Erah looked tentatively around, but didn't seem petrified as Rea would have thought she would be.

All around her the Marching Night grew quiet.

"Do not stop the party on our account," Laz said. "I have promised Erah there will be singing and dancing and much food."

Roash started to play his drum and Jestia started to sing as if they had planned it. Rea sat next to Katrina with her bowl of food.

Not too surprisingly, Erah seemed captivated by the witch's voice. Laz sat her at the table beside Rea and went to get food for both of them. Katrina leaned around Rea.

"What do you think, Erah?"

Erah smiled at them both took her finger and pointed to both of them then touched her heart and said, "Happy."

Katrina nodded and looked at Rea. "Yes, very happy."

"Jestia sings pretty," Erah said.

"Yes," Rea said, with her mouth full of food, "and it may be a spell, but I don't think it is."

Laz set a bowl of food in front of Erah and she started eating as she always did.

Across the table Fleat looked at the girl, laughed and said, "She is definitely one of us."

Erah smiled at him with most of a lobster tail stuffed in her mouth and started making yummy noises. When she had chewed it all up, shell and all, and swallowed it she looked at Laz, "This is better than bear; kill this for me."

"Take the shell off like this." He showed her.

She took it out of his hand and ate it. "It is even better!" she said.

Fleat looked from Erah to Laz and mouthed the words, "You are next." Laz was suddenly very interested in his food.

When they had all finished eating they moved the tables against the walls, and there was dancing to go with the singing.

Erah had listened to them sing and watched them dance longer that Rea expected her to stay, but early in the evening she'd had as much as she could take, and she had Laz walk her home.

They had just finished dancing to the fifth song in a row; Rea more fell into than sat in her chair. She looked at Katrina and said, "If you want to do anything more than dance tonight, that is it for me and dancing."

Katrina smiled at her. "I am glad we did this; I think everyone needed something to celebrate, but now I am ready to have you all to myself."

Rea stood up, took her hand and helped her to her feet, then started leading her out of the hall.

The others all started to whistle and tease them.

"I wonder where they are off to," Fleat said.

"To see if we can put each other through a wall," Rea said, and started to pull Katrina up the stairs after her.

More instruments had come out all night and then slowly they had gone away. Jestia still felt like singing, so she just kept doing so till the last musician told her he could not strum one more string. There were only a half dozen of them still in the hall, and when the music stopped they all got up and headed for the latrines and then bed.

Jestia was tired but didn't feel like sleeping, so she went upstairs to walk around the catwalk. When she walked past Rea's door she smiled; it was quiet in there now. It hadn't been an hour ago, but it was now.

Jestia was still humming the last tune she had sung when she walked out onto the catwalk.

The sentry nodded at her as she walked around going in the opposite direction. Jestia had thought about taking a lover; the woman was gorgeous, she was single, and Jestia could have her if she wanted her. But the more she thought about it the less it appealed to her. She'd had plenty of sex without any emotion attached to it; none of it was any better than what she could do with her own hand, so what was the point of involving another person maybe causing a bunch more drama. She'd had enough drama to last her a lifetime already, and she was most probably going to live hundreds and hundreds of years. She needed to pace herself.

Something caught her attention and made her look down over the rail. She stopped walking and saw Laz walking back into town. She smiled. *I never thought that girl would ever want to be around more than a couple of people at a time at best. When she buried the mummy because he wanted her to, that was huge. But coming to that party... She trusts him completely, and he is completely smitten with her. Look at him. It is the middle of the night, he is near skipping, and I'll bet all they were doing was talking. I used to have that, now I don't, and if I don't think about it I'm fine, but when I do I feel empty. But this place...this place is helping me. Here I have purpose. They need me now. They care about me and for me. They know I am hurting and they rush to bandage my wounds many times a day. Eventually I will go home, and when I do I will carry all these memories with me. I will carry these people in my heart and remember they are my pack.*

216

She pulled the stone from her pocket and wished it to be its original size. *There is a mine full of these. I can go any time and get as many as I want, but this one will always be my favorite because Laz got it for me just because I told him needed it. I had a brother I never bonded with. He died, and the only thing I ever grieved was that I never really knew him. I am closer to Rea and Laz than I ever was to him. Poor Katan, we will never know what he might have become because our father's drunken whoring killed him. And she knew...that Ufalla knew that...and she still chose to become my father. Round and round I go; I talk myself out of a funk then talk myself back in. But I am better; it doesn't last, and today... Today was a brilliant day.*

She looked at the stone in her hands and let herself feel the full weight of it; she let its power mingle with hers. She stood and for a minute just drank in the energy of the Everything. She let it wash all negative thoughts from her mind. Then she walked back in, set the stone on her dresser and went to bed while all she wanted to do was sleep.

Laz undressed and crawled into his bunk; all three of his bunk mates were asleep. Two of them were still in their Katabull sate which meant they had been drunk when they passed out. The third was the one who snored so loudly nothing could wake him up, so Laz hadn't even worried about how much noise he made. He took a deep breath and let it out, glad for the warmth of his bed. He had been on his way home from Erah's cave before he realized he should have worn his cloak. The hike to her cave had been chilly, but the hike back had been teeth-chattering frigid.

Winter was soon to show its teeth, and he was both excited and apprehensive about it. After all he had lived his entire life—except for the last few weeks—on a tropical island. When he'd gone to the Jethrik Territories to fight the Hive it had been early summer and warm. He had never seen snow. When the Great Leader had come in the snow the year before he hadn't been with them because his monkey had been acting sick. Since Riglid and Kaden, his father and Hared had been going, Tarius had told him to stay home and take care of the monkey. Pogo had been fine; just no doubt ate something that he shouldn't have. When

Laz found out they had all played in the snow he had wanted to wring that damned monkey's neck.

Laz was already wearing more clothes than he ever had in his life. He was excited to experience something new but worried that the cold might be more than he wanted to endure especially when he was so cold right now.

As he started to warm his thoughts went back over the day. He was very happy for Rea and Katrina. Riglid and Kaden had done an exchange a year and a half ago. Kaden's family had never been to a Katabull exchange or party, and they had been a little shocked, but a few drinks in they were as loud as any Katabull there.

His younger brother Jaden fell in and out of love so many times they no longer even bothered to learn his boyfriend's names because by the time they did he would be gone and there would be another one. Every time he was crushed, moody, and just bad company till he fell in love again and did it all over again. His father assured Laz that Jaden would grow up someday and find someone and settle down, but Laz wouldn't be surprised if he was as old as Fleat when that happened. It seemed to Laz that Jaden enjoyed his life the way it was; Jaden thrived on drama.

When Riglid had taken a human lover and then bound himself to him, Laz had been worried about him. Humans weren't Katabull; they weren't as hearty, and they didn't live nearly as long. Riglid was very serious and loved with his whole heart; if anything happened to Kaden, Riglid would be like their mother was when his madra died. But when he said as much to Riglid, he had said he wasn't afraid at all because he loved Kaden but knew he would outlive him. That he would enjoy every minute he had with him and have his memories when he was gone. Unless he felt he couldn't handle it, and then he would have Jestia split his years with Kaden as the Great Leader had done to Jena and their mother had done to Hestia.

Jestia was Riglid's back up plan. All of them had grown up around Jazel, but Jestia—even more than Jazel—easily did things that shouldn't have been possible. It happened so often that a conversation about whether Riglid should bind himself to a human ended with his very serious brother saying—as if it was as easy as tying his boots—that if he was worried about outliving his husband he would just have Jestia give Kaden half his life.

It wasn't till he saw how Erah reacted to Jestia's magic that he remembered how extraordinary magic really was. They rerouted a volcano, so what. They sent storms to drown a keep and stepped on a well of power and all glowed blue—happens every day. His mother gave half her life to her lover—big deal. The Great Leader's baby had three parents—all in a day's work.

When I saw the look of absolute awe and rapture on Erah's face as she saw even the smallest of Jestia's spells, I went back to a time when seeing Jazel make a light in her hand and set it in the air was a huge deal. How quickly I took for granted all the many things Jestia does. We all do because she makes it look effortless.

Poor Jestia. Her world has come apart, yet no one seemed happier to see my sister bound to Katrina. No one seemed to enjoy the party more. Love is never a sure thing. I know that, but my heart is pounding in my chest and even when I was walking home freezing my balls off my blood ran hot because I am in love. Now I even understand why Jaden acts so goofy all the time. When you are in love you know hundreds of things could go wrong: they might not love you back; they might fall out of love with you; you might fall out of love with them; it might all blow up in your face like Jestia's marriage. But you don't care because all of the "I just don't knows" is what makes it so wonderful.

Laz had actually been shocked when he had been able to talk Erah into going to the party with him. He was more surprised that she wanted to stay as long as she did. She was enjoying the singing the dancing and mostly the food. Which she had eaten more than he did, and he ate too much. There were a couple of times that she was overwhelmed and hid behind him or his sister, but for the most part she was more than alright; she was actually enjoying herself. At one point the look on her face told him she was about to get too much of a good thing, When he asked her if she wanted to leave she had said yes please, but as soon as they were outside she started talking about everything she had seen and asking questions.

What were they playing that made music? When he told her "instruments" she then wanted to know what the different ones were called. She asked about all the different foods and the songs and the stories, and...

When they got to the cave he said he should really get back to the party, but when she asked if he wouldn't like to have a cup of tea first he said yes, and... Well, he didn't get back till everyone except the witch was in bed asleep. He had seen her walk into her room as he came to the top of the stairs.

When they walked into the cave Erah got a candle she kept by the door, took it to the fireplace and lit it. Then she put it on a table in the middle of the room.

"That's new," Laz said of the table.

"Jestia made it for me and another chair." She pointed to it. "So I can have company for tea." She stirred the coals, threw some wood on the fire and put the kettle on. It wasn't cold in the cave at all, and he guessed that was why he was so surprised when he walked out of it into the late night cold.

"You know why she is so proper don't you?" Laz had said, taking a seat at the table.

Erah looked at him in a way that told him she had no idea what he was talking about, so he mimicked Jestia as best as he could. "Ohhhh...everything is so messy and way too crude. We must fix it all up and make it pretty. Your hair is a mess, Erah, here let me fix it. Your clothes are too baggy; let me make them fit. Now isn't that better?"

Erah laughed and he grinned then said, "She is like that because she is a Princess. Her mother is the queen of the Kartik, and someday Jestia will take the throne and she will be Queen, and then... the Nameless One help us all she will outlaw dirt and grease and make the horses shit in bags."

"But she is your sister."

"Her mother is Rea's madra and my mother's mate." Erah looked confused, which Laz guessed she had every right to be. "And you might as well know that Tarius the Black and her wife Jena have a baby with my father's husband. So Tarius and Jena are my stepmothers and their cubs are my brothers and sisters. Though in all of the world the only ones I am blood related to are my brother Riglid,

Tarius, Jabone, the babies Diana and Arvon, and maybe Elven—who is at least as old as Fleat." Then for reasons he couldn't have explained he told the names of everyone he considered to be family and just how they were connected to each other and him till her eyes were glazed over and he was sure she was more confused than ever he ended with. "They are all my family."

By the time he had finished they had already drunk two cups of tea.

"That's a lot," she said then she looked sad. "I had only Pandy."

"But now you have all of us," Laz said. "And Pandy is always with you in here." He pointed to his heart. "That is where I keep my madra and fadra."

She nodded, then the frown left her face and she was grinning from ear to ear as she said excitedly, "A song is just a story you sing."

"Yes exactly," Laz said. "And some songs the only story they tell is a feeling."

That was the point at which he decided he wasn't needed at the party, so he couldn't blame his staying on Erah because he was the one who just kept thinking of things he could talk about until he realized, *Gods and spiders, I am doing exactly what Katrina said she did. I don't want to just keep talking, but I do just to have a reason to stay with her because my feelings for her have turned into love.*

He had just kept talking about everything and nothing. She didn't seem bored, but finally she yawned just because it was very late and she was tired. Laz had said he'd better get back. At the door she had hugged him and he had hugged her back, but this time it felt different.

Mostly he admitted because after drinking all that tea her very tight hug almost made him pee himself. As she walked back in and closed the door he ran to the nearest tree and marked his territory. Then he had all but run home because of the cold.

Now in his bunk under his covers he was warm again and his thoughts of Erah warmed him more until he fell asleep.

"Babies up a tree!" Darian yelled. He ran to the bottom of the tree they were climbing. Pogo was on his shoulder. "You bad babies better come out of that tree right now."

On his shoulder Pogo was jumping up and down giving the babies what for, too. Darian looked around; they had all gone to the beach, and he realized only now how far they had gotten away from where their parents were. His madra and brother were running down the beach as fast as they could go.

"They will not get here in time. Pete, shift at once and go after them."

Pete shifted and was halfway up the tree when Arvon lost his grip on Diana. She lost her hold on the tree and started to fall. Pete made a grab for her but missed.

Darian stuck his hand up and yelled out, "Sister not fall, sister not fall, sister not fall!"

By the time his madra got there Diana was just hanging in the air and Pete was climbing down the tree with Arvon.

"Darian just cast his first spell!" his madra said excitedly. Darian's mother and their fadra were coming. Hared got there first.

"That's great, Tarius," his fadra said, "but our daughter is crying and about twelve feet off the ground."

And Diana was crying, too. "It's alright sister," Darian said. "You didn't fall, but maybe now you will learn not to climb trees."

"Much better hanging in the air than splattered on the ground," his mother said, as she stopped under Diana and looked up. She was trying to catch her breath. "You are alright, Diana."

When Diana saw their mother and heard her voice she stopped crying.

Pete came down the tree and handed Arvon to Jabone.

"Thank you Pete," Jabone said, and patted Pete's head. To Arvon Jabone said, "Boy, are you in trouble, mister."

His madra gently pushed his mother out of the way. "Darian, can you drop Diana into my arms?" she asked.

"Tarius, I do not like the word 'drop' in the same sentence as our daughter's name," their fadra said.

"Can you, Darian?"

He didn't know. He had just been so scared he had shouted and wished her not to fall. He looked at where she hung there, no longer screaming but still scared in a way he had never felt her be scared before. He lifted his hand and wished her to be in Madra's arms and then said, "Diana come down. Diana come down. Diana come down."

The baby dropped, and his madra caught her easily. Diana grabbed his madra's neck and held on tight. Their mother moved to rub Diana's back, and their fadra walked over and kissed her on her head.

Darian walked over, looked up at her, and caught her eyes. "Now maybe you will learn not to go where he tells you to."

He turned and caught Pete's eye. "Come on, Pete. Let's go swimming."

Pete nodded and they started towards the water.

Halfway there Darian ran back and tapped his fadra's shoulder. "Fadra, hold my monkey."

Then he ran to catch up with Pete.

"Is she alright?" Hared asked.

"Yes," Tarius said. "But she's still scared."

"Good."

Tarius spun her head to look at Jena in disbelief.

"I mean it. I realize you Katabull think fear is a horrible thing, but a little fear goes a long way towards stopping babies from doing stuff that could get them killed."

"I'm sorry, mother," Jabone said. "I was supposed to be watching them; I turned to look at the ship coming in for just a moment."

"A moment is all it takes for these two, or those two for that matter," Hared said, pointing at where the boys played in the serf. "And we cannot watch them every minute of every day. Jena is right, Tarius, maybe Diana needs to learn a little fear. Jabone's cub is always Katabull; our baby isn't even all Katabull, yet she thinks she has to do everything he does."

Tarius looked into her daughter's blue, blue eyes and said, more to Diana than to them, "She must not do such dangerous things. She must accept that he can do things she can't... Someday she will be a fierce Katabull, but for now..." Tarius ran her hand over the toddler's auburn hair. "For now we might have to let you be afraid." She handed the baby to Jena and started walking down to where the boys were playing in the ocean.

"Darian," she called, and he came trotting over.

"Am I in trouble?"

"Should you be?" Tarius asked with a smile.

He shook his head no.

Tarius started to sit on the ground, but the porters came running over with her throne and set it right where she was going to sit.

"Thank you." She sat down and patted her lap.

Darian trotted right over and crawled into her lap, getting sand and water all over her. She didn't care; the same would have happened if she had sat on the beach anyway. She hugged him tightly to her and looked out at the water. "You are a very good big brother and uncle. Thank you for always watching out for them"

"Well you can't watch them by yourselves. There are only six of you between those two babies, and they are a handful."

That was rather the pot calling the kettle black, but Tarius grinned and kissed the top of his head. "Yes they are. So, Mister Wizard, how do you feel?"

"What do you mean, Madra?"

"You just cast your first spell. Are you tired? Do you feel weird?"

"Should I?" Darian asked.

"I don't know, but sometimes when wizards and witches cast spells it makes them tired, and you are very young. I love you so much, Darian."

"I love you." He nodded and leaned up to kiss her on the cheek. "You worry too much, Madra."

"Do I?"

"Yes you do. I will be alright. Can I go play now?"

She nodded and he climbed off her lap. "Send your brother back to me."

In seconds Pete was standing in front of her. She patted her lap and he climbed up to sit on it and hugged her neck.

"You give the best hugs, Pete," she said. "You are the very best big brother and uncle ever."

"But I didn't catch sister, Madra." He looked close to tears.

"You couldn't, Pete. I saw you try. She was way too far away from you. Sometimes it doesn't matter what you do, it only matters what you meant to do, and you went on up and got Arvon. You always watch out for Darian, and son, on a good day that is a full-time job." She smiled at him and hugged him tight. "You are very quiet, Pete, and because of that you don't always get as much attention as crying babies who won't stop climbing trees or your brother who talks so much he even talks to whales, monkeys and feral humans. But many days it is your smile that most warms my heart, your face I most want to see. You give so much and ask so little. Your parents loved you very, very much; thank you for letting me love you, too."

She kissed his cheek and he hugged her neck again.

"I love you, Madra."

"I always know that. Now go and play."

She watched him run down the beach to play with his brother. *Neither of them has even an ounce of my blood flowing in them, yet I feel the same for them that I do for the children that are my blood. Their souls touch mine in a different way—in some ways a closer way. I just saw something I can't ignore. Those two will finish what I have only started. Did we bless them when we took them or curse them? No, without us to teach them they would not be ready to face whatever they will face. It is time for me to not just put swords in my sons' hands, but to start training them for combat.*

Rea woke, stretched, then moved to wrap herself around Katrina. The air was cold, the bed was warm, the woman in bed with her was warmer, and getting up could wait.

Katrina rolled in her arms till they were face to face. "You know what I just thought of?"

"No, what?" Rea kissed her quickly.

"If you kiss me again, I will not be able to think at all."

"Will it stop you from talking?"

"You know it will not." Katrina pulled herself more tightly to Rea. "None of our parents know that we are bound to each other."

"So?"

"Think about it for a minute. Usually when you are going to make an exchange the first people you tell are your parents. Two cubs have been born here, and no grandparents."

"But there are old people fighting to hold them all the time," Rea said.

"True, but it's not quite the same. Next time the Great Leader is here I think I will ask her to bring my parents the next time she comes."

"Or you could go on one of our ships in the spring to visit home. Maybe some of the others would like to go as well."

"Would you go with me?"

"I don't think I can. I'm captain. Who would run the colony? But you wouldn't go for long. It is a three-day trip, tops, and if you stay three days you would only be gone nine days total. I think I could live without you for that long."

"But I don't know that *I* can live without *you* that long." Then Katrina was all over her, and holding her off would have been more work than Rea wanted to do so early in the morning.

When they finished coupling Rea sat on the edge of the bed and pulled on her pants. She turned to look at Katrina. "You know, Katrina..."

"What?" Katrina prompted, and got on her knees on the bed to wrap her arms around Rea and rest her head on her shoulder.

"If you were gone even a day I would miss you."

"I know that, my love, and if I was gone for nine whole days I would spend the whole time thinking about what my homecoming would be. It might be worth it to go just for the 'I'm home' sex." She let Rea go, climbed out of bed and started to dress. "Don't you ever get homesick?"

"In the winter when it is so cold and there is nothing to do," Rea said, with a grin. "But my woman has built a library, so if I get bored I will lay around in bed and read about doing things I can't be do because it is so cold. Oh, but wait! You are my woman, so my bed will be warm but no doubt I won't be able to read because she who built the library because she loves books will not shut up or keep her hands off me long enough for me to read a stinking book so... I will not get homesick at all."

Rimmy watched as Tarius put a practice blade in Pete's hands then stood him up on her feet in front of her. She placed his hands in the right spots on the sword, put her hands over his, and started to walk around with him slinging the sword. Till now all any of them had done with him or Darian was grab practice blades and let them run at them swinging as they blocked their blows. It was an exercise that taught a cub how to find the holes, and when Pete occasionally hit one of them they were proud of him and he was excited. The cubs always watched them practice, and occasionally Tarius would show them how a blow was thrown or blocked.

Tarius put a blade in her cubs' hands as soon as they could walk, but now Tarius was actually training Pete.

"He is only nine," Hared said. He had walked up behind Rimmy and then he leaned against him, resting his head on Rimmy's shoulder.

"I was just thinking I was surprised she has waited this long. He is nine already. The years get away from us my love," Rimmy said.

The look on Pete's face was pure ecstasy.

"He was made for the sword," Hared said.

"Why do I hear unease in your voice?" Rimmy asked.

"Have you not noticed how tense Tarius has been since Persius and Hellibolt's last visit?"

Persius came with Hellibolt to visit his daughter and grandson about twice a year now. While Persius had mostly played with the cub, Hellibolt and Tarius had gone off to have one long discussion after another.

"I have," Rimmy said.

"And do you know why?" Because Hared didn't.

Rimmy did; he knew exactly why. But though his son was now her runner in his stead, Rimmy still did not tell the things Tarius told him because of his past position. He carefully weighed what he knew and what he could tell.

"Persius has set up a network of spies in his country to find Amalite missionaries the same as the queen did here. He thought it was good that they have found and killed so many members of the cult, but when he told Tarius how many they had found... Tarius thinks the fact that there are so many means that they might have acted too late."

"What are you saying, Rimmy?"

Rimmy forced a smile he didn't feel and said, "It is Tarius, Hared. You know how she is. One is too many and three means there will soon be a war."

Tarius lifted the boy from her feet and set him in the ground.

"Hared! Come here take a practice blade and let me see what Pete has learned."

Hared ran over and took a blade.

As Hared sparred with their son, Rimmy was not surprised at all to see that Pete had learned nearly everything Tarius had just showed him. Pete had always been a fast learner, and he always listened to every word Tarius said.

It was good that she was training him; it was the reason she was that bothered Rimmy. She wouldn't talk about it except to say she'd had another vision and felt it was time for the boys to learn to fight. And this was what he knew about Tarius. If what she was saying was enough to worry you, then what she wasn't saying was much worse.

When she finished Pete's lesson and called Darian over and started to train him as well, Rimmy knew that what she wasn't saying was even more than he thought.

Darian walked over to Rimmy. "Father, please hold Pogo. I go to learn to be a battle mage like Jestia."

Rimmy took the monkey and it ran up his arm to sit on his shoulder. He watched the five-year-old walk over, pick up a practice sword, and run over to his madra.

"Gods and spiders, I hope not like Jestia," he mumbled.

The monkey looked at him and started chattering. "Shut up, you damn monkey."

Chapter Fourteen

Jestia stood with Rea and Katrina on the catwalk with twenty other members of the Marching Night who had crowded out there when the sentry had yelled down that it was starting to snow.

Jestia had never seen the snow. The others had been here over two years, so this was their third time to see the first snow fall of the year. Yet the fact that so many of them rushed to see it showed that they still saw it as a novelty.

As she watched the big flakes fall faster and harder she was reminded that her magic came from the world. Magic happened all the time. She took a deep breath, let it out, and then spun around in it looking up and letting the cold flakes hit her face. She started laughing. "This is amazing."

"It always is until you are slogging through it every day for months, and then it loses its appeal," Rea said. Yet when Jestia stopped spinning and turned to look at Rea she was smiling. "I'm going to bring Erah something to eat before the snow gets worse."

"It will snow harder than this?" Jestia asked.

"Oh, it's just getting started. Come on." Rea led her to the other side of the catwalk. She pointed. "Look that way, do you see the port?"

"I can hardly see the buildings across the street," Jestia said in excitement.

"The storm is coming in from the ocean." Katrina had followed them. "All the biggest snow storms seem to start in the ocean."

"Can I go with you?" Jestia asked Rea.

"Are you going to pop us there?" Rea asked, making a face.

"No, I want to walk in the snow storm."

By the time they got to the cave there was already three inches of snow on the ground and they were covered in it.

They knocked on the door and Erah yelled, "Come in!"

As they walked through the door Jestia did some spell that removed all the snow from them. Rea took her cloak off and hung it up out of habit anyway. There were piles of dried plant life, bark, mushrooms and fungus everywhere. Rea had seen it before and knew what it was—all year the girl collected food from the forest; as the first snow fell she did an inventory of what she had then stored it for the winter.

"What's all this?" Jestia walked over and picked up some dried root.

"It's food," Rea said. She walked over and handed Erah the bowl of food she had brought her.

"This is not food; it's mandrake. It's a medicinal plant."

Erah tapped at her head. "For bad head, bad blood." She sat down and started eating the food Rea had brought her. "Tea is on."

"What about this one?" Jestia held up a bundle of what looked to Rea like green sticks.

"Bad belly," Erah said.

"And this?" Jestia held up what looked like dried white flowers.

"Fever."

"Erah, did Pandy teach you this?"

It was obvious by the way she looked at Jestia that she had no idea what she was asking her.

"Where did you learn about plants?" Jestia asked.

"I just know." Erah shrugged. "I walk through the forest. The plants tell me what they can do."

"Plants talk to her. That's not crazy at all," Rea mumbled. She would have sat down, but every surface was covered in dried stuff.

"What do you mean?" Jestia asked Erah, ignoring Rea.

"I walk through the forest. I will see a plant. I will touch it, smell it, and I will know what it's good for. Good to eat, good to drink, good medicine."

"How do you know?" Jestia asked.

"I see it in my head," Erah said. It was clear she didn't understand what Jestia didn't understand about that. Which was really funny since Jestia was always and forever spouting things no one could understand and then looking at them all like they were imbeciles because they just didn't get what seemed so simple to her.

Jestia picked up another bunch of herbs, held it up towards Rea and said, "This is how she made it out here all those years. She knows plants."

She looked at Erah. "That's your magic, Erah. You know what plants are good for without anyone telling you. Rea can't do that. I'm the most powerful witch the Great Leader knows, and I can't do that. I had to learn it. I can't just grab a plant and know what it's good for."

Jestia seemed really excited. Rea wasn't really sure why till Jestia turned to Rea and said, "Don't you get it, Rea? This is an apothecary, and she knows what plants will heal which ailments if any of you get sick."

"With just a little work I could teach Erah how to make potions and powders. She could teach me about plants you have here that we don't have at home some might even be better at curing different ailments than what we have. It would give you something else to trade with the mainland. Alright, go home. I'm going to stay here and work with Erah."

Next thing Rea knew she was standing on the catwalk in five inches of snow. "Dammit, Jestia!" She quickly went inside. After all her cloak was still at Erah's.

She went to her room and grabbed her other cloak. When she went downstairs no one was there but Fleat. "Where'd everyone go?"

"Out to play in the snow," Fleat said. "You'll get no work out of them today. I'm guessing since you came from upstairs and I didn't see you come in the front door that Jestia popped you home."

"Yes, well I was in the way of her figuring out everything she can about Erah's magic ability which... Well Jestia wasn't interested in it at all till today when she figured out it has something to do with being able to find medicinal plants." Rea shrugged. "I might have learned more but you know Jestia was too excited about what she wanted to do to explain it to me so she just sent me back to get me out of her way."

Fleat laughed. "Well at least she didn't make you walk home in the snow."

"But she sent me home without my heavy cloak. Now I have to run around and check that everything that is supposed to be put away is put away, that everything that needs to be stored out of cold has been, because as you said I will get no work out of any of them today. And I have to do it in this rag I wore out two winters ago because my cloak is still hanging at Erah's."

"What you need is a coat. Surely you have some nice fur from one of your many kills... Oh, that's right, you've only killed one thing the whole time we've been here and you gave its hide to the Great Leader for her to make a tent." Then he made an attempt to imitate her voice which had him talking in a falsetto much higher than anything that had ever come out of her mouth. "No Great Leader I want you to have it. We have so many skins here. I will doubtless kill three more bigger than that one next week."

Rea smiled and shook her head. "That is not what I said, you mean old fart. But a coat would be nice, and I am wishing I wasn't so quick to give away my only hide. I bet I can talk someone out of a nice bear skin."

"If you listen intently to her and ask her nicely I'm sure your woman would make you a coat from it."

"It would be easier to just ask Jestia to make the skin into a coat. You know if she isn't too busy training Erah."

"A hedge witch would be a good thing for the colony to have. Your coat may have to wait," Fleat said,

Rea looked at Fleat and grinned. "Be nice to Katrina and listen to her, make the coat myself or... just wear this raggedy cloak." She slung it on went to the door and went through. As she was closing the door she could hear Fleat laughing. She wondered how many more times she would get to hear her friend laugh.

Before she had a chance to get maudlin she heard the sound of Katabull at play. They were smacking each other with snowballs, making statues from it, running around and skidding in it, sometimes falling on their asses. The whole time yelling at one another and laughing.

When they all got to a point where they were too cold for it to be fun they'd run inside and warm up. Then many of them would come right back out and play some more. They had done it with the first snow every year since they got here. Rea thought maybe they needed to name it and make it into a real celebration with a feast. She would make the checks she needed to make, and then she would play with them.

She had just finished making the last of the checks on the docks and walked back into town when a huge snowball crashed into the side of her head. She spun towards the direction it had come from, and there was Laz. Her brother was so covered in snow that she nearly needed to sniff him to recognize him. It was still coming down, and he had obviously been playing in since it started. He was a big kid on most days, and this was his first time to see snow. She shook her head to get the snow out of her ear. Then she bent down, made her own snowball, and chunked it at his junk. He moved his hands quickly to protect the family jewels then dove to the ground, rolled, came up and threw another one at her. This one she dodged away from.

They were soon joined by others that Laz had obviously been playing with when he broke ranks to come after her. It was a free for all that left them with skin stinging and no few bruises. At one point Katrina ran up behind her and tackled her to the ground. They rolled around in the snow for a minute before Rea wound up on top—which was her favorite place to be.

Laz ran up to them. "I'm going to go see Erah."

"What you're going to do is freeze your ass off," Rea said. "You are covered in snow and most likely wet to your skin."

"I was going to change my clothes first and warm up a minute." He started to run towards the keep.

"Bring my good cloak back with you please!" Rea yelled after him.

"Will do!" he yelled back, and then he was gone.

Rea looked down at Katrina. Rea had both of her hands pinned. Rea smiled at her. "You don't always have to make it so easy for me to win."

Katrina started to struggle underneath her, gave up and smiled at her. "I wish I was letting you win."

She tried to get loose again, so Rea let her go, stood up and put down a hand to help her. Katrina took her hand, and Rea pulled her up and into her arms and held her.

"I'm cold. Are you cold?" Rea asked.

Katrina nodded.

"Then let's go home. I'll warm you up if you warm me up."

She winked, and Katrina laughed, took her hand and started dragging her back to the keep, so Rea ran and made Katrina work to keep up.

By the time Laz got to Erah's he was cold again. The snow had slowed down but was still falling. He was walking in what he guessed was about six inches of the stuff. He knocked and heard Erah's voice tell him to come in. When he came through the door and closed it behind him Erah ran over and started not so much brushing as pounding the snow off of him.

"Oh, what are you doing here?" Jestia said, sounding put out.

"I was about to ask you the same thing," Laz said, every bit as put out.

"I'm teaching Erah to mix potions," Jestia said.

Erah was busy taking Laz's cloak off. Then when she had hung it on the elk antler she had hung by the front door as a kind of coat rack, she took his hand and led him to the fire. He held his hands close to the fire and warmed them.

Jestia sighed. "Argh! It is hard enough to make her focus without you here distracting her."

"I am making medicine," Erah told Laz. "Look." She walked over to where there was a new set of shelves covered in jars filled with the things she had dried. There was a small work bench in front of the shelves, and on it was a small mortar and pestle made from cornelian from the old mineshaft. "Jestia made me apotho-hairy."

"Apothecary, but that is closer than she's gotten yet, so you might all just have to deal with going to the apotho-hairy to get your herbs and potions," Jestia said.

Of course Jestia had made all this stuff. How else would Erah have gotten it, but why?

Reading the confused look on his face Jestia said, "I didn't get the herbs, Laz. Erah had them. I told you she might have a little magic. Well, it turns out her gift is finding medicinal plants. It's how she saved Pandy, how she kept her alive as long as she did, and it's how she could survive out here alone. If Erah touches a plant she knows what it's good for, or if it's poison. Well, I might as well go. Now you're here it will be the two of you just staring at each other with lust in your eyes."

She looked at Erah. "I will come and continue your training tomorrow." Then she was gone.

It might have been nice if she had given him some warning; he would have had her bring his sister's cloak back to her. Though he guessed as cold as it was he wouldn't mind having both his and hers to go home in.

Erah walked over and hugged him. "First snow," she said.

He hugged her back. When they parted he walked over to sit at the table and Erah put the kettle on.

"It's my first snow ever," Laz said, still excited about it.

She gave him an odd look.

"Where we come from it never snows. It never even really gets cold, not cold like it does here anyway."

"The Kartik, I know."

Laz smiled. "That's right, the Kartik. It's about three days by sea that way." He pointed.

"I know." Well of course she did. Pandy had been a Kartik bard, so Erah probably knew almost as much about the Kartik as he did. "You've been here before. It snows here a lot."

"But I've never been in the Territories in winter before. The first time we came here in the cold there was no snow, and last time my family came when there was snow I was not with them," Laz said. She nodded. "Everyone tells me I will get tired of it, but right now... To me it's like magic, a new adventure." He looked at the cornelian mortar and pestle thinking it was awful fancy for a hedge witch who lived in a cave. "You know, Erah, you don't have to do everything Jestia tells you to."

She sat down across from him.

"I want to learn. If I learn then I can help the colony. You and Rea are always bringing me food. Jestia did all this to my cave. Now I am much warmer and no smoke. I would like to give back. I know about plants, but she is teaching me how to mix the different plants together to make potions for even more illnesses. How to grind them to make powders."

"I'm sure you will be very good at it. Garrett is a decent medic, but he is more about taking care of wounds. He can give people powders, but I don't think he even knows what's in them much less how to make them. It will be huge for the colony to have someone to go to when they are sick but don't need to be stitched up." Laz got up walked to the window and looked out. "It's beautiful, and you know what I noticed walking here, it's so quiet."

"It will get quieter. In hard winter the forest sleeps. The bears sleep, the porcupines sleep, but the wolves do not sleep, and they are hungry," Erah said. "Since you have come there are not as many wolves, or bears or lions." She brought him a cup of tea and pressed it into his hand. She stood at the window with him and looked out. "The Katabull have killed so many."

"Tarius said it is not because we have killed them out, it is because of our latrines," Laz said, with a smile thinking about the conversation.

"Latrines?"

"Where we crap. Tarius said the predators quit coming through our town because we have eaten so many of them. She said when they get close they can smell our crap and they think, *Something bigger and badder than we are has been eating our kind, run away, run away, run away faster.*" Laz laughed and looked down at Erah. "To the people outside the compound, the Great Leader is the picture of the kingdom warlord; very serious, stern, a fierce warrior. But among our people she is very wise, loving and really, really funny."

She looked up at him. "Can you tell me a story, Laz?" She took his hand and held it. She still didn't talk much. He was always worried he was talking too much, but she never seemed to want him to go, and she never told him to be quiet. He was no bard by any stretch of the imagination, but if she could get him to tell a story she would sit, watch him, and listen intently to every word as if he was the greatest bard who had ever lived.

"I can," he said. "But I'm really not very good at it and I feel...I feel like I talk way too much and you never get to talk."

"You are good." She let go of his hand, got up and went to make more tea. "Laz, since Pandy died... I talked to myself all the time, but no one ever talked back. When I could no longer remember what Pandy sounded like... for so long the only voice I ever heard was my own. Then you all came here and I heard you but couldn't understand you. You all know so much about everything, but all I know is what Pandy taught me and how to live in this place. That is why I want to learn whatever Jestia wants to teach me. When you tell me stories, the sound of your voice reminds me I am no longer alone. I learn things about other people and the world that I don't know." She brought the tea over, sat down, and looked at him expectantly.

Laz smiled. "What kind of story would you like to hear?"

"Tell me one where the Great Leader is funny."

"I know just the story, though my brother Riglid doesn't think it is funny at all... See the water in the compound had turned white. The Great Leader took Riglid and went to check the spring we get our water from..."

When he had finished the story Erah laughed and pounded the table. "It is funny because she only pretended to be dead."

Laz nodded and realized that Pandy had taught Erah to have a sense of humor that his brother Riglid did not have. "Riglid's husband Kaden tells it much better, but when he does Riglid gets so mad he leaves. My brother Riglid is very serious but very brave, and there is no one I love better. There is nothing Riglid wouldn't do for the people he loves."

"I would do anything for you, Laz," Erah said

He smiled. "And I would do anything for you, Erah."

"I asked Rea about coupling," Erah said.

"Well at least it is something she's an expert on," Laz mumbled, some embarrassed.

"I asked Jestia, too."

"The Nameless One alone knows what Jestia told you."

"That men stick their thing in you, jump up and down a couple of times, grunt a lot, then ask if you liked it. If you lie and say yes you have done it right." Erah grinned. "But then she said she doesn't like boys because they spit."

"Ahh...is there a reason you are telling me this?"

"I thought you should tell me about coupling."

"Me? But ah..."

"Or you could just show me."

Laz lay there holding her and refused to ask her if she liked it. *Stupid Jestia. And I can tell my sister told her about coupling because she wasn't afraid and she knew things I did not know.*

"I love you," he said. It was something he had learned from losing both his parents so young. You said what you felt when you felt it.

She turned in his arms and kissed him on the chin. "I liked it, and it's not a lie."

Laz smiled and kissed her on the forehead then said, "Then according to the witch you have done it wrong."

"I don't think I did."

She rested her head against his chest, and in seconds she was asleep. He wasn't far behind her.

When he woke it was dark, and he woke because Erah was rubbing herself against him. "Again," she said.

"Erah... My sister will be worried about me; she will come looking for me."

"No because she has already been here and she brought enough food for both of us. When she saw you were in bed she said to tell you..." She cleared her throat. "...do not try to come home after dark; it is too cold. And do not impregnate that girl."

Laz laughed and shook his head. "I would not." He kissed her, shocked that she would rather couple than eat. Of course afterwards when he got up and went to the table he found that her bowl was already empty. He realized his sister had come in daylight and he had slept right through her entire exchange with Erah. Playing in the snow and then being with Erah had made him tired enough he had not even heard Rea come in. Of course he had been completely relaxed and not on guard at all.

Erah took his bowl. And he laughed. "That is my food; you already ate yours."

"I was going to put it on the hearth to warm it. I would not eat your food." She sounded almost insulted. She set the bowl on the hearth to warm it up. "It is bear and squash with peppers and garlic..." Then she named every spice that was in it.

"How do you know that?" he asked. Most of them were spices that had been brought here from the Kartik.

"Jestia told me their names, and I could taste them in the food. I just know." She shrugged.

He smiled and wondered if she had enough magic that she might at least live as long as he was going to.

"You should live here," she told him. "I do not snore, and my bed is bigger. It is warmer here."

"I will live here if you will go to town with me and eat with the others from time to time."

She seemed to think about it for a minute then smiled and said, "I can do that."

Rea had just sat down with Katrina to eat when Laz walked in with Erah.

"I told you so," Rea said to her mate, who had insisted Laz would not spend the night with Erah nor would he bring her for breakfast.

Rea watched as Erah pounded the snow off herself and then watched as she pounded the snow off Laz as well. Then Laz walked over and handed Rea her cloak which she hung on the back of her chair.

"I didn't know it would take you so long, or I would not have asked you to bring me my cloak," she said, grinning at her brother. Of course she didn't mention that she had forgotten to get it when she was there the day before. "Good morning, Erah."

"I coupled with your brother, so now you can call me sister," Erah said.

Rea watched as her brother's face turned bright red.

"Well, at least she understands how the Katabull pick family," Jestia said, as she walked in the hall. She looked Laz up and down, grinned and said, "I knew I should not leave you two alone." Jestia got a bowl and got in line.

"I wouldn't want to do it with you there," Erah said, making a face. Then as if she had done it every day of her life she went and got a bowl and got in line.

Fleat laughed. "Oh boy," he said to Laz. "You have got your hands full."

"Well not right this minute," Rea said.

They all laughed.

"Come on knock it off," Laz said.

He left to get a bowl and stand in line behind Erah. She grinned up at him and he smiled back. Rea was happy for them.

Fleat shrugged looked at Rea and said, "I must tease him at least as much as I do you and Katrina, or he will think I don't like him as well."

"You could like me less, old man," Rea said with a smile.

"Could I?" Fleat asked.

Jestia looked from Laz to Erah. "I can't even act surprised. Well, I could but," she shrugged and looked at Erah. "So, did you forget everything you learned yesterday?"

Erah looked confused, "About what?"

"Medicine," Jestia said slowly, and grinned as Laz had turned red yet again.

It was funny because she wouldn't have thought he would be easily embarrassed. In fact, she knew he wasn't. *It is because he loves her, but is afraid of what we will all think because after all she is mostly a wild human. I will let him off the hook.*

"We love who we love, Laz. It doesn't matter what anyone else thinks. And if you ask me, and really who else's opinion matters, you are well matched."

Laz looked at her in shock. "Thank you Jestia," he said.

"Yes, well don't expect me to be nice all the time. It hurts me, but while I'm in the mood... You know the others are only teasing you because they approve. If they didn't; they would not tease you. They would tell you that what you are doing is wrong because you Katabull are blunt as hell."

Laz nodded and smiled. "I will not tell anyone you were nice."

"Good. I have a reputation to uphold."

She looked at Erah then. "When we have eaten, you and I will go back to the cave for your next lesson. Laz will not go because he will distract you and you have much to learn in a short period of time."

"Are you thinking of leaving soon, Jestia?" Laz asked.

"I would not commandeer one of your ships to go home, and I am not quite ready. Tarius will come in the next few weeks with supplies. When she does I will be ready, and I will leave with her." It was finally her turn, and she filled her bowl quickly seeing that Erah's mouth was watering. As she moved away so Erah could fill her bowl she turned to Laz. "I can't afford to stay here licking my wounds. My next task is at hand, and to do it I will have to go home first."

Laz watched Jestia walk away and turned to Erah who was trying to get absolutely as much food in her bowl as would fit. "That couldn't be good."

"What?" Erah asked, starting towards the table moving slowly to keep from spilling her bowl.

Laz started to fill his. As he followed her to the tables he answered. "When Jestia says something like that there is more in what she doesn't say than what she does."

"Ask her what she means."

"She will not answer, Erah, because she can't. It is hard to explain; almost as hard as it is to understand."

"So are you," Erah said with a grin.

He went over what he had just said and decided he couldn't argue with her. Erah sat next to Jestia and pointed to the seat next to her; he sat beside Erah where she indicated he should.

"So," Fleat started. "Your mother sleeps with the queen, and yet it is you two who let your women order you around."

Laz tried to think of a comeback, but he didn't have to because Rea said, "Old man I have seen you have an argument with your hand, so don't act like you don't let your partner pull you around by your junk." They all laughed, including Fleat.

"See?" Jestia said.

Laz smiled and nodded.

The Territories

Chapter Fifteen

Tarius sat on her throne at their fire pit outside their hut. Diana and Arvon were playing with sticks in the dirt at her feet. Jena had taken Darian and Pete to the lake, so the monkey was on her shoulder. She looked across the fire at her uncle who sat on a chair.

"Are you sure, Elven?"

"I have given it a lot of thought," he said. "I have been happy enough these last few years getting to know the family I thought I had lost. But I lived alone a long time. Though I love you all there are a lot of you, and the cubs are a delight, but… It's a lot of noise."

Tarius smiled. "Surely not my cubs."

"Especially your cubs." Elven laughed. "And more so your grandson."

"I can't promise that the Territories won't be as noisy," she said.

"I have heard you and others talking about how different and how wild it is. I would like one more adventure before I am food for the worms. And let's face it; no one really needs me here. But *there*…there is much I could do and teach much I could them. Do not sit there and tell me you yourself will not go there when your days are numbered because I have heard you tell your grown son as much."

Tarius nodded. "But when we leave port in a few weeks we will be getting there just as it starts to get bitterly cold. Perhaps you should wait till we go in the spring."

"I could die before then, and… I really want to see this snow you have all talked about. Are the Marching Night's quarters not heated?"

"They are." She smiled and nodded. "You will travel with us when we go, then. I will miss seeing you here, but if you don't die too soon I will see you whenever we go to the Territories. However I must warn you, with the exception of my grandson and this damn monkey the rest of the noise will be on the voyage with us."

"The adventure will begin," he said with a laugh.

Diana stopped playing, walked over to Elven and crawled up in his lap; he hugged her. She was trying to show him something she had in her hand, a dirt clod or a stick. Elven pretended to be very interested in whatever it was.

"No offence, Tarius, but this one here, she is the one I will miss most. The one I will most look forward to seeing if I live long enough for you to come back to the Territories." He kissed Diana on the top of her head and she kissed him on the cheek then she got down and went back to play with Arvon. "When I see her, play with her, it takes me back to a time when our pack was whole. When Shandra was alive and you were her cub that I played with."

"And of course," Tarius said in a whisper, "she is the most beautiful of all of my cubs."

"Because she looks like both you and the beautiful Jena and only slightly like that guy Hared," Elven said.

"I heard that old man," Hared said, walking up and adding a couple of fish he had just butchered out to the pot that sat over their fire. "We will all miss you. Because with you gone who will be here to tell us that we are all doing everything wrong?"

"Or that we are stupid beyond belief," Rimmy said, walking out to dump the vegetables he had just chopped up into the pot.

Jena had dumped all the herbs in the pot before she left. What had Tarius done towards getting dinner ready? She had watched the cubs. Hared, Jena and Rimmy had all gotten off easy.

"Oh aye," Elvin said with a laugh. "It is a duty I do not take lightly. No doubt you will all perish without me. Except Diana who is smarter than the rest of you."

"She is that," Hared said.

Diana once again stopped playing with Arvon. She walked over to Hared.

"Fadra, pick me up," she said.

"Please might be nice," Tarius told her. But of course Hared had already picked her up.

She looked into the pot then at Hared. "Done?"

"Child you slay me," Tarius said. "You act like you are starving, and yet not that long ago we all ate lunch."

She looked at Tarius and shrugged. The monkey picked that moment to start screeching, so Arvon climbed up her leg, up her body and onto the shoulder the monkey wasn't on and started chattering back at him as if noise were a contest.

The reason for the monkey's chattering became obvious when she looked up and saw Darian and Pete coming at a run. They were both dripping wet, and they stopped a few feet in front of her.

Darian said to the monkey, "Pogo, be quiet. You know that Madra said she would eat you if you screamed in her ear again."

The monkey shut up and held his hands over his mouth. Arvon pointed and laughed at the monkey.

Tarius said, "You shut up too, mister."

Tarius looked from Pete to Darian. "Where is your mama?"

"She is coming," Pete said, but it was the way he said it.

"What did you do?" Tarius demanded of Darian.

Darian walked over and took the monkey from her and Arvon screeched nearly as loudly as the monkey had to show his disapproval.

"What did you do?" Tarius demanded of Darian. She stood up, took Arvon off her head and set him on the ground.

"She isn't hurt, and it was an accident," Darian said quickly.

Tarius could see Jena coming up the trail then. She was wet from head to toe and so mad steam was nearly coming from her ears.

"Your sons!" Jena yelled when she was in hearing range.

Tarius looked at them in turn. "Since you are my sons and not hers, what is it you have done?"

"It was an accident," Darian said again. Then as Jena got closer he went to hide behind Rimmy, so Pete did, too.

"I will not protect you from your mother's wrath; she can be mean," Rimmy said.

Hared nodded in agreement.

"What did you do?" Tarius demanded of Darian again.

"We were just trying to build a raft," Darian said, shrugging.

Tarius turned to look at Pete, and he broke. "Mama was laying on a rock by the water. She told us not to get her wet."

"Then why is Mama drenched?" Tarius asked.

"We tied a bunch of logs together. When we flipped it in the water it got Mama wet," Darian said. He shrugged. "See? An accident."

Jena arrived then looking like a drowned rat. She pointed at the boys who were still hiding behind Rimmy. Tarius knew better than to laugh, but Hared was not as smart.

Jena turned on him fire in her eyes. "I will rip your tongue out of your head."

"See what I mean?" Rimmy said to the boys, and they nodded.

"I told you I didn't want to get wet. This is my new dress," Jena said.

"It was an accident, Mama." Darian said.

"Was it? Because when I saw what you had built I told you not to flip it in the water and get me wet."

"No, you said we couldn't get it in the water without flipping it in and getting you all wet," Darian said.

"Son," Tarius sighed. "Can you not see that is the same thing? Look at your poor Mama. She took you to go swimming, and all she asked was that you not get her all wet."

"Sorry, Mama," the boys said at once.

"No dinner for you," Jena said.

Darian looked in the pot and then turned to Pete. "It's fish." Pete nodded. They were obviously alright with missing dinner.

"You will eat dinner, but not until you have done all our laundry," Tarius said. "Since you like the lake so much and since you think it is alright to dirty Mama's clothes you can take the clothes down to the lake and wash them."

"But it was an accident!" Darian cried.

"No, an accident is something that couldn't have been prevented. Now march, mister."

Under Darian's protests of unfair treatment he and Pete went in the hut to get their laundry basket as Jena went to get dry clothes and head for the shower grumbling the whole time about Tarius's sons.

Elven started to laugh. "Oh, yes, I will definitely miss all of this." He got up and walked away.

When Fleat woke up he found he had more trouble getting out of bed; his left leg didn't want to work at all. The left side of his face was numb, and when he tried to move his left arm it was in no better shape than his leg was. Getting dressed was a chore, so was putting his sword on. *I cannot do this, I just can't.*

Rea woke early, as she often did, grabbed a spear, and headed out to do some hunting. Erah said it was mean bear season. Apparently before they gave up and went to sleep for the winter the bears were more aggressive but also more sluggish.

She wouldn't mind getting herself a mean bear. Of course at this point in time she would have been happy to kill a damned rabbit. Hell, this time of year Erah was trapping a rabbit or a racoon every other day. Rea didn't even see animals. Hell, she rarely even saw their tracks. Her brother Laz had gotten a bear the week before, and he was all about showing her the nice bear skin coats both he and Era had. Because of course Jestia had taken one look at the skin when it was still wet and at Laz's request made two coats from it. What would have normally taken weeks had been done in minutes. Jestia could very easily spoil them all, and Rea wanted to get a bear so she and Katrina could have coats before Jestia left. It would make it a lot of work, take weeks and not be nearly as nice as the coats her brother and his woman had.

The first snow had melted. They'd had a week without snow on the ground, and now eight inches had fallen in one night. Rea hoped the snow would keep the bears from smelling her and make it easier to find their tracks.

She hadn't been in the forest long when she found bear tracks, big ones. Her heart started to pound a little faster as she started following them. Soon she found herself less than a stone's throw from a huge brown bear who bared his teeth at her and charged. Rea called on the night and ran forward to meet it, which had the bear turn midstride and run the other way. But he couldn't get away from a Katabull honed in on its prey. Rea jumped on the bear's back, and drove her spear between its shoulders down into the animal's heart. She rode the animal till it started to fall then left her spear in it and jumped clear to land on her feet in the snow. The bear fell over and was dead—a clean kill. She was excited, but not so much so that she didn't remember to thank the bear for its life. She skinned it out, thinking she and Katrina were going to have the best coats yet. She had just finished gutting it and was about to yell so everyone would know she had made a kill and come to help her finish butchering it and pack it out when Erah came running through the woods. She took hold of Rea's arm and started pulling on her.

"What?"

"Come now."

"Are you kidding me, Erah?" Rea looked at her kill.

For answer Erah jerked on her arm and then took off. Rea ran after her, suddenly afraid something had happened to her brother. She saw a dark Katabull-sized spot on the forest floor, and she ran so fast she easily passed Erah. When she got there she skidded on her knees to a stop beside him. She saw it wasn't Laz, but her relief was short lived when she realized it was Fleat.

When she looked back she could see where his tracks changed from the weight of a Katabull to the weight of his human form and knew that meant he was close to death.

Erah stood behind Rea jumping up and down. "I was checking my snares. I saw the old one walk into the forest. He wasn't walking right so I followed him. He shifted then he fell. I heard you make your kill, so..."

"Thank you, Erah."

Rea took Fleat's hand and looked into his eyes. "My brother, what do you want?"

Fleat forced a smile that only curled half of his lip. "Tell them I died in a horrible hunting accident."

Rea nodded, lifted him onto her shoulders, and carried him all the way back to her kill site. Erah followed her carrying Fleat's spear. Rea laid him in the snow beside the bear. She looked into his eyes.

"You had killed this bear…"

"But that is your kill," Erah said.

"We will never tell anyone that, Erah."

Rea turned back to Fleat. "You had killed this huge bear."

"It is not that big," Fleat said.

"Yes it is." Rea ignored the tears running down her face. "You killed this huge bear, skinned and gutted it, and then your heart just stopped. We found you here by your kill."

"I was barely alive, and I said that you, Rea, should keep the hide," Fleat said. The light started to leave his eyes, but he fought back, caught her eyes and held them. "This time has been the best in my life, and you are the best friend I have ever had."

"And you are the best friend I ever had, Fleat."

He was gone, but she was sure he had heard her. She rocked back in the snow and started to cry.

Erah got down on her knees and hugged Rea. Suddenly Rea realized Erah was crying almost as hard as she was she pushed away from her and looked at her.

"You hardly knew him."

"I cry for you, Rea," she said, sniffing and wiping her nose on the sleeve of her new coat.

"Thank you, Erah." Rea dried the tears off the woman's cheeks and forced herself to stop crying. "He was very old, and he wanted to die before he could do nothing. He wanted to die in the forest surrounded by the trees. I cry only for myself and not for him. This is what's best for him, and I have to be alright with that."

Erah nodded. "It's alright to miss him."

"Thank you, I already do."

Rea stood up out of the snow and put down her hand to help Erah to her feet. Rea started yelling; she knew in minutes several members of their pack recognizing her voice would show up to help her with her kill.

"When they get here remember that this is Fleat's kill. Do you understand, Erah?"

Erah gave her a confused look. "But you killed the bear."

"I told you, Erah, never to say that. Fleat killed the bear. This is Fleat's last kill. It will be easy for them to believe that because I never kill anything. It is important that people think Fleat killed the bear, Erah. He wished to die in a horrible hunting accident."

"Why?"

"No Katabull wants to die of old age. We want our death to be worthy of a story. You like stories, everyone likes a good story. Fleat deserves to have a story about his death that's worthy of the life he lived."

"I am going to go get Laz to see Fleat's kill." Erah patted Rea on the back then took off running towards her cave.

Rea looked down at the face of her friend, bent over and shut his eyelids. Her tears started to fall again. She let herself cry for a minute and then stopped as a thought blasted into her brain. *For a breath I was sure the body in the snow was my brother. If it had been Laz that would have been a tragedy for me, my brothers, my madra and fadra... and Erah. Everyone who loved Laz would have been devastated because he is so young and has a whole life to live. But Fleat, Fleat lived a long life, a good life filled with adventure and love. He fought the good fights and lived to see not just his children but his grandchildren live longer than Laz has lived yet. And here at the end of his life when many just sit and wait to die, become a burden to those around them, he came here. Without his knowledge and guidance we could not have done all that we have done, and I would not have learned how to lead my people. His death is not a reason for me to cry. I know that; at a Katabull memorial we don't mourn their death we celebrate their life. That was so hard for me when it was my mother because she was still so young. But Fleat...his memorial should be a true celebration because few live as long and do as much as he did. For a breath I thought my brother was dead. And it could have been him; it could be me. Every day we are alive there are many ways to die.*

When someone lives as long as Fleat did... He cheated death many, many times. If I live as long I hope I live as well. I hope some silly young girl cries for me and then realizes that she shouldn't.

She found her knife where she had dropped it in the snow when Erah called for her, and she started to quarter the bear. *Life goes on. I will quarter this bear. We will take it home, cook up the heart and the liver and a couple of huge chunks for our breakfast at the keep. We will take the rest to the smoke house, smoke it, and the whole community will eat on it till it is gone. If Fleat were here he would eat with us. He is gone and so doesn't care that I cut up the bear right next to his body. Were he alive he would be the first one to tell me life goes on.*

She had taken her human form back and had just finished quartering the bear when Erah and Laz showed up. Not far behind them Katrina and four other members of the Marching Night ran up.

"What happened?" Her brother asked looking from the bear meat, skin and gut pile to Fleat's body.

That was all it was, a body, it wasn't Fleat anymore. Any more than her mother's body had been her once her spirit was gone. That was made worse because her mother's spirit had left, but her body had lived several days after that. Fleat's death was clean; he lived until he died.

Katrina walked over and embraced her, ignoring the blood all over Rea's hands. She cried, and Rea patted her back getting blood and pieces of flesh all over Katrina's cloak.

"What happened?"

"Erah and I were checking her traps when we heard someone make a kill. We walked towards where we had heard the noise, and when we got here Fleat had just finished gutting the bear. He was still kneeling. He looked at me and said, *Even I, though I am older than dirt and rocks, am a better hunter than you are. You can have the skin for coats for you and your woman since you will never get one yourself.* I asked him how he got the bear and he said in his Katabull form he had run up on the bear, the bear turned around scared and ran from him, so he chased it, jumped on its back and ran his spear into it between its shoulder blades down into its heart and then he rode it to the ground. When he finished talking he stood up and when he did he shifted to his human form and fell over. I went to him and he said...

"To Rea he said, This has been the best time in my life and you are the best friend I have ever had," Erah said. "And she told him he was her best friend."

Rea swallowed a lump in her throat and went on. "Yes and then he was dead."

Katrina was still crying, and Rea was still patting her back.

"I am freezing; we need to pack the meat and Fleat back to town, dig a grave and bury him. We can discuss his memorial later as we eat his bear."

They had brought a litter to carry the meat back to camp. They put Fleat on it and threw the bear skin on top of him. Two of them carried Fleat as the rest of them grabbed the bear meat stuffed it in burlap bags and started back to town.

"You know what Fleat would say right now?" Roash asked from the back end of the litter. Laz had the front.

"What?" Laz asked.

"That we should be careful or we will bury the bear and smoke his body."

"That's terrible," Katrina said. "Which means that's exactly what he would have said." And then it looked like she might start crying again but instead she came back and became a drag on Rea's arm as she tried to carry an entire back leg of the huge bear. When the others were well a head she Katabull whispered to Rea, "I know you killed that bear."

"I didn't; Fleat did."

"Save it for everyone else. I know you left with your spear to go hunting this morning. I know that is Fleat's spear Erah is carrying which has nothing on it while your spear which I am carrying was covered in blood."

Rea turned to look and her spear was clean.

"I wiped it off on your cloak—it was already dirty—when no one was looking. Fleat was in no shape to kill a rabbit much less a bear. Plus, Erah hardly talks, and for her to jump in... she didn't want you to lie about that part of the story, too. She wanted us to know what he really said to you."

"You must never tell anyone, Katrina. It has to be his story. It has to be; it's what he wanted."

"I will never tell a soul, but I needed you to know that I know because it's an amazing thing you have done for him. You have worked so hard to get another kill—and that is not just a big bear it is a huge one. I find that I am crying more at your thoughtfulness than I am our friend's death. Rea, I could not love you anymore than I do right now. You are the most amazing person I have ever known. And you found a way to do it and still get us the skin."

Rea smiled at Katrina and whispered, "I did not do that. That really was Fleat's idea, and he did it without saying anything mean, though... he did make a point of saying the bear wasn't that big. But it is; it's huge, right?"

"Huge," Katrina said, then moved to help her carry the bear haunch. "Otherwise you would not need help carrying it."

Katabull only buried their dead because it took too much wood to burn them and leaving them out for nature to take was too messy. Besides in the Kartik where there were no natural predators bigger than a mongoose the worst that would happen if you left a body lie out was that it was very messy. Here it might get the local predators to thinking Katabull were on the menu. They had made an area on the north side of town in the tree line where they buried their dead.

So as they buried Fleat he was surrounded by ten of the older colonists who had "died in hunting accidents" probably just like Fleat had. None of the others had been Marching Night; this was the first time they were burying a member of their own pack.

Erah had kept watch in case some bear, lion or wolf might decide to sneak up on them as Rea, Katrina, Laz and Roash had taken turns digging the hole. Then they threw his body in and covered it. She and Laz picked up a big rock and stuck it over where his head was. They covered the head so they knew not to dig another hole there and because it discouraged animals from digging up the head. Then they headed back to the keep for breakfast. There was no ceremony for burying the dead. It was a nasty task, and they just wanted it over with.

Rea went in the washroom to clean up before going for food. Katrina had followed her. "And that is another thing," she whispered, her lips nearly touching Rea's ear as Rea was washing her hands in the basin. "You are covered with hair, blood and guts, and you wouldn't be if all you had done was quarter the bear. While Fleat was clean as a whistle."

"You are almost too smart, Katrina, and now I have to go change my clothes before I eat so no one else will notice."

"I will go up get you clean clothes and then take the dirty ones to the wash," Katrina said.

As she turned to go Rea reached out and grabbed her hand. Katrina turned to face her.

"If we had not made the exchange. If I didn't know that I am yours and you are mine, I could not have taken his death."

Katrina smiled at her, leaned in and kissed her gently on the mouth. "If I didn't know that I am yours and you are mine, I could not get up in the morning or go to sleep at night. You are my everything, Rea."

She left, but she'd be right back. Rea smiled and said, "Thank you, Fleat. Thank you for everything, but mostly right in this moment thank you for Katrina."

Jestia woke up to more than the usual noise of the kitchen downstairs which meant someone had gotten a major kill. She hoped it was elk or moose and not bear, but if it was she'd just make it taste the way she wanted it to and eat it anyway.

She got dressed and headed downstairs. As she got closer to the bottom floor she could hear it in their voices; something had happened. There was sadness but also excitement. When she turned the corner and didn't see Fleat sitting at his usual spot she knew what it was. When Rea walked out of the wash room freshly washed and in clean clothes, it was obvious looking at her eyes that she had been crying. Jestia walked over, hugged Rea and started crying like a baby.

She couldn't imagine why she was so overcome with sadness. She had known he was dying knew it was going to happen soon and she didn't know him as well as the others did. He had been ancient; it was his time to go and all that. Yet her heart felt heavy at the thought of not seeing him again. *I am still so raw and... I am feeling their communal sadness. I didn't shield myself against it. I should have as soon as I sensed something was wrong, and I normally would have done it without thinking. I am still not back to my old self.* She put up her shields and started to calm down. Rea was patting her back so hard her teeth were rattling.

Jestia let her go and pushed away from her.

"Are you alright, Jestia?" Rea asked her.

Jestia nodded. "I am sorry about Fleat, Rea, and sorry about the way I reacted. I forgot to shield myself. I walked into a wall of everyone's grief and was overwhelmed for a minute."

And then the teapot was hanging in the air and it poured into one cup and then the other. "Anyone want some tea?" Jestia sighed.

Erah actually got out of the chow line to come and take one of the cups out of the air. She made yummy noises and downed it. "It's very good."

"Well hold it up and it will pour another one. No one makes tea like my cousin Eerin does."

Jestia was embarrassed by the way she had acted and more embarrassed because she had transported the teapot without trying. Then something dawned on her.

"Wait a minute! My magic shouldn't work across the ocean, and this is not the first time I have made tea in the Territories. I can't even mind speak to Tarius or Jazel from here. Why did I make tea... well steal Eerin's tea? How can I steal his tea from across the ocean?"

She realized they were all just looking at her like maybe she had finally completely lost her mind. Except Erah, who was holding the cup up to get more tea. Jestia made a quill appear in her hand, grabbed the pot as it had just finished pouring Erah's cup full and wrote a note on the side of it. When she put the pot back into the air the pot and the cups vanished.

Erah, who had been in mid drink looked startled and then put out. She went back and got in the chow line.

"What was that all about?" Rea asked with a smile.

"I wrote my cousin a note," Jestia said. She moved to get in line, and Rea got in line behind her.

"I meant the teapot and all the going on about the teapot," Rea said with a smile.

"My magic shouldn't work across the ocean. That's why Tarius brought me here in the first place. I never even thought about it before, but that isn't the first time I have made the teapot appear in the Territories. Now here's the thing about the teapot. I never even try to make it happen. In fact, it usually seems to happen when I am the most stressed out and not even thinking about magic. And it is always Eerin's tea, so he has to have just made a pot. Maybe that is the answer; maybe it's a mix of his magic and mine. Neither one of us tries to make it happen; it just does, but why and how across the ocean? When I try to work magic across the sea, nothing. I have to use birds to send messages across the ocean. But the teapot... That's Eerin's teapot, and he is in Montero. It doesn't really make any sense."

Rea shrugged. "Everything doesn't have to make sense."

Katrina got in line behind Rea. She had also just cleaned up and put on clean clothes. "You have obviously both just washed up and dressed in clean clothes. From that I can assume that you were both dirty. Since I know from the business in the kitchen and the smell in the air that someone has made a recent kill, and I know that Fleat has died, I can further assume that you got dirty either helping to butcher the kill or burying Fleat. Since I know the two of you, I can make a guess that it was probably both."

"You are right, Jestia, but what does that have to do with the teapot?" Rea asked.

"Things have to make sense. That is the reason religion is so dangerous. It asks people to believe things that don't make sense. The Amalites are such a scourge because they willingly embrace something that makes no sense and which makes them easy to manipulate. There has to be a reason that teapot comes across the ocean and back without me even trying yet I can't throw a spell across it no matter how hard I try. It has to make sense. If I can figure out the why and how of it I may be able to throw a spell across the ocean."

"But... why would you want to?" Katrina asked.

"Maybe I wouldn't want to, but maybe someday I would need to," Jestia said. She filled her bowl and made a face. "Bear heart?"

"Fleat killed a huge bear right before he died," Roshe said from where he had gotten in line behind Katrina.

"And we have to suffer by eating it's heart," Jestia said, making a face.

"We like heart meat, especially fresh," Rea said.

"Lovely." Jestia turned it into elk. It would have the same properties of bear heart but the taste and the feel of elk. She looked at it in her bowl and thought. *Elk is Ufalla's favorite. When I think of her it still hurts, and I still don't know what I should do about her. Even if I still want her or if she still wants me. But I no longer want to kill her, so I must be getting better.* She took a deep breath then went and set down, suddenly having very little appetite.

Rea sat down next to her. "Jestia, will you sing at Fleat's memorial?"

"Of course I will."

As she sat and listened to them decide who would tell stories, who would sing, and who would dance, she ate her elk/bear heart meat. As she did she tried to figure out why she could make the teapot cross the ocean.

Chapter Sixteen

They were sitting at their fire outside their hut when Riglid came running up and told her. "The queen is coming with Mother and one wagon."

"It's not like Hestia to come without sending a Harold first," Tarius said. Then as she stood up from her throne she looked at her wife and said, "You suppose she found out about Jestia and Ufalla?"

"I'm sure I don't know why she would suddenly come here if she did."

"Riglid, go and meet Hestia and Radkin and bring them to our fire."

He started to leave at a run, but she jumped up and said, "No, wait! I will go with you."

She turned to Jena. "I will not be able to sit and wait for them to get here. It will drive me nuts waiting to find out why they are here and what's in the wagon."

"Then you'd better run," Jena said, with a smile.

Tarius kissed her quickly on the lips and then took off at a run Riglid had to work to keep up with.

Tarius and Riglid met them just as they rode through the front gates. The two Katabull who stood watch at the gate ran up to take their horses. Before they reached them Radkin got off her horse, walked over and helped Hestia off hers as she normally did—by basically lifting Hestia off her horse and setting her on the ground.

Tarius and Riglid walked up to hug them both in turn, then Tarius said, "Not that I'm not glad to see you, but what's going on and what's in the wagon?"

"My cousin Eerin showed up at the castle three days ago with a message from Jestia she had apparently written on the side of a teapot. It said that I should send books to the Katabull colony in the Territories," Hestia started. "When I asked him where Jestia was that she couldn't come to the castle to tell me herself... What the hell is Jestia doing in the Territories?"

"Didn't he tell you?" Tarius asked.

"He said she and Ufalla had a fight," Radkin said. "But that didn't make any sense because they fight all the time."

"Not like this they haven't," Tarius said.

Then to the two men in the wagon she added, "Please take the wagon down to the docks and my people will load the cargo right onto the ship. Riglid will show you the way."

"What happened?" Hestia asked again.

"I don't know if you were aware, but Ufalla had been drinking a lot…" Tarius told them all that had happened as she led them in the direction of her huts. "…and so I took Jestia to the Territories. When I left she had me leave her there because she still didn't trust herself. I plan to go back to the Territories at the end of the week mostly to get Jestia, but if she still doesn't think she can be here I will not bring her back."

"She was going to kill her," Hestia said. "You really think she would have killed her?"

"Oh come on," Radkin said. "If I did that to you, you would want to kill me; don't pretend that you wouldn't, and I would certainly kill you."

Hestia immediately walked over and took Radkin's hand. "You would, would you?"

"You know I would," Radkin said, and the queen wrapped herself all around Radkin.

Tarius rolled her eyes, shook her head, looked at Radkin and said, "You are right. She is aroused by the damnedest things. But let's be honest, our first instinct would be to kill our cheating, lying, mean-ass drunken mate, but we would take a second to think about it and talk ourselves out of it. Mostly because we'd have to get our weapon and think about a plan of attack… but not Jestia. If Jazel hadn't shown up when she did Ufalla would be dead because Jestia was getting ready to throw a ball lightning spell at Ufalla's head."

"I knew that girl was no good for Jestia," Hestia hissed.

"When you thought that they were very good together, and you know it. Things happen in relationships, and they were both very young when they fell in love. Ufalla is still young and stupid. She let her ego rule the day and did idiotic and hurtful things. None of us can swing too big a stick at them because when we were young we all made many mistakes and caused much hurt. Perhaps their biggest mistake was to get so serious so quickly, but... That is also what young people do, and sometimes it all works out. Here is what I know; if we meddle or try to tell them what they should or shouldn't do, they will do as they damn well please anyway. Then whether it is what we wanted them to do or not they will still blame us if it doesn't work out the way they wanted it to."

"Gods and spiders," Radkin grumbled. "Why do you have to be so annoyingly wise?"

"It's a gift," Tarius said, with a grin.

"For you! A curse for us," Radkin mumbled.

"Should I... *we* go to the Territories with you?" Hestia asked.

"If you wish to come you may, but I don't know that there is anything you could do because... Well, I just told you why. If Jestia is herself again I will be bringing her home anyway, and if she is like she was when I left her there... Even if you should talk to her she wouldn't hear you. As you know she can be really mean even when she doesn't mean to. You don't deserve her bad temper just because you want to help her."

"And you will tell her we had this very conversation because *you* she will talk to about anything," Hestia said. "I would like to help her, but the worst mistake I made when I was young was that I wasn't a very good mother. Now when I would like to be I can't help her because she still doesn't really trust me."

"That is not it at all, Hestia. She does trust you now. She talks to me because I understand her, and she me. I love Jena with my whole heart and my whole soul, but she will be the first to tell you that she often doesn't understand what I mean when I say things. I never say anything to Jestia, and she never says anything to me that we don't understand. Our connection does not diminish your relationship with her or hers with anyone else. Ufalla didn't understand that, and...now there is a huge mess. But it is *their* mess not ours."

Hestia looked at her and then Radkin. Radkin smiled and said, "She does not think it will help for you to tell Ufalla off or beat her senseless."

"But if you must you must..." Tarius said.

They had reached her fire pit. Rimmy, Hared, Jena and the cubs were all outside waiting to greet them.

Hared and Rimmy brought their table and chairs outside. As they sat down to eat, their two little boys sat on some of the chairs they kept outside around their fire pit which had been set on the corners of the head of the table where Tarius sat on her throne with Diana in her lap. Had they had time to prepare, they could have eaten in the Great Hall, but this worked on short notice.

"I am three," Diana told Hestia, holding up the right number of fingers.

"Very good!" Hared cheered and clapped his hands.

He turned to Radkin who was sitting beside Hestia. "She is very smart."

"Yes, our daughter is a genius," Jena said with a laugh. "After all, she stopped letting Arvon drag her to the top of trees just as soon as she nearly fell to her death and Darian had to catch her."

"Pete tried to grab her but he missed. So I caught her," Darian said. He handed the monkey on his shoulder a piece of fruit which it greedily took and started munching on dripping the juice all over the boy in the process.

Hestia looked at the size of the boy and the size of his sister. "That is amazing. How did you do that, Darian?" Darian was after all a human while his sister was the Katabull, so he was only about a head bigger than she was.

"How do you think he did it?" Tarius said. "Magic of course. He didn't want her to fall, so he cast a spell."

"How old is he now?" Hestia asked, surprised.

"I'm six," Darian said. "My birthday is right after the babies."

"He talks to whales and monkeys," Pete said.

Hestia smiled at the boy. He was her cousin's only child, and they had all been there the day the boy had lost both his parents to Amalite scum. Had they lived he would have grown up in a palace, but his mother had been Katabull so he was. He had been fostered by Rimmy and Hared and now he was part of the Great Leader's family. They loved him like they did their own and because of that he loved them.

"He talks to everyone and everything," Tarius said to Pete. "Like Jestia he talks all the time."

Pete grinned at her and she kissed him on the forehead and went back to eating.

"I don't talk too much, Madra," Darian said. He took a bite out of a chicken leg then with his mouth full said, "I talk just the right amount."

"Yes, well don't talk with your mouth full," Jena said.

"But Mama, it is his best trick," Tarius said.

Diana didn't have her own plate; she was eating off Tarius's, which became obvious when they both went after the same piece of chicken. They played a little game of tug and war till the toddler laughed and Tarius let her have the chicken wing.

"Someday that cub..." Jena said, pointing at her daughter and when she got her attention smiling at her, "...will have to eat from her own plate."

Diana grinned back and shook her head. "No I will eat Mother's food." She was a beautiful child with strange coloring, bright blue eyes, bronze skin and auburn hair. Then Diana was growling, and when she did her expression looked so much like Tarius it was scary.

Whenever Hestia saw Jena and Tarius with their children it always sparked a deep longing in her. She wished she could go back in time and be a real mother to Katan and Jestia. How much different all of their lives might have been. *I didn't know any better; that is my only excuse. I raised them the way I was raised which I hated.*

They had sat and drank tea and talked for a while after dinner, and then she and Radkin had headed for the wash house. As they were walking back to their huts Hestia saw the girl hiding in the shadows watching them.

"We have a spy," Radkin whispered in her ear.

"I saw her. Should I... should I go talk to her?"

Radkin looked thoughtful. "What would you say to her?"

"I don't know, but tonight I was reminded that I don't want to be judged for the mistakes of my past. When I look at how she's standing I don't believe she likes what she did, either."

"I will wait for you here," Radkin said. Because of course it was a rare occasion when Radkin didn't feel like she had to guard Hestia. Though Hestia was more than capable of taking care of herself.

Hestia walked towards Ufalla and there was a minute where it looked like the girl might bolt and run. Why? Because Hestia wasn't just the girl's mother-in-law, she was the warrior queen of the stories Ufalla's generation had grown up hearing. "How are you doing?"

"Ahh... I'm fine... no, no I'm not. I know I have no right to ask, but... have you heard from Jestia?"

"Sort of. She sent a note to Eerin asking me to send books to the Territories," Hestia said. "She is not at the castle if that's what you want to know."

"I did wonder if she might use one of their ships to come back to the Kartik and if she was at the castle or even in Montero. The Katabull will not let me leave here. I guess I deserve it. They don't trust I will not go right back to doing what I had been doing before I got caught. Jestia hates me." She sniffled. "Do you hate me, too?"

"I don't hate you; I hate what you did." Hestia smiled because it was, after, all a thing Katabull said that humans usually didn't understand. "We all make mistakes when we don't know any better..."

"But that's just the thing. I knew it was wrong and I did it anyway. Worse than that, I think I did it in the first place because I knew it was wrong."

It was hard to be mad at the girl when she looked so miserable. "And you know what, child? We have all done that, too." She sighed. "Just today I was reminded that I have made my own mistakes that hurt Jestia. I don't have to tell you that because I'm sure you know. It would be wrong for me to take the moral high ground right now. I can't tell you whether she will forgive you or not because I just don't know. But I can promise you this because she is so much like me—if you have any chance of getting her back you had better not *ever* abuse her trust again because if you do she may not kill you, but she will be over you completely, and she will make you wish she had only killed you."

When Hestia walked back to where Radkin was waiting for her Radkin took her hand. "Well?"

"Tarius is right. Yelling at her would have been a waste of time. She is already busy torturing herself. Made me once again wonder why people do things that take chunks out of their lives and then... Well I remembered I made choices that took huge chunks out of mine. I knew why I did it at the time, but now when I know better and look back at my choices they don't make any real sense. It might be nice if we didn't have to learn things the hard way. Better yet if our children could learn from our mistakes instead of making every stupid mistake we made and three we never did."

"I know, right?" Radkin laughed and shook her head. "I find that I am more surprised Laz left that damned monkey here than I am that he stayed in the colony. When we were all there I could see the way he looked at the place. And though Rea made all of our lives a living hell for years, and maybe Laz's more than the rest of us, in part that was because he was always running after her cleaning up her messes. Laz and Rea have always been very close."

"Should we go to the Territories with Tarius?" Hestia asked.

"Woman, do you have any idea how cold it is there right now?" Radkin laughed.

"I'd kind of like to see this snow they keep talking about," Hestia said, squeezing her hand. Radkin squeezed right back.

"And right now three of our kids are there," Radkin said, knowing. "We will go in the spring and maybe next winter. I don't want mine to think I am checking on them and don't trust them. And I don't have to because Rimmy will spy on them for me. As for Jestia I think we need to give her space for a whole different reason."

Hestia nodded; she knew Radkin was right.

They got to their huts, Radkin opened the door and they walked in.

"And there is work I left on my desk unfinished, so that we could get the books and bring them..."

"Which as I told you, we could have sent the wagon; we didn't have to come with it," Radkin said.

"We did because I was tired of the work on my desk and just wanted to be here for a while."

Radkin moved to hold her, and Hestia lay her head on Radkin's shoulder. Radkin said, "When we stopped in Montero and Jazel would tell us no more than Eerin had, I have to tell you I was expecting something much worse than Jestia was just trying to kill Ufalla and had to be taken to the Territories."

"Me too," Hestia said, with a sigh. "Remind me why we had kids in the first place?"

"Well, you needed an heir for the throne, so that's better than my excuse—that we wanted them. They are so cute when they are little and relatively easy to take care of. No one ever warns you what a pain in the ass they are when they are grown."

So it turned out that the hardest part of training Erah was that Erah couldn't read at all. Jestia had figured the girl couldn't read, but she hadn't realized what a huge stumbling block it was going to be. Everything from marking the herb jars to naming plants and writing out potions was near impossible. Jestia couldn't make her read with a spell because Erah hadn't learned to read in her original language. It made sense. Pandy had been a translator but they would have been taught to speak and understand the language; they wouldn't have worried about them reading or writing in it because only the priests had been literate. Amalites didn't allow the common people to read or write. Learning was in the same boat with witchcraft, the arts, and being queer or Katabull—all were an affront to the Amalite gods.

The best Jestia could do was show Erah a word, sound it out for her, and then make a picture of what it was appear over it when it was applicable.

Laz was more than willing to help teach her. It turned out that even without Jestia's magic Laz was still better at it than she was. He had unlimited patience with Erah;

Jestia not so much. She liked to think things and then have them be done, not to have to explain them a dozen times.

She would teach her all she could and leave a book on potion making and one on different herbs. If Laz would keep teaching Erah to read, Jestia was sure with Erah's natural gift she could probably figure everything else out on her own.

Jestia had decided to walk the trail to Erah's today because she actually liked walking in the snow. She wasn't going to be in the Territories long enough to get tired of it; she just wanted to soak it all in.

Rea had said she expected Tarius within the week. Jestia hated to admit it, but she didn't really want to leave. She liked the colony, and she had gotten really close with Laz, Erah, Katrina and of all people, Rea. She was going to really miss them, especially Rea.

She would miss the comradery of staying in the Marching Night's keep; she still thought it was a stupid-assed thing to call it, but she enjoyed the interaction in the hall when they all came to eat. The smell of cooked food filled the air and they would all sit and talk. In the morning it would be their plans for the day. Midday it was often as not everything that had gone wrong as they tried to do what they had planned to do that day. In the evening it was everything they had done and still had to do, what they had accomplished that they had planned, and what they had not.

They would all eat, they would tease each other, joke, sometimes sing, dance and play instruments. Sometimes one or more of them would tell a story. The Marching Night had always been bard heavy because their leader was such a great bard.

She felt like she was not just part of them now but an important part of them. If she didn't know she needed to go home she wouldn't have gone just to deal with Ufalla. *She has gone from being the most important thing in my life to being something I barely consider. I didn't do that to us; she did. I am going to miss this place and these people. I think I will be like Laz and feel like I am not going home but leaving it. I don't really have a choice, though; I have to go back. I have to go back because of what I have learned here.*

She wasn't paying attention, just walking along, and they were on her before she knew it. Three wolves—no problem for her—she could just go ahead and pop to the cave or turn them all inside out. She didn't have to do either thing, though, because Rea came bounding through the snow all katted-out, spear in hand, and killed all three of them faster than Jestia could cast a spell.

I take them for granted, but there is nothing as magnificent as the Katabull. I can feel the edges of her power because it extends much further than a Katabull's body, and... That is why magic won't work on them. Their own magic is a barrier to other magic; it repels it.

Rea turned to look at her and grinned. "Look what I did."

Jestia laughed at the child-like glee in Rea's voice. "Yes, and faster than I could throw a spell. Very impressive."

"I was trailing them, trying to get close enough to make my move, but when they decided to eat you..." Rea shrugged and stuck her spear in the snow.

Jestia looked from the spear to the bearskin coat Jestia had made Rea from Fleat's kill, and knew. "Fleat didn't kill that bear, you did," Jestia said.

"Shhhh!" Rea said. She looked around. Then even though there was no one near them whispered, "I told Erah not to tell anyone."

"Erah didn't tell me. I just put it together." Jestia looked at the three dead wolves and made a face. "The only bad thing is now we will have to eat them."

"They are not so bad with plenty of rub and well smoked," Rea said. "The skins are nice."

Rea pulled her knife and started skinning one.

Jestia watched her for a minute and then said, "You hadn't killed anything in over a year, yet you told everyone that Fleat killed that huge bear."

"He was my dear friend; he wanted to have a good story. Now look Jestia how the Everything has blessed me. I killed three wolves! That will redeem me as a hunter."

And that was the thing. Jestia knew how important it was to a Katabull to be a good hunter, and she knew how badly Rea wanted their respect. The fact that she would let them all think she continued to fail to give Fleat a good death story was a selfless act of love.

"Bring me the skins, and I will at least tan them for you," she said. Then Jestia popped off.

When Jestia vanished, Rea figured she decided not to walk to the cave after her close encounter with the wolf pack. She shrugged and continued to skin the animal out. She had finished skinning and gutting one and had started on the second one when she heard a noise, looked up, and saw that about ten members of her pack—including her mate—were running her way though she hadn't yet called for their help.

She stood up and yelled, "Is something wrong?"

"Jestia told us how the wolves came at her and you killed them faster than she could throw a spell!" Roushe yelled back.

In seconds they were all there.

"We wanted to see," Katrina said. "And help you butcher them out. Those are big wolves; how did you get them?"

So she told them and they were impressed and excited. They helped her butcher them out. She whispered in Katrina's ear, "Remind me to thank Jestia."

"She was very excited in a way I didn't expect her to be over dead wolves." Katrina smiled and kissed her cheek. "She said you were magnificent, but I don't need to see you kill three wolves to know that."

"If you hurry, you will be able to help them. They are..." Jestia pointed. "...that way."

"Thanks, Jestia." Laz took off out the door then ran back in and grabbed his coat and took off again.

"I hope she got the hungry ones," Erah said. "They watch me all the time waiting to see if I will make a mistake. They often steal my kills out of my snares. Was one of them black?"

"Yes." Jestia nodded.

"Did he look like this?" Erah made her eyes go wild and barred her teeth, curling her lip back.

Jestia laughed. "If he did, he was a goofy-looking thing and hopefully he died before he could reproduce."

"There are a lot more rabbits," Era said, pointing to a pot boiling over the fire. "Since the Katabull killed so many bears, wolves and lions, there is a lot more to eat. The elk and moose and deer are back in great numbers."

Jestia heard what the girl didn't say. "Are you telling me there didn't used to be so many predators?"

"There were hardly any till after Pandy died. When I first found Pandy there was not much to hunt for, not even many fish. Pigs everywhere, but we could only get the little ones, and the big ones were always trying to kill us. Then they all died. I don't know why, a sickness I think. Before Pandy died there were a lot more rabbits, martins, porcupines, squirrels, racoons, foxes, and the river was full of big fish. We ate well. After Pandy died there started being more and more bears, then the wolves and the lions. Soon not enough small game, not as much fish. But since the Katabull come, there is a lot more small game, lots more fish."

Which was exactly why Tarius wanted to spread her people out. People left an impact on the land that lasted decades. The cycle Erah had just explained brought that point home in a big way. This land had yet to balance itself since the Amalites—as they always did—so completely raped the land here.

There were few predators when there were so many Amalites because they ate everything the predators would have eaten. They never even tried to live in tandem with the natural world because, after all, that was what their horrid gods were for. They kept hogs as their main source of meat; nothing ruined the land like pigs did. When the pigs had destroyed and eaten everything they got sick and died which was a blessing for the land. Smaller predators would have come to dine on their carcasses.

When the Amalites and their pigs were gone the native animals and fish replenished, but with nothing to keep them in check. This brought the predators back till there were then too many predators, so fewer fish and small game. Eventually the predators would have been forced to leave or would have gotten sick and died. Then the cycle would have started again. People ruined everything in the blink of an eye never seeming to realize that it would take the land decades if not centuries to right itself from their misuse.

Tarius had sent so many of her people here to colonize in the first place to save their piece of the island from being overhunted and overfished. She hoped to manage the land of the Territories and build a self-sufficient, sustainable community here. The plan was to make things better here, not worse.

She had also sent them here to save her people from extinction if something should happen to the island which... Well it did. Only the wall Tarius had her people build saved them from absolute annihilation.

Then Jestia realized something that sent a cold chill up her spine. *She is building up a Katabull compound here, because she believes they will be needed here someday.*

"What's wrong Jestia?" Erah asked.

"I just realized that my friend already knew something that I thought I was clever to have figured out."

Erah gave her a confused look and Jestia smiled.

"It's alright, Erah. No one but Tarius ever really understands what I say."

Erah went to the pot and stirred it. "This rabbit is done."

"Do not stick that in my mouth; I just ate," Jestia said. "Feed yourself and then let's get to work. Tarius will be here soon and shortly after that I will have to go home."

"I will miss you, Jestia."

"And I will miss you and this place and these people. I have to go, but I will be back because I don't think I could stay away now if I wanted to. This place will always call to me."

The Territories

Chapter Seventeen

Darian had tried to throw himself a world-class fit when she told him he couldn't take the monkey.

"Son, there is a reason Laz didn't take him with him. He would not be safe there. You know he will run off first chance he gets. There are too many things to eat him, and it's way too cold," Tarius said. What she didn't say was that with three kids to watch she didn't think they needed to add a monkey to a three-day voyage.

When the monkey started chattering at her from her son's shoulder she almost told the damned monkey that was exactly why he wasn't going.

"I will not go if Pogo isn't going," Darian said. And stomped his foot for emphasis.

"Then you can stay here with your brother," Tarius said, as if it didn't bother her at all. She went back to packing her bag.

Darian had looked confused then said, "Mama will not leave me here."

"Jena, Darian wants to stay with his brother when we go, is that alright?" Tarius yelled down the hall towards the main room.

"Fine with me. One less thing to worry about," Jena yelled back at her.

A look of sheer panic crossed Darian's face. "You would leave me here, Madra? You'd leave me here!"

"Child, you slay me. You are the one who didn't want to go. You know I must go, and it isn't like we are leaving you alone. You will be with your brother, his wife, Arvon and your monkey."

"I didn't say I didn't want to go," Darian said. "I said I didn't want to leave Pogo."

"Well, Pogo can't go, so if you will only go if Pogo will go..." Tarius shrugged.

Darian stomped into the main room where she could hear him talking to Jena.

"Mama, you won't leave without me, will you?" he said.

273

"The monkey can't go, Darian," Jena said, firmly.

"But Mama..."

"Don't but Mama me. I heard your Madra tell you no, and you need not ask your fathers. When the monkey belonged to Laz, Pogo stayed with your brother when we went to the Territories. You didn't complain then."

"But he wasn't my monkey then, and Arvon was with us. Now Arvon is staying, and Pogo will like him better than me when I get back."

"No he won't..." She heard Pete say. "...because Pogo can't understand Arvon. You have to go because I am going, and I need you to go with us. And *snow*, Darian, there will be *snow*."

Even with Darian in the other room Tarius could almost hear his mind working. Finally he said, "Pogo can stay with Jabone, and I will go, but I will be sorely grieved."

Tarius laughed.

"Madra, I can hear you!" Of course he could; his hearing was better than a Katabull's.

"As you should." Tarius stopped packing and walked down the hall towards the main room. "You will be sorely grieved? Where did you hear that?"

"You said it in a story," he said. "And I will. Madra. I will be sorely grieved to leave Pogo."

Jena looked at Tarius and smiled. "He is your son."

Diana sat on the floor playing with some blocks Rimmy had made her. Without looking up she said, "I am sorely grieved, too."

"And what about that cub there, Jena?" Tarius asked with a smile.

"That one is Hared's for sure because she has no idea what she has said and is just talking to hear herself speak." Jena grinned back.

"I heard that," Hared said. He could hear it all in he and Rimmy's room where he was packing. Of course Jena wouldn't have said it if he couldn't hear her. What would be the fun in that?

"You can't be sorely grieved, Diana. He isn't your monkey," Darian said.

Diana looked at him and rolled her eyes.

Jena laughed and looked at Tarius. "And now she looks just like you."

"I wouldn't let a bear eat him. I would keep him warm. I will be sorely grieved…"

"Son, for the love of the Nameless One stop saying sorely grieved, and the monkey isn't going. You can stay here with him if you want," Tarius said.

Darian took in a deep breath then let it out and said in a defeated tone, "I will go or Pete will be…"

"Do not say it!" Tarius warned, pointing her finger in his face.

"Sorely grieved," Diana said, clapping her hands.

"What's that, what's that!" Tarius jerked her up, grinned in her face and said, "I said don't say it, don't!"

Diana cracked up then grabbed the braids on either side of Tarius's face, drug her head towards hers and kissed her on the cheek. Tarius looked at Darian, smiled at him and he stopped frowning so hard.

"I am glad you are going with us." She cracked up then. "I would be sorely grieved if you weren't."

Pete started to laugh, and in spite of himself Darian started to laugh, too.

"Now you are all mine," Jena said.

Jena would never leave one of her cubs at the compound and go to the Territories even if Tarius would. She and Tarius knew Darian wasn't going to just leave the monkey, so they had come up with this strategy. It was a lot easier than having a huge scene as they were trying to board the ship that would have ended with Tarius wrestling the monkey off Darian's head. Then grabbing the boy and carrying him onto the ship kicking and screaming.

Jena continued packing for all the cubs as Tarius sat down on her throne and drug all of her cubs into her lap. She started to tell them a story. One she made up about all three of them—and even the damn monkey. She wove their different personalities into the way they acted in the story and highlighted each of their special skills. They were fully engaged, which kept them out of Jena's and their father's hair so that they could finish packing for the trip.

Considering the weather they'd be heading into, it was a lot more than they needed for a summer trip.

The story Tarius told didn't just entertain the cubs; it entertained Jena as well. No one could weave a tale the way Tarius did.

Jabone and Kaseria came with Arvon. They were there to say their goodbyes, pick up the monkey, and avoid a big goodbye on the dock which would likely as not have Darian, Diana and Arvon all crying. When Arvon saw what Tarius was doing he took off running, climbed right up Tarius and sat on Darian where he sat on Tarius. Kaseria and Jabone were respectfully silent so as not to interrupt Tarius's story. As if it was the plan all along Arvon was suddenly in her story, too. He showed his excitement by chuffing and clapping his hands.

Jabone slid up to Jena and whispered in her ear. "Look at Kaseria. She is as excited as the cubs to listen to Madra tell a story."

"After all these years..." Jena whispered back, "...whenever she starts a story I still can't help but listen."

The stories she told them were pretty complex for cubs. The characters faced dilemmas, problems. Tarius had them fighting monsters and going on quests. They only ever succeeded because they worked together and used the different gifts that each one of them had. They were wonderful stories.

They are... They are more than stories. She is teaching them... No, more than that, she is preparing them. Suddenly the story had an ominous feel to it. Jena shook the thought from her mind. *It doesn't because they always succeed. They are always all safe because they work together and use the gifts each of them has. She is training not just Pete but Darian to sword fight, and it scares me more than a little that she thinks they need to be fully trained so young.*

Jabone whispered in her ear. "She used to tell Tarius, Ufalla and I the same kind of stories when we were little, and we were no less enthralled."

Jena whispered back. "Do you think they helped you? When you were in the Territories I mean?"

He seemed to think about it a minute, then he smiled and nodded. "You know what, Mother? They did help. I can even remember telling the others that we would not make it if we didn't work together." He looked thoughtful, then said, "I will tell my son that story."

"Whatever the world throws at these cubs; they will be ready for it," Jena said. "We will all make sure of that."

The second day at sea it started to get colder, and they put on more clothes. Though Darian had promised to be sorely grieved he obviously was not as he ran around the ship hanging on his madra's arm, suddenly very interested in what everything on the ship was and how it worked. Pete trailed along behind them, and if history served he was learning at least as much as Darian was.

Jena was so glad not to have Arvon with them. She loved him but away from home Diana was much easier to keep up with alone. Arvon could be a handful all by himself.

To Jena's shock and the compound's dismay Tarius had once again left Kaseria in charge. When Jena asked her about it, Tarius's answer was very... Well Katabull. "She really hates to do it which makes her perfect. She is crazy, but she won't do anything crazy while I am not there because she knows it would reflect on her alone. She will do just what has to be done, no more and no less. She did a good job last time and did not start any wars just to have someone to kill. She was born to lead."

"Yet you just said she is crazy."

"And what am I?" Tarius asked.

Jena had smiled. "I see your point."

But she didn't, not really. Of course she also didn't understand why they all thought Kaseria was so crazy but guessed it was probably because she didn't act like any other Katabull.

It was a good thing she enjoyed sailing because Tarius had insisted on going to the colony three to four times a year.

She said they needed to go at least that often just to make sure something horrible hadn't happened to them—a drought or some sickness. So the ship was always loaded with fruit and vegetables, grains and medical supplies, as well as anything else Tarius thought might make life easier for them in the Territories. This time they also had two cases of books the Queen had brought and enough practice swords to last them for years. Cold weather was something the Katabull of the Kartik were not used to. Being stuck in because of cold she imagined that was why they wanted the books. She remembered many cold winter days when she had laid in her bed reading a book. And no part of the Jethrik got as cold as the part of the Territories they had decided to build the colony in. Just outside the capital where Jena had grown up, they rarely saw snow and only in the coldest part of winter. The colony had snow off and on mostly on for nearly three months. Jena had added some books she had that she hadn't looked at in years to the load.

Why Tarius had insisted on all the practice weapons she didn't know because she didn't want to, so she hadn't asked.

The kids just loved to play in the snow, and since they were normally only in the colony for a few days, Jena enjoyed it, too. By the time they were leaving she was always more than ready to go home where it was warm and she didn't have to wear so many clothes.

Diana was all but asleep where she sat beside Jena on a chair on the deck. It was set against the wall of the cabin which helped sheltered them from the wind. They had on heavy cloaks, and they were warm enough. Jena was about to take Diana below deck and put her down for a nap when Tarius called out.

"Jena, come quick and bring the baby!" The tone of her voice said it wasn't disaster but something she wanted them to see.

Jena got up, picked Diana up, and ran to the stern where Tarius and the boys stood. When she got there Jena could see six dolphins trailing along after them.

Tarius took Diana from her and pointed them out to Diana whose eyes got big. She smiled down at Jena.

"Look, Madra, look!"

Jena smiled. She had been sure Diana would call Tarius Madra because the boys did, but she didn't. She never did.

"I see, baby."

"Madra saw them and Darian called them in," Pete said, excitedly.

Jena looked at Tarius for conformation. She smiled and nodded.

"I'm going to go get our fathers and uncle Elven," Pete said, "Can you keep them here, Darian?"

"I will." Then to the dolphins Darian said, "You will stay and play while my brother gets our fathers and uncle, won't you?"

One of the damn things got up on its tail, and Jena swore it nodded.

"You are all very pretty. See, I told you it would be fun for you to ride in the wake. You don't have to worry; Katabull don't eat dolphins and whales."

The dolphins started making a strange sound like a cross between a whistle and chattering that Jena had never heard them make before.

Tarius laughed and slapped Jena on the back hard enough it rocked her and said, "I didn't know they could call out like that."

"I talk to fish?" Diana said to Tarius.

"They aren't fish ,baby girl," Tarius said. "They are dolphins. They are like whales; they breath air like we do."

"I talk to dol-pins?"

"You can, but they will not understand you. That is Darian's gift."

Pete ran up beside them with Hared and Rimmy only slightly behind him. Elven was, of course, bringing up the rear.

"They are beautiful," Rimmy said. "I have never seen them so close."

"Has anyone ever seen them this close?" Elven said, and he laughed and shook his head.

"They make noise," Tarius said.

It was then that Jena realized they were all as excited as the kids were. Jena reached out, and took hold of Tarius's hand and squeezed it.

"Darian, can you get them to talk again?" Tarius asked.

"Can you please talk to us again?" Darian asked, and this time all the dolphins started to make the same noise.

It was so loud Darian had to cover his ears. Slowly it died down again.

"Dol-pins!" Diana shouted. "Talk to me!"

Hared turned to look at her and smiled. "My sweet girl, it is enough that they have talked to us and you got to hear it."

Diana nodded her head and grinned at him. She had a mad love for him and he for her. Rimmy had fathered two children and had raised four cubs; these three were his second family. And Tarius had given birth to Jabone. Hared had three children, but Diana was the only one that had his blood. Jena had four children, but Diana was the only one she had given birth to. She loved all her children the same, but Diana was just different. When she looked at her she could see herself, but she could also see hints of her father and her aunts. She imagined it was the same for Hared who had lost both of his birth parents in the Great War.

Tarius turned her head towards the ship and yelled, "Riglid! come here at once."

In seconds Riglid was there; Kaden was well behind him.

Jena smiled when she remembered all the times one of them had teased Riglid about marrying a weak human man or Kaden about being a weak human man while Jena was standing right there.

"Look." Tarius pointed.

"Dol-pins, Riglid, dol-pins," Diana said.

"Dol-*phins*," Hared corrected.

"Teach her later, Fadra. Look at that." Rimmy pointed; one of the dolphins was dancing on its tail.

Jena squeezed Tarius's hand again and caught her eyes, but Kaden looked up at Riglid and said what Jena was only thinking.

"Without you my life would have stayed very narrow."

Rea watched as the ship sailed past the break water and then into the harbor. Beside her Jestia was jumping up and down like an excited cub.

"Calm down, Jestia. I told you once they are in the harbor it will take them half an hour to dock and put down their gangplank."

Jestia nodded but didn't stop jumping around. "I don't really want to leave, but I have to, and... There are about a hundred different things I want to talk to Tarius about. But mostly I just need to see her and hug her."

It had snowed again last night, adding two inches of clean snow to the four inches that had been there already, but when Rea looked down at the ground where Jestia was standing there was about a two-foot circle that had been stomped completely flat until it was a thin sheet of ice.

"Do you maybe need to pee, Jestia?"

"No… Why would you think that?"

"With all the jumping around…" Rea looked with meaning at the ice disk Jestia had created at her feet. Jestia looked at it, looked at Rea and grinned.

"I'm really excited."

"No one would have guessed," Katrina said.

"Hey, Three-wolf killer," Laz said, walking up and shoving Rea with his shoulder. "Don't crowd the docks. We all want to see the Great Leader."

"I hope Fadra and Riglid are with them," Rea said. Then she looked at Jestia, who was still jumping around like she had wasps in her pants.

"Could you not just pop on the ship?"

Jestia hit herself in the head with her palm, then popped off, no doubt headed for the ship.

"If patience really is a virtue…" Katrina shrugged.

Jestia popped up right next to Tarius on the deck.

Tarius laughed and hugged her. "What took you so long?"

Jestia hugged her back. "I forgot I could pop onto the ship as soon as I saw it." She finally let Tarius go and stepped back.

"How are you little sister?" Tarius asked.

"I no longer want to kill her, so I think I'm doing as good as I am going to for a while," Jestia said. "You will not believe what I have learned since I've been here. Except I think you probably already know the most important parts."

Tarius looked at her and smiled. "You fell in love with this place."

"I did, and the people here, but I am already getting tired of the cold. I have to go back to the Kartik because of what I've learned since I've been here."

"What, about Ufalla?" Tarius asked carefully.

"I still don't know what if anything to do about her. I have learned not to care about her as much which is better for me, but I don't know how that will be for her. She is not with you?" She looked around quickly; she felt pretty good, but she didn't want to deal with her wife not right now.

"Couldn't if I wanted to. Jazel put a spell on her that throws her off of any ship she steps onto. Besides, I would not ambush you with her especially not when I didn't know how you were doing. Which... I have missed talking to you and seeing you. I have been worried about you."

"How is Ufalla?"

"Pretty broken. She finally realizes that what she did was wrong, but even that was a process. When I got home from here the whole compound had been shunning her. I didn't ask them to do it; her behavior was such they just did it. But I did tell them not to let her leave if she came there, which they also did. I think being shut away from everything and everyone made her really have to look at what she had done and why. She still loves you."

"Seriously, I don't know how I feel about her. At this point the best description I can give you is numb. I went from having my thoughts consumed with her to hardly thinking of her at all. I still don't know if I am going to just separate myself completely from her or keep her. If I do keep her, what the new rules will be because it's pretty clear that what we were doing wasn't working —at least not for her."

Tarius nodded. "We all make mistakes, Jestia. I don't think it will serve you to hate her, but I would never insist that you forgive her, either. It is not something you have to decide one way or the other right away."

"And that's exactly what I have decided. I will either take one look at her and know what to do, or know that I still don't know. Either way I'm alright with it because my pain has been dulled, and I no longer wish to see her head explode."

"So, what has been going on in the colony?"

"Well I will not tell you most of it because it is not my news to tell, but Fleat died in a horrible hunting accident; Rea can tell you more about it. She has handled it pretty well, but it is clear she is still a little lost without him. You know because she needs a wise but mean-ass old man to tell her she is doing everything wrong and who basically makes fun of her all day every day or she doesn't quite know what to do."

"Well then I have brought my uncle Elven just in time."

Tarius had been standing right behind the helmswoman when Jestia appeared in front of her. Everyone else was at the bow waiting for the ship to land trying to see who they could make out on the dock. So as they disembarked no one but she and the helmswoman where aware that Jestia was even on the ship.

As she and Jestia started down the gangplank right behind Jena, Jestia said, "I have the strangest sense that I am doing this backwards."

Jena had started, turned quickly to look at Jestia, almost fell, and Tarius had to catch her.

"Sorry," Jestia said to Jena.

Jena took a deep breath and let it out. "I was not expecting to hear your voice behind me," Jena said. She looked at where Tarius still had hold of her arm and smiled at her.

"My hero." Then she kissed Tarius quickly on the lips. Tarius released her arm, she turned and started back down the gangplank.

"You know you two have ruined us," Jestia said.

Tarius knew what she meant, so she smiled. "It wasn't a plan, you know."

"All of us that have grown up knowing the two of you. To us your relationship is what real love is. We all want it, but it isn't actually attainable. I know no one else that has what you two have. That is part of what I have done here. I have let go of the example that you and Jena set."

That made Tarius a little sad because she wanted everyone she loved to have what she had with Jena, but she knew they couldn't. Her sadness was short lived because then she saw Rea, Katrina and Laz greeting Rimmy, Hared and the boys.

She heard Rea tell her fadra, "Katrina and I have done an exchange; please do not make a big deal..."

Rimmy let out a great roar then picked Rea up and spun her around. When he finally released her he grabbed

Katrina up, spun her around, too, and yelled out. "The best news ever!"

Tarius stopped and took hold of Jestia's arm to stop her and give them all room to have their moment.

Seeing the smile on Tarius's face she said, "And see? Those two work because they don't expect too much from their union. They enjoy it for what it is, and that is what I learned from them. I don't know if I can ever do it, but I'd like to think I could."

"Every person is different, Jestia, so every couple is so different. What works for Jena and I will not work for anyone else," Tarius said. "But I think I should remind you that I once betrayed Jena. She, too, wanted me dead, and we got over it."

"You know what I had forgotten that."

"And see, we never do. We never forget that we once lost it all but got it all back and then some. Things are rarely as dark as they seem."

"What of the coming war?"

"There is and always will be a coming war as long as the Amalite gods are prayed to, Jestia. Even in those times there is and will be light mixed with the darkness. We have a lot to talk about, but first let me greet my people, learn what they have been up to, who has been born, who has died, and who has found love. Then you will tell me what you have learned, and I will tell you what I have."

They started walking again as at the bottom of the plank Jena embraced Laz and he her.

"So, I must ask, did you know that Laz had a crush on Jena?"

"Always." Tarius turned to her and smiled. "Why do you think when I decided she and my cubs needed a body guard I choose him? I knew he would never let anything happen to her or them that he could stop."

"That's what I thought."

Jena didn't realize how much she had missed Laz until she saw him. She ran up to him, embraced him, and so did all three of her cubs. "I have so missed you," Jena said.

"And I all of you," Laz said. He backed away from her, the cubs were all still hanging on him and he looked down at them, smiled and asked. "Who has my old job now?"

"Tarius has not chosen anyone yet, but then we have also not left the compound except to come here. She said you could do it again while we are here," Jena said then whispered to Laz. "But you know I can take care of myself because, though people seem to forget it, I can actually use the sword I carry. It isn't just for show. One of these cubs can already shift, the magic one is already throwing spells, and the little one could talk a grown man to death."

As if to prove it, Diana climbed up him to hang on his neck even as the boys finally let him go. "I saw dol-pins, Laz."

"Dol-*phins*," Hared told her.

"That's what I said, Fadra. Dol-pins," Diana said, then turned back to Laz and rolled her eyes.

"As I was saying, I saw dol-pins. They sang and danced. Darian talks to dol-pins and monkeys. He was very bad because our parents wouldn't let him bring Pogo."

"See what I mean?" Jena said.

"I wanted to bring him so you could see him Laz," Darian said.

"No, you wanted to bring him because you were being a willful brat," Jena said. She had learned when he could barely talk that there was no sense sugar coating anything with Darian. He saw anything remotely patronizing as an insult and would tell you as much.

"I do miss Pogo but Darian, he should never come here. If it was safe for him to be here I would have brought him myself and kept him here. Just last week our sister killed three wolves at one time that were stalking Jestia of all people."

"Stupid wolves," Jena said, with a chuckle.

"Yes, Jestia said she had just seen them and didn't have time to either cast a spell to pop herself out of there or turn them inside out when Rea appeared and killed them all faster than she could cast a spell. When Erah saw the hides she said it was the wolves she called The Hungry Ones, and she was glad they were all dead."

"Jestia made Erah talk?" Darian was excited. Laz nodded. "Good! I can talk to her."

"You could talk to her before," Laz said, and ruffed his hair.

"But I couldn't understand her," Darian said. Then he seemed to notice the snow. No doubt because more started falling and he yelled, "Pete, there is snow! We must play in it."

"Me too," Diana said, climbing down Laz's body.

"No!" Tarius boomed. "You can play after we have eaten. Rea says there is a meal waiting for us at the keep."

"We can unload the ship when it stops snowing," Rea said. "You know, if it does."

As a whole they started moving towards the keep, her cubs looking like they were being marched to their deaths. Laz reached down, grabbed a handful of snow and threw it at Pete who brushed it off his chest then grabbed himself a handful of snow made a ball out of it and threw it at Laz. But Laz ducked and it hit Tarius in the back of the head.

Tarius turned quickly and the look on Pete's face gave him right away even before he said, "I'm sorry, Madra."

"No, I am sorry because I forgot for a minute what it is like to be so young. My cubs, go play in the snow for a minute and then come to the keep to eat." Tarius turned knowing eyes on Laz and said, "Your brother will happily watch you."

Laz didn't actually mind staying to play in the snow with the cubs at all. He took hold of Darian in one hand and Diana in the other. "Come on, Pete. Let's move away from the docks and go to the center of town where there is lots of room to play and the snow is cleaner." When he got there he set them loose, and they were all throwing snow at each other running and purposely falling down in it.

He more felt than saw her. When he looked up Erah was standing behind the corner of one of the houses, watching them. Laz smiled at her and waved towards himself, telling her to join him. "Come on, Erah."

"Yes, Erah, come play with us," Darian said.

Erah nodded and walked to meet Laz.

Darian trotted over, and Erah bent over to hug him.

He hugged her then stepped back and hollered, "Sister! Come and meet Erah."

Laz watched as the toddler struggled to walk through the snow. She was already absolutely covered in it. When Diana got there she hugged Erah around the knees.

Erah gave Laz a puzzled look, and Laz smiled and said, "Diana never knew a stranger, and she isn't afraid of anything."

"She doesn't climb high in trees anymore," Pete said, running over. Erah hugged him and he hugged her back.

"Why not?" Laz asked Diana.

"I fell and Darian had to save me," Diana said. She let go of Erah and stumbled off to play in the snow and Pete followed her.

"She is very pretty," Erah said to Darian.

"Yes, she looks like Mama," Darian said. "Do you like talking?"

Erah nodded, which made Laz laugh. She seemed to figure out why he laughed and said, "Yes, I like talking. I have a little magic."

"You do? What can you do?" Darian asked, excited.

"I know plants."

Darian smiled. "That is good. I know animals, and you know plants, and Jestia knows everything."

Erah nodded again.

Darian was obviously torn between playing in the snow and talking to Erah.

"Go on and play. You will have plenty of time to talk to Erah later."

Darian ran off to join his brother and sister. Laz put an arm around Erah and pulled her close. "My father and his husband, my brother Riglid and his husband have all come. Everyone has gone to the keep for a late lunch. When the cubs get worn out or cold I am to take them to the keep. I would like for you to meet my father and my brother Riglid. Will you come with me and the cubs?"

"Is Tarius the Black there?"

"Of course. These are she and Jena's and my father and Hared's cubs."

"I will go with you," she said.

A snowball hit him in the chest and splashed on to Erah. When he looked, Darian had obviously thrown it and was working on another one as Pete launched one. Erah jumped down on the ground, started making a ball and launched it with accuracy at Darian then immediately hit Pete with one. The boys laughed.

Diana was trying to throw snowballs, too, but she was mostly just throwing snow. More of it was going on her than anywhere else. They were in no danger of her hitting them, that was for sure.

Realizing Erah was a better shot than he was, Laz got on his knees in the snow and started making snowballs and handing them to Erah. Erah hit one of the cubs with every snowball she threw; the cubs hit them only a couple of times. Laz called a stop to it when he realized Diana was getting cold, of course she was the one who most didn't want to go inside.

Laz had picked her up and started walking towards the keep with the boys and Erah following them.

"B..b..but I'm n...n...not c...cold," she said.

Laz pointed at her chattering teeth and blue lips. "That's what cold feels like, you little dummy."

When he looked back the boys were on either side of Erah, holding her hands. Darian was, of course, talking.

Laz had just come in with Erah and the cubs. Laz, who was carrying Diana, took her right to the fire.

"This one is cold as a toad," he yelled at Jena.

Jena got up and walked over to check her even as Darian and Pete crowded in at the fireplace.

"I'm not c...cold," Diana told Jena.

It was a lie. Tarius could see the cub's lips were turning blue from where she sat at the great table.

"Child, you slay me." Jena took her from Laz and stood Diana close to the fire to warm her up. She looked at Laz and said, "Let me guess. She didn't tell you she was cold; you had to guess."

Laz smiled and nodded.

Tarius could feel the girl looking at her. She was a little surprised to see her in the keep in the first place around so many people. Erah stood towards the back of the room away from everyone, but she was there and though she felt cautious she didn't seem to be afraid. Tarius watched as the girl checked out her throne then looked from her finger to her sword and back.

"I see you have noticed you have an admirer," Jestia said. "Turns out Erah was raised till she was about eight by a Kartik soldier who had been badly wounded and was left behind during the Great War. That Kartik soldier was named Pandy and she was a bard. Think of the stories that bards were telling at the time of the Great War. All stories about you and Jena, but let's face it of the two of you, you are the most interesting."

"Not to me," Tarius said with a grin. "I have to tell you, though it will doubtlessly swell your already swollen head, that I have missed you and do not feel quite whole when I can't see or talk to you any time I want."

Jestia smiled. "And I will tell you, though it will swell your already huge head, that not being able to talk to you was the only thing I really missed while I've been here. I was glad not to have to study my magic or run the spa or the alchemy. I was happy not to have to face Ufalla and all her dysfunction. But it was frustrating, and... I did not feel quite whole when I couldn't just see or talk to you whenever I wanted. And as long as we are blowing your head up anyway... Erah, come here and meet Tarius."

Erah walked up slowly and stood several feet away from Tarius.

Jestia pointed to the seat on the other side of Tarius. "Sit down; she doesn't bite."

"Well that's a lie," Jena said, with a laugh.

"I do not draw blood. Not on those I like, anyway," Tarius said to the girl with a grin.

Erah sat down beside Tarius and just looked at her. When Tarius smelled the girl she turned to look at Laz who looked away and pretended to suddenly be all about helping Darian off with his coat.

"So, Erah, I assume you can talk now." The girl nodded and Tarius chuckled. "You were alone a long time. Do you know what a family is?"

She nodded again.

"Well, like it or not, you will never be alone again because now you are part of my family. Isn't that right, Laz?"

"Yes, Great Leader," Laz said.

"He has bad manners," Tarius told the girl. "You can just call me Tarius."

Across the table Rimmy gave her an odd look. Tarius sniffed, then looked from Erah to Laz, but it was Riglid who figured out what she was saying. He laughed, got up from the table and went and hugged Laz.

"What's this? My brother has chosen a weak human mate?"

"She's stronger than your husband." Laz laughed, patting Riglid on the back.

"Prepare yourself, girl," Tarius warned.

Rimmy ran over and hugged the unsuspecting girl. He looked at Tarius. "Thank the Nameless One; I thought that boy would be alone forever," Rimmy said. Then looking at his daughter and her mate said, "Not one miracle but two."

"Thanks, thanks a lot," Rea said then. "Fadra, let Erah go. You are scaring her."

"Are you afraid of me?" Rimmy asked Erah.

Erah smiled and shook her head no.

"I thought you said she talks now." He released her, ran over, pushed Riglid out of the way, grabbed Laz and hugged him, lifting him off the ground.

"I can talk," Erah told Tarius, but that was all she said.

"Get this," Jestia said to Tarius. "The wild girl has magic ability..."

"I hear her humming," Tarius said.

"She knows about plants," Darian said. He crawled up in Tarius's lap. He wasn't Katabull, but when it came to climbing all over her he wasn't any different from her other cubs.

"Dammit, Darian, I wanted to tell her."

He just shrugged, ignored Jestia and turned to Erah. He patted the side of Tarius's face. "This is my madra, that is my mother. Rimmy is my father and Hared is my fadra." He pointed as he told her who they were. "I had other fathers, but they died in a horrible hunting accident. That's my brother Riglid and his husband Kaden. You will like Kaden. He tells great stories but not as good as Madra…"

"Son!" Tarius laughed. "Let the girl breathe."

"I was just telling her about our family. Oh!" He climbed down and ran over and climbed up on Rea's lap and then started telling Katrina the same thing he had been telling Erah. Even though he knew good and well that Katrina knew who everyone was. Katrina was Marching Night, and he had known her his entire life.

"Apparently overwhelming people that is how Darian welcomes them to your family," Jestia said.

Kaden had sat on the other side of Jestia. "Well that's what he did to me," he said with a laugh. He looked around she and Jestia at Erah. "Welcome to the family. I would introduce myself, but I'm sure Darian has already done that."

Erah nodded at him. She then looked at Tarius, and Tarius understood what Jestia meant about getting a swollen head. The girl was not afraid of her; she was in awe. "Your finger is in your sword."

"It is. So is Elven's." Tarius nodded her head in his direction.

"And my cheating, lying, drunken wife's," Jestia said.

"Still bitter then?" Tarius asked.

Jestia shrugged.

Elven had just filled his bowl and parked across the table. "So much noise. People talking all at once," he grumbled.

"We are happy, Uncle Elven," Riglid said. "Laz has chosen a mate and our sister has made an exchange."

"Yay! Another human." Elven grumbled. "Soon there will be no pure Katabull, just a bunch of half breeds. It's all going to end in tears, I tell you."

"Well, you're a delight," Rea grumbled back at him.

"You with the smart mouth. Who are you?" Elven asked.

"I'm Rea. I'm captain of the Territories."

"Really? Because I thought Tarius was in charge," Elven said.

"Rea is in charge of this place. I am only Great Leader of the people; someone has to run things while I am not here," Tarius explained.

"And she's the best you could do?" Elven looked at Rea. "I meant, who do you belong to?"

"I'm sure Darian would be only too glad to tell you," Jestia grumbled.

"She belongs to me," Katrina said.

"Woman," Rea hissed. "I am not a thing."

"Hey, dimwit," Elven said to Rea. "I meant, who are you related to?"

"Who are you calling dimwit, you senile old fart?" Rea snapped back. "Rimmy is my fadra. Radkin is my madra..."

"So you are not Tweed's daughter."

"I am. Tweed was my father," Rea said.

"But..." Elven sighed as if with relief. "I am not blood related to you."

"Who the hell do you think you are?" Rea got to her feet and glared down at the old man.

Tarius could almost see the twinkle in Elven's eyes; he had found someone suitable to spar with.

"That's right," Rimmy said. "Rea was fortunate to have left for the Territories when a darkness fell on the compound and Elven arrived." He let go of his son and moved to look at his daughter. "He is Tarius's uncle. It turns out Tweed was Tarius's nephew, and so Laz and Riglid are blood related to the Great Leader, Diana, Arvon, Jabone and, unfortunately, by marriage to Elven."

"Who shall become your problem," Hared told Rea, "because we are leaving him here or... he will go back and we will all stay."

Rea looked at Tarius and Tarius just smiled.

"I am sorry, Great Leader... That you are related to such a barnacle on the butt of the planet," Rea said.

As she turned to glare at her uncle, Tarius saw the girl smile.

"Now see here, girl..."

"That's Captain Girl to you." Rea snapped back.

"Captain, Oh my captain," Elven started.

The room went stone silent.

"Finally there is quiet." He grumbled something and went back to eating.

When Tarius looked around her, Rea and nearly all the Marching Night in the room were near tears, and she knew why.

Rea glared daggers at Elven, but before she could tear into him Tarius said, "No one told him, Rea, and he didn't do it just to be mean. Though he is a shithead on good days. It is the chorus to a very old song. I know because my fadra used to sing it. It is why Fleat said it, and it is why Elven did. Now tell us all about Fleat's horrible hunting accident."

Rea took a moment to compose herself then moved to the front of the room, paced back and forth, and then as they ate their breakfast Rea told the story of Fleat's final moments. Across from her Tarius could see the moment at which Elven realized how raw the girl's feelings were over the loose of her friend and mentor.

When Rea had finished telling the story they all clapped and roared.

When it quieted down a little, Jestia leaned in till she was touching Tarius's ear and whispered so low only she could hear it, "I'm going to tell you because I know you will never tell and because Rea has become the best friend I have in this world besides you. Fleat didn't kill that bear..." Then Jestia told her what had really happened. "Erah knows, too, and I'm pretty sure Katrina knows because she is smart as a whip."

When Jestia had finished, Tarius turned to Erah and said, "Thank you Erah." The girl looked confused and Tarius explained. "For being there for Fleat and for Rea. And for giving my stepson the mate he has always longed for."

She nodded again.

"She is still not very vocal, but she usually talks more than this," Jestia said. "It is because there are so many people."

"She doesn't talk because how could she get a word in edgewise with this bunch," Elven grumbled. "The only one who talks more than Katrina is the witch."

And how did Elven know Katrina? Because she had come to stay in the compound with her parents after she was well enough to leave Montero and the smoke had cleared—literally and figuratively. Katrina had hung out most of the day around their fire pit. No doubt because being around Rea's family made her feel like she was closer to Rea.

"Old fool," Jestia hissed. "I will turn you into a toad. No, that would be redundant."

Then she turned and whispered to Tarius with a tear in her eye, "You are right. He is a perfect replacement for Fleat."

It wasn't hard to talk Kaden into using his bardic talents to entertain everyone. Once he had started telling stories Jestia knew she wouldn't have to worry about Erah leaving any time soon. Still she asked Rea to make sure the girl didn't go home.

When everyone was fully engrossed in the story Kaden was telling Jestia and Tarius snuck outside. Then Jestia popped them off to the cave.

Tarius looked around, took a sniff and said, "So I can smell that Laz already lives with the girl."

"My guess is they will make an exchange as soon as he is sure she knows what it really means."

Tarius nodded. She had guessed as much. "I wouldn't mind living here... and the energy."

"It is even greater since I moved most of the rock from the cave-in..." Jestia told her about finding the spell book and the pages and what had happened when she finished. She showed Tarius the stone pendent. "So I was supposed to come here."

"It might have been nice if you had just been curious and so wanted to come with us."

Jestia smiled and hugged her neck. "That is exactly what I told Rea. This is why I have so missed you. We think with the same brain." She let her go and said, "Follow me and I will show you where all the energy comes from."

She walked out the door she had put in the back of the cave and made a witch light. When Tarius saw the wall of cornelian she didn't have to ask where the energy came from. She walked up and put her hand on it.

"Imagine what it would have been like before the Amalites..." They both spit. "...gutted the mountain to sell the stones."

"No doubt to arm their people for the Great War. What you have said, Jestia, about Triad… it is not the first time I have thought it. When you first told me what you read, how in our last lives our mother was from Triad, that this place we call the Territories was Triad before it was the Amalite…" She took her hand off the wall and turned to face Jestia. "The Amalite religion did not start here. This was the Katabull's homeland, and it was the Triad homeland. It was not the Amalite's homeland. That being the case. Where did they come from? The same place they are coming from now. They are infiltrating the Jethrik, but they are not coming from here. Nor did they come from your uncle's monstrosity in the Kartik. The Hive didn't have missionaries, and the Amalite people here… There have been no uprisings. In fact, in a lot of ways they seem happier than the rest of us to be rid of their hateful religion."

"They are coming from somewhere," Jestia said. "But where?"

"Before the Great War, when we rid this land of them, the Amalites hit the shores of the Kartik hard. That is how the Marching Night came to be. We worked the shores, killing every Amalite landing party. Your mother used to pay us for their scalps. Being unable to attack our country they then went after our shipping lanes, capturing our trade ships. You know how we captured their ships and took them for our own because you have heard the stories."

Jestia nodded.

"Yet when we hit the ports of the Amalite there were still hundreds of ships here. At the time I thought it just meant they had a much larger fleet than we had thought, but now… I don't think the ships that attacked us ever came from here."

"You think you know where their actual home land is?"

"Not exactly, but… It's about their ships. The Kartik is a seafaring nation, and yet the Amalite ships were bigger and better made than ours. I thought it was just because they had more and better wood to work with. Now I realize they had bigger and better boats than we did because they have been at sea even longer. They originated on an island, and on that island…"

"...there are more of them than we can count." Jestia took in a deep breath and let it out. "That explains some of what I have seen."

"And my visions as well. We must find this island and rid the world of them once and for all."

"But first we must drive them out of the Jethrik again," Jestia said.

Tarius pointed at the amulet around her neck. "And now you have the tool to help us do that. This part of the cave is not warm, and we should get back before we are missed. Jestia, would it be wrong for me to take stones for myself, Jena, my grandson, and each of my cubs? Would it decrease the energy of this place?"

"No, there is a hidden vein of the stone almost as big as what the Amalites took out. I brought you here because I think you should all have one, but I should tell you I have already chosen one for Arvon." She watched as Tarius carefully chose stones, small ones the size of a quail egg. Her hand seemed to be hovering over a larger one the size of a hen's egg. "Yes, that one for Darian."

Tarius took a deep breath and let it out. "Yes, I was afraid of that. The stones protect, don't they?"

"And they heal. Pandy... that was the soldier that raised Erah. Her injuries were such she shouldn't have lived. If it weren't for Erah's special gift—giving her plants to help keep her strong—and this cave, she wouldn't have lived as long as she did."

"But she lived long enough to give Erah everything she needed to thrive and to be a person." Tarius picked up the stone then rose, putting them all in her pocket. "If I had to pick a woman for Laz I could not have picked one as right for him as Erah is. She is not like Jena, but they have a similar energy. What I see when I look in his face is that she has healed him from losing his parents the same way Jena healed me from losing mine."

"So, what is wrong?" Jestia asked.

"Really Jestia?" Tarius laughed, though she obviously was not amused. "What is wrong? I wanted to be done with this. I thought we were done with this more than once. First there was the Hive, and then there was Rorick." She spit. "I lost my parents, Laz and Riglid lost their fadra, Jena lost her father. Hared lost three of his parents, and poor Pete lost both of his. People lost their lovers, their friends, their children—all to the Amalite menace." She spit again. "I don't want that for my children, for any of my children, for *anyone's* children. I don't want death and fighting and loss for me or you or them. I want to raise my cubs, watch them grow up..."

"Stop right there, Tarius. You will raise your cubs and train them, because you know that is the best way for us to put this dog down forever. I will take care of what has to be done in the Jethrik when it is time to do it. When that is done we will find this island of Amalites. Then we will go and destroy them. We will not go there till we are all strong enough and know enough that it will not be us losing our loved ones, it will only be them. You know I don't have to tell you that Darian will be as strong a wizard as Hellibolt ever was. Tarius, it never dawned on me till I was here and the teapot showed up—and it wasn't the first time...remember in the Hive? I don't know how to make it happen yet, but apparently my magic can reach across the ocean. When we go against them this time, it will not just be fighters, it will be a Katabull army, and we will bring every witch who can throw a spell. We will go when I can throw a spell across the waters that blows up ships and towns. We will unleash what they have done to the world tenfold, and when their island is a smoking hole and their kind finally dead, we will still have many days to enjoy the sun."

Tarius nodded. "I still don't like that we have to do it."

"But we don't have to do it today, Tarius."

"I am cold as a toad," Tarius said.

So Jestia popped them back just outside the keep. It was still snowing. Tarius held up her gloved hand and caught a few flakes.

"Well, this should make my cubs happy."

"What about you?" Jestia asked.

Tarius turned to her and smiled. "I'm happy, Jestia, just worried. On the day I am not worried you'd better check to see if I have a fever or am dead."

Chapter Eighteen

Elven had parked himself close to the fire for most of the day. Rea had noticed a lot of the old people spent most of the cold weather under covers or by the fire. Fleat had told her every joint in his body ached when he got cold.

All day long Tarius's cubs would talk someone into going out into the blowing snow with them and then come back cold and huddle around the fire. When they did Diana would walk right over, crawl up into Elven's lap and start talking to him. Yet the old man who made out that everyone talking at once annoyed him grinned like a fool the whole time the baby was talking.

When she warmed up Diana would climb off the old man, find Rea, take her hand and follow her as Rea did the things she had to do. Rea had purposely left a bunch of minor repairs that had to be done inside to do when the weather was bad. Diana would sit and watch what she was doing talking and occasionally trying to help.

At one point as Rea was stuffing some moss in a crack with her knife to stop the wind from blowing in, and Rea had laughed more at herself than the cub. She had gotten so used to only half listening to Katrina that the cub's constant prattle didn't bother her.

"You talk as much as my wife does," she told Diana.

"No one talks as much as Katrina," Diana said. She was really funny because she talked with wild, sweeping hand gestures just like Rea's fadra did, but the expressions on her face were the same as Tarius's. "Katrina never stops talking."

"True, but she is the most beautiful woman in the world," Rea said.

"She is pretty, but the most beautiful woman in the world is Jestia," Diana said.

The tone of her voice made Rea turn, look at her and laugh. "Well, it isn't hard to see what side of the bread you want buttered. Still you're a little young, and it's a whole lot weird for you to crush on Jestia. I mean she is..." Rea thought about it for a minute. "...she was your mother's twin in another life, and without her you wouldn't even be born."

"I have told her the same thing," Jena said, walking into the room where they were. "Though if I'm honest I was more destressed that Diana no longer thought I was the most beautiful woman in the world."

"You are very beautiful, Madra, but not like Jestia. She is all..." Diana started throwing her hands around trying to mimic Jestia throwing a spell. "...like that."

Rea laughed. "If you say so."

"Diana, come and leave your sister alone now. She is very busy."

"But I am helping," Diana said, but followed Jena out of the room anyway.

"I'm sure you are helping...right into twice as much work. It's time for a nap."

"But I'm not tired."

"Yes, I know. Just like earlier you weren't cold," Jena said.

Rea smiled, finished stuffing moss into the cracks, and then went back to the main hall to warm up. It was already that time of year; they worked in shifts now—running out, doing what needed to be done, then coming back and soaking up the warmth.

Kaden had stopped telling stories, and as soon as he did Erah had left and of course Laz had gone with her. Till she noticed they were gone Rea had forgotten she was watching them. She hoped Jestia was done with whatever she was doing.

Rea was presently surprised to see that fadra and Hared, Kaden and Riglid were still there sitting around the table talking to Katrina. Well, listening to Katrina was more like it.

Elven was still sitting by the fireplace. He looked to be about half asleep, so she thought about yelling just to make him jump.

"Where did Jena and the cubs go?" Kaden asked.

Rea took a seat next to Katrina. "She took them to lay down in our room for a nap. The boys were all for it, tired from playing in the snow..."

Rimmy interrupted, "...but Diana kept insisting she wasn't tired, but she will be the first one asleep."

"Whether it is time to go to bed at night or take a nap it is always the same thing with that cub," Hared said, with a smile you couldn't have wiped off his face.

"She is so much smarter than the rest of you," Elven said. "She is afraid to sleep and leave you lot in charge."

Riglid leaned towards Rea and she him so that he could whisper in her ear, "Diana's the only person he actually likes."

Rea nodded and said, "I had noticed that."

"If I am going to live here will I get my own room or have to share with three or four rude idiots?" Elven said. "If it's time for cubs to nap, it's for sure time for old men to lie down."

"But if you go who will entertain us with their wit and wisdom?" Rea asked. "Come on; I will show you to your room. You will have to bunk alone as we are all out of rude idiots who will put up with a shriveled husk of a man." She stood up. "Follow me. I will shuffle so that you can keep up."

"Really? I thought you walked that way because your mother dropped you on the head when you were a baby, Captain oh my Captain."

"Just come on, you horrible wart on a monkey's ass," Rea said.

The old man picked up his bag and followed her right to Fleat's old room.

"So a closet?" he said.

"But with a window," Rea said. "Or you can bunk with four idiots who snore and fart all night if you'd rather."

"What a great room!" Elven walked over and sat on the bed. He looked at her. "I think we can work well together. What do you think?"

Rea smiled back. "Oh, aye, like a barnacle on a boat's ass."

He laughed as she walked away.

Jena walked out of the stairwell. "Have they unloaded the ship yet?"

"I was waiting for it to stop snowing. Why?" Rea asked.

"Well we have all the usual stuff, but we also have enough practice swords for everyone in the colony. Don't ask me why. Tarius insisted on them. And two cases of books the queen sent that Jestia requested," Jena said.

"Books!" Katrina yelled. She jumped up and started jumping around. She ran over and hugged Jena and then she hugged Rea. About that time Tarius and Jestia walked in the front door and Katrina ran over and hugged Jestia then took off running for the docks.

"What's going on?" Tarius asked with a laugh.

Rea grinned. "Jestia must have done her greatest spell ever; Katrina is speechless."

They stood at the dock ready to board the ship. Jestia looked at them all standing there in the snow to say good bye. She found she couldn't think of any of the things she had so wanted to say to them.

Everyone else had already said their good byes and boarded the ship. She had purposely arrived late to have this moment alone with them, but now she found she couldn't find the words, and there was a catch in her throat.

Then she heard Tarius's voice in her head, "Just speak from your heart, Jestia. Just speak the words of your heart."

"I will miss you," Rea said. "You have helped us all so much."

"Thank you, Jestia," Erah said, and then she was hugging her neck. Laz was right; the girl was strong. Erah hung on her and started to cry, and Jestia patted her back.

Jestia looked from Laz to Rea to Katrina. "I am the one who should be thanking you. When I came here I was broken, angry and dangerous. Your friendship and your patience with me helped to heal me. Laz, you are more like a brother to me than my own brother was. Katrina, I have never known anyone as honest with their heart as you are; I do not think you talk too much. Erah, stop crying and go hang on Laz so that I can speak."

The girl did, now crying on Laz's shoulder as Laz pounded her back till her teeth rattled.

"Erah, I learned much more from you than you did from me."

When she turned and caught Rea's eyes she had to fight down the ball of tears she found in her throat. "You are more than a sister and more than a friend to me. I have to go, or I would not leave this place, but mostly I would not leave you. The conversations I had with you...the time we spent together...I don't know what I will do about my problems, but I know I will make the right decisions because of what you told me, because of the example you set for me. I will be back. I will be back *often* because I won't be able to stay away from all of you or this place."

Rea rushed forward and hugged her. She was crying but said nothing; no words were needed. When she finally let her go she stood back and said, "We will always be waiting for you, Jestia. Always looking forward to the next time you grace our shores. Your friendship is a blessing I didn't know I needed till I had it."

Laz let go of Erah, walked forward and hugged her. "I will miss you, my non-blood kin."

When he released her, Katrina hugged her and whispered in her ear, "Thanks for everything." She looked with meaning at Rea.

"You are more than welcome."

"Oh for the sake of the Nameless One, let the witch go already," Elven said. "Let's go back to the keep before I freeze my ass off."

"Without your ass what will you talk with?" Rea said. She looked at Jestia and smiled and Jestia smiled back. "You know, old man, no one asked you to stay. Or can you just not find your way back to the keep alone?"

Laz and Erah, Rea and Katrina, stood on the dock waving till she could no longer see them. Then she stood at the stern looking at the land. It was beautiful all covered in the new snow that had fallen last night.

"Are you alright, little sister?" Tarius asked at her shoulder.

"It is hard to leave them and leave this place. I know you know because it is the reason you did it. This place will be key to the final war."

Tarius's silence told her she knew.

"I know I have to go home. I know my destiny is there, but I'd rather stay here. In no small part because I'd like to at least delay my destiny." Jestia turned to look at her. "I had thought that I could never be closer to anyone than I was to Ufalla, young Tarius and Jabone. We grew up together; their friendships were always so dear to me. But the friendships I made here with those four seemed so much more real, so much more important—almost as important as my relationship with you."

"We are lucky if we get to keep the friendships of our childhoods at all. Children grow into adults, they move away, and they find new lives. We make those ties when they don't know who they are and we don't know who we are. The friendships we make as adults are made between people who truly know who and what they are. We have made our mistakes. We have gotten better or worse, but we know who we are."

Jestia nodded. "Are you telling me why I grew such a bond to them or why Ufalla and I grew apart?"

"I am saying why I think it's different is all. I could be wrong; I'm sure it happens on occasion. Not very often but sometimes." She turned and started walking towards the helm. When she arrived, the helmswoman moved aside and let Tarius take the wheel.

Jestia stood in the stern watching the land till there was nothing but water. She was cold but not too cold. After all she wore the wolf skin coat she had made from the black hide Rea had given her. *I will not need this at home, but I will take good care of it for when I come back to the colony.*

Ufalla was working picking mangos with her younger brother and sister when Jabone came running up to her. Before she could ask what was wrong Jabone said, "My madra's ship is coming."

"How far out?" Ufalla asked.

"Far enough for you to wash the sweat and dirt off and put on clean clothes."

And that was just what she did. Then she ran down to the docks to wait. She could just see the ship, and now she had plenty of time to think. "Maybe I should go back to our hut or hide from her all together."

"She may not even be on the ship," Kaseria said, helpfully from where she stood holding Arvon's hand. Arvon obviously couldn't see the ship because he climbed up his mother to sit on Kaseria's head.

"What do you want to do, Ufalla?" Jabone asked.

"I want to see her. I want to run to her, take her in my arms and beg for forgiveness. But mostly I don't want to hurt her anymore. Maybe just seeing me will hurt her. Maybe she just couldn't stand to even see me. Maybe I shouldn't be here when she gets here."

"Well I wouldn't be," Kaseria said.

"Kaseria, you aren't helping," Jabone said.

"I'm just saying given what Ufalla did and who she did it to she's lucky to be alive. Maybe she shouldn't push it," Kaseria said. "If you ever…"

"Please do not tell me yet again the many horrible things you would do to me if I ever cheated. Especially not in front of Ufalla. Can you not see she is nervous enough?"

Kaseria shrugged then took Arvon off her head and followed him as he went to climb up a tree.

Jabone bent down and whispered in Ufalla's ear, "It is a good thing our son has a Katabull primary or he never would have lived through my wife's mothering."

"And you'd better never cheat on her or she will kill you for sure," Ufalla whispered back.

"Oh, that was the least of it," Jabone said, making a face.

"Seriously, Jabone, should I be here at all?"

"I think if you want to be here you should be, and if you don't you shouldn't. Madra always says…"

Ufalla cut him off. "Listen to your belly." She nodded her head. "That settles it; I am going to go to our huts. When you see her, please tell her where I am and that if she wants to see me I will be there and if she doesn't… She can pop off to Montero without me. I will not follow her."

She left at a near run. Once home she sat at the table in their main room and waited. The ship had still been a long way out, so it could take a long time for Jestia to get there if she came at all. There would be a lot of people there to greet the Great Leader's ship; Jestia would have to wade through all of them. Or she might just pop right up there or go straight to Montero.

Ufalla got up and got a glass of water sat back down and waited. Now her belly was all tied in knots. She wondered whether she should have listened to it in the first place seeing as now it was acting like she had made the wrong choice.

Ufalla had just decided that she had made the right decision but that it was clear that Jestia didn't want to see or talk to her at all when the door opened and Jestia walked in wearing a short blue wrap-around dress.

"When I left the Territories I was wearing fur from head to toe, and now I am too hot in this." She turned looked at Ufalla and caught her eyes.

Ufalla didn't look away, though it was hard. There was still so much hurt in Jestia's eyes.

"I am not going to kill you, so you can stop looking at me like that." She walked over and sat across the table from her.

"I am just glad to see you, Jestia," Ufalla said. "I am so sorry. I have missed you. I screwed everything up, and..."

"You sure as shit did. I have had a lot of time to think about it, Ufalla. Tarius reminded me that she betrayed Jena, that Jena wanted her dead and they got over it. But you know what? It's not the same at all. Everything that Tarius did she did because she loved Jena. For only a second Jena wanted someone else to kill Tarius. She didn't start to do it and have to be stopped by a friend. Weeks didn't pass with her still wanting to see Tarius's head explode.

"You wanted me because I was...all of this. Then once you had me you couldn't stand that I was...all of this. So you got drunk, talked shit to me, and banged whores. That's exactly what my worthless father did to my mother. You know—because I told you and no one else—that he is the reason my brother is dead and I am stuck being the heir to a crown I don't want."

"I am so sorry, Jestia. I didn't think about that. I didn't think at all. I was stupid, alright? I was so stupid that if you never want to live with me again, if you want a divorce, I understand. If you can never forgive me you are within your rights. You deserve better than me."

Jestia took a deep breath and let it out slowly. Then she stood up and started for the door where she turned and looked at Ufalla. "Do you love me?"

"I do. Hate me if you need to, but never doubt that I always have and always will love you."

"Until I got to the dock and saw you weren't there and Jabone told me where you were and why, I still didn't know whether I still wanted to be with you or not. I did something to you without asking that I shouldn't have done; I gave you half my life. I thought it was a gift. I didn't realize at the time what a curse it is for a human to have even half of a witch's life. Like you I didn't think; I just did it. If you have a child, you will outlive it. Your friends, your siblings…all will likely die before you do. I did that to you, and I'm sorry. I didn't realize any of those things when I did it. I was completely consumed with only one thing—I couldn't imagine my life without you. When I searched the dock and didn't see you, I realized that I still can't.

"I don't know what our lives will be like from here on. They can't be what they had become. I don't know what rules need to change, but I absolutely will not put up with any of your drunken crap ever again. I don't need you; I never will. But I want you; I want *you*, not the thing you became. I am going to walk outside and transport myself to Montero. If you still want me, know that they will let you leave now and you can meet me at home."

Ufalla stood up quickly, but by the time she got to the door Jestia was already gone. Ufalla ran to the pasture and got her horse, and in minutes she was on the road to Montero.

The Territories

About the Author

I started writing at twelve as an escape. The situations I have lived through are the stuff of which my fiction is born. My relationships with the many and varied people I have come into contact with over the years is a catalogue of characters from which I pull.

I am Jewish but consider myself spiritual not religious. I have studied every form of spirituality and try to live a spiritual life. I don't always succeed, but I do try.

My wife of over thirty years and I own a small farm where I raise milk goats, rabbits, chickens and a garden. I raise—depending on the weather and bugs—between forty and sixty percent of our food mostly organically. By "mostly" I mean if it looks like I will lose an animal I will do what I think is necessary. We make no trash; we use or recycle everything.

I lived for fourteen years of my life without electricity or running water. I had my only son naturally with no drugs. Though I was married off at sixteen (in an attempt to keep me from being gay) to a thirty-four-year-old man who immediately took me to New York and stuck me in a drug den for a month, I have smoked a total of five joints in my life. I have never done any other drugs.

My son was a prescription drug addict for nine years.

I have worked every shit job you can imagine from pulling car parts in a junk yard and cleaning rich people's houses to home health care. I ran an industrial plane and have logged timber using a team of mules. I have worked at saw mills, framed houses, and poured slabs. I am a carpenter and a rock mason. I can run (install) electricity, and I can plumb (I hate plumbing). I have also built more than one house using only hand tools and a chain saw. I like to hike and cave, and I love the ocean.

I fought heavy weapons (and trained other fighters) with the SCA (The Society for Creative Anachronism) for about twelve years. During that time I broke several bones (mosty mine), and I have a seven-inch plate and eight screws in my left arm as a result of a bastard sword blow. Elizabeth Moon talked me into fencing many years ago and I still do that, but I sold all my armor and heavy weapons a few years ago. Erin Grey talked me into trying Tai Chi to help with my CFS, so I have now been doing a mixture of Tai Chi and Chi Gung every day for the last five years.

Mercedes Lackey helped me get my first short story sale in *Marion Zimmer Bradley's Fantasy Magazine*. That sale opened the door for other sales to MZB, one of which was included in a German-language anthology, and the royalties came in steadily for many years.

CJ Cherryh line edited the first two chapters of *Chains of Freedom* and taught me more about writing doing that than I had learned to that point.

I'm not just name-dropping here; I'm giving credit to people who helped me who certainly didn't have to. Over the years I've come to know many very famous people, and here's what I know for sure—we are ALL the same.

In the writing community the person who is the most famous and makes the most money is often the least talented or deserving—not always, but often. In our business who makes it and who doesn't is often determined by nothing in the world but dumb-ass luck. That being the case, the near worship we see of the "famous" is something I just don't get at all.

The truth is I always think bios are sort of a waste. Anyone who reads my work knows more about the real me than I could ever put in a bio. If you want to talk to me, find me on Facebook. If you see me somewhere, come right up and talk to me. I am just like you. Luckily, I have a job I love, and the reason I have this great job is that people like you let me.

Friend me on Facebook, or if you prefer you can contact me through my personal website www.selinarosen.com, or Email me at selinarosen@cox.net.

About the Cover Artist

John Kaufmann has over twenty years of experience in the commercial field where he enjoys creating art for the education and advertising markets. He is an avid reader and loves creating Astronomical, Sci/Fi, and Fantasy art for art shows and publishing. John's work appears on numerous fiction book covers1 and has received top honors at art shows and conventions in the US and Canada.

NOTE FROM THE EDITOR: John's Yard Dog Press covers include *The Burden of the Crown, Leopard's Daughter* (by Lee Killough), *Gods and Other Children* (by Bill Allen), *The Guardians* (by Lynn Abbey), *The Burden of the Crown* and *The Twins* (books 3 & 4 of the *Sword Masters* series) by Selina Rosen, and this cover, which is book 5. He has also created covers for Dragon Moon Publishing in Canada, including the covers for *Sword Masters* and *Jabone's Sword*, books 1 and 2 in the *Sword Masters* series by Selina Rosen.

More Great Titles by Selina Rosen

The links provided are for the Kindle Editions.
If there is no link (yet), then go to www.yarddogpress.com
and check to see if there is an electronic edition
available or order the print edition.

Fiction (Novels):

The Bitter End
Black Rage
Fire & Ice
Getting It Real
The Ghost Writer
Hammer Town
How I Spent the Apocalypse
Not My Life
The Pit
Reruns
Strange Robby
Vanishing Fame
Weirdough, Inc. with Sherri Dean
Why I Blame Trump on Jesus Yes, it's fiction ☺

Novellas:

The Boat Man
Material Things

Short Fiction Collections:

Adventures of the Irish Ninja
The Bubba Chronicles
Deja Doo
Permanent Solution to a Temporary Problem

Non-Fiction:

It's Not Rocket Science: Spirituality for the Working-Class
Soul

Series Novels:

"Bad" Series (Suspense)—With Laura J. Underwood
    Bad City
    Bad Lands
    Bad Seas coming soon. Keep checking at YDP

The Chains Series (Post-apocalyptic military SF):
    Chains of Freedom
    Chains of Destruction
    Chains of Redemption

Drewcilla Quah Books (Bawdy Space Opera):
    Queen of Denial
    Recycled

The Host Series (Evil vampires and a lesbian rabbi vampire hunter):
    The Host
    Fright Eater
    Gang Approval

Sword Masters Series (Epic Fantasy with lesbian protagonist):
    Sword Masters
    Jabone's Sword
    The Burden of the Crown
    The Twins
    The Territories

www.ingramcontent.com/pod-product-compliance
Lightning Source LLC
Chambersburg PA
CBHW030645260626
47157CB00007B/2497